THE MAVERICK AGENDA

The Maverick Agenda

A novel

by

KENN ODDECK

BOOKS

Adelaide Books
New York/Lisbon
2018

THE MAVERICK AGENDA
A novel
By Kenn Oddeck

Copyright © by Kenn Oddeck

Cover design © 2018 Adelaide Books

Published by Adelaide Books, New York / Lisbon
adelaidebooks.org

Editor-in-Chief
Stevan V. Nikolic

For any information, please address Adelaide Books
at info@adelaidebooks.org

or write to:

Adelaide Books
244 Fifth Ave. Suite D27
New York, NY, 10001

ISBN-10: 1-949180-12-3
ISBN-13: 978-1-949180-12-1

Printed in the United States of America

One

MY LOVE FOR FANCY GADGETS started the minute I realized my parents' obsession for all things electrical could never really be healthy, and, had to be some sort of highly addictive substance abuse cleverly disguised as science. The two are highly passionate physicists who never stop gawking at machines.

Not only did they have a time-consuming hobby, but, ever since I can remember, it's all they've lived and breathed for, and many a time, didn't even seem to know I existed. I was left to my own means. It was driving me crazy.

This went on until the eve of my adolescent years, when, suddenly emboldened by the wild prospect of approaching teenagerhood, I decided to emulate them by taking devices apart.

At first, I tinkered away at little things—discarded watches and toys, nothing anybody would miss. This didn't bring me immediate attention though, but by then, I was having so much fun at it, that I lost sight of my original goal, which was to snare my parents. Surprisingly, I quickly acquired a taste for reverse engineering. The talent to go with the same, however, was another matter altogether.

As I got bolder and took to probing and jabbing away at larger gadgets and more-complex machines I had absolutely no business at all looking into, weird things started to happen. A particularly bizarre incident involves my parent's favorite radio. On splitting this up and then creatively putting it back together again, I decided on a whim of inspiration to try and sell it on eBay. And wonder of all wonders, it sold! But when the paying customer got back to me and told me my unique creation actually doubled as a lovely designer toaster, I was shocked and zapped to the very core of my being. This new functionality had never been my intention at all. Create a designer toaster? Never in a million years! I just wanted to spice up 'my' radio, that's all, I swear.

So of course, for hours on end after that, I battled with feelings of self-doubt, suffered panic attacks, spent days trying to breathe new life into my battered ego, and even imagined my tinker days to be over for good.

Meanwhile, the radio was gone. The good old days of music ricocheting off the four walls of the living room, was a thing of the past. Upon noticing how suddenly quiet it was within their home, Mom and Dad went in search of their missing radio. I slithered away and went underground for a week.

They searched high and low for their prized possession. I believe by then it was industriously toasting bread for its new owner across town. Lucky bugger! As for me, my nightmares came in the form of toasters. I lost all interest in bread. My legacy was in tartars.

When Mom and Dad eventually caught up with me, they put me through a series of such intense interrogations, that when I finally cracked and told them marmalade would never be of any use to me ever again, they were seriously puzzled, and discussed my mental health for days.

Eventually, though, lack of music got to them. And so, they were back at it. Night after night, they would come home from work and grill me about the whereabouts of their missing broadcast receiver. For just as long, I mumbled unintelligible words about eBay and big dreams.

They lacked evidence. But were rich in suspicion. And copiously grumbled on and off for a while.

Days went by before things got back to normal.

Old habits die hard. When I noticed they no longer missed their missing radio, I rejoined the land of the living, and, of course, took up tinkering again. This time around, I was messing about with Mom's brand-new blow-dryer when—I swear this happened—instead of spewing forth the old familiar heat we are all so accustomed to, it suddenly shot out long jagged bolts of brilliant-orange lightning. To say that I was stupefied would be a complete understatement. For two straight days, I simply sat there, stock-still, and stared at it in action.

A friend later told me I had inadvertently invented the ray gun. Me? Can you believe that? Fantastic! I was over-the-moon! I was absolutely ecstatic! I also remember collapsing on the spot from sheer joy.

Sometime after that, motivated by candid advice freely whispered into my ear by my alter ego, I went straight down to the registration office, hoping to secure a patent for my little fire breather. When the patent officer asked me to demonstrate what my little invention could do, I gleefully did so, and to my utter disbelief and total humiliation, a wild fire suddenly broke out in that small office, sending the patent officer screaming and crying out for dear life. I was instantly horrified at what had just happened.

It didn't take long for the fire department to appear out of nowhere. I, the new genius, was shoved to the sidelines. These brave boys courageously battled the little inferno to near exhaustion. All the while, I scientifically watched and took meticulous notes as things quickly got out of hand. By the time the coast guard came to assist them a little while later, I was so shaken by what had transpired that the new colors playing on my features had me totally camouflaged in my hiding place in the neighboring building across the street.

As luck would have it, my little invention only scorched half the patent office. I later learned this half contained only the prototype inventions nobody in their sane mind ever wanted realized. So, if you ask me, I did the whole world a little favor, me and my little ray gun. Still, I ended up in the local penitentiary for the night. Crap! Nothing but misconceived ingratitude in this world. I've been trying to recover from the horror of it ever since.

Anyway, I was released. Within a week, I was back to old habits. I can't quite tell how many times laptops and electric kettles zapped me to within an inch of my death. Nor do I care to recall how I must have looked with my hair statically charged and straining up toward the heavens. But one thing's as sure as hell: I was bad news for electrical appliances.

Up until then, my parents hadn't yet gotten wind of what was going on behind their backs. Apart from their zeal for electronics, they are also avid movie lovers, those old folks of mine, and almost always have their noses stuck before their television in the living room, tearfully watching the latest romance movie on their most beloved DVD player, which almost always seemed to be under lock and key when they were not around. Now, one thing you may not know about me is that locked things have always attracted me like bees to nectar. Naturally, it wasn't long before I was watering at the mouth, and even shorter still till I started tampering with the lock. And true to my nature, I eventually found my way around it. For me, this was like early Christmas. Slyly looking left and right, I quickly made away with my new loot, tightly wedged underneath my armpit.

Suspecting me, my confounded parents acted quickly. They paid me a visit in my tinker kingdom, in the toolshed out in the backyard. The minute they saw what I was doing to their DVD player, they turned as white as sheets, then started to gurgle and moan uncontrollably, as though inventing a new language. There I was, strange instruments in hand, feverishly jabbing away at their most beloved movie player. The machine was whining and whirring and churning out smoke, a sight that had Mom and Dad coming apart at the seams. Obviously, in their vast experience as physicists, they had many times come across the sounds and sights of technology in deep trouble. The look on Papa's face! And Mama's scream! I knew there and then I was dead meat if I didn't act fast. Suffice to say, my legs started pumping furiously of their own accord, and before I knew it, I was tearing past them, my torso straining desperately to catch up with my legs. I wasted no time getting as far away from them as possible.

They smothered and fumed for a day. I kept a safe distance. When I figured they had simmered down a bit, I sent them a text message explaining my side of the story. In it, I earnestly reasoned with them as best as I could, pointing out that I, their little special boy, was on the path of some great and noble discovery, and if they could just bear with me, hang in there, so on and so forth, they would be really proud parents someday. I was sure to change humankind forever, I told them excitedly. By then, they had gone a whole day without a movie. So severe were their withdrawal symptoms that, apart from many four-letter words and bloodcurdling screams, they were barely coherent. Best to stay away from them a whole week, I remember thinking, while pensively shaking my head at their complete lack of understanding. How could they not see? I was a genius in the making!

I moved in with the only one willing to take me in at the time, the very person who told me I had invented the ray gun. Great! For a whole week, he pumped my head full of the emptiest thoughts of grandeur humankind has ever known. "You will be famous, buddy," he told me over and over again. "This is the start of something big! Keep going. You are almost there."

I did just that. I kept going. What can I say? My ego was well and truly stocked.

A month later, and thanks to my continued efforts, the junkyard out back had grown to such gigantic proportions, that Mom and Dad simply couldn't ignore it anymore. They decided it was time to take appropriate action. Life, as I knew it, was about to change drastically.

They sent me to a no-nonsense psychiatrist with a string of Ph.Ds and an ironclad reputation for pulling off the impossible. My psychology needed a firm hand, they reasoned. I'm still smoldering over this blatant slight to my sanity.

Lucky for me, Dr. Ferdinand, the psychiatrist, has a truly special son. His boy never gets out of bed, never shows an interest in anything other than sleep, food, and has the largest appetite for the dullest string of sitcoms this world has ever seen. When Ferdinand happily told my parents that such curiosity as that which I possessed is highly commendable in a young person, they lost their marbles overnight and ended up being his patients by the very next morning.

Over the course of several months, they watched many of their prized possessions draw their very last breath at my hands. For just as long, they grieved bitterly before the mountain of junk out in the backyard, and trust me, this was a sight to see. They beseeched the gods, the skies, and the heavens to give me a new hobby. In vain. Their little monster—that would be me of course—just kept going. I was unstoppable.

Apparently, I was also very bad for their health.

When they started carrying out memorial services in honor of dearly departed and sorely missed electrical gadgets, I thought my eyes were playing tricks on me. Parents aren't allowed to crack like that, I recall thinking, and had wasted no time reporting this state of affairs in clandestine whispers to Dr. Ferdinand. He of course just couldn't wait to witness such strange behavior for himself. He immediately convinced me to let him sneak into the house in the middle of the day. Once hidden in an upstairs bedroom, he proceeded to spy on my unsuspecting parents through the window. His eyes almost popped right out of their sockets at the spectacle before him. There were my parents, before the scrap heap, doing the crazy, looking insane, getting worse by the minute, and totally out of control. In his shock, Ferdinand's head and entire torso were poking out of the window, but Mom and Dad were so busy doing their bizarre thing they wouldn't have noticed even if he'd fallen right out of the window and into the backyard.

Ferdinand was aghast. He wobbled over to the only chair in the bedroom and sat down heavily, shaking his head and asking what had become of the world.

I was shaking my head just as pensively, agreeing with his every word.

In all his years practicing psychiatry, not once had he ever seen anything so peculiar. He said he needed to think. So, I gave him some thinking space. During his deliberations, he kept mumbling to himself while his eyes darted about the room in a frenzy. Now this was something new. This really got me worried. Who was I supposed to call next? Another psychiatrist? When his body started to shake like an electric kettle about to blow its top, I ran out of the room screaming for Mommy and Daddy, and when I looked back, Ferdinand was hot on my heels, bearing down on me like a bad phantom in a nasty nightmare. Panting frantically and afraid for my life, I quickly took refuge behind my terrified parents.

Only when the ballistic doctor started to address Mom and Dad did I realize he was not after me at all, but simply couldn't wait to go to work on my wayward parents. Next thing I knew, he accused them of trying to kill my creativity and create another person like his lazy son. My outraged parents said they couldn't comprehend his dislike of such a sweet boy like his, who damaged nothing, touched nothing, did nothing, and, for crying out loud, most important of all to my parents, said nothing, not even in response to a simple "Good morning." I was appalled my parents wanted me to be dumb. Ferdinand couldn't believe my parents found his son appealing, and the tension between doctor and patients could have split the world in half, I tell you. In the end, he ordered Mom and Dad into straitjackets for life, and almost went insane when other doctors didn't agree with him.

After a week of straitjackets in a correctional facility, my old folks came back sound, sweet, fully rehabilitated, and full of praise for me—their industrious little lad—only to witness my unique brand of reverse engineering all over again and lose it on the spot. Just five minutes back home, and they cracked like coconuts. They simply burst into tears and wept for days on end.

Dr. Ferdinand did his best to console them. Several times, I even happened on them while he was doing his virtuous work out there before the mountain of junk, trying to make them come to terms with its monstrosity. "Your boy will be an Einstein someday," he would tell them as I passed by to feed the mountain of junk with more metal. He would smile at me, and I would smile back, and my parents would wail as if there had been a death in the family. "So be proud of him," Ferdinand would continue, ignoring their caterwauling. "Chin up, stand tall, smile wide. I wish my son was like David." At this, Mom and Dad would quiet down a little but only for a few seconds, staring in utter disbelief at the newly dead and totally unrecognizable gadget I'd just deposited. They would pick up where they'd left off the minute Dr. Ferdinand started sharing with them his most amazing quotes from Dr. Freud's good books on the mysteries of the mind. These were truly moving moments. I think I even shed a tear or two.

One thing is certain: Dr. Ferdinand played a great role in shaping my emotional being. I am still not sure if that is a good thing or bad. I guess time will tell.

Several years later, as I set my sights on reverse engineering my parents' brand-new, life-size, curved-screen Samsung TV, Father learned of my intentions, screamed like a banshee, and for the first time in his entire life, instantly fainted out of sheer shock. He was out cold for several minutes. When he came to, he and Mother, both pale and forlorn, quickly agreed history shouldn't be allowed to repeat itself with their new window to the world. They held an emergency strategic meeting on the spot. The decision, when it came, was unanimous. It was high time to get rid of their little monster once and for all. And by George, it was time to do it quick.

Not long afterward, they devised a plot on how to accomplish that. This involved chartering a Commando plane. On the lure of a family vacation, they flew me halfway around the world. Then, upon faking engine failure and mortal danger, they strapped a parachute on my back, stuffed a few documents and a passport in my pockets, and airdropped me out of the plane while making me promise I would survive to continue their Elbert surname, come rain, or shine.

I was in shock. I was in the middle of mourning my parents. I was also hurtling toward the ground like an avenging missile, intent on creating untold havoc on the ground below.

As I plunged down to the University of Applied Sciences in Jena, Germany, I discovered the documents in my pockets were a letter of acceptance at the same university, a monthly allowance agreement, and a letter from my parents insisting I pursue a course in business engineering, since I was so fond of tinkering. It was at that precise moment that I grasped what had just happened. I had been ditched. The engine failure had been fake. And Mom and Dad were probably dancing up there in the plane, while drinking champagne and laughing their hearts out, even as I tearfully released the parachute and sailed down to my new fate.

So that's how I ended up being a student at this university on the other side of the world, far from loved ones and friends, far enough away that I couldn't accidentally happen upon any of my parents' future gadget acquisitions.

I had been dropped like a hot potato. Being abandoned like this really got me fuming. With an enormous chip on my shoulder, I began plotting my elaborate revenge. This took the form of avoiding classes, loitering and jaywalking the streets of Germany at all hours, with the express intention of completely ticking off my kooky parents. I even engaged in the most seriously brain-dead partying that I could find, all in the name of sweet payback. My face became a regular sight at almost every sizzling social event far and wide. I would party and dance and rave all night, wake up at noon in dire need of hours of recovery time, and do it all over again as soon as the sun went down in the evening. Life became one long, sleepless, woozy stupor.

When Mom and Dad finally got wind of my activities, I screamed loudly for sheer joy. My revenge, I decided, had been appropriately enacted. To commemorate the moment, I even threw a really big start-of-summer party. I invited all my new friends. They came with their friends' friends and a whole bunch of other people I had never met in my whole new life. It was fun getting to know them all. And boy, did we have a ball. I partied myself into a hangover that lasted two days and eight hours.

On the second day of my hangover, Mom and Dad sent me a scathing e-mail. This angry piece of writing only served to split my sides with laughter, until I came across the shocking sentence in which they vowed never to send me another dime if I got kicked out of university. In that one second, my whole world turned upside down. That was when I realized first-semester exams were close, and I was nowhere near ready. I flew into a panic.

Desperate to keep my cash flow from freezing up, I moved into the university's grand library on the very next day with nothing but a simple plan; I was going to save my party life. Dead serious about keeping my beer money coming, I embarked on a crash-course learning program of truly epic proportions.

Studying for exams on short notice is a disaster, I quickly learned. I barely survived the first day. By the end of the second, a splitting headache had me feeling like my brain was being split in half. A day later, the pulsating migraine I was nursing was so severe, that I couldn't see clearly, let alone think at all. Reading became torture. When I started moaning in pain while squinting at my books, an overzealous librarian suddenly materialized, stood stock-still, and began surveying the studying students with ever growing suspicion. Everyone knew she was waiting to pounce on the source of the sound, which, by now, was welling up in my throat, clamoring ever so desperately for sweet release.

I was fought to hold it in. I guess this must have shown. She peered at me as if daring me to even squeak. The sheer strain of trying to squint her into focus is what did it in for me. I let out one single blast, a pitiful moan so shrill and sharp, that after jumping a clear five steps back and quickly recovering from her fright, she simply screamed, "Dear God," and then, "Get out!"

I was unceremoniously thrown out for disturbing the peace. Can you believe that? Disturbing the peace! Dear heavens. I was just trying to read!

So anyway, there I was, before the library, frozen to the spot in disbelief, nursing a splitting headache, and staring a tragedy of epic proportions in the eye. This was all too much for me and my best-laid plans of keeping my party cash flowing. I saw stars and blacked out on the spot.

When I came to, I was in the university hospital. A calendar on the wall informed me another day had gone by while I was out cold. To make matters worse, my lips were bandaged. On seeing my confounded look, a deeply disturbed doctor kindly explained to me I had fallen on said lips when I'd blacked out the other day. Then he loudly asked himself how one could manage such a feat in the first place. Of course, since I couldn't answer, he reassuringly tapped me on the head while telling me not to worry, I would be back on my feet in a month. A *month*? What of my exams? And for Pete's sake, what did bandaged lips have to do with getting back on one's feet?

I had my own unique way of dealing with this unwanted convalescent prescription that probably defies logic. I went shopping on Amazon.com, then, an hour after my parcel was delivered, I looked just like one of those top agents in the old spy movies, complete with a fake beard and sixties-style wig, all nicely complemented by the bushiest set of sideburns that I could find on Amazon. No one had the slightest chance of recognizing me as I broke out of the university hospital in the middle of the night. My veins were coursing with adrenaline.

I felt great! I felt invisible! Maybe even a little invincible. And of course, I was on an impossible mission. With the clock ticking. I had exams to beat.

Devoid of a library and with the exams just around the corner, I came up with a fantastic new plan to save the day. This great idea involved implementing statistical analysis in four simple steps. First, analyze the material the professor had covered during the semester. Second, note all comments on what was likely to be tested. Third, eliminate content covered in past examination papers. Last but not least, create a list of likely questions with answers and memorize them for all I was worth, a week before exams. Simple, straightforward, easy, brilliant. I burned this stuff so firmly into my brain cells that for seven days I dreamed of nothing else.

Exams finally came. I took them. A month passed. I simply couldn't believe my ears when the results were announced. I was completely stupefied. Not only had I absolutely aced them, but I had scored such a high grade that I was the top-ranked person in a class of forty geniuses. Now who would have thought that possible? Simply fantastic! Ever since, I have been employing the same strategy with relative success for the last four years.

Two

AS YOU HAVE BY NOW probably worked out for yourself, I am not studious. Just a strategist at passing exams with as little input as possible. This strategy, however, doesn't always work out well. I found this out on two previous occasions: the first, Professor Cole's Machine Elements exam and the second, a re-take of the same. In both cases, engineering logic and complex calculations were called for. I'll probably go down in history as the first student who ever memorized calculations in hopes of passing exams with flying colors. Can you believe that? Memorizing $4 - 3 = 1$? And what if the professor changes the question to 4-2? Will I still say the answer is 1? So much for being a genius. Needless to say, I flopped harder than a falling tree.

THIS CAMPUS has a rule that allows each student to repeat a maximum of three exams three times. Failure to pass an exam on the third try means goodbye campus, goodbye student life, goodbye brilliant future, and, in my case, goodbye party life. It's this last I would miss the most. And since I have already struck out twice, this next attempt will be my third and final try. So, for the whole of this final semester and, quite frankly, for the first time in my young-adult life, I have been a true student worthy of mention. No more memorized questions and answers, no more lazy-boy approach, no more shortcuts. This time, I am doing it right. So, here I am. For days on end, I have been stuck in my room, studying. Hour after hour I have been combing through my books nonstop, with a feverish intensity in my eyes. There is a mountain of material on my desk, a mug of cold coffee beside it, and an incessantly ticking table clock to my right. For all intents and purposes, I am dead to the world. Right now, I live only for the most mind-blowing knowledge-acquisition attempt ever known to man. I look like Einstein. I smell just like sweaty Hulk after a pretty bad smashup day. I am in dire need of a shower. All the while, the sands of time slip away at an increasingly alarming rate. Tomorrow is the day of reckoning. I still have about sixty pages of machine calculation procedures to work through.

Outside, people are partying as they have been doing the whole summer. It seems as if the whole world is completely oblivious to my struggle. Shouts of excitement ring through the neighborhood. This makes it difficult to concentrate on the task at hand. Over the past weeks, I have spent a lot of time looking out these very windows and cursing avidly. Life is passing me by. And I'm stuck with books. I want to cry. But I don't. Instead, I man up.

I study all evening. Around midnight, after I finally get a shower, I fall into a troubled sleep and dream of menacing machines and horrible calculations for hours on end. At five, a nightmare takes root and won't let go. Something to do with one of the machines I murdered at my parents' home. It's haunting me, hell-bent on payback. I wake up in a cold sweat, scream in fear, recall the machine is dead, and proceed to curse in anger. *Dead things shouldn't disturb my sleep, dammit! Well, I can't go back to sleep now.* I decide to hit the books again.

The critical hour is almost upon me as morning dawns. I breakfast on cereals and strong coffee as "Chariots of Fire" plays on the radio and burns its way into my memory. *Oh God,* I cannot help thinking. *It's the final countdown.*

FUNNY HOW SUCCESS or failure after four years of studies can be decided in a paltry one-and-a-half-hour period of time. I am sitting in an examination room on the second floor in the business engineering building, pondering what fate has in store for me. My heart is also racing out of control. I am fighting to stay calm. A no-man's-land of about two meters separates all the desks in this examination room. Normal standard examination procedure, intended to curb cheating. About forty of the sixty places are occupied by equally nervous fellow examinees. Quiet chatter from the terrified students reverberates across the room. Some have given in to last-minute cramming in the hope of scoring an extra point or two. I, naturally, belong to this frantic breed of creature still looking into books. On the other hand, a few other students opt to distract themselves from the looming exam in incredibly imaginative ways, thus managing to let off some pent-up steam. Silly jokes and clowning burst out spontaneously here and there. A girl trying to free her spirit from her body twists herself into such an impossible yoga position, that I fear it may be permanent and she may never get out of it. At least, it appears to be giving her the much-needed respite from the exam tension plaguing her. Her face melts, and is suddenly serene. Nice. The rest just sit like statues, frozen, as though struck by lightning and never again capable of movement. I smell fear in the room, including mine. We are a flock of sheep waiting for slaughter.

Before me lies Professor Aldrick Cole's text on machine elements. We are expecting him to walk in any minute now and set the proverbial bloodshed in motion. I am fervently poring over the more-complex machine-elements calculations when the chatter dies down to a low minimum, and suddenly, I know without a moment's doubt that the critical hour has indeed arrived. My heart skips a beat. I look up to see Professor Cole marching toward the lecturer's table, small cardboard box cradled in his hands. The box draws my attention. I stare at it intently. There isn't an iota of uncertainty within me. I know what it contains. Our exam papers. I try not to shake with fear.

TEN YEARS OF LECTURING have taught professor Cole one fundamental truth about young exam students: they are simply not to be trusted. At this moment, he is staring intently at each one of us in turn. He studies our faces, notes our chosen seats and chosen exam neighbors, and immediately starts to contort his face like a prize pit bull. It's a wordless inquisition to draw out the cheats. The silent interrogation is intense. Obviously, he smells a rat. I almost melt under his stare before suddenly finding the scene outside the window quite attractive. I look outside, riveted, as though watching an amazing movie. I even manage to raise an eyebrow in stupefied wonder. This is quite an accomplishment, given just how dull and boring the scene outside actually is. It's high summer, and despite it only being eight o'clock in the morning, the heat outside is already unbelievable. Thanks to the ventilation system running at full throttle in here, our exam room is pleasantly cool.

I almost jump out of my skin as Professor Cole booms out, "Mark Forester, Daniel Hoffmann." As usual, the professor's words are drawn out, thoughtful, captivating, authoritative. "One of you will have to take the empty seat two rows back."

Mark Forester totters between a nervous breakdown and a total collapse. Giggles emanate all around at the sight of his ridiculous appearance. "Old billy goat," he says with great feeling. Laughter breaks out from all within earshot. Reluctantly, he moves to comply with the professor's request, fully aware his chances of cheating just went down a good notch.

"David Elbert?" calls out the professor.

My soul freezes as I hear my name for the first time on this fateful day. Even my make-believe movie outside the window cannot help me anymore. I am shaking like a leaf in high wind. "Yes, Professor Cole?" I stutter, fully conscious of the fact this is my third and final chance to pass this exam. Unfortunately, Professor Cole knows this too. He also knows this is when students move heaven and earth to cheat and steal exams, so he is fixing me with such an intense gaze, that every molecule of my being feels pinned down to this particular space-time I am sitting in. I feel inside out, upside down, smashed and trashed, and totally drained of all thought for at least two lifetimes. Only a bewildered look survives on my face.

"You," he says loudly, "will be sitting right here at the very front." He points at the desk right in front of his table. As an afterthought, he adds, "Any cheating material on your person I should know about?" His question evokes a few laughs.

I turn pink. "No, sir," I answer.

"Good. I will not make engineers out of cheats. You understand?"

"Fair enough," I say. Then I giggle at the hilarious thought of me flipping through a gigantic encyclopedia right in front of Professor Cole, who would be watching me with wide, unbelieving eyes as I copied everything the encyclopedia had to offer onto his exam paper. What a laugh. I would love to see that in a comedy someday.

On my way to the front, I take a good look at my fellow examinees. No close friends here, nothing but a sea of strangers, junior faces I have seen here and there on the university's grounds. I spot one or two kindred spirits who, like me, are retaking this exam. We avoid eye contact, choosing to enjoy our shame in private.

The professor continues setting mayhem to well-laid plans of examination cheating, and I cannot help wondering how many enemies he will make on this day. Minutes tick by. At last, happy with our seating arrangement, he says, "Put away all study materials. Switch off all mobile phones." A ruckus ensues as we comply. He looks around, ascertains there is nothing other than pens and pencils on our desks, and dishes out the papers.

This is the moment for which I have been studying my brains into a near coma the whole semester. I had only four courses this semester: Product Innovation, Design-Manufacturing Interfaces, Management of Research & Development, and, last but not least, Machine Elements. I have already taken exams in the first three and expect good grades. It's this last, Machine Elements, which has me concerned and currently sweating blood and brain cells in equal proportions.

Professor Cole sees me bleeding and hurries to pat me on the back. "You can do it," he says.

I wish he would just give me a gigantic encyclopedia instead. If he did, I would bless his name for all eternity the rest of my life. I swear.

"You have ninety minutes," he booms, turning to face the class. "You may turn your exam papers over. The clock is ticking."

And so is my heart. Desperately. I turn my paper around and soon lose myself in exam fever. My anxiety slips away as I notice just how well prepared I am.

Fifty minutes into the exam, Mark Forester gets up, shoulders sagging, face drooping, eyes lost. He walks to the professor, belongings and all in tow, exam paper in hand. Professor Cole has been expecting this for the last fifty minutes. Now, he looks at his watch and then at Mark Forester, a single clear question written all over his face: *Why in goodness' name fifty minutes? You could have thrown in the white towel in five.* Mark Forester hands in his blank exam paper. He walks out the door, completely dejected, all the while cursing Professor Cole earnestly. Mark will be back next semester for a second attempt. As for the rest of us, the scribbling race is on, and everyone is fighting tooth and nail for a favorable position at the finish line.

I spot a few desperate faces when Professor Cole nonchalantly says, "Thirty minutes to go."

I cannot believe I am not worried. For the first time since we started, an amazing smile creeps onto my face. I have answered twenty questions fairly accurately, and my pace is good. I ignore the buzz of adrenaline through my system as we receive yet another time appraisal fifteen minutes later.

Before we know it, Professor Cole's voice is booming out again. "Stop! Put down your pens and pencils! Anyone still writing will get an F on the spot. Do you hear me, you miserable lot? Don't jot. Not another letter. Or I swear, I will come down on you like thunder and lightning and Thor's hammer all at once. Who wants a zero? Who's still got a pen in his hand? Keep writing, I dare you."

Several pens slap hard on the wooden desk surfaces as fear of the ominous zero grade takes hold among the exam students.

"Daniel Hoffmann, are you still writing?"

"No, sir, I swear I stopped when you started barking," says Daniel Hoffmann in self-defense as he sends his pen crashing into the ceiling above us.

Laughter rings out at his choice of words.

Gravity is a bitch. His pen comes down hard, missing my face by a mere centimeter. I stare at Daniel in shock, but the reeling lad only has eyes for the professor as he tries to discern if he's about to receive a flat zero for adding a few extra seconds to his exam time. But the ax doesn't fall, and the danger passes. He lets out his breath in relief.

It takes Professor Cole a while to collect all the examination papers. The minute he is done, he lets us out. And as is the nature of students the world over, we regurgitate the whole experience and compare notes in earnest. I am smiling from ear-to-ear as I walk out of the exam room in a sanguine haze.

THE UNIVERSITY'S CORRIDORS are wide, and, for the most part, hemmed in by yellow walls throughout the whole of campus. I negotiate the never-ending maze while trying to sort out my feelings. Four years! Now it's finally over. I walk by a cleaning lady to my right who is busying herself with the polishing of glazed windows. My rubber-soled shoes hardly make a noise on the marble floor, and there is a slight spring in my step. My cell phone starts to ring. It's Mom and Dad, curious to know how I fared. I tell them the good news. I caution the results are not yet out, but they are already planning a party in my honor, in my hometown, to be held within the next couple of days. I plan to be present in spirit.

Dad bellows his congratulations at me, while Mom punctuates his comments with her shrill screams of joy. Just another day in the Elbert family. Nothing to worry about. Before long, Mom asks if I am dating that nice girl I brought home last summer. This opens Dad up, who starts reminiscing about his first date with Mom. Minutes later, they are discussing every last detail of their lives. This goes on for what feels like an eternity before they release me to get back to my own, now very promising life. Tonight, I am thinking of partying till the doctor comes. But first, I am hungry. It's time for me to get some lunch.

Given the soaring temperature today, I chose to dress as lightly as possible—brown shorts, a matching flannel shirt, dark-brown socks, and low loafers. I look good. I feel fresh. The heat hits me like a furnace as I walk outside. All around, hurried students with tottering stacks of books rush past, offering only the briefest of nods and the faintest of hellos. I was like them not too long ago, pressed for time and short on words. With the exams now behind me, I am as free as a lark and pondering ways to spend my newly acquired free time.

I make my way into the cafeteria with food on my mind. Already, the hard-core lunch action is well underway in the large and elaborately designed dining facility. Long queues to the left slowly inch their way toward the food counters up front. Most of the dining tables are occupied. In every direction, there are students, professors, and a handful of administrative stuff. In other words, the regular lunch crowd at a university. All around, low chatter reverberates across the hall. The food seems delicious. Everyone's chewing in earnest.

A good number of these patrons are rushing through their meals for obvious reasons. Time is precious, knowledge is power, and they want to acquire more. Their every hand movement to and fro between plate and mouth leaves no doubt what's topmost on their minds. Books.

I take a seat with a good view of the entrance as I wait for Elise Amsel. Like me, she has been a student of this university for the past four years. Unlike me, she's already embarked on her final leg of undergraduate studies, the thesis-internship initiative. Elise has always had a thing for marketing. When Daimler offered her a dream marketing thesis-internship at its subsidiary in Frankfurt, everyone expected her to say yes. What a surprise it was when she said no. She ended up taking an intellectual thesis study here at the university's marketing department. She has become my most favorite person in all of life, and quite frankly, my very best friend.

Absentmindedly, I take in the lunch crowd as I wait for her to walk in. Most of the students appear to be discussing the ongoing examinations. And their professors keep clandestine surveillance, with many struggling to hide knowing smiles. The numerous voices merge into a continuous hum. In tune with this is the constant clinking of cutlery on china. Hypnotical, transcendent, almost as if it were a deliberate lullaby. My eyes half close. My breathing slows. I am acutely close to falling asleep.

FOR ENTIRELY DIFFERENT REASONS, however, I almost stop breathing as Elise walks in through the door. She's in her early twenties. As usual, a mysterious yet pure allure of innocence hangs about her. She surveys the room, one elegant hand stroking her long scarlet hair, held in a ponytail. A shimmering violet blouse clings to her feminine torso. Below it is a tight black miniskirt that accentuates her firm figure. She's gorgeous. I breathe out slowly, as I get up and walk over to her.

We exchange greetings and a hug. The standard friendly hug. I let her go a few moments later. She stands back, an appraising look in her eye. "You look happy," she says.

"I have every reason to be," I respond.

She raises a delicate eyebrow in a silent question.

"I aced it this time," I say excitedly.

"You said the same thing last time."

I turn a bit red with embarrassment. "This time, it's different."

"Sure?"

"Positive!" I gulp nervously nevertheless and do some quick math of the possible grade I will get.

She's still looking me in the eye, critical, analytical, evaluating my every expression.

I start to relax a bit, as my mental grade-calculations begin to appear more promising.

She's quick to notice my growing confidence. Appreciatively, she nods. "Good, David. That sounds really good. I was a little worried for you there."

"Really?"

"Sure, damn ass," she says with a quiet smile that warms my heart.

"Good," I reply.

"That I was worried?"

"No, that you care."

She blushes, and with a demure finger pointing at the food counters, sets us in motion in that direction. We say nothing for a few seconds. Her beauty and confident stride draw a couple of looks from both sexes. Clearly, the guys desire her. The girls, on the other hand, want to be just like her. She is about five inches shorter than I am. She's almost always smiling, constantly vibrant, and forever sparkling. It's certainly not surprising that everyone notices when she walks into a room. At this very moment, her light-brown eyes glitter with merriment. I try not to read too much in them, for fear of falling in love.

We pick out and pay for our meals. At the back of the dining hall, a table is presently vacated. We quickly walk over and converge on it.

For Elise and I, lunch proceeds at a leisurely pace. The two of us have no exams to face. So, for now, we take time to savor our meal. I bite and sigh with the pleasure of eating a juicy piece of roasted lamb. The roasted potatoes look enticing too, so in one fluid motion, I stuff a piece in my mouth, all the while eyeing the fried cabbage suspiciously. I suspect I am a carnivore and only eat vegetables because my doctor insists they are good for me. Potatoes sometimes look like meatballs, so I have learned to give them a break. Besides, they make French fries. And who doesn't love French fries? Cabbages, however, have always given me the hibbie jibbies since childhood. I push mine to the very edge of my plate and make a mental note to keep my distance.

Elise seems particularly overjoyed with her choice for today's lunch. She went with French fries and sausages, the scent of which is making me a bit jealous. She purrs every time the mayonnaise dipping melts on her tongue. More than once, she vows never to eat anything else her entire life, and I almost dump my meal and go for the same. I strongly suspect I'll be raiding McDonald's this evening.

Over lunch, we talk. I get into a detailed and exhilarating account of my session with Professor Cole this morning. Elise is laughing to the point of tears. The "old billy goat" bit almost completely floors her. We laugh about it for several long moments. It's a full minute before she regains her composure and calms down again. She sure is a lovely sight.

It takes a while. Eventually, the lunch crowd thins. Many of the students still have a multitude of pending exams, so off they go to the library, where for much of the day, they will remain holed up as they do battle with their books.

How many of us will wonder why they studied in the first place? The job market is a tricky place, and a few are bound to fall between the rails. I try not to wonder what the future holds for me. It's best to stay positive. We continue to eat as the dining hall empties.

"Have you decided on your thesis yet?" Elise asks between mouthfuls.

"I believe so," I tell her. I've been putting this off in the past, intending to deal with it after today's exam, and now, I suppose, the time has come for action. A cateress comes about, replaces an empty salt shaker, and reveals a toothy smile. I let her get out of earshot before replying, "I have narrowed it down to the three most promising offers."

"Which are?" Elise asks curiously.

"Controlling in an automobile manufacturing company, purchase logistics at a synthetic producing company, and output optimization for an automobile subcontractor."

"Which is up your alley?"

"I guess I will go with output optimization," I say.

We covered this last semester in Management Methods of Production. All that it needs, apart from the prerequisite background knowledge, is a knack for creativity and an eye for detail. I believe I have both in abundant measure, and that's why I'm drawn to this choice.

"Where's the company?" Elise asks.

"In Apolda. Thirty minutes by car from here."

She spoons thoughtfully through her delicious strawberry dessert. Not far away is a young student couple holding hands dearly. They whisper the occasional word to each other. If I am not mistaken, they are forever lost in each other's eyes. Clearly, a sweet love is going on between them. Their lunch seems to be forgotten, and they seem oblivious of everyone else.

Elise takes them in for a moment. Then she turns to me with a wistful look in her eye. "Will you be moving out of town?"

"No. That would be too much trouble for too little gain at the moment. I am staying right here, in my present apartment."

I spot relief in her eyes and then hope. A fraction of a second later, both emotions are gone. She is quickly her old self again, full of jokes, teasing, easy, nothing other than super friendly. But I'm not fooled anymore. Evidently, something is brewing inside of her. Could she be harboring feelings for me?

We kid around a bit more after that. There is a mysterious twinkle of mischief in her eye. A tender feeling towards her ignites inside of me, and for a second, I believe she sees it. We both slowly avert our eyes. The moment passes. But the knowledge remains. We have a soft spot for each other. I try not to get overly excited about this new discovery.

Shortly afterward, we part ways.

Three

I DRIVE AN OLD piece of junk that, over time, has become the subject of my worst nightmares. This relic from the past does little for my image or self-esteem. It's slowly beginning to define my reputation in ways that make me scared to show my face anywhere. It quickly attracts undue attention everywhere I go. I also firmly believe it isn't doing my overall health any good either. So just to play it safe, I tried acquiring a health insurance policy in case of car poisoning, but to date, no luck. It's an old Mazda that's going on its very last breath. For some time now, I've been driving it about with a busted ventilation system. My friends think I'm crazy. I can count on the fingers of one hand the times I have had girls in my car. Not even one of them has ever gotten in a second time. And since this is college, you can very well see how stigmatized I have become. I fear this has marked me for life. I have been meaning to get my car fixed for close to three years now. As always, the reason for my procrastination has quite simply been money.

Since my parents throttled down my funds to cut down my copious lifestyle, I have been hopping from one student job to the next, barely keeping my head above water, and wondering when I will be done with this drudgery and can step over into true living. Life on a shoestring budget is no romance affair. Apart from a modest accommodation, three square meals a day, inexpensive partying and cheap beer, I've had to do without many things, a real car being one of them. Not surprisingly, I have been dreaming of graduation followed by a fat paycheck and a brand-new Mazda, one that's blessed with an excellent ventilation system, nothing short of state-of-the-art. The latter completely fills my mind at this very moment. I would give anything for high-tech ventilation on this particular day.

I find my car soaking in the day's heat at the university's open-air parking lot where I left it earlier this morning. To tell you the truth, I am bitterly disappointed. I was really hoping that some crazy junk collector would have stolen it by now, or that it would have been towed away for its lack of aesthetic appeal. Sadly, none of this happened. It's still here, sending me vibes, waiting for me, hoping to continue its none-reciprocal, none-beneficial relationship with me. *I hate it!* I stare at if for a second or two, before resignation sets in.

With great apprehension, I let myself in. A curse escapes my lips as I very nearly suffocate from the oppressive heat within. A mighty sigh then follows suit, knowing I have absolutely no choice in the matter. I have to drive this furnace. Moaning loudly, I pull out of the parking lot and make for home.

The B88 takes me out of town. I pass a number of pleasant-looking public parks laid out within the city. They are dotted with sun worshippers and nature lovers, many of whom have long since retreated into the shade of trees in the hope of gaining a little respite from the blazing sun. I wish I could be out there too, but I can't—not just yet anyway. There are urgent matters to attend to.

As I drive, my brain churns. For five kilometers, I think about my future, my hopes and dreams, and the constant wish for the dawn of a better tomorrow. Everything I have done till now has been to get me to this point. What comes next?

I leave the B88 and rumble onto Erlanger Alley. The interior of my car is not much unlike a sauna. The heat is stifling. I am sweating profusely as I turn left onto my home turf on Drachendorfer Street. The two-way road is deserted. On either side of it is a strip of parking. Beyond these and facing each other across the street are two rows of six-story apartment blocks in different shades of yellow, red, and green. I draw to a stop and park before the first one on the right. As I walk up to it, I wonder for the umpteenth time whose decision it was to paint it a bright orange. The building stands out like a clown would among kindergarten kids.

My student apartment on the second floor is like any other the world over—forty square meters containing a sleeping niche, a kitchen, a bathroom, and a small living room where I spend most of my time when at home. I have turned one-half of the living room into an office. The other half has a couch, a TV, and a small music blaster. This concludes the extent of my wealth and personal possessions to date. It's embarrassing. I try not to think about it.

At this very moment, I am in my little office. The window beside me overlooks a little park. In it are countless flower beds filled with lilacs and roses in full bloom. Couples frolic nonchalantly among the flowers, carefree, happy, unaware of my troubled heart. The source of my discontent happens to be Elise, who is currently weighing heavy on my mind. Since this afternoon, I've been thinking of the two of us as one. Is there a chance of this happening? Does she even know I harbor feelings for her? I battle with questions of love for a bit, then shake my head and discard this train of thought. No use thinking about it. My focus goes back to the task at hand.

Everyone knows carrying out a thesis internship in a company is about the surest way of getting one's foot in the door and landing a fat dream job. And since Displaytek Systems Ltd.

is rumored to be a rising star in the electronics world, I chose it as a possible candidate for my thesis study. My first run-in with the company took place during a job fair held on campus three months ago. It was an exceptionally hot day, just like this one. For this reason, all the companies' stands were set up in a cool hall not far from the campus diner. There were twenty companies present on that day, each vying for bright young minds while creating awareness for their array of services, products, discoveries and inventions. I was in seventh heaven.

At Displaytek's stand, things got serious the minute they learned I was to be a future business engineer. "There could be a thesis-internship opening at our company," one of them cautiously mentioned to me.

This was wonderful news. I was all ears.

They then inquired about my grades. I laid it on thick, painted myself Einstein-like, and promised them the stars and half the neighboring galaxy if they take me on. I was on a roll.

They were over the moon. For minutes on end, they bubbled excitedly about nothing else other than the great discovery of David Elbert. They were ecstatic.

One could see it in my smile. I have never felt so intelligent in my whole life.

When we got down to talking about the intricate workings of their amazing gadgets, the tinker in me was suddenly wide awake, and revving to go.

They had my full attention and knew it.

We have been exchanging e-mails ever since.

Right now, while looking out my window, I call them to follow up on their offer. The receptionist picks up on the third ring. She introduces herself as Caroline Henke and remains professional, discreet, and to the point.

"David Elbert," I say confidently into the phone. "I am a thesis-internship student applicant. Personnel is expecting my call."

She leaves me at the mercy of a waiting melody. I drum my fingers to its rhythm for several seconds. She puts me through.

Anje Tille's melodious greeting chirps in. Although we haven't met, I feel I know her a little bit already. As I said, we've kept in touch. For weeks, we've danced about the prospect of my putting in a few months at the company.

I let her know I'm done with my final exam, and now happen to be looking for some real action. She wants to know how many thesis offers from competing companies I am considering. Two, I tell her.

She tells me they want me and cannot wait to get their hands on me, my fresh knowledge and schooled perspective, brilliance and youth, as well as my driving force. I am giddy with anticipation of what could be.

"Have you reached a decision yet?" she asks.

"Indeed, I have, Mrs. Tille."

"And?"

"I would love to come on board at Displaytek," I let her know. "I'm ready to meet the rest of the gang."

"Super. We will take good care of you; you just wait and see."

I'm counting on it. I agree to show up at her office the next morning at nine. For a minute longer, we engage in a bit of social chatter, then hang up.

MY PLANNED visit to Displaytek has me too excited to sleep. I surf the net instead, looking for more information on the company. I already know the fundamental basics, thanks to Anje Tille's numerous brochures. The flood of information I find on the Internet, however, is amazing. Displaytek's CEO, Duncan Beike, is reputed to be a brilliant machine engineer whose greatest desire was to start his own company. Duncan wanted instant success. To achieve this, he needed a game changer. Being a born tinker, he made up his mind to invent something monumental. It's at this point I recall my near miss with the blow-dryer. I moan forlornly as I imagine what a marvelous ray gun it could have been. I stare at the image of Duncan Beike on the screen, while pining over lost riches for several seconds. It's a while before I can read on about his amazing success.

After graduating at the top of his class, he set up a lab of sorts in the barn at the back of his parents' house and got down to some serious tinker business. For several months, he did nothing but fiddle away like a mad scientist. Rarely did he come up for fresh air. He had his meals brought to him, and it's rumored to have gone days on end without a shower. He was a man on a mission. Being alive with brilliant ideas is not an easy and peaceful way to live. One is constantly buzzing with fiercely sizzling energy. The desire to create. The desire to invent. The scent of that next great discovery, always fueled by the power of a dream. Duncan was passionate about capitalizing on that dream, come rain, or shine. He didn't stop working, no matter what.

At first, it was touch and go, trial and error, scrunch and scrape for funds and support. There were many sleepless nights and hair-raising explosions. When fires broke out, he doubled as a fireman. I stare in wonder at the accompanying pictures of him with singed hair. I fantasize until I see myself looking just like him, singed hair and all, on the verge of a monumental scientific breakthrough and a solid patent for life. It's a few minutes before I come back to reality.

Duncan's one of a kind, I read on. Despite all the various setbacks, he didn't give up. He worked out the kinks. He straightened out the problems. Months poured into a year. Little by little, his dream project grew. It wasn't long before his futuristic automobile head unit began to take shape, its main feature being an extremely large holographic touch screen.

When the big breakthrough finally came, Duncan Beike was as excited as a fresh daddy with a newborn baby, so goes the report. His groundbreaking invention had just opened its eyes to the world and taken its first ginger steps. Just like a new daddy, Duncan had celebrated. He had eaten birthday cake the whole night and partied till morning, just like I had intended to do with my ray gun. Duncan and I, we must surely be birds of a feather.

By afternoon of the same day, he had a patent. Lucky bugger! A day later, Displaytek Systems Ltd. came into being. Six months after that, the first batch of automobile head units hit the market. They were an instant hit, and Duncan Beike became a celebrity overnight. Ten years later, his company is now eighty employees strong, and growing.

I wager he makes a ton of money, lives like a king, and is chauffeured about in a ridiculously long limousine, just like one of those celebrities I see on TV. Tomorrow, I'll be signing a thesis-internship contract with his company. I may not be starting a company of my own, but I will be walking the corridors of one whose CEO dared to dream big. On this night, I dream of riches beyond my wildest imagination. I stay up for a long time, and do not fall asleep until the wee hours of the morning.

Four

THE ROAD THROUGH Jena's city center is teeming with the slow-paced midmorning traffic. For twenty minutes, I meander on Fuerstengraben Street and then slowly on toward the outskirts of town. Here, it's peaceful. Traffic is thin. On either side of the road, a vast expanse of forest extends as far as the eye can see. Every few feet, sunlight finds a gap in the thick foliage and breaks through unimpeded. When this happens, its brilliant beams cascade through the air and splash resplendently onto the superhighway. Already, I can tell it will be another super-hot day. And unfortunately for me, my ventilation is still as dead as a doornail. I roll down my window for some relief. The respite is little. I stick my head out for more. The breeze is lovely, but I can't maintain the position. So, in comes my head again, and it's back to the stifling heat-business once more. I drive on, thoroughly disgusted.

The green forest presently gives way to vast fields of open farmland. A strip of trees in the distance, snakes through farms, indicating the presence of a river in their midst. Though beautiful, the landscape barely registers on my now troubled mind. Anje Tille is expecting me at this very moment. Sadly, I'm still on the B87, ten minutes away from Displaytek. I still have another fifteen kilometers to go. Nothing is as unforgivable as being late for an interview. With deep worry lines firmly grooved across my brow, I floor the gas pedal. The Mazda shoots forward. We, my car and I, are gunning for Displaytek. Before long, I turn southwest in Apolda and head toward my destination.

THE MASSIVE tract of land seventeen kilometers northwest of Jena houses a budding industrial area that, over time, has become home to several manufacturing companies. A number of these are famous, and many are reputed to have been highly active in truly monumental scientific breakthroughs. I spot a few big names, and a thrill runs through my bones. I'm in the heart of technological development. How great is that?

As Displaytek comes into view, I take in its impressive appearance. I even let a "Wow!" escape my lips. The building is four stories high, with light-blue walls and rows of windows interspersed by dark-blue pillars. Neon letters on the roof spell out Displaytek. The sign, which stands tall, must be without a doubt brilliant and impressive at night. I've got to come back here at night sometime. It dawns on me I'm gawking, so I rein in my emotions.

I leave my car in the parking strip designated for visitors and follow a short, meandering path, that takes me through well-manicured lawns up to the majestic building. A receptionist with an inviting smile and sparkling eyes urges me over. "Caroline Henke," says the name tag on her right breast. It's nice to finally put a face to the name. I introduce myself. She knows why I'm here. She asks me to follow her, which I do. We are on the move, stepping into an elevator.

We surface on the fourth floor, Displaytek's top and final floor. I learn from Caroline that many of the people here simply refer to it as the executive floor. "Here," she says, "is where the business end of things takes place."

"Aha! Very impressive," I say. *Goodness, I sound and feel like a true schmuck.*

We walk over a plush cream carpet in a well-lit hallway. My feet are comfortably cushioned, my steps muffled, and I can't help noticing the golden silence that hangs heavy in the air. Closed doors on either side with nameplates on them betray a variety of offices and professions. I barely take note of them, as I'm focusing on the encounter about to take place.

We zero in on the door immediately before the elevator— "Personnel and Legal Services," according to the nameplate. A quick knock and we step through into the office. Two women are seated at desks facing each other. Five meters of open space lies between them, and daylight streams in through the window in the far wall. Caroline announces my presence and vanishes quickly, leaving me alone with the two.

"Anje Tille," says the middle-aged woman at the desk to my left.

"We finally meet," I say, upon recognizing the melodious voice and familiar name.

Smiles and handshakes cover up the fact that we are sizing each other up. She is wearing an olive-green business suit, and her hair is severely pulled back into a knot. I'm in black cotton trousers and a white shirt. A tie dangling across my front, is firmly noosed around my neck and seems to be choking me to death. She looks austere, while I am dressed to impress.

I think I'll fit in here quite nicely.

The young woman in a yellow blouse and blue jeans at the other desk quietly introduces herself as Christine Gay, the company's legal representative. Waves of warmth stream from her soft gray eyes, which are covered by amazingly thick-rimmed glasses. Her smile makes me feel welcome, cherished, and appreciated. She has the loveliest head of golden hair I've ever seen. The way it casually cascades over her shoulders and down to her slender waist is truly awesome. I try not to spend too long looking at it, otherwise, she might think I am creepy.

Instead, I will my eyes to grow a healthy interest for the room's interior.

Most of the office is decorated in white—white walls, white shelves to the sides along walls, white carpet, white ceiling, white picture frames, and even the desks are white. The only other place with this much white, I earnestly believe, is the Antarctic.

"Please," says Anje Tille, "do take a seat." She nods at the two chairs across from her desk. I sink into one.

"Any trouble finding Displaytek?"

"None at all."

"Good. It's a maze out here. Some get lost, you know? Never to be found again." She smiles weakly at her lame joke.

My smile mirrors hers.

Suddenly she is all business. A folder with my name on it lies before her. She opens it and, with a mighty jerk forward, starts to rummage through my documents. I sent her these a while ago. Curriculum vitae, application letter, my various grade slips, and so on. She furiously churns through them wildly, sending several sheets of paper straight up into the air. They all swirl about her head as though caught up in a small hurricane. Her brow is knitted in concentration. The sound of ruffling paper fills the office. I watch, mesmerized.

Her hand surfaces with a slip of paper. She starts speaking before her eyes focus on it. "Your thesis subject is…" She pauses, skims the document, discards it in disgust, and stirs up another little hurricane as she dives into the folder for what she wanted in the first place.

I know my thesis subject by heart, as I've been glancing at it almost every hour of every day since Anje e-mailed it to me. I've had days to analyze it. I took time off studying for exams, in order to research it. I've spoken to professors about it and even done a little preliminary work on it. I could recite it to her, word for word. But, at this moment, I'm tongue-tied. I watch the little hurricane swirl unimpeded. It comes dangerously close to the edge of her desk, and for an instant, I hold my breath, fearing my documents will sail off into the air, never to be seen again.

At last, she finds what she is looking for. She holds the document closer to her eyes, squints at it, and then says, "Aha, here we are." She squints some more. "Analyze the production processes and suggest improvements with a view to increasing output," she reads. "There!" A smug satisfaction possesses her face as she absentmindedly discards the piece of paper. It floats under her desk.

Christine Gay, the legal representative, seems to have lived through one too many of these such moments. She's been keeping a keen eye on the whole ordeal, hoping intensely nothing lands on the floor. With a sigh, she comes over, fetches the sheet of paper, and places it with mock ceremony on the desk before Anje, hoping the latter will get the message. Anje doesn't even notice her.

I look from one to the other in growing amusement. Anje's voice pulls me back to the issue at hand. "Ready to take this on?"

"As ready as can be," I say. I hope my smile is reassuring. I could swear my face is made of plastic.

She scrutinizes me, trying to determine if I'm good for the company or acrid poison. My plastic smile resists all attempts at dire readjustment. All I can do is hope I look intelligent. She eyes me suspiciously and then chooses to give me the benefit of the doubt.

A second later, she throws herself into a small but passionate discourse about the reasons for the thesis internship and why they need me. Her lips are a blur as she races through what Displaytek hopes to gain from me in the end. "We want to increase output, optimize production, improve things, and make changes, that sort of thing, you know?"

I don't know but answer in the strong affirmative, nevertheless, as though I know everything.

She consults my grade slips and then suddenly looks up at me. "Says here you were the best in your class for Management Methods of Production?"

My question-and-answer strategy at preparing for exams come to mind, and I almost choke on my tongue. As helpful as they were back then, this shortsighted approach to my future career life is now coming full circle on me. My facade of intelligence almost crumbles as I plow through with my best poker face I can manage. "Yes, I was."

"And you also have a firm grasp of automated systems?"

I recall that the simple Introduction to Automated Systems was only a one-semester class. Do I have a firm grasp of the subject matter? I fidget a little, barely holding back a hard swallow. Because I'm still under Anje's glaring scrutiny, I answer as firmly as I can, "Yes."

"Hmm" is all she says, and next thing I know, her elbows land on the desk, and her chin comes to rest on her balled fists. She stares at me ever more suspiciously, openly analyzing me, probably in an attempt to get me to break out in a cold sweat. I think I'm almost there. Christine Gay suddenly finds something to read and is very busy all at once. Her ears remain piqued, however, and I realize she is listening very closely, as though expecting a bloodbath any second. A stream of sweat does finally find its way down my face.

Anje Tille is once again engrossed in my grade slips. She reads just under her breath, "Layout of Work Systems and Factories, best grade. Electrical Engineering, best grade. Fundamentals of Business Administration and Economics, best grade. Design Engineering, best grade. Dynamics, best grade..." She breaks off to resume staring at me.

I slink lower in my seat. If my question-and-answer study strategy comes to light right now, I am a dead man; I just know it. I try to tell her just how many books I have read in my life and just how clever I am. She is a living polygraph and does not stop looking for lies. I sweat and gulp like never before and blame it on the heat outside.

"My my, Elbert," she finally says, as I run out of words to fluff myself up with. "We got ourselves a prize bull here," she coos. "You will do just fine at Displaytek; I can tell." With that, she breaks into a broad smile. Her eyelids are down at half-mast, and her voice is remarkably melodious. A goofy smile appears on my face too.

Then things happen quickly. One moment, half her pupils are visible. The next, she's earnestly rummaging through paperwork as though her life depends on it. She snaps up a document and raises it to her eyes. Several single-sheet documents take to the air in the wake of her hand and then flutter lazily back to the table once more. Nothing falls under the table. It's a miracle. Christine breathes a sigh of relief, as Anje waves her prize in my face. "The contract," she says matter-of-factly.

The document is several pages thick. I stare at it apprehensively. Christine watches closely, ready to give legal advice if need be. Anje goes into her routine. She explains the contract, my intended relationship with the company, and what they expect of me. She waves the contract here and there as she speaks. I do not let it out of my sight, except, of course, when responding to a comment, or agreeing to a condition. We agree that the contract is between Displaytek Systems Ltd. and me; that my name, date of birth, and address are all true, belong to me, and are correctly spelled; and that I am who I say I am and not an imposter. I have to swear I am capable of meeting the demands of the thesis study and that I will heed my supervisor's advice to the best of my ability, or so help me God. She stares holes into me until I actually repeat three times that I will most definitely heed my supervisor's advice, no matter what. Now, I am scared. Who is this supervisor? What breed of animal is he? And what actually lies in store for me?

The last few pages of the contract detail my legal responsibilities to the company. I am obligated to secrecy, and anything I invent or discover during the course of my thesis will become the property of Displaytek. Somebody somewhere thinks the world is full of Einsteins and Duncan Beikes, and that I'm probably one of the above. How sweet.

I spend two minutes of my life scrawling my signature on several dotted lines throughout the document. Just as I'm done, Anje becomes aware of the shocking state of her desk. Unexpectedly, she lets out a shrill yelp. I'm two feet in the air as she flips into a tizzy and springs into action. Almost simultaneously, her hands shoot out in all directions as she gathers up the scattered documents. This is evidently not a onetime occurrence. Christine has been expecting this and watching me, waiting for my reaction. Unbridled laughter plays in her eyes as she struggles to keep a straight face. At least someone is having fun. I'm scared silly and still pumped full of adrenaline. Anje's shrill mode is one of a kind. Composure will be a long time coming.

I look over to Anje, remnants of fear still streaking from my eyes. Her brow is knitted, her eyelids are fluttering, and her hands are a flurry. The clutter dwindles. In no time, her desk is once again neat and tidy. My copy of the contract lies before her, and hers is locked away. She slips mine into an envelope and pushes it over as she says, "Congratulations. You are now a part of our team for the next few months."

"Thanks," I say. My voice is shaky.

Christine giggles and then blames it on what she is reading.

"Do you have any questions or queries?" Anje asks, suspicious eyes darting between me and her legal representative.

"None I can think of."

"Should you have any in the future, feel free to come over."

"I most certainly will, thanks." I intend to avoid her like the plague.

"Your supervisor is waiting for you at reception. Use your time here well, and deliver an enlightening and successful thesis study. We are counting on it."

"I will give it my best shot," I reply.

Her duty is done. Suddenly she is acting like I am a gate-crasher. I get it. It's time for me to go. The two ladies wish me all the best. I take my leave.

A cool breeze sweeps through the executive corridor as I wait for the elevator to resurface. Now that the meeting with Anje Tille is behind me, I am relaxed and receptive to my immediate surroundings. Apart from the personnel office I just came from, I spot a bookkeeping office, controlling office, sales and marketing office, as well as the CEO's domain at the opposite end of the corridor. The corridor opens into a well-appointed circular vestibule right in front of the CEO's office. Luxurious couches are strewn across the plush cream carpet, and a kitchenette is tucked away to one side. Two restrooms for the different sexes take up the other side.

I walk into the vestibule and stare at the CEO's door. I will it to open, but Duncan Beike doesn't come out. I know he is in there because he has a Do Not Disturb sign hanging on his door. What normal mortal has a Do Not Disturb sign hanging on an office door? *Maybe this is a special attribute of the tinker humankind,* I muse. And what if he's tinkering in there right this very minute? How I would love to watch! How I would love to engage him in tantalizing conversation about his tinker escapades! He is a walking treasure trove of fascinating tinker anecdotes, of this I'm sure. Give me half a chance, and I'll squeeze every last one out of him. Who knows, one day, I might even end up an accomplished tinker with my own successful company and just as many tinker anecdotes at my fingertips for those dazzling office parties. There is hope for me yet. I have a very sloppy and dreamy smile on my face, as I turn about and make for the elevator.

In the reception area, a tall man impatiently paces the floor under the watchful eye of Caroline Henke. His snug-fitting designer jeans and blue shirt visibly outline the contours of his lithe body, which he obviously loves to show off. Every now and then, he runs a hand through his vibrant black hair or over his clean-shaven face in ever-growing agitation. A big red writing pad dangles from his other hand. Behind the receptionist hangs a giant clock that has his undivided attention. As my footsteps ring out on the tiled floor, he turns, notices me for the first time, and calls out, "David Elbert?"

"Yes?"

"You've kept me waiting here five minutes already?" A look of horror is firmly planted on his face. Apparently, I'm late, and, unmistakably, he has things to do.

"Sorry, I just left Anje Tille's office."

His thin lips crack into a slight smile. "Kevin Koch, your supervisor."

"Nice to meet you," I respond. I look for the animal in him but don't find it. *Maybe,* I think to myself, *it will pop up later.*

"So," he says with a last look at the clock, "I am a technical-college graduate with a major in production, and in case you are wondering, I know my way around technology and technical issues pretty well." He's establishing his authority. Fine by me. I am just here for a thesis internship, so I can graduate with honors and land a fancy job with outrageous pay somewhere out there in the big bad world. God forbid I step on anyone's toes in the process.

"Been here three years now, you know?" he continues. "Most of it as the company's production scheduler."

I know not what to say other than "Aha!"

He lets me know life's been good. Very good in fact. To him, especially, he emphasizes with a coy smile, but also to the company as a whole, he points out. Over the years, the company has been blessed with steady growth. Sales are up, know-how is at an all-time high, and they are all making good money. Still, there's lots of room for improvement, and dark clouds are hovering on the horizon. Competitors have grown in number and strength. "Bad times are brewing," he says ominously. "An all-out war for the market share is imminent. It's time to prepare for a storm." He hunkers down a little as though in need of a warm coat. I look out just in case maybe since the last time I looked, the weather has changed without my noticing it. Nope! Nothing new out there, not a single dark cloud on the horizon, just the same blazing sun high up in the sky. It's a proverbial storm he's referring to, I now know for sure. And judging by the stern expression on his face, it's going to be huge, and it's coming pretty soon.

Kevin starts to explain Displaytek's current and most pressing concern, a little matter of a client demanding more output. So, he says, the company is looking for bright young minds to bring it to the next level. And here is where I come in. He will guide me, show me the ropes, and be there for me if I need him. The bulk of the work will have to be mine, though. After all, I need this in order to graduate, isn't that right? I answer in the affirmative.

All the while we have been talking, he has been giving me a quick tour of the company. A lot of work obviously went into its design. The offices are stylish and modern, fitted with simple yet elegant decor.

Kevin succinctly introduces me to selected persons before quickly steering me onward. We rush through the materials procurement office, the goods receivables, and the storage facility on the first floor. We spend a few more minutes in the production department on the second, then ride the elevator to research and development on the third. Everywhere we go, everyone is hard at work. A number of passageways and vestibules boast eye-catching futuristic sculptures designed to motivate and awe. The whole look is sophisticated and ultra-modern. It's the perfect setting to work in. I'll definitely love it here, I quickly realize.

The guided tour sadly comes to an end without a visit to the executive fourth floor. I was hoping for a personal introduction to Duncan Beike, so I am heartbroken. We go back to the cafeteria for a quick cup of coffee. Once seated, Kevin peppers me with all sorts of questions. He is a curious man who wastes no time finding out who I really am and what makes me tick. He starts off by filling in the usual blanks. Where did I study? What did I study? Do I have kids? Am I married? Why Displaytek? His tongue is guarded. Mine flaps nonstop. The questions are diverse and endless. I try to watch my answers.

Without warning, he quickly gets down to business. "We are currently producing about 1,100 automobile head units a month," he says out of the blue. He then presses his thin lips together and waits for my comment.

The new topic of conversation has caught me by surprise. It takes me a handful of seconds to rally. "What's your target figure?"

"Four hundred percent increase in output." He once again presses his lips almost seamlessly together, and I sense the weight of his words in the air. He eyes me, waiting for a comment.

I screw mine, trying to look very intelligent. "Anything done toward this end?"

"We have carried out a number of optimization modifications to date …" He pauses, wincing at unpleasant memories.

I pounce on this titbit, prompting more info, knowing I'm on to something. "And?"

"Little or no impact on production efficiency or output, I am afraid."

We both remain silent for a moment. I revisit my classroom lectures, looking for something clever to say. "How is the competition doing in comparison?"

His brows squint as he formulates an answer. "Most producers in the industry are old-timers, know what that means?"

"Not really." I am getting into my flow, enjoying this busybody conversation and craving more of it. This time, I am eyeing him as he speaks.

"They've been around for a while. They use standardized parts to create standardized products, which they produce in impressive assembly plants acquired over many years. Undoubtedly, they outgun us on any given day. They can produce several thousand units a month without breaking a sweat." He sighs as though this is all very unfair and there is nothing he can do about it.

"Despite this, you mentioned sales are up?"

"Yes, that's true. Product differentiation's the word, and we have Duncan Beike to thank for this," he says with a weak smile. "You see, no other R&D team the world over has quite gotten the hang of his groundbreaking and most futuristic automobile head unit. The large holographic touch screen is not only a lovely beauty, but a true marvel of advanced technology. Reverse engineering it is a nightmare and developing one from scratch is such a big headache that everyone is asking how Duncan Beike pulled it off in the first place. They can't quite get it right. Don't get me wrong; they are tinkering furiously, and one day, they will get there."

"And when they do, you fear they will flood the market?"

"That's right, and put us out of business."

We both fall silent at this. He is lost in thought. I sip my coffee nervously. For the first time, I see what I'm up against. Increase production and secure a bigger market share before the patent runs out. It's a tall order. And since Displaytek wants to tap into cutting-edge production knowledge, they came to campus, fished about, followed the trail of best grades, and ended up with me. So here I am doing sixty seconds with Kevin and hoping he will not notice how nervous I am.

"Come in early tomorrow," Kevin says in a low voice, still deep in thought. "I have scheduled an orientation program for you, you know? To help you acquaint yourself with our production systems and processes."

"Will do," I respond. So, there it is, as clear as writing on a wall. My Displaytek adventure begins tomorrow. There is a tingle in my tummy, a mixture of excitement and disquiet. It's still too early to tell which emotion will gain the upper hand. I fill myself with hope for the best, and mentally prepare myself for the days ahead.

Kevin has lots to do. He announces it's time for him to get back to his post. We drink up and part ways fifteen minutes later.

Five

DISPLAYTEK'S REVERED operations-scheduling section lies within the west wing of the production department. I arrived at seven, and I'm now seated amongst the busy members of the picking team. We are at six tables in a tight three-by-two formation. Four of the team are seated at their places, working independently. Ludwig Beck, their leader, hovers over me, closely watching my every move on the large monitor. Since morning, this bald man in his late forties has been showing me the ropes of their operational activities.

He gives me a set of instructions to carry out. I punch them in on the keyboard, and the computer goes to work. The image on the monitor suddenly changes to columns of data. I study the words and figures. Ludwig points excitedly. He's speaking nonstop, explaining everything. I'm beginning to connect the pieces.

Staying focused on Ludwig's little lecture isn't easy. Primarily, because of the odd bunch of picking personnel gathered here with me in this well-lit open office. In one way or another, every single one of them is an incredibly amazing if not truly shocking source of distraction. Probably the worst is the mountain of muscle seated to my immediate left. Hans Hartmann is—huge! This scary freak of nature should never have happened, I am convinced of this. To make matters worse, he's a bodybuilder. And since his immense size apparently isn't enough for him, this imposing giant has seen it fit and proper to work out right here in the office, amidst his workmates. In his right hand is a small palm-size biceps developer about the size of his fist. Since the day begun, he's been gleefully pumping away at it with one hand. The other hand earnestly pecks at his keyboard. Working muscle while getting work done, seems to be his normal modus operandi, judging by the lack of interest his colleagues are showing. Every now and then he poses, flexes, steals a glance at his absurdly huge biceps, admires the way they are seriously poking out of his tight-fitting T-shirt, and is immediately deliriously dizzy with joy. I try not to look but find myself powerless. I am simply riveted.

Ludwig is still rattling on. He goes into a fastidious monologue so full of technical terms, I find myself fighting to keep pace. "Our Enterprise Resource Planning System uses the Complete Production Order Method to credit materials," he says, trying to keep his voice low. He needn't bother. I am the only one paying attention to him, and he knows it. "This is how we credit materials to reflect true stock levels. So far so good?"

I nod. He smiles and bows theatrically, clean-shaven scalp catching the light and glinting for a second. I am momentarily blinded and partially amazed such a thing is even possible.

Sitting motionless across from me with his elbows on the table and head in his hands is a stubble-cheeked black-haired man who hasn't moved a hair's breadth since I first saw him. There's a large book open before him. He appears lost in earnest study. Suddenly, he snorts loudly. Then all at once, he's snoring consistently.

Damned! Here in the office? Am I the only one seeing this? I look around, and to Sleeping Beauty's right, notice the puny little guy with the strangest facial features I've ever seen on a person. And he's super excited! I watch as his maroon eyes, already too large for his oblong head, gain a further centimeter or two in diameter. He smiles, and blood-red lips pull way back, revealing shiny teeth, puffy gums, and a violently snaking tongue overcome by the thrill of what he's about to do. I quickly learn he goes by the name of Timothy Lang, but everyone simply calls him Timo. And boy, he loves to be a comedian.

The minute he realizes Frank is asleep, his face embarks on a journey through a series of expressions that, try as I might, I can't even begin to describe. One thing is for sure: mischief is about to take place.

He pulls out a feather from nowhere. Then, in short quick jabs that can only amount to the fabled guerilla tactic fashion, he sets about tickling Frank in the face. He attacks him on the cheek, and then sits stock-still, doing his best imitation of a statue. Giggles break out all around as Frank's hand comes up fast. Wham! He slaps himself so hard on the face he almost topples off his chair. The snoring stops. He's suddenly completely awake, looking through beady eyes, searching our faces, trying to figure out what the hell just happened. It's a sidesplitting spectacle. I am doing my damnedest not to laugh. At the same time, I struggle for focus, since Ludwig is still talking. It's a losing battle.

Timothy heaves with suppressed laughter. He stares at his monitor and then sneaks a sideways glance at Frank. The way he does this, tips us all right over the edge. We roar with unrestrained laughter, then double over at the sight of Ludwig trying to suppress his mirth by rocking back and forth on the balls of his feet, and Hans, poor Hans, howling like a dog and clutching at his ribcage like he's about to die, nearly does it in for all of us. It's a circus. Frank, quite naturally, wants none of it. He simply ignores us and goes back to "reading." Timo can't wait for him to start snoring again.

A WHILE LATER, an exciting discussion on the intricacies of materials crediting flares up when Ludwig poses a question to me. Everyone has something to say, apart from Sleeping Beauty, of course. We talk about actual stock levels, their book values, how to equate the two, and their significance to the purchasing department. Mostly, I listen, and twice, I comment. Nick Neumann makes a number of contributions. He's an ambitious type blessed with big ears, sharp eyes, a long nose, and full lips, which he constantly keeps severely pressed together when not talking. Must be one of those types who think best when doing that funny lip thing.

It soon becomes clear his knowledge is as formidable as that of Ludwig Beck. Unlike the others, who are simply dressed in jeans and casual shirts, he's wearing black cotton trousers and a white long-sleeved shirt with a tie. A matching suit coat hangs from the back of his chair. I learn that Nick Neumann has big career dreams. One day, he plans to move up the ladder into Ludwig's position. To get there, he's leaving no stones unturned and has his life well mapped out, down to the very last item of clothing. He might be a useful ally. I could learn something from him. I'll have to wait and see.

The discussion peters out, with everyone going back to their regular duties. Ludwig, however, is not done with me yet. "Do you know how many production orders are initiated each day?" he asks.

How could I? "No," I answer.

"Many."

"How many are many?"

"Depends."

"On what?"

"Quantities per order. But that's beside the point." He runs a hand over his naked scalp, polishing it some more. It shines brighter.

"What I am getting at is this: for each order, assembly work is carried out, and materials are used up."

"Naturally," I interject needlessly.

He ignores me. "As a result, a materials credit slip is generated."

"A what?"

He dashes over to his desk and comes back with an in-box tray, which he ceremoniously places before me. From it, he picks up a materials credit slip and holds it before my nose. I get cross-eyed trying to read it.

"Oh, that!"

"Yes, that," he responds flatly.

"What about it?"

"For every accomplished production order, a materials credit slip will land in this tray on your desk," he says matter-of-factly, pointing at the tray.

For the first time, I notice it's overflowing with a huge pile of credit slips, probably accumulated over many days. His last words register with a bang. I stare at the endless hours of grant work heaped up before me. In growing shock, I barely manage to ask, "Did you say my desk?"

"Yes, David. You want to learn, don't you?"

"Certainly, but I —"

"Perfect. Materials crediting is the best place to start. I have shown you the ropes. Think you can handle it?"

"Yes, but ..."

"Fantastic! Music to my ears! Since you know what to do, by all means, David boy, do have fun." With that, he goes back to his desk. A big satisfactory smile commandeers his face and won't let go. He just dumped his grant work on the new rookie.

Just like him, his team is loving every moment of this show. They all grin at me, bursting with amusement. At that moment, a few things suddenly become very clear to me. This is a defining corporate culture. I am being initiated into the production department. This must be a standing ritual, repeated on every new rookie that comes along. Absolutely no way around it. So, this is the way my foray into the corporate world begins? I am a little disgusted. "Hooray, David. Such a promising start," I say sarcastically under my breath. It takes me some time to shake off the let-down.

A few minutes into my labor, Hans Hartmann is eager to talk. He taps my left shoulder, darts his eyes secretively about, and then beckons me to draw closer. I oblige, welling with curiosity.

Our heads almost touch. "Real lady-killer," he whispers, blatantly jerking his thumb toward Frank Krueger. So much for secretive. The faux pas is not lost on Hans though. Like a periscope, he raises his head and scopes the room, scanning for detection. No one is paying us any attention. So, he breathes easier and stoops down again, in my direction. It's back to whispers.

"Our lady-killer here," he says, again with the thumb-jerking, "usually parties all evening. More often than not ends up with a girl for the night. Sleeps through the first hour of work almost every day." He nods knowingly, gives me a long list of party locales Frank is known to frequent, then asks if I would like to be his wingman to any one of them. Before I can answer, he flashes a super wide grin at me as he sits back and suddenly changes the topic by saying, "What do you make of this?" He's pointing at his left arm, the biceps of which are now contracted. The bulging muscles fill out his T-shirt nearly ripping it apart. It's not unusual to see the bodies of weight-lifters vibrating from the exertion of constant exercise. For some inexplicable reason, this is not happening with Hans, though he's been at it since seven this morning. I generously compliment him on his marvelous workout and watch him swell a further notch with pride. His sunny smile spasms with the strain of posing but doesn't fade. A muscle pull on that body would be a colossal disaster.

I've been crediting material slips for two hours straight. The pile in my in-box dwindles quickly, making me come across as an assiduous neophyte. I would like to say I'm enjoying this, but that would be a lie. It's simply something that must be done. I go at it as if I would love to do nothing else my entire life. I neither slack nor waver. I keep this up for a week.

Dead ahead and a handful of paces from where I am seated are four offices, two to either side of a narrow corridor. Their glass walls give price to everything within. Kevin has the nearest to the left, and the production manager has the other beside his. The ones to the right are currently unoccupied by personnel. They seem to be doubling as storage and are filled with all manner of junk.

I can clearly see Kevin and the production manager from where I sit. On this day, Kevin is dressed in jeans and a blue shirt, while the fiftysomething production manager is in a dark-blue suit. Their line of sight is just as unimpeded as mine. They can clearly see the goings-on in the open office where my colleagues and I are seated.

At this very moment, both are on the phone talking earnestly. They are looking this way, their gazes resting on me. It doesn't take me long to deduce that I am the subject of discussion. When I notice how grave their faces are, a feeling of disquiet comes over me. I try not to worry as the hairs on my nape slowly rise.

Am I doing something wrong?

Minutes later they set down their phones pensively. I watch with growing unease as Kevin steps out of his office and looks at me. He hollers, "Mr. Wolfgang wants a word with you, David. Right away."

I nod, act calm, but my heart is doing a racy drum solo. I drag my leaded legs into the production manager's office. A nameplate on his mahogany desk lets me know he is Matthias Wolfgang. Up close, I notice the prominent whites on the sides of his grizzly-gray hair. The man has a considerable number of years under his belt. He looks distinguished too, and authority oozes from his every pore.

Quietly, he offers me a seat. I settle down across from him, on the other side of his desk, alert and weary all at once. My eyes wander to the family portrait hanging behind him. It's huge, preposterous, and sorely out of place. He narrows his eyes as I take in his colorful family. A wife, a teen daughter, and a slightly older son are grouped around his seated frame. None of them bear the slightest resemblance to each other. A mix-and-match family if ever I saw one. Matthias Wolfgang tries to gauge my opinion of his brood. After a moment, he asks, "How's materials crediting coming along?"

The monotony is killing me, and I hate the crap. "Great," I respond.

"Having fun?"

"Hardly."

"You are working hard at it."

"Yes."

"Why?"

"I cherish work?" This came out as a question, though this was not my intention. I read somewhere in a progress-review guideline that this is the right answer to give. I watch him keenly.

His eyes soften. He chuckles. "Really? Just a simple workaholic, huh? Nothing to prove?"

"Let's just say I'm driven."

"By what?"

"Success."

Again, he chuckles boisterously. "Trust me, young man; materials crediting won't bring you millions."

"What will?"

"Deliver a good thesis, graduate with honors, and find yourself a real job in a glamorous outfit. Then pray its manager dies quickly of old age. With luck, someone will recommend you take his place. And with further luck, the board of governors will agree."

"Sounds bleak," I comment fearfully. "Is it really that bad?"

"Life is tough," he answers gruffly. "And finding oneself in a life that's glamorous? Well, that depends on plain old luck," he says, almost growling. "That's just how it is. Trust me; I know." His eyes take on a distant look as a long, wistful sigh escapes him. I get the feeling his past is riddled with countless attempts at climbing the corporate ladder. He's got his sights set on serious money. Clearly, Matthias Wolfgang craves the lifestyle of the rich and famous. His eyes burn with ambition. Someday, he will rake in the millions. Till then, he makes do with production management. This isn't bad, just demanding and time-consuming, and that's just the problem. He wants to sit on a luxury yacht, sipping rum and watching the sun cross the heavens, and then go in for a dip as the last sun rays vanish over the horizon, he lets me know.

He shakes his head, trying to shake off the fantasies and return to the present. Within seconds the dreamy side of him vanishes, leaving behind the competent, ever watchful time-driven manager.

"Let's map out a strategy for your thesis initiative, shall we?"

"I am game," I say.

He places a call to Kevin, who then quickly joins us in his office. Together, we spend an hour beating out a detailed plan for me to follow. Through it all, I get a glimpse of the company's tall expectations of me. I am slightly overwhelmed. Displaytek is awaiting a monumental miracle. I start to wonder if I'll ever deliver.

Six

My actual internship is set to take place under the excellent tutorship of Bianca Winkler. According to Kevin, she's a gifted assembling genius. I'm dying to meet her.

The blond-haired woman picks me up at my desk and sets off at a brisk pace in the direction of the company's east wing. She is speaking as we go. There are many thingamajigs she'd love to show me. I can't wait.

Five minutes later we arrive at her domain. "This is the sprawling production hall," she says in a voice filled with pride. Her hands spread out to encompass the entirety of the scene before us.

My eyes roam appraisingly over the fifty or so identical workstations. They are set in neat rows of five on either side of a narrow aisle. An odd assortment of assembly workers seats at them. Very few look up. Most are too busy to pay us any notice at all. It doesn't take a genius to figure out why. Behind each one of them is a humongous mountain of queued work. They have a lot to do. The sense of urgency is palpable. The shortage of time, apparent.

At the front of the hall is a massive wooden shelf that can hold close to a hundred such containers as those in the various queues within the hall. I am quick to realize the purpose of the shelf. It holds freshly scheduled work entering this chain of production. At this moment, it only has a dozen or so containers in it. Bianca steers us in its direction. She picks up one loaded container from it, turns abruptly about, and motions for me to follow her. We end up seated at her workstation in the center of the production hall.

"So, how much do you know about assembly work?" she asks, smiling broadly at me.

Although my knowledge of transistors, resistors, LEDs, semiconductors, processors, synthetic materials, metals, metal machining, dynamics, electrical engineering, and more, has improved in the course of my studies, my knowledge of how all these individual parts function in a machine as a whole still needs a bit more work.

I frankly admit this to Bianca.

She immediately slips into an emergency lesson on aggregate machines and Assembly 101.

I feel my knowledge quickly rounding off.

She is a good teacher.

Occasionally, I get distracted by all the action going on around us. A number of machines and gadgets fill the air with sound, giving testimony to the earnest activities going on within the production hall. I make out the intermittent whirr of automatic screwdrivers at several workstations. Parts click as they clinch together in the moment of their assembly, and a quality control machine growls as it checks out the contours of finished products. Two employees a few rows back are engaged in an intense discussion over the integrity of an assembly part.

Everywhere I look, sleek futuristic automobile head units in various stages of assembly attract my attention. Bianca catches me staring about and admonishes me. I should focus my attention on learning, she says. I do just that.

We are at it for an hour. Suddenly, she fixes me with her gray eyes and says, "Time to take the rudder, David."

I knew this moment would come. Barely calm, I approach the huge shelf up front, drawing to a stop before it. I take stock. Next in line for production are fifteen X28 automobile-head-unit monitors. The very same type she'd just assembled for my benefit. I grab the tray-size container. It feels heavy in my hands. I stare at the single parts within it. My thoughts are a little bit sporadic. Exhaling slowly, I turn about and walk all the way back to Bianca. It's time to show her what I've learned so far.

Once more I'm seated beside Bianca. I get into action.

The bubble of activity in the hall fades as I lose myself in the task at hand. The screen goes onto the flange. I clinch it in place, then drive the screws home. She watches closely as I fit in an FPGA circuit board, bolt spacers, and main circuit board. The hobby tinker in me is alive and kicking. This is fun! I am smiling broadly as the subassembly finally starts to take shape.

Minutes later, with the final touches in place, Bianca announces an assembly time of ten minutes. I want to scream for joy. She, on the other hand, is wearing an expression that says my performance is acceptable for a rookie, but would never be acceptable for a professional like her. The quality is quite perfect, though, she concedes grudgingly. I glow from this compliment and sit taller. Bianca laughs.

Input cables, output cables, VGA and SKS cables dangle freely from my tinker output. The whole subassembly has a surreal look, like a flattened face with electronic dreadlocks. It's giving me the heebie-jeebies. Still, I take a mental picture and marvel at my first ever professional assembly.

At Bianca's bidding, I repeat the process with the remaining pieces. An hour later, I am done. All fifteen X28 monitors are fully assembled and on display.

"Grab your container," Bianca says. "It's time we brought these to Arnold."

ARNOLD is a burly man in his late fifties who occupies a crowded workstation in the extreme right-hand corner at the back of the production hall. His face, white mustache, white goatee and white hair, would make him a natural choice for Santa Claus.

I am certain I have never seen him before. A quick look around his workstation tells me why. Arnold is a man under siege. Unbelievable amounts of work awaiting his attention surround him from all directions, making it practically impossible to spot him at all. There's certainly enough here to keep him busy for many months. Cautiously, without disturbing him, Bianca queues my subassemblies at his workstation. Then we quietly turn around and leave.

"We kind of favor batch production around here," She says to me once we are back at her workstation. "Know what that is?"

"Certainly," I respond, trying to sound offended. "How could I not?"

"Excellent," she says, "Once an order is started, its production progressively goes through one workstation to the next, in a seemingly haphazard manner. In the end, a finished automobile head unit usually leaves the production hall," she tells me in a matter of fact voice.

"Usually?"

"Sometimes, rework is needed. At other times, the piece cannot be salvaged. In which case we scrap it," she answers.

I take note of this. She then goes on to say successful completion may take days, weeks, and sometimes even months. It becomes clear as she talks that the major issue of contention in this company is the unending backlog. It cries out for attention. It needs redress. They are actively looking for answers.

WE BREAK FOR LUNCH at midday and head down to the cafeteria on the ground floor. An air conditioner croons at the center of the ceiling, set high above a spacious scattering of dining tables and modest chairs. I amble over to the food counter at the front, where I select a plate of short boneless ribs, potatoes, black truffle gratin with mushrooms, and a glass of orange juice. I settle with my goodies at a place in the back with a good view of the abstract paintings running along the midsection of the yellow walls. Sunshine streams in through large tilted windows. Its warm light falls partly on the tables and its dinners, and partly on the sparkling gray-and-white tiled floor. The food is delicious.

While we eat, Timo entertains us with a parody of endless jokes. We giggle and laugh, comment and jest. Seeing everyone so merry, Frank Krueger decides to make a play for Christine Gay in the melee. He soon finds out this is easier said than done. The legal representative has her sights set on someone else, who, as unbelievable as it may seem, doesn't seem to realize she exists. For weeks now, after catching the love bug, Christine has been stealing glances at the unsuspecting Hans Hartmann, and going through such a plethora of feverish emotions that it's a wonder they haven't consumed her entirely yet. From burning desire to a steady dreamy look, the list is endless.

I've observed this blossoming affection for days, and clearly noticed one thing: Hans Hartmann has absolutely no idea he's got a stunning admirer. Every lunch break since I started here at Displaytek has been the same. He walks in, orders a meal, takes his seat, and starts to eat. While he does, he admires himself. All that muscle, the power, coupled with boundless testosterone. It's making him delirious. Today, this self-admiration has gotten even worse. With each spoonful to his mouth, he checks out his bulging biceps. He flexes. Muscles ripple. Christine swoons and then tries to hide her delight behind her cascading brown hair. All three of them, Frank,

Christine, and Hans, are lightheaded with delirium, albeit for different reasons. I watch the love triangle and struggle to hide my smile. The deeds and antics of the others in the dining hall only serve to exacerbate my mirth that much more. It's a circus like no other, a festival of colorful personalities. *Boy, I'll really love it here.*

Seven

TO GET MY FEET WET in this business, I decide to pay an impromptu visit to the company's storage hall. Ergon Klein, the stock manager, eagerly walks with me through the long rows of shelves towering way above our heads. He starts to feed me oodles of information. Every few feet, he points at selected pockets of the small fortune and happily explains what they are. He lets slip their obscene prices. I stare at the hundreds of parts and subassemblies. At least ten million dollars in here, probably more. It's impressive.

Ergon never stops talking. Apart from the frequent short visits of the picking team, hardly anyone else comes down here, he says. Most of the time, it's just him and his stock against the world. Clearly, this explains Ergon's exuberance.

He continues to chatter nonstop, lighting up like a Christmas tree when I inquire about minimum and maximum stock levels. This leads to a spirited discussion on tied-up capital, opportunity costs, purchase-trigger stock levels, and safety stock levels amongst others. Ergon is impressed by what I know.

He pulls out a thick wad of printouts from the breast pocket of his gray overalls and eagerly shows them to me. Hundreds of little jagged line charts come into view. "This is how I keep track of all physical stock levels," he says.

I study the piles of paper.

He hops from one foot to the other.

From the corner of my eye, I catch Ergon's excitement going off the scale. He wants to discuss his printouts with me but realizes I'm still busy scrutinizing them. Reluctantly, he lets me be.

We are on the move again.

A few seconds pass in silence.

Further down the aisle, minimum stock levels catch my attention. With a start and a choke, I swoop my head in for a closer look at the warn out charts. Unable to rule out user error, I finally turn to Ergon and ask, "Can this be right?"

There is a questioning look on his face.

I point to the alarming figures.

"Ah!" Comments Ergon, "I was wondering when you would notice."

"They are completely off the charts," I reply, incredulity written all over my face.

Ergon sighs. "Just covering our bases," he says heavily.

"Is stock-out a threat?"

"More than you can imagine."

I raise my eyebrows as I ask, "Delays in deliveries?"

"Sadly, yes."

"Has this ever caused loss of clients?"

"Once," says Ergon. There is a pitiful look in his eyes as he relives this sad memory.

I yank him out of his thoughts with a further question. "How many months of production do these stocks cover?"

"Depends," he says.

"Highest figure?"

"Four to five months."

"Five months!" I stop dead in my tracks. Ergon follows suit. The disbelief in my voice hangs in the air between us.

"For which material, in particular?"

"Central processing units."

"Why?"

"Why CPUs?"

"No dammit. Why five months? I know stock-out is an issue. But five months? That's ridiculous!"

"Supply-company politics, I am afraid. Setting up equipment for each production-change takes time. Time, as we all know, is money. So logically, suppliers want to do this as little as possible. Result thereof? Five months of deliveries dumped on our doorstep. This means for a whole five months, our suppliers don't want to see or hear from us. During this time, they are geared up to produce some other CPU brands for some other clients."

"Phew. Five months!" I let this play in my mind for a while before asking, "And what's the monthly rate of turnover?"

"Zero point one two."

"You don't say! Only twelve percent goes into production each month?"

"I wish it wasn't so, but that's the way it is."

"Goodness gracious me!" The words come out under my breath, barely audible. "That means eighty-eight percent of the stock idles away, day in, day out, for a whole month?"

"You make it sound like a disaster!"

"What else could it be?"

"We're rich," Ergon says in defense before adding, "but yeah, liquidity does get a little tight now and then. I get a whiff of this sometimes, mostly when I put in a request for a new toy. Like last month when I asked for a Yale MTC10-15 forklift. I got a flat no for an answer. Crumbs!"

Ergon must have aced drama in high school. His mouth is theatrically twisted. He looks like he's about to cry. I am entertained but don't get a chance to enjoy it. He's rattling on again.

"One of these days," he says, "I'll get the CEO to try to manage the inventory with the tools I have. We'll see how much fun he has with that." He smiles into the air as this scene plays out in his mind, causing a chuckle to escape my lips.

"Talking of inventory," I say, morphing my face back into a semblance of seriousness. "Isn't there a way around such massive stock buildup?"

"If there is, we've yet to discover it," Ergon lets out quietly, thoughtfully, while looking about at the gold mine around us. A barely perceptible streak of some unknown fear is streaming out of his extra-large eyes.

His premonition of doom sends a cold shiver down my spine. I'm beginning to fear what I've walked into.

A second later, he's his old self again.

We chat for ten more minutes, mostly about his charts.

As I finally make my departure, he lets me know his door is always open.

I promise to be a regular visitor.

I walk out, with only one thought on my mind: *Eighty-eight percent of stocks completely idle for a whole month! No activity taking place, no value being added, nothing!* What a waste. I am unable to stop thinking about this for the rest of the day. I even dwell on it through much of the weekend.

Eight

I'VE DECIDED not to use my troubled car until I get it fixed. Starting this week, it turns a new leaf as I leave it to gather heat and dirt in equal measure out in the parking lot before my apartment.

Nick Neumann gets wind of the fact that I am looking for a carpooling opportunity and rushes in to save the day. He quickly offers to pick me up every morning until further notice. I jump at the offer.

On this lovely Monday morning, he parks before my orange apartment block and then goes on a honking spree for every minute I don't materialize before his car. I cringe at the sound. His horn is unbelievably loud. I worry about my neighbors. Some of them, not surprisingly, start to curse and swear bitterly. A horrendous cry for blood comes from the apartment across from mine. A muscular giant lives there. Granted, he's only a three-quarter-version of Hans Hartmann, but nevertheless, he's a monster. The type who readily breaks one in half simply for smiling at him. I'm tempted to spring out the window. Just in case.

A mad sprint out of my apartment out into the open sends me shooting like a bullet right into Nick's car. I stare out the window, looking for any sign of iron Mike, my neighbor, and only slump back with relief into my seat when I realize the coast is clear. Nick coughs politely. The memory of his horn is still ringing in my ears. I glare at him. As usual, he is wearing a metallic-gray suit, white shirt, and matching tie. He chuckles at me dismissively, turns the key, and the engine catches. The Volkswagen Tiguan lurches erratically forward, and with that, we are on the move, cruising down Drachendorfer Street. We quickly leave the multicolored six-story apartment blocks behind us.

A light shower begins to fall as we breeze through the light morning traffic. The radio is on. We listen silently to the music streaming from the car's surround speakers.

After several minutes, Nick lowers the volume, turns toward me, and asks, "How are things?"

"Good," I say. I have no idea what "things" he's talking about. Doesn't matter.

"And work?" he asks again, running a hand through his jet-black hair.

"Couldn't be any better," I reply succinctly.

"Hm," he says.

There is an air of superiority about him that makes me stifle a smile.

His brow then creases slightly, as though something is troubling him. "The thesis initiative?" he asks. His jet-black eyes look worried.

"Taking shape," I answer.

Then, out of the blue, he says, "I was this close to university too, you know?" His thumb and forefinger are an inch apart from each other and an inch from my face.

"What happened?"

"Wrong priorities in high school, I guess."

"Aha." I recall my high school priorities and wonder how I ever made it to campus. *Music, parties, staking out the mall and hanging out at McDonald's, girls ...*

"Had this girl ..."

"Yeah?" My interest is piqued.

"She dumped me."

"Must have been hard," I empathize quietly.

Nick shrugs. "All in the past now. But back then, my world fell apart."

"Happens more often than you think, to a whole lot of people."

"I know. Thing is, I really hit rock bottom."

"Yeah?"

"Yup. And so, did my grades."

"Shit happens."

He looks at me, nodding in sage acknowledgement. "Took me a while to figure that out, though. By then, I had howled right through my remaining time in high school and failed practically every test I took. I've been trying to make up for it ever since."

"How?"

"Hard work," he answers. "At the office, at home, books, distant-learning programs, you name it."

"Sounds harsh."

"Necessary, that's what it is."

As tough as an ox, this young man. A real fighter who doesn't give up easily. Me, I would simply play the lottery while sipping rum for the rest of my life and hope to hit the jackpot. End of story.

He suddenly looks me dead in the eye and says, "Thanks to all this hard work, I now know a lot of things."

"Yea?"

"Oh yeah, things that could be useful to your thesis," he says mysteriously.

"Like?"

"Principles of production, fundamentals of production theory, process models, VLOOKUP, IFERROR ..." He rattles on for nearly two minutes, but I hear nothing new. It's all familiar.

I nod and make supplementary comments. Then comes the bomber.

"Say, what if I lent you a hand with the whole thing?"

There it is again. That word, *thing*. I sigh as I ask, "Which thing?"

"The thesis, of course."

"You must be kidding!" My heart skips a beat at the thought of such academic suicide.

"I'm not," he says happily, completely misinterpreting my statement. "All you have to do is place my name in the glossary, and we will call it quits. What do you say to that?"

"I ..."

Nick, however, is not yet finished with his elaborate plan. He has big dreams. And he's just getting started.

"What the heck, forget the glossary," he says. "In small print, just under your name on the first page will do just fine." He smiles brilliantly.

"Ooh God!" I am as white as a sheet.

A dreamy look clings to his face as he pushes on. "The two of us, we will be great, I tell you. And the thesis, it will be perfect! With my name as coeditor, can you just imagine that?" He goes starry-eyed like a lover in the middle of ecstasy. The car rockets past an unsuspecting motorist and almost comes broadside with another. I yell to snap him out of it. He swerves. Tires squeal. We barely maintain our lane as he rectifies the car. My heart is galloping like mad, and he simply turns to me and says, "Hey, you look like you've just seen a ghost. What's up?"

Where do I start? The fact that I find myself fearing for my life? Or the blatant disregard of faculty thesis statutes? This last was playing in my mind like a horror movie before the road scare.

Nick snaps me back to the present. "Can I be your co-author?"

I look in dismay at the overzealous lad.

"Will you put my name down under yours?" he asks in an undulating voice overcome by excitement. "Will you do this for me?"

It takes several minutes to explain to him why this won't be happening. Not today, not tomorrow, not ever.

The glitter in his eyes die. His smile slowly but surely turns soar. Nick sulks and pouts through all of three kilometers, finally throwing all caution to the wind and driving more dangerously than ever before. I scream soundlessly in terror. He thinks I am mouthing the music and pumps up the volume. Music creeps back into his soul. I hang onto my seat for dear life, and watch horror-stricken as he bounces like a DJ on his, all the way to Displaytek.

I AM STILL shaking slightly from my ordeal at Nick Neumann's hands as I zero in on Arnold within the production department. He is bent low over his desk. I hear him mumbling away to himself as he feverishly jabs and stabs with various instruments at a sub-assembly before him. The many columns of stacked containers filled with works-in-progress awaiting his attention say it all. Time is the last thing he has to spare.

I approach him for a few lessons on principles of quality controlling.

He, however, is tied up until 1:40 p.m.

I promise to come back then.

Since my session with Arnold doesn't start for another five hours or so, I get myself excused and walk outside into the light of day. With Nick's permission, I drive off in his car. Previously unexplored roads take me past several companies and one or two manufacturers I have never seen before. In between these little eye treats, my thoughts keep coming back to my forthcoming study. There are many production models and premises, principles and statutes, rules and regulations, and a whole load of hypotheses I must sift through before I can be clear on which direction my study will take. There is a lot of work ahead of me.

At lunch hour, I pop into the Hotel am Schloss's restaurant on Jenaer Street, where I order country beef strip loin and French fries in spicy ketchup. Arnold's probably in the middle of his morning's workload, so I am in no hurry. Besides, the meal is delicious. I take my time to enjoy it.

The restaurant's amazing struts and ties keep me entertained for a bit. Time passes slowly. The lunch crowd grows.

By Eleven, I've moved on to my second Cola. Though conversation picks up in the busy restaurant, it's in no way disruptive to me. The minute my plate is cleared away, I replace it with my laptop. I also pull out two university texts: the first, a lecture in product innovation. The second, a study in industrial manufacturing. I open both to relevant pages of interest. And lose myself in study.

Minutes turn into an hour, then two. A quick glance at my watch lets me know it's time. Time to get back to Arnold.

I DRIVE BACK to Displaytek and walk into the production hall at exactly 1:35 pm. Arnold points me to a chair beside his. We get to talking.

After several minutes of him dazzling me with the depth of his knowledge, we dive into the actual physical part of quality controlling: inspecting subassemblies for chips, cracks, scratches, blemished surface treatment, correct assembly, and the flow of continuous current in all circuits.

Arnold proudly hangs a stethoscope about his neck the minute we are done with the subassembly inspection. I have no idea where the stethoscope came from, or what he uses it for. He's now the spitting image of a smiling cardiologist at a heart clinic.

Though an eccentric, Arnold is essentially a simple man who has worked this job on a regular basis for the last ten years. Thanks to the passage of time, he's gathered a body of work-place-specific knowledge that's amazingly rich and incredibly extensive. He happily lets me know this body of knowledge is called work experience, and although no fresh student comes equipped with the good stuff, he assures me that by the end of this day, and with a little help from him, I will be the most experienced student on our side of the At-lantic. I smile, knowing how fantastic this claim is. Despite this, I find myself wishing with all my heart and soul for some truth in it.

Nine

EARLY TUESDAY MORNING, Kevin shows up at my desk and engages me in a lively discussion. It's a test, to see how much I've assimilated thus far.

On realizing I'm enjoying this exchange, he changes tactics and tries to scare me with what's yet to come. "Two more *crucial* processes in the X28," he says, dead serious.

"Which two?"

"Programming and cleaning."

"Anything I should know?" I ask cautiously.

"Study the company's expansive product spectrum. That'll help," says Kevin.

I spend the rest of the day elbows deep in research.

OUT OF CHARACTER, Elise decides to call me shortly before midnight. I've been sound asleep for at least two hours when the ringing phone wrenches me out of my dream. I shoot up and stumble out of bed in near panic. It's dark. I'm disoriented. I find my cell phone on the fifth ring.

"Hello? Who's there?" I ask, groggy, slightly pissed, and still half-asleep. My voice doesn't sound like my own.

"It's me," says a voice I fail to recognize.

"Me who?"

"Elise, of course. Who else?"

"Someone died?"

"No."

"Are you sick?"

"No."

"Pregnant?"

"David!"

"Then why call me at this ungodly hour?"

"Couldn't sleep; that's all."

"That makes two of us now," I say, yawning, practically nodding off as I ask, "What's the problem?"

"Should I only call when there's a problem?"

I sigh and cut her some slack. "Okay, Elise. What's on your mind?"

"We had a good time on campus, didn't we?"

"The absolute best. Many memorable adventures," I say softly. "You miss it?"

"No ... yes ... I mean ..."

I picture her in my mind's eye, wringing her hands. This could prove interesting. Elise is never at a loss for words.

She continues, "Could we have another adventure again?"

"You mean all of us—Karl, Uwe, Leni, you, and I?"

"No."

"No?"

"Eh ... just the two of us."

It's several seconds before this sinks in. My heart starts to race. Now I am fully awake. My eyes grow huge and they desperately try to take in everything in the dark bedroom.

"David, are you still there?"

"I ... yes ... I'm still here."

"Well, then?"

"I ... um ... sure, Elise. I would love that."

"Good. Been to Prague?"

"No. You?"

"I've been dreaming about it for the last year, and, well, since exams are now a thing of the past ..."

"You want to go."

"Yes. With you."

Her voice is soft and endearing as she says, "with you." My heart flutters deliciously. A bittersweet feeling comes over me. Right then, I realize this is what I've been missing all my life. This poignant feeling. Obviously, Cupid has me in his sights and crosshairs, bow and arrow raised. And he's about to draw. All at once, my breathing goes out of control. She hears me panting desperately.

"Are you okay?"

"Sure," I croak. "Just need a sec." I find some water on the bedside table and gobble it down. My voice is finally recognizable to me at last as I ask, "So when should this adventure take place?"

"How does this weekend sound?" she asks.

"Like music to my ears," I say, practically singing.

"Excellent, David. This will be a lovely expo," she croons. "I just know it."

I start in disbelief, wondering if I heard her correctly. "Did you just say expo?"

"Yes I did," says Elise. "Marketing Expo. I thought I mentioned it." She giggles sweetly. Clearly, she very purposely kept this bit of information for last. "What else did you think we were going to do in Prague?"

"Oh, I don't know, maybe have some fun?" Exasperation distorts my voice a further notch.

She giggles while explaining just how great it will be, that I should trust her, expos are a way of life, and I'll love it."

I sigh as she guides me through all the arrangements we need to make for the trip.

Ten minutes later, she lets me get back to bed.

For a while, I struggle with mixed feelings. Are we just friends? Could we be more? Or is she simply looking for a chaperon to ward off the bad boys when we are in Prague? I analyze our phone conversation and come to no solid answer either way. Finally, her lithe body and light-brown eyes take up the whole of my brain capacity. It's a while before I fall asleep again.

9:20 a.m. It's Thursday morning. I take my place beside Jonas Haas. The programmer looks a little surprised. I learned earlier students on thesis missions are known to avoid his workstation like the plague, so he's now openly wondering what's wrong with me. What should I make of this?

Right now, he's engaged in an epic battle with his emotions. Something's happening to his rosy cheeks. They are trembling spasmodically. He attempts a smile while trying to make up his mind whether he should warm up to me or not. Great! Marvelous chap. A truly amazing personality. This one's a keeper.

Suddenly he's aware of the ticking clock. He nervously runs a hand through his umber-colored hair. As he spontaneously skips all pleasantries and ignites into a wicked smile, I realize I'm in trouble. My own brilliant smile falters, then slowly dies out. Knowledge overload is clearly imminent. I'm about to get my brain cells fried.

In a nerdy voice that's more of a squeak, Jonas Haas gets into action. He tells me about BIOS, operating programs, their development, and how they get uploaded and written into the central processing units of machines. He uses many abbreviations. Every now and then, I ask a nerdy question and watch his excitement shoot through the roof as he sets off on a new round of intricate explanations. I didn't want to believe it at first. But now I'm more convinced of it than ever before. His eyes are glowing like diodes. Damn, this is uncanny.

Half an hour later he asks, "Care for a practical demonstration?"

"Thought you would never ask," I say excitedly.

"Lovely," says Jonas. "Prepare to be amazed."

I draw to the edge of my seat, square my shoulders, and wait for it. A tingling sensation creeps over my forearms as Jonas Haas powers up his computer. *Magic is about to unfold,* is all I can think as he grabs the first container in the queue before his workstation. By the time he shows me the batch inside, my internal compass is flipping about so insanely, I dare not breathe. It's tinker hour once more.

Fifteen units of X28 monitor subassemblies, same as the ones Bianca and I assembled, same as the ones Arnold and I later gave a clean bill of health now lie before us. He expertly hooks one up to his computer and starts to download a program into it.

Mr. Squeaky Beady is suddenly a flamboyant orator. As his face lights up, his lucid delivery transforms a dreary topic into a science fiction wonder. All the while he's talking, he's going through the motions. I get to see how he turns a puzzle of random metal and wire into intelligent objects capable of carrying out simple instructions like GPS guidance. It's an act of creation. It's amazing.

We work for two hours straight. I'm almost sorry when the session comes to an end.

Ten

I emerge from deep sleep into a state of partial wakefulness. My whole being is rejuvenated. I feel awesome. Reluctant to get up just yet, I languish between the sheets and let my mind lazily float from one idle thought to another.

It's Friday. This is the day Elise and I have been planning for! At four o'clock today, she and I will drive off to Prague as planned. True, she says this is just a marketing expo trip. But will the business side of it cover the whole weekend? Sweet promise lingers in the air. The prospect of fun with Elise is looking better by the minute. I'm burning with anticipation.

I get out of bed and skip into the bathroom. There's a song in my heart and a whistle on my lips. I yodel as I shower. I laugh with joy as I quote Romeo and Juliet. Water splashes everywhere. I fear something strange is happening to me.

Fifteen minutes later, I gulp down a slapdash breakfast and dash out of the apartment. Carpooling with the reckless driver Nick Neumann doesn't faze me out in the least bit. In fact, I am still in high spirits and full of beans as I arrive at my desk within the walls of Displaytek. Sinking down to it, I get on with the task of looking busy.

Thoughts of the coming weekend interrupt my concentration several times on this day. It's hard to focus on work. And time seems to be standing still.

More than once, I catch myself staring at the clock, looking for any indication of the passage of time. I can barely wait for the day to end.

At ten, I decide to meditate with my palms clasped together, elbows spread out on the desk, and my neck held out as straight as that of an ostrich. As much as is humanly possible, I will myself to be as catatonic as a wooden board. Nice. Calm washes over me. And God forbid, am I falling asleep at my desk?

This new development doesn't go unnoticed by Frank. He's staring intently at me, wondering if at last he's found a kindred spirit among Displaytek's industrious population. God help.

Somehow, I make it through the day. At four o'clock, with my nerve endings sizzling, I dash into Displaytek's toilets and excitedly change into brown Bermuda shorts and a checkered shirt. I look like I should be on a sandy beach somewhere, and not just walking out the doors of a notable company. Nick is kind enough to drive me into the heart of town.

Elise's car is for all intents and purposes, enough for only one person. Her. Okay, yeah, I'm kidding. It's a two-seater. Nevertheless, it's not far removed from the size of a toy. When she suggested we drive to Prague in it, I flatly refused and wouldn't back down. And since she has absolutely no intention of ever getting into my Mazda, we reached a compromise and decided to rent one.

She and I meet as planned at the Douglas & Sons car rental in the east of town. We settle for a white VW Touareg. Shortly after five, we drive off in a white VW Touareg. I am behind the wheel. It's a three-hour drive to Prague.

We cruise out of the city center, then zoom past Gera, Glauchau, and Chemnitz, plus a couple of other smaller towns whose names I do not know; carry on to Dresden, which is set on a wide plain; and then drive through Dohna before moving on to Liebstadt. Each town shrinks to the size of a thumbnail behind us, before disappearing out of sight.

We talk, flirt, and smile a lot. From time to time, I steal furtive glances at her. She is the spitting image of a love goddess in her short red summer dress and matching shoes, sparkling ruby earrings, and the loveliest set of brown eyes I have ever seen on any living creature. More than once, my feelings threaten to break free and take charge. I want to tell her how much I need her. Somehow, though, I just can't seem to find the right words.

The border comes up at Schwarze Pockau. Countless housing blocks and business premises stretch out as far as the eye can see on either side of the Vladivostocká, which takes us into the heart of Prague. Baroque architecture and gothic structures rise in every direction we look.

"It's amazing," I say quietly to Elise.

"It's enchanting," she readily agrees. Her lovely brown eyes burning with excitement.

The two of us are dying to explore it all.

We book ourselves into the Iris Congress Hotel, then board the elevator to the third floor. I turn pink the minute we walk into our suite. The bed prompts an involuntary whistle out of me, and when I hear Elise's gasp beside me, I turn to see her face completely drained of color. We are both staring at a Casanova affair, complete with a handful rose petals strewn all over it. This bed is made for just one thing, and the implication is not lost on either of us.

Elise recovers quickly. Just like me, she is now doing her level best to avoid looking at the bed. She croons over the enticing adjacent bathroom, falls in love with the view outside the window, and tries to get me interested in the flat-screen TV hanging on the wall a few paces from the foot of the bed.

I'm hardly listening though. I'm thinking of tonight. That bed and all the red within this room has raised my libido. The monster's awake and doesn't want to go back in. I am thinking keenly of sex.

Desperate to yank me out of my thoughts, Elise picks up the phone in a mock room-service call and speaks to an imaginary room service attendant. It's very good acting. But I just can't help it. My mind is elsewhere. And my eyes keep going back to the bed.

Suddenly I hear Elise say, "I'm hungry."

"Yeah?" I ask, looking over at her, somewhat distracted.

"Yeah." She replies. "Let's go eat. Right now."

"Okay," I sigh, the spell finally broken.

We vacate the suite in a hurry.

I'm curious how this evening will play out.

We hail a taxi outside the hotel's doors. Its driver, a boisterous Czechoslovakian with about ten English words to his vocabulary, insists on picking our restaurant and tells us to relax, saying we will have a beautiful time this evening. He drives only six kilometers away to the street Smetanovo Nábřeží and then points to the entrance of an imposing red chateau to the right. We pile out of his taxi. An unintelligible English farewell later, he shoots off into the distance.

We walk into the Bellevue restaurant. A friendly concierge guides us into a pleasantly appointed dining room. The windows are wide and arced. Exquisite chandeliers hang from the ceiling. Merry diners eat, laugh and talk the night away.

The concierge hands us over to a happy waitress who then shows us to a table. Like all the others here, it's covered with a cream cloth and set with brilliant napkins and polished cutlery. At its center burns a hospitality candle. I like the atmosphere here. Elise too, says it's great. We thank the waitress as we take our seats.

Starting with soup, we work our way through salad, and then an appetizer. The main course eventually shows up. I put away a succulent knuckle of lamb coated with pink garlic puree in no time at all. My desire to belch is overwhelming. Across from me, Elise does battle with a giant prawn. It looks deadly. My livid fear of sea creatures almost gets the better of me as I watch her tackle it.

Several minutes later, as she pops the last of the poor creature inside her mouth, I sigh with relief and call for champagne, intent on celebrating her victorious duel, only to have her admonish me then turn around and request red wine instead. I go with the flow.

Dusk falls. I sip my wine contentedly.

"Change is coming," Elise says softly.

"How do you mean?" My sixth sense is piqued. I look into her face intently, trying to read her mind.

"Now that we are almost ready for the job market," she says.

"Ah yes," I agree solemnly, then add, "What do you think the future has in store for us?"

We look at each other quietly for a moment. She wants to go into marketing, and I want to go into production. This much is clear to both of us. Beyond that, neither of us has a clue as to what direction our lives will take. It's a scary thought. Not knowing what awaits one. To get some insight, we kick a few ideas back and forth, hoping for a premonition of what lies ahead. Meanwhile, diners come and go.

After nearly two hours of talking about everything under the sun, we finally make our departure.

The air outside is warm. A gentle breeze has picked up. Trees and shrubbery rustle ever so slightly in its gentle wake. Above us, stars twinkle in the cloudless sky.

I am slightly tipsy from the red wine, and so is Elise. We decide to clear our heads with a short walk. A few feet west of the exquisite Bellevue restaurant is the 270-mile-long Vltava, whose gentle waters ripple slightly as it streams by.

Both Elise and I are talking freely as we walk along it. Our guard is down, thanks to the red wine. And that king-size bed is on both our minds once again. We hail a taxi and head back to the hotel.

Elise takes a ragged breath and looks me deep in the eyes as we ride the elevator up to our floor. No one here but the two of us. I take her hand in mine. The passion that has been building inside us all night suddenly flairs out of grip. My heart is beating wildly as I snake my arms about her slender waist and hold her close.

She moans.

I sigh with longing.

We reach the third floor and somehow, I'm not quite sure how, we make it to our suite. I'm burning with desire. We stumble into each other's arms as the door shuts behind us. My lips lock onto hers. "Please, Dave," she whispers, eyes smoldering with passion. I pause in concern and look deep into her pleading eyes. She is begging me not to tease her, asking me to get on with it. My hand snakes over to her left breast. I dive in for more sensuous kissing and even forget to breathe. She's moaning with pleasure. We tug desperately at each other's clothes.

I guide her toward the bed. We fall onto it in a jumble of hands and legs. The heaving of her chest. Her raspy breath. The sweet scent of her feminine desire. I breathe in her sensual aroma. She wraps her legs around me and takes my probing tongue deep into her conquered mouth, never getting enough of me. Her muffled moans taste so good. I sink my tongue deep into her mouth, and soon, both our tongues are fencing furiously with each other, fighting for the beautiful prize of her absolute delirium. "Such sweet surrender, you beautiful gorgeous thing," I whisper in her ear.

Her muffled moans fill mine, as I tease her beyond all endurance. We remain suspended in time and space for what seems like an eternity. Then make slow, sensual, mind-blowing love, time and again, for most of the night.

The sun comes up early on Saturday morning. Elise slips into a short light-green summer dress. It fits like a glove. She's stunning. Jeans as usual for me. A black shirt covers my torso.

We make our way to the expo taking place at 5. Května 65 in Holešovice, a quaint little suburb just off the Vltava in the north of Prague.

The expo's venue is a massive structure of concrete and glass. It's surrounded by numerous parking lots interspersed with patches of green lawns.

We spend much of our time in a huge hall on the ground floor. It's teeming with people, exhibitions, shows, discussions, and marketing exchanges of all sorts. Elise is quite active. I'm merely a bystander.

Late afternoon, we go for a walk. It's a lovely day. The sun is shining. The air smells of roses. And we never stop kissing. This is quickly getting serious. I absolutely love it.

Eleven

It's mid-morning of mid-week, approaching ten. The gang and I are at our little island of tables. Before me are my notes. I'm partially reading while half listening to the incessant chatter of my equally depleted comrades. We all need to recharge. Three hours of nonstop work will do that to a man. Any minute now, we'll be heading out for our coffee break.

I'm counting down the seconds to the morning break when Kevin calls and drops a bombshell. I'm to be part of an urgent telephone conference in an hour, he says over the phone.

"What's it about?" I ask.

"An unexpected delay in goods receivables," he replies. I try to get more out of him, but he doesn't say much more. He's swamped, short on time, and quickly hangs up.

One look through his glass wall quickly confirms this. His cell phone is firmly pressed to his ear. Urgent words go back and forth between him and his caller. His desk phone is buzzing. And he's furiously punching away at his keyboard with his free hand.

The same level of activity is going on in the office next to his. Matthias Wolfgang is just as inundated. This doesn't look good. Something's amiss. My apprehension is growing.

I query Ludwig, Hans, Nick, Frank, and Timothy, but none of them has a clue as to what's going on. I'm devoid of information. I'm in the dark. This is beginning to freak me out a little.

My coffee break is quick and restless. I'm back at my station in less than ten minutes. I need to prepare myself for the coming conference as best as I can. Hence, I read up on materials procurement.

The appointed hour eventually arrives. I dial the conference number. While waiting for a connection, I glance over into Kevin's and Matthias' office. As expected, they too have their receivers raised to their ears. They must be logged into the conference. And Kevin appears to be speaking.

His voice comes through loud and clear the minute I get a connection. He's introducing himself. Name, rank, and company. The usual. Several others follow his example. I do not know half the people on the line. They are not from Displaytek, but a supplier company known as Screen Systems Ltd.

Beside me, Timothy says something funny, and the whole picking team seated at our group of tables breaks out into laughter. "David Elbert, thesis-internship student at Displaytek," I say into the mouthpiece, taking advantage of a moment of silence in the ongoing telephone introductions.

"Sweet jumping Christopher!" booms Duncan Beike. "Who the heck let a rookie in on this?"

I stutter and stammer, but not a word escapes my lips.

"My idea," Kevin replies, briefly explaining how my study and this discussion are interconnected.

The correlated importance of both to Displaytek is not lost on our CEO. He gives a mighty grunt. It sounds like the beginnings of crackling thunder.

I am quickly forgotten as the next person suddenly speaks up. "James Bright, CEO, Screen Systems Limited."

"About time," booms Duncan. "Let's get rolling. Mr. Bright, could you please?"

"Yes, certainly," replies James. "I would like to start with a sincere apology for this debacle." He sighs heavily as though the weight of the world is upon his shoulders. "As you are all aware, a system malfunction at our plant disrupted our production activities. As such, screen production has ground to a halt. I am very sorry, gentlemen, but we are momentarily incapable of honoring our delivery obligations."

"How long till this is fixed?" growls Duncan in a low and threatening voice.

Another long sigh. "That's just it," replies James. "We cannot tell."

Duncan's trademark exclamation of shock rings out with brutal force. "Sweet-Jumping-Christopher!" He roars into the phone.

I cringe.

The personnel seated about me perk up and attempt to listen in. They heard him too.

"What's that supposed to mean?" An angry and exasperated Duncan continues.

James Bright struggles with an explanation.

Duncan doesn't like it.

The two CEOs are locked in a dual discussion.

Everyone else on the telephone conference remains silent. No one says a word. No one dares to breathe.

After several seconds spent trying to appease our CEO, James Bright finally moans miserably and adds, "It's a massive plant with millions worth of high tech. We just cannot seem to find the problem," he says dejectedly. "Teams of diagnostic engineers have been working round the clock for three days now. Tons of money and lots of time have gone into this salvation endeavor. Still, we have come up empty-handed. All systems check out, but the damn plant just won't come to life. What more can I do?"

I almost feel sorry for the poor chap.

"Lars," Duncan asks, "what's the latest on our screen stock levels?"

"The X28 is in bad shape," says the head of materials procurement.

"How bad?" Duncan asks. There is a threatening note in his voice, like the very last thing he wants to hear is more bad news, or so help him God, someone will get fired, maybe even completely dematerialized. If I were Lars, I wouldn't answer. I would simply run out of the office screaming blue murder and never come back.

But Lars is not like me. He's really brave. He puts his neck out there by saying, "We are eating into safety stock as we speak. In three days, these too will run out."

"Jumping kangaroos!" cries out Duncan.

I shrink in my seat and wait for thunder.

"Three miserable days?" To my surprise, our CEO sounds like a man on the verge of a clinical breakdown. Now this is unexpected!

James Bright simply moans. It's a pitiful sound. A strait-jacket and short stay at a mental institution may not be far behind. His world is unraveling fast.

"If Screen Systems Limited isn't back on track by then," Lars continues, practically the only stable voice on the line at the moment, "the X28 production will grind to a halt."

Pin-drop silence follows his words. I dare not breathe. I picture Duncan Beike in his office, his phone pressed to his ear as he stares at his Van Gogh, which I am made to understand hangs on the wall to his left, eyes squinted, weighing his options, trying to find a solution, sweating under the pressure, doing his level best to stave off madness. "Okay," he sighs at last. "So, the X28 is bad."

"Yes, really bad," echoes Lars.

"What about screen stock levels for the other products?" Duncan asks. His words are slow, fearful even. The air crackles with tension.

"Order levels on four have long since been surpassed," states Lars.

"Which four?" Duncan asks.

Lars rattles off four product names.

Duncan curses loudly and then breathes heavily into the receiver, thinking. "Mr. Bright," he says at last, "any available stocks on your side?"

"A little, but all reserved."

"How long," Duncan asks in an authoritative voice, "have we been doing business together?"

"Ten years."

"And have I given you cause for concern in all this time?"

James sighs. He knows what's coming. We all know what's coming and listen with piqued ears to his answer.

"No, not that I can think of," he says.

"We pay up front for a third of all goods receivables," continues Duncan, intent on driving the nail home. "Just as a goodwill courtesy to you. Do we not do this?"

"True, Mr. Beike. For that, I am forever grateful."

"And we pay on time for the rest. Don't we?"

"Yes, you do, Mr. Beike. No argument on that."

"Good. I would like to call on this goodwill now."

"How?" Though submissive, James is clearly apprehensive.

"I'm sure you can work out a ration plan with your other clients. Pry some of those stocks loose. Send them our way. We need them."

"And what do I get in return?"

"A happy client, that's what," says Duncan. "We love doing business with you, you know? We are dying to keep things that way."

"Oooh," James moans, finally at his wit's end.

I have a feeling he's had this very conversation many times this morning with many other clients. There must be a whole lot of other manufacturers out there clamoring for additional supplies. Now, he is deflated and sounds absolutely defeated.

Those in his entourage suddenly find their tongues. They come to his rescue and make many promises. They will solve the riddle within a week and get rid of the problem. They will come back to us with good news, come hell or high water.

We wish them Godspeed.

Screen Systems Ltd. gets off the line. At Duncan Beike's insistence, we stay on to compare notes.

"This timing couldn't have been any worse," the head of sales says. "Orders are at an all-time high."

"It's a major disaster," Duncan agrees heavily.

I can hear the nervousness in their voices. I listen and keep my mouth shut, hoping to learn a few lessons on disaster management.

"If this goes south," says the head of finance, "we will be looking at an astronomical loss."

"And don't forget the legal bills and punitive damages," Christine Gay adds.

Fear of these legal monsters jogs everyone's mind all at once, igniting the birth of new ideas. Suddenly, diverse views are aired. A strategy begins to unfold.

Within a few minutes, and while still at the conference call, a think tank is set up to look into Displaytek's raw materials procurement procedure. What's working? What's not working? Which improvements can be made? Which alternative procurement strategies can be pursued?

Duncan suggests getting the think tank started off with a couple of ideas. The telephone conference turns into a quick brainstorming session. I share a few solutions I've learned in the past four years as a student, which quickly improves my reputation in the eyes of the CEO. He suggests I be a part of the think tank.

Fantastic! Things are finally looking up.

FOR A WEEK, telephones ring off the hook. Management dashes from one meeting to the next. I see Kevin only twice during this time. On both occasions, he unequivocally lets me know he has absolutely no time for me. There are fires burning everywhere. He's straining to put them out.

His interest in my study falls into the background. It doesn't take me long to realize the obvious. I've been left to my own devices. Just as well. I needed time. I need to consolidate my position. There are volumes of technical stuff I should work my way through. Needless to say, I dig my feet in with renewed vigor.

SATURDAY, eleven-fifteen in the morning. A heat haze shimmers off Drachendorfer Street, creating the illusion of a vast sheet of water hovering over its surface. The apartment blocks on either side of this street are faring no better.

On this day, the heat is merciless. No cars drive up to the complex. No one walks in or out. The whole place appears abandoned and lifeless.

A few rays of sunlight manage to filter in through the tightly drawn curtains hanging over my window. They stream into my apartment, eventually falling onto my study desk within my designated open office space.

Elise and I are farther in, within the living room section where it's cooler. She's sitting on the couch before the TV. Pink mini shorts and matching T-shirt for the barest of modesty, make up her entire attire. This way, she doesn't get too hot on this sweltering day.

I am sprawled out beside her in a white vest and black checkered shorts. My head is resting on her lap, framed by her hands. I'm staring into her eyes. She's quizzing me relentlessly, eager to know where I see myself five years from now.

I give her the usual cliché answers on social status and prestige. Lots of money, big home, powerful car, and throw in a yacht for good measure. She doesn't buy this last bit. She knows I don't know the first thing about yachts, or anything that floats on water for that matter. Plus, she's doubtful I'll ever be able to afford one.

She next asks about what kind of family I would like to have in the future. When I tell her about all the kids and schools of grandchildren I dreamt about in my teenage days, she springs up in shock, and I end up on the floor with a mighty thud. She spends the next five minutes explaining to me how there's no way on God's given earth that she's ever having any more than two kids.

"Aha, so this inquisition is all about you and me playing happy family for life?" I ask excitedly.

She blushes and quickly changes the subject.

I tease her endlessly, calling her Mrs. David Elbert, or wife, more than once.

She loves it. Elise is practically glowing with joy.

Soon, the subject of living arrangements comes up. As dusk falls, the idea to move in together slowly begins to crystallize.

Twelve

Among the maze of R&D laboratories and high-tech equipment on Displaytek's third floor is a rather unobtrusive presentation hall set all the way back within the expansive building. In it, Brandt Artificial Intelligence is set to show us their most recent ground-breaking innovation.

I try to figure out what I know of the Ltd. company. For one, they are our supplier. Two, they are by far and wide the most advanced producers of digital processors. Word on the ground is they not only love to invent, but each time they create something truly brilliant, they immediately make a bee-line for all their leading customers, to dazzle them with the magnificent wonders of their fertile minds. For this purpose, a Brandt Artificial Intelligence engineer, a Dr. Fiddle, is here at Displaytek on this very day. Kevin assures me he's quite the goofy character. I'm in for a very special treat today, he says.

I'm burning with excitement as I head for the presentation.

THE HALL I WALK into is built like a small student lecture hall with a door to the right opening onto the stage up front. On the stage is a small table, with a podium not far from it, and, in the far corner, a sturdy, waist-high mahogany cabinet. The audience section, sprawled out deep into the room, rises back through the hall in stadium seating. About forty seats in total. Co2 extinguishers hang at strategic distances along the walls. I even notice a massive fire escape door. I head up the stairs and take my place.

Today, twenty of Displaytek's finest are gathered here. Duncan Beike and his comrades from the executive floor are seated in the first row. The rest of us are in the second, with Kevin and I next to each other at the center.

Light chatter and conscious laughter fill the hall for a bit until Dr. Fiddle opens the door to the side of the stage and pokes his head in. It comes along with half his thorax. There's a large box wedged under his left arm. He clears his throat, twangs the red suspenders crisscrossing his chest, and it's action the minute he steps through the doorway. "Brandt Artificial Intelligence Limited has outdone itself once again," he says confidently as he marches purposefully into the room. His straw hat threatens to fly away. He grabs it and pushes it firmly into place, all the while excitedly looking at us through large eyeglasses as he swiftly walks on. Without the suspenders, his extra-large black trousers would be an untidy pile of material down at his ankles. And his ample gut, which mother of all wonders sticks out almost half a meter, is threatening to be the only thing I'll ever notice about the man from hereon after.

Somehow, I get my eyes to focus on the box in his hands.

A second later, his voice captures my full attention. "We have improved our digital signal processors a hundredfold," he says boisterously, finally coming to a stop at the center of the broad stage. He sets down his box on the table before him, never once losing stride in his speech. "Software, hardware, the works, this little component here," he says, fishing out of his trouser pocket a prototype digital processor not much different from the ones we are currently using here at Displaytek, "is a marvel of technology," he concludes, turning it this way and that in the air, making sure we get a good look at it.

He beams at us, his audience, and then proceeds to unwrap his box. "Behold, my latest invention." There is a note of reverie in his voice.

We hold our breath as he lifts something out of the box. It's roughly the size of a football. For lack of a better term, I am on the verge of describing it as a miniature UFO when the good doctor beats me to a description.

"Ladies and gentlemen," he says dramatically, gingerly setting the object on the table beside him, "I present to you … my first ever … one and only … self-made, man-made, truly amazing, flying saucer."

Damn it! I knew it! He's built himself a UFO!

For a second or two, total silence prevails. Then a torrent of questions suddenly erupts, drowning out Dr. Fiddle's further comments.

It's several minutes before the furor dies down and we can hear his voice again. "Damn, I am good!" Dr. Fiddle cries out excitedly. "I just knew this would get your attention. Look at you lot." He laughs exuberantly. All his teeth are visible, including the molars. His eyes are glowing as he drinks in our response. We are like kids looking for the alien that just landed.

"By the way," he says, lovingly patting his interstellar explorer, "this little baby here is controlled by the newly improved digital processor I just showed you. Watch its performance in this little marvel I bustled up. Then buy it, use it, fit it into your automobile head units, and watch it work wonders for all of your products. Rest assured of one thing: my processor is a sensation. This, you are about to witness for yourselves."

At this, excited chatter picks up and spreads out like wildfire among us.

Dr. Fiddle, however, is not done and flaps his hands about to get us quiet again. "Just one more thing." He looks at us uncertainly and then abruptly spills the beans. "I cannot vouch for my baby's propulsion unit. You see, it does not come from Brandt Artificial Intelligence," he says, smiling apologetically. No sooner has he said this, when he pushes a button on a remote control, jumps a clear five feet back, and, with an expression of mortal fear, quite suddenly and very quickly ducks for cover, disappearing behind the sturdy cabinet.

Panic breaks out. The scene is like that of an imminent bomb explosion as the baby UFO prepares for takeoff. All I can think is that this little gadget is not a magnificent galactic explorer anymore, but rather a very deadly, loudly ticking time bomb, one that's about to go off with a mega boom any second now.

The galactic explorer begins to huff and puff. Then, wobbling dangerously, it slowly rises off the table to begin its maiden voyage. Dr. Fiddle suspiciously peeks out at it from behind his cabinet. He makes the sign of the cross as his baby starts to give off a high-pitched tone. "This is it," he screams, and then disappears even deeper behind his protective cabinet as though Armageddon is imminent.

That's all the rest of us still seated can take. We hit the floor and await a supernova. I catch myself saying my last prayers. My heart is beating out of control. Suddenly, the UFO shoots out in our direction. It wobbles above us. I'm moaning as if I'm dead, eyes staring fixedly at the galactic explorer as it does a few erratic gymnastics above my head. It freezes in midair, and I freeze. For one long second, it's like both of us are waiting for the other to react. Then in the next instant, it's shooting back toward its creator, only to collapse once more onto the table, its steely back shivering and trembling uncontrollably. We wait for an explosion. Seconds tick by. None comes.

I've never held my breath for so long before. My throat is constricted. *"But I'm alive,"* I realize, as I finally let out my breath in a long, high pitched, wheeze, as I continuously think to myself over and over again, *"I'm alive! I'm still alive! Oh thank you merciful God."*

Every single one in the room is just as badly shaken, but slowly coming around.

Likewise, Dr. Fiddle rises up from his hiding place. He straightens his clothes and then his face. He fiddles about with his red tie for a second. His fingers are shaking, but they in no way correspond to his rosy voice as he says, "Wasn't that lovely?"

"Ooh God!" My moan is hardly perceptible. The way my heart is hammering, it's a wonder it hasn't broken through my chest yet. My shaky legs won't carry me. I remain on the floor for a good five minutes.

AT KEVIN'S BEHEST, I spend the rest of the afternoon in a one-on-one with Dr. Fiddle. I get to learn more of his eccentric ways. Together, we study electronic charts, discuss digital processors, and even do a little software programming. It quickly becomes clear Dr. Fiddle loves talking. He exhausts the topic of the digital processor in no time, and next thing I know, he's talking about hard disk drives.

"Brandt Artificial Intelligence doesn't produce them," he concedes. A different supplier, one specializing in memory technology and data storage media, provides this compo-nent. He tells me not to worry though, to relax, because he's here and will shed light on how a hard disk drive functions as memory. "I know a lot about everything," he whispers quietly before revealing he has a confirmed IQ of 170.

I am talking to a genius and didn't even know it.

He articulately explains the drive. For clarity's sake, he also uses a lot of hand gestures, just to make sure I follow his logic. With ears and eyes, I listen keenly. Every now and then, I ask a question.

Dr. Fiddle takes great pleasure in showing me how an actuator arm stores terabytes of information on the platters of the drive, and how information goes back and forth between it and the processor.

"My digital processor is the brain," he says proudly. "That's where the thinking takes place; that's where codes are executed. Right now, we at Brandt have gone a step further. We are working on the next generation of processors."

"Further improvements?" I ask.

"Oh yes. These will be better, faster, smarter," he says smugly, then adds, "They'll be brains—artificial brains but nevertheless brains, just like yours and mine."

"You're kidding. Are we talking about artificial neurons, cerebrum, cerebellum, medulla, and so on?"

"Yep," he replies matter-of-factly.

I am astounded.

"After their development," continues Dr. Fiddle, "they will be capable of independent thought within set parameters. No more programming, just thinking machines. Now how about that for a breakthrough? Super, don't you think?" He is momentarily lost in glorious dreams.

I do my best not to recall his nearly exploding UFO and quickly change the topic.

We talk about various things such as low and high pass filters, and transistors. Together, we spend oodles of time admiring circuit diagrams and calculating everything from transistor impedance to bias.

Suddenly he jerks upright. "Oh—my—God! Look at the time!" It's shortly after two-thirty, and he has another engagement at three o'clock. "I must go," he says abruptly.

I walk him to the reception hall and out into the parking lot. I wish him farewell and good luck. He tells me to keep my eyes and ears open for his new breed of thinking processors.

I hate to see him go. It's not every day I get to meet a genius. Hopefully, our paths will cross again someday.

Kevin is lurking in the reception hall as I make my way back into the building. He makes a show of studying the furniture, the floor, and the ceiling.

The minute I'm within reach, he jumps my way and shoots myriad questions at me.

I barely have time to answer.

"How did it go?" he asks.

"Great."

"Really?"

"Yeah, why?" I ask.

"What did you learn?"

"A lot."

"Like?"

"Well, let's see… radios, processors, amplifiers … and lots of windy calculations … Did you know transistors are the main components of amplifiers?"

"Kid stuff!" he replies. "Every engineer worth his salt knows that."

I am tempted to tell him I am still gathering salt.

"So, what do you think of engineer Dr. Fiddle?" he asks.

"The man could probably go toe-to-toe with Einstein," I reply.

"Yeah," he says wistfully, and from the dreamy look on his face, I quickly surmise he's probably imagining what it would be like to be a genius. He spots my amusement and loses the silly grin in an instant. The questions come back in a torrent.

"Ready to get on with your study?"

"More than you can imagine."

"How's it coming along?"

"Super."

"Indeed?" he wants to know.

"Certainly!" I reply as though affronted by the question.

"Excellent. Nice to hear." He smiles and then gestures in the direction of the production department. "Shall we?"

We make our way to the operations-scheduling section while discussing my next agenda. As we walk to our stations, I fill him in. Thanks to Bianca and her comrades, I am now well versed in the intricacies of monitor assembly, quality control, programming, and product cleaning. Today, Dr. Fiddle has walked me through the finer workings of car radios, related processors, hard disk drives, and DVD units. None of these baffles me anymore. I am finally ready for the end-product assembly, I tell Kevin.

"Super, David. Simply terrific!" he exclaims, clapping my shoulder with an open hand. "You have set a nice pace, boy. Keep it up. Keep me posted. And above all, remember…"

"Yes?"

"The clock is ticking."

TIME, FOR ELISE, crawls to a standstill this week. She has just completed her thesis study. A while ago, she received her results. Her exam was a roaring success. It's now official. She'll be graduating summa cum laude. Her shrill scream of joy at this good news is still ringing in my ears.

Her parents are proud of her. I'm proud of her. We are all just such a proud bunch of happy people, that we just don't know what to do with our emotions. We are still trying to figure things out. It might take a while.

To celebrate, we go on a daylong ice cream binge that nearly ends in overindulgence. Sometime during the same day, she mentions she's thinking of taking on a master's. But after a short afterthought adds, "Only after a much-needed sabbatical."

Life is hers for the taking, she says. Since success has her name written all over it, why rush it? A change of activity is just as good as a rest, she reasons, and that's exactly what she'll do. That's exactly what she needs right now. Thing is, she still doesn't have a clue which activity she should take up during this sabbatical. However, she will search. She will wrack her brain cells. She will find one. She is sure of it. Until then, all she wants to do is idle about, lie in the sun, and enjoy life a little.

I cheer her on and wish I could do the same. I still have a long way to go till I get to where she is.

Thirteen

I MEET UP with Elise in the heart of town late afternoon of the following day for a round of refreshing drinks and light conversation. A few minutes into our tête-à-tête, she suggests an impromptu visit to a real estate agent she recently learned about. "Handal Hoams," she lets me know, reverently speaking out the agent's name.

It's been a hard day at Displaytek and I'm dog tired. I tell her the only thing I want to do is go home and unwind. She won't take no for an answer. She leads me into the sweltering heat outside, sweet-talks me into her tiny red car, then proceeds to placate me as I sit in a tight squeeze beside her as she hits the gas. My knees are jammed against the dashboard. My head is pressed against the ceiling. I sigh, resigning to my fate as the bumpy ride begins.

We zip across town on a ten-minute drive to Landgraben Street. I get the jarring of a lifetime.

"The agent's office is in that building over there," she says exuberantly the moment we arrive.

I look up to see her pointing excitedly at the Tenkon Towers.

"Let's go up honey," she adds, lithely jumping out as she speaks.

Before I know it, we are at the agent's office.

Handal Hoams is actually a nice enough guy—soft-spoken, middleweight, robust health, rich black hair, a clean-cut metal-gray suit, and shiny shoes. His walls are plastered with pictures and information on housing properties of all kinds. On a table near his desk, is an extravagant model of an upcoming housing project he seems particularly proud of. The project is indeed grand. The model is supposed to impress and win the heart of anyone walking through his doors. Since I am dog tired right now, my heart is as cold as stone. I am certain I cannot be won over by anything he might have to say. Tough luck, Mr. Hoams. All I want is a nice bath and a warm meal in my apartment.

I frown at him.

He smiles back, acting like Mother Teresa.

He slips into an easy Q&A session the minute we are seated before him: What brings us to Jena? Do we love it here? Working? Married? How about engaged? Elise talks freely and badgers me with her elbow to do the same.

All at once, Handal shows an unnaturally keen interest in our pet status. Do we have a dog? No. How about cats? No. Have we ever had either in the past? Yes, for Elise; no for me, except for a Labrador my parents had when I was a kid. I am happy to say it didn't stay with us for long. I sold it to my uncle the minute it punctured my football with its obscenely scary teeth. Elise stares at me in shock, wondering how callous a boy can be and if she should even be in a relationship with me in the first place.

"Damn beasts," Handal says with feeling. "Nothing but the devil incarnate. Lucky you. All you lost was a ball. Any idea how many millions in property damages these little beasts cause each year?"

"No, no idea," I say.

"Do you want to know?" he asks.

"Not really," we both tell him, anxious to avoid the tirade about to happen.

He tells us anyway.

For two minutes, we get to hear all about nasty animals with the meanest vandal streaks ever known to man and all about the malevolent things they did to him and his company. He works himself into a state, and somewhere along the line introduces delinquent tenants to his list of woes.

We nod and exclaim in amazement. We tell him how sorry we are he had to suffer all these wicked things. Elise clicks her tongue at non-present dogs, and I nearly hiss as the incredible list of misdemeanors Handal has witnessed grows longer and longer and even more disturbing. He's truly distressed. This is slightly rubbing off on us. He realizes this, and tries to calm down.

Minutes pass before we get down to any real estate business.

"So," says a partially grief-stricken and slowly simmering-down Handal Hoams finally, "what kind of home are you looking for?" At this point, he's suddenly smiling, emboldening, urging us to get dreamy. A twinkle appears in his eye. "A home is a man's soul, you know?"

I'm still thinking of dogs. But—wait a minute—what's this about souls and homes? I believe I've read something of the sort in a fortune cookie before.

The phrase is wacky in any case, and I stare at Handal suspiciously as he continues, "Spare no expense when choosing a home, and you'll be happy for the rest of your life."

Yeah, right. Me, the mortgage, and bankruptcy. I hear you, pal. Nice try.

Elise, however, is doing just as he requested. She's dreaming. And by George, she's not sparing any fantasies. Her eyes change shape and size spontaneously and quite suddenly, before going through a series of iridescent colors in the blink of an eye. Every once in a while, she looks at the grand penthouse project and sighs. Now this turn of events is worrying. I fear my girl has set her heart on a celebrity home. And I'm pretty sure I can't afford one. Here comes trouble in paradise.

Now that Elise is hooked, Handal engages in some nasty foul play. He whips out three large real estate catalogs filled with hundreds of beautiful homes, the likes of which we've only seen on TV. This sends Elise clean over the edge into irrevocable grand-home frenzy. She starts to salivate. Seconds later she is hyperventilating, and when her large deer eyes zero in on me, I'm all but ready to buy her the moon and countless other satellites as well, if only someone could put them up for sale. But first, I need the Midas touch.

Handal spots my dilemma. He quickly reassesses my financial situation and comes up with a final verdict on the depth of my wallet. "Shallow pockets," I think I hear him whisper under his breath.

I shake my head vehemently and gabble something about working towards being a self-made man in the near feature.

This doesn't slow Handal Hoams down in the least bit. The brochures with celebrity homes disappear in the blink of an eye. From the back reaches of a desk drawer, he fishes out a puny little catalog and slaps it onto the table. It looks more like a child's scrapbook. Dog-ears are its most distinguishing feature. It's certainly seen better days. I am baffled by it, and Elise looks dazed, probably from the shock of its appearance. We are both lost for words.

"You will love these cozy little homes," Handal says with a wink. The catalog fluffs in the air as he triumphantly waves it about. Then he goes into action, talking fast, flipping pages, a well-oiled routine practiced thousands of times before.

We can barely keep up. Several times, we tongue-twist ourselves on a string of yeses and nos. It's a brutal pace. In no time, we whittle down the fifty possibilities to four. The first is a prestigious apartment in the heart of town. The second is a split-level home with a paved driveway and green lawn not far from the university. The third and fourth are two semidetached houses, one to the east, the other to the west of town.

The homes are modest and clean. Though every last one of them appears to be in good state, not a single one is a dream home. Elise's lip curls up spectacularly at this fact. She's downright disgusted.

It doesn't take us long to make arrangements for visual property inspection. Ten minutes later, we depart for Elise's apartment. There goes my love life. I have a feeling she won't be dotting on me this evening.

On Kevin's request, I show up at Gustav Graf's workstation early the next day to lend him a helping hand. The chubby little man is behind schedule and quickly running out of time. His high-seated eyebrows squeeze together as he squints at me. "Can you assemble?" he asks.

"Somewhat," I answer, in light of Bianca's and Arnold's lessons.

"Good. Read this," he says briskly, handing me a little booklet.

I grab it and notice it's a standard methods-time measurement guideline. The ins and outs of his trade are sure to be detailed within.

"In thirty minutes," says Gustav solemnly, "you'll be my extra pair of hands. Today, we decimate my backlog, capish?"

It's a huge backlog. I nod hesitantly as I sink into the seat beside him.

Gustav has long since picked up where he left off. His fingers are a flurry. He's hard at work. He's also constantly muttering to himself. Snippets of his one-man conversation reach me every now and then.

"This place can drive a man crazy, huh?" I say, smiling broadly, hoping to loosen his tension.

His reply is a grunt. He beckons me to get on with my reading. I'll need it, he says.

I watch a second longer as he loses himself in his work once again. This time, his mouth stays shut. Clearly, there will be no conversation at this workstation. *Oh, well. Nothing to do but get on with it.* I start to read.

THIRTY MINUTES LATER, he calls out the time and then places a similar set of components before the both of us. "Just follow my lead and go with the flow," he says.

And so, the action begins.

For fifteen minutes, I ape his every move.

We pick; we fit; we screw on and clip in. Gustav's voice is ever-present. He's full of technical advice. I surprise myself by being able to keep up.

We take a short recess and continue half an hour later. By lunch break, I'm creating value like a true professional. At the end of the workday, and to my utter surprise, the outcome is almost too good to be true. We actually did it! We assembled a hundred goddamn units!

"Well, I'll be damned," says Gustav.

I act cool, like everywhere I go, good things happen.

"The backlog, however, never goes away," says Gustav sadly. He stares forlornly at the queue of work awaiting his attention.

I do the same. It towers over us like a hopelessly beached sperm whale on a super-hot day. Gustav wrinkles his nose at it as if it's already starting to reek. He sighs heavily as he puts his tools away. Once again, it's time to call it a day. We leave his workstation and join the flood of workers exiting the building.

IT'S THURSDAY, CLOSE TO MIDNIGHT. Drachendorfer Street is dead and quiet. Apartment windows for several blocks down the road are dark and silent. With good reason. Most students are fast asleep. The rest are obviously out partying the night away.

Unlike either of the two groups mentioned above, I happen to be sprawled out on the couch in the living-room section of my apartment. The light is on. I'm still up. The TV is on mute. And I'm surrounded by lots of material. These include charts, scientific tables, printouts, and untold volumes of scribbled personal notes collected over the last few days during my research at Displaytek.

For hours, I've been sifting through all this information with a fine-tooth comb. I'm looking for opportunity. Anything that stands out. Something that'll give me a starting point. Anything.

Outside, the wind blows with brute force. Every so often a windowpane rattles loudly. My concentration begins to wane.

Just when I think I'm done, I spot it. "Damned," I mutter out loud on making the connection. "Why didn't I see this before? It's so obvious." I stare at the alarming trend. "Manufacturing lead time. Two months, give or take another." *Three months at most? So high? This is a disaster!* All at once, my mind is abuzz. This is the development opportunity I've been looking for.

I shoot up and pace across the room excitedly. *This is it,* I think to myself, as a to-do list slowly crystallizes in my mind. First, I must find out every point at which production time goes to waste. Second, I have to eliminate those wastes with extreme prejudice. Of course, in order to achieve this, I will need process flowcharts. That being said, the only man who can provide me with the same is Collins Becker, the company's product engineer. *Okay then,* I think in my hyper state. *Okay. All I need to do now is pay Collins a visit.* I look at my watch. Twelve-thirty AM. *Right now, I need to get some sleep. Then first thing tomorrow, I'll be knocking on his office door.* I'm sizzling with energy. I burn with feverish excitement for a while longer. I make a few more plans. At about two, I finally get to bed.

Fourteen

The brick-walled office of the product engineer is situated within the R&D department. I walk into it on the second knock to find the thirtysomething man the very picture of intense study. He's seated at his desk, reading in earnest.

Though only seven thirty in the morning, Mr. Collins Becker is already hard at work. And despite the early hour, his black hair is tangled, ruffled and messy. I'm quick to notice his full brown beard is in complete contrast to his black ruffled hair. It's certainly clear one of the two is dyed. I'm hard-pressed to tell which.

"Come on in," he says brightly, looking up to reveal a pockmarked face well in advance of his age.

"Thanks."

He points to the chair across from his desk.

I stride in and flop into it, then start talking. I let him know why I am here and what I hope to gain.

He wants to know where and what I studied.

"Business engineering, huh?" he reiterates.

"Best decision I ever made," I confirm.

"Why?" he's curious, looking at me questioningly, waiting for a reply.

Why does anyone ever study anything? Money? Job? Fame? "I want a promising career," I tell him off the top of my head.

"And you hope to find it here?"

"I'm just here for this thesis internship," I respond cautiously, unaware of where this line of questioning is leading to.

Collins' right hand shoots up to his chin. He sort of rakes his fingers through his brown beard, then quite suddenly gets up and goes around his desk. The dark-blue suit he has on is a perfect fit. His brightly colored tie, which not only happens to be a nice touch, but is also a little overkill, lends him a lovely flare of personality. I certainly do not fail to notice his confident stride.

"Process flowcharts, huh?" He questions, repeating my request out loud.

"Exactly," I respond.

"Tell you what," he says excitedly. "Instead of just giving them to you, I'll go one better."

"Oh yeah?" I'm wondering what I have gotten myself into.

"I'll fill you in on product family engineering," he says with an exuberance that's not lost on me. "How does that sound?" He asks, eyes glowing excitedly as he comes to a standstill directly in front of me.

Medium in size, about as tall as I am, I quickly estimate.

With one little plunge, he plants his butt on the edge of his desk before me. A fatherly smile plays on his face as he looks down at me, awaiting my answer.

"Perfect," I say uncertainly, but clearly too wary of giving any other answer.

"Great," says Collins, sizzling with positive energy. "Let's get started then, shall we?"

He fetches a product from the glass-fronted display case along the wall to his right, then gets into a tale of R&D struggles so horrendous in nature, that I'm speechless at the end of his tale.

Collins, far worse, is literally blue in the face. No joke. I can see the color. I think about fetching a doctor. I also start to rethink this whole corporate lifestyle thing: the agony, the pain, the struggles, and pursuits. Why do I want all this stress? I'm on the verge of dumping my chosen path when Collins mentions the money.

Suddenly, he's bright and lively once more, spurred on by visions of untold riches and endless wealth.

In seconds, I am caught up in the same daydream.

Collins by now is speaking on about raw data research. He lets me know how this very nearly gave him an ulcer.

I'm empathy in the flesh, my voice loaded with feeling as I tell him I wouldn't wish that on anyone.

"So, there you have it," Collins concludes. "Research into the development of this gadget here," he says, flipping the gadget in his hand a few times into the air, "was a real bitch."

I nod in agreement as though carrying the same battle scars, even though I wasn't present for it all.

We pay our respects to his horrifying recollections with a moment of silence. Eventually, I ask, "What of subsequent development?"

"Took a lot of experimentation," he says simply.

"Nothing good comes easy."

"Yeah." He sighs, and I lose him to more memories for another second. "In the end, though, the breakthrough finally came, and we were able to greatly improve on Duncan Beike's original model." He laughs for the first time.

"What of success?" I ask. "Did it come about immedi-ately?"

"No. Took a while. First came requests for product mod-ifications. You know, specific designs to meet specific needs?"

"Aha. Product engineering, you mean?"

"Exactly. That's when I was put in charge of this department, and that's when the astounding magic really started to unfold." He spreads out his arms to encompass the modern products on his desk. His eyes sparkle like little stars. He excitedly shows me the basic platform they derived from the very first product Duncan invented. He goes on to demonstrate how they used it to create product families. "Ten different product families in all," he says. "About six members in each family. In total, fifty-six different products catering to a variety of niches in diverse markets. Impressive, huh?" He glows like a bulb.

I nod in a frenzy, totally overcome by the moment.

Suddenly he decides we are comrades-in-arms. He would do anything for me if I asked him to, he says. "No matter what it is, just ask, and it's yours."

I repeat my earlier request. Process flowcharts, dear Collins, and I'll be on my way.

He hands me a stack of fifty-six sheets, each one comprehensively documenting the process flow steps in the creation of an automobile head unit. "The data you need is all there," he says solemnly.

An awkward silence follows, in which he looks at his babies and fondles them while weighing something on his mind. Finally, he looks up at me and says, "I hear you are out to improve the production process in this company?"

"Yes. That's my goal." Something about the question and the way he asked it has me a little worried.

"The road ahead will be bumpy and treacherous," he cautiously warns his new comrade-in-arms.

An irrational rash of goosebumps covers me on hearing this. Tentatively, I ask him to elaborate further. He instead changes the topic.

In the span of just a few minutes, he discusses this and that, the weather and life, earth and space, philosophy and art, till my goosebumps start to lose steam and wilt, eventually merging back into my skin. I'm once again breathing easier as he gets up and wishes me good luck in my undertaking. That's my cue to let him be. The visit is over. We shake hands like old comrades. I let myself out.

Back at the production department, I get down to work. There's a ton of qualitative and quantitative data to sift through. At the back of my mind is Collins Becker's whispered warning. The very one responsible for the rise of my goosebumps a few minutes earlier. There is a storm brewing in my future. I try not to dwell on this fact, and instead focus on things to be done. For the rest of the day, I remain deeply buried in systems and process evaluation.

YET ANOTHER flat-viewing session comes to a dead end. Like the five before it, this one too ends in disappointment. We weren't inspired to conclude the deal, and are now wondering if we'll ever find a suitable place to call our own. Lucky for us, Handal does not take this personally. He's a real professional, I'm happy to say, and even right now, as we ride in his car toward his office building where we left our own vehicle, he's hopeful, and still searching his mind, looking for exactly that which we're after, that one special gem in a million, an exceptional love nest that we'll be truly proud to call our home. Within budget, of course.

True, this last prospect's failure got him down a little bit, but he quickly recovered. He is once again the same old talkative Handal Hoams that we have come to know and cherish. The man has nerves of steel. I like that.

Not only that, he's also as patient as a chameleon. He's determined to end up with happy clients. In his book, he tells us, every happy client is one more spreading out the good word that he can be trusted and relied upon to meet expectations, and nothing could be more important to him and his real estate business than this one goal. Attaboy, Handal. Exactly my kind of man.

At this very moment, while steering through light traffic, he's giving us a well-rehearsed speech on unfailing optimism. "It's all about keeping your spirits up," he says. "New opportunities always come knocking on one's door," he lets us know. "All one has to do is reach out and grab them."

I wonder if he's telling us to make up our damn minds and grab the next piece of property he shows us. In any case, the man's a sage with a musical voice, and is almost singing as he says, "I'll find you your dream, do you believe me?"

Sincerity pours out of his eyes in gallons and splashes into his rearview mirror, reflecting right into our eyes and finding its way into our hearts. He reassures us with the confidence of one who has done this countless times before. His smile is endearing as he speaks. Our replies sound like a chorus to my ears. "Yes, Handal," we say to one thing; "No, Handal," we reply to the other. We find ourselves trusting him with no reservations at all.

It's close to evening. Traffic picks up somewhat as we approach the city center. Handal is driving south on the stretch of Highway 88 that curves along the Saale River, between Jenzigweg and Am-Anger Streets, while keeping up a constant banter on a variety of topics. Set back away from the highway on either side, are a string of flats, residential areas, and business premises that zip past the SUV's windows as we hurtle along.

"There's plenty happening in the real estate market since the euro arrived," says Handal. "Business is booming. Clients are as many as grains of sand on a tropical beach." He points out several properties as we zoom past. He talks nonstop, never once slowing down to catch his breath. He's procured a lot of homes for private persons. Thanks to him, many companies and corporations are luxuriating in splendid buildings on beautiful grounds surrounded by pretty neighbors. "Like this one," he says, bobbing his head sideways at a brown three-story building to the right. "And this one." He indicates a yellow four-story building a few meters down the road to the left. He's still got many more properties to let or sell, both business premises and private homes, and each has its own story. He's full of anecdotes on every one of them, and even shares one about a former homeowner who had a blind dog and deaf cat, and the epic chasing and fleeing that went on between the two in that home. The poor homeowner almost had a nervous breakdown, Handal recalls amidst our laughter.

The real estate agent presently veers into another beautiful neighborhood on Saaleufer Street. A non-quintessential building on the driver's side catches our attention. Two stories, fifty meters long, twenty wide, flat rooftop. It sits on a generous piece of real estate that swoops down to the river below. The many trees around it rise up to a great height, obscuring our view. Despite them, we get depressing glimpses of peeling paint and broken windowpanes.

Handal sadly points at it as he drives by. "Letting a building like that fall into a state of disrepair is a crime," he says with feeling.

"One of your clients?" Elise asks.

"Yes. The Tentaq Company Group."

"Unbelievable!" I say, my face a study of disbelief. "That group is making headlines and swimming in endless money. Are you saying they're broke?"

"Let me explain," Handal says. "Here is where they started out."

Our jaws drop. We stare at the building as it slips out of sight.

"That was fifteen years ago," Handal says.

"What happened?" I ask.

"They outgrew it, needed more room."

"When?"

"About eight years back. That's when they asked me to find them a new place within the city center."

"And you got them one?" I ask.

"Oh yes. You bet your marbles I did."

"Ah, the Pine Towers," Elise says knowingly.

"Exactly," replies Handal.

"And this old place?" I ask.

"Still belongs to Tentaq. I've been looking for a tenant or buyer on their behalf ever since."

"Why doesn't anyone want it?" Elise inquires in a voice overflowing with incredulity.

"It's not in the heart of town, I guess. And people looking for a home consider it a monstrosity. Fifteen years have a way of chopping at the asking price." He checks us out in the rearview mirror to see which of us has fallen for the bait.

Elise and I are staring out the window, not yet quite hooked. So, he adds a juicy morsel, keeping his eyes on the rearview mirror. "It's now dirt cheap."

And that's when Elise bites. "How much?"

"Six hundred thousand, all in."

"All in?" she asks.

"The land, the building, the trees, and the bees." He smiles at his lame joke.

I am horrified at the thought of spending over half a million for anything.

Handal, ever the astute salesman, knows this, so he centers his efforts on Elise. "It's a once-in-a-lifetime opportunity," he tells her. "Can you imagine building your dream home from the ground up, next to a lovely, plush river in this beautiful neighborhood, on seventy square acres of prime property acquired for a song? The neighbors, far out to the right and left, did the same thing—bought cheap and built dream homes from the ground up."

This man's dead serious. He's truly hoping to shed off this property on us.

Suddenly, it's an all-out sales pitch, and Elise's consent is the prize. I slink deeper into my seat, afraid of the outcome.

"I want to see it," Elise says unexpectedly.

"Sure thing. When?"

"How about now?"

"Now?" Handal and I chorus in surprise.

"Yes, now. Please," she says. There's a glint in her eye and excitement in her voice. Elise's been searching for something to do in her sabbatical, and the look on her face right now tells me she may have found it.

I think of the monstrosity we just saw, and my skin tingles in warning. Handal is grinning from ear to ear and having trouble sitting still. He takes the very next right turn and goes around the block before Elise can change her mind. We circle back onto Saaleufer Street and begin our approach to the ghost house. Dusk is gathering fast. Seconds later, we branch off into the abandoned building's driveway.

An eerie silence hangs over the dilapidated building. We walk up to it in different states of emotion. Me, fearful; Elise, excited; and Handal, ecstatic. He seems to be thinking that he finally might be able to get rid of the derelict structure on a couple of unsuspecting youngsters.

Chipped and broken stairs lead up to the front door. They are bare, their decorative tiles having long since vanished. The door refuses to budge at first. It only creaks open when Handal and I lean on it in a concerted effort.

"I'll have the door fixed by tomorrow," says Handal. Clearly, he's optimistic about a sale.

I flip the light switch and start terribly. No response, no power. Of course, Handal came prepared with a torch and explains there has been no power here for a while now. Elise follows closely as we step in the doorway. After a minute's hesitation in the hallway, we forge our way deeper. Countless corridors take us past a maze of dark rooms and sealed-off restrooms. No furniture, no plumbing, nothing. The floors are littered. Impressive graffiti adorns the walls. Cigarette buts lie everywhere.

"Teenagers," Handal says in disgust. He quickly remembers what's at stake and resumes smiling as if his face has never known a single frown his entire life. "Tentaq wants to get rid of this property really bad. They are willing to negotiate."

He waits for us to speak, but we're still busy taking in the disaster.

We go upstairs. Same story. Dozens of rooms and corridors. Litter and graffiti. More broken windows. Endless beer cans. It's a dump, and I am downright disgusted. Elise, however, if I'm not mistaken, must be seeing a vision of a stunning celebrity home or something of the sort. Her face starts to glow as she stares about with unseeing eyes, and when her breathing starts to quicken, so does mine, albeit for opposite reasons.

"Elise?" I call to her, now heavily concerned about the implications her current emotions may have on my future house and home.

She doesn't hear me, doesn't respond.

My girl is lost in virtual reality. By now, I'm nearly half out of my mind with the prospect of living here for the rest of my natural life, even if it will be with the girl of my dreams at my side. I try again, this time louder. "Elise darling?"

"Yes, sweetie?"

"You are giving me the jitters."

"How, honey?"

"That look, like the world's about to get a remake."

"Relax, honey. Just thinking."

"About?"

"Our new home."

"Jumping Jupiter!" My voice is weak with shock as I come to a standstill.

"Two hundred thousand, take it or leave it," she says, suddenly turning to Handal.

"Never in a million years. Four fifty," Handal counters.

More figures go back and forth between the two. Somewhere in between, my life hangs in the balance.

"Three hundred, and that's final," Elise says.

Handal cries like a severely wounded cat that's fallen into a pail of salt. "Three fifty, dear woman, have mercy!"

"Three hundred, and I am not backing down, mister," says Elise, legs akimbo, ready to do judo.

"Jeez! Do you want to take away my livelihood? Three fifty, Handal repeats, eyes wild and desperate as though staring at a gigantic meteorite making for his head. I would be bursting with laughter if only they were not discussing sums of money I can only dream about.

"Okay, Handal. You win. Three fifty it is."

Handal grumbles but is fooling no one. He is clearly euphoric, and right now, he is absolutely convinced there never was a business genius and negotiating guru quite like him before.

"Are you okay, honey?" Elise has her eyes on me for the first time since the bidding started.

I am as pale as a man in a haunted house. I pull her to one side and whisper in her ear, "Elise ..."

"Yes, David?"

"You do know I don't have that kind of money, don't you, sweetheart?"

"Don't worry; I have that covered."

"How?"

"My dad."

Great. Her rich father who's a doctor. How could I forget? "I haven't met the man yet, and he's all ready to buy me a new home?"

"Don't be silly, David. He doesn't know he's buying us one. Not yet, anyway."

"Elise … darling … that's absurd." My lips continue to work, but no other sound escapes them because nothing else comes to mind. So, I clump up and let my eyes do the talking. Hers join in, and we have a silent conversation.

I am scared of the hundreds of thousands, I tell her wordlessly.

She accuses me of haggling over peanuts and wrinkles her nose at me.

We maintain eye contact for several seconds, neither of us backing off.

Finally, Elise sighs and says, "Okay, David."

"We walk away from this?" I ask in surprise.

"Oh no, we are certainly not doing that," she says matter-of-factly.

"Then what do you mean by 'Okay, David'?"

"I'll just ask Dad for a loan," she says simply. "That way, you can keep your pride and pay him when you are good and ready. Is that better?"

"I don't see how," I answer in shock. "I don't even have a job yet."

"You will be graduating soon."

"Fat chance of me earning half a million in my first year."

"Stay positive, David. Good things come to the hopeful, you know?"

I don't know, and I don't want to know. "I think you mean good things come to those who wait?"

"Davvvviiiddd?" Her drawl reaches an octave or two higher toward the end.

"Yes, darling?" I am attentive and obviously submissive.

"We are getting this place, okay?"

"Yes, darling." And that's that. My worst nightmare has just come true. We are buying a dump. For close to half a million. *Oh-God-Almighty!* And as if that is not bad enough, we'll be moving into it. *I am dead, I tell you, dead-and-buried.*

"Relax, honey," says Elise, seeing how much paler I've just become. "Everything will be fine. I took a course in house construction while at high school. When we are done vamping up this place, it will be a jewel by the river. I promise you, sweetheart; just wait and see. This will be great!"

I wish I could share her optimism. In my book, a dump by any other name is a dump. Worse, in this case, it's a really expensive dump. But all I can do is sigh and listen on in a stupor as Handal and Elise discuss the property in greater detail.

Fifteen

SUMMER'S COMING ALONG QUITE NICELY. In every courtyard, there's a grill party. In every park, a picnic. Vibrant tunes of music and laughter ring clear across all neighborhoods. Everyone is having the time of their lives. Everyone, it seems, but me.

I know this feeling. I've been here before. Longing for fun but unable to participate. Back then it was because of books and exams. Now it's this thesis study. *I need it if I'm to graduate.* I have my work cut out for me.

For the last several days, both at home and at work, I've been studying the development process of Displaytek's fifty-six products with a keen eye and a critical mind. I've been looking for flaws and inconsistencies. Anything I can get rid of. Any improvements I can make.

Metaphorically speaking, every last event from the placing of a washer to the fixing of a screw, has come under my magnifying glass. I've been thorough and objective. I have analyzed and evaluated and judged and then condemned or approved every last event, right down to the finest details.

At this very moment, my desk in Displaytek is buried under assorted paperwork on products and procedures. I've had my nose in them since clocking in early this morning.

I stare at the data. How best can I rearrange the processes? Try as I might, I can't shake off the notion that I'm missing something. All this information is spinning around in my head when it suddenly hits me. *Why not cut out unnecessary events?* This thought has me abruptly sitting upright. With wide-open eyes, I gaze out into nothingness as my brain churns. *This could work! Shorter manufacturing lead time. Why didn't I think of this before?*

I twitch in my seat with the realization of where all this is going. *A breakthrough! At long last!*

I plot down all the changes that I need to make, changes such as circumventing unnecessary transport, eliminating queues, whittling down administrative tasks to an absolute minimum, and striking out redundant quality controls.

This is it! I know it! This is how to cut back processing time. This is how to win more time for what really matters: the actual creation of value.

In growing excitement, I get to work on my plan. While I do, soft staccato plays in the background. It's Ludwig and Nick, pecking away feverishly at their keyboards. Hans Hartmann is here too. For some reason, this mountain of muscle is finding it hard to work on this day. Something's been troubling him. He finally gives up thinking about it and leans over to me and whispers, "Say, David, do you have a moment?"

"Yes, Hans. What's up?"

"What do you know about love?" he asks.

"Little. Why?"

He looks right and left, moves in closer, and lowers his voice even more. I can barely hear him. "It's Christine Gay."

"The legal representative?" I try to hide a knowing smile.

"Shh!" He looks about apprehensively, but nobody heard my words. He dives in for more intense whispers. "Yes but keep your voice down." He hesitates for a moment and then says, "I think she's hitting on me."

I do my best to look bewildered, but of course, I've known this for a while now. Every other person in Displaytek knows it. Quite clearly, Christine has a thing for Hans. This gray-eyed beauty with waist-long brown hair has been hacking away at him for the better part of a month now, and finally, it would appear, Hans is beginning to see the light. He lets me know that muscles, he understands. Physical pain, he can tolerate. But love? How's he to handle this creature? He asks for advice.

I tell him I'm more or less in the same boat as he is. It's very new territory for me as well, I say, and add that I find myself in completely uncharted waters sailing in the dark, entirely without a compass or any other means of directional orientation.

His eyebrows shoot up in absolute bafflement.

I simply shrug and leave him desperately trying to make sense of my statement.

Evidently, love scares the living daylights out of him. Since my answer's been less than satisfactory, he gets hold of lover-boy Frank for more urgent whispers. Together they huddle in a corner for several minutes to discuss love's pros and cons. Now this should be interesting. I'm curious to find out how this saga plays out.

NOT SURPRISINGLY, about a zillion production orders are scheduled on this very day. Only half of us are present here within the operations-scheduling section this very moment. The other half are in the store, picking parts for all they are worth, intent on covering their day's quota before the morning runs out.

I pay them a little visit at eleven o'clock. Frank Krueger is relaxed, casual as ever. He's pacing himself as always while he works. "No point in suffering a burnout this young," he's known to say. Stress is not his way. He's always taking things easy.

Timothy Lang, on the other hand, is practicing jokes to an invisible audience. Nothing out of the ordinary there. Somehow, he manages to squeeze in the time to perform his mandatory duties as well.

Since I still have a lot of blanks in my gradually forming strategy, I approach the two young lads and present them with a hoard of questions. Both are kind enough to accommodate me. They're full of valuable insights. They tell me what I need to know.

Sixteen

We found the contract papers in my mailbox early this morning. It's now become an irrefutable fact. Elise and I are finally the proud owners of a derelict building overgrown with weeds and swamped in trash.

What a notable Saturday this is turning out to be. I moan in pain. Elise cries for joy. We both hug each other dearly, albeit for different reasons. I'm still struggling with the idea of turning this decrepit place into a home.

After lengthy soul searching, I politely reject Elise's offer to let her father foot the bill for the place. It's not mere pride that motivates me at this point. More than that, I'm intent on making a good first impression on the father of my sweetheart.

When all's said and done, purchasing our future home took all of Elise's savings and a sizable bank loan in my name. I'm still reeling from the bank's terms and conditions of doing business. How could I ever let Elise talk me into owning this place? I simply cannot come to terms with the monstrosity of it all. I mean, I am, for all intents and purposes, penniless, and running on fumes. Yet here I am, taking out a sizable loan on an oversized hovel. I must be mad.

At Elise's insistence, we pile into her small car and drive like mad to our new acquisition. She's convinced I will be able to see it in a new light now that we own it. "This is the start of something big, something bright, something truly amazing," she says to me ever so softly. Her voice is extra sweet. Her baby-doll eyes drink me in as she casts her spell on me. I think I'm about to get hopelessly wrapped around her little finger.

Off the top of her head, and practically the minute we get there, she has a name for the dump. "The White Rose," she says proudly, her voice drenched in adrenaline. "The White Rose Residence. That's what we will call it, David, do you agree?"

I stare at her in horror and then at the landfill. Nothing rosy about it springs to mind, but my head simply bobs in agreement of its own accord. I'm tempted to chop it off for this unforgivable betrayal.

As if on cue, Handal appears out of nowhere, dressed in his usual metallic-gray suit. He praises Elise's astute decision to buy the property. He loves the name she has given it. He labels her a crafty businesswoman and then stands back to watch her glow like a jellyfish. My fingers are itching. I want to wring his neck. But my sweetheart won't let me anywhere near him.

Elise and I take to scouting around in this corner or that of the dumpy White Rose. We soon learn that Handal is a sport too, and loves nothing more than to tail us about. Wherever we go, he remains hot on our heels. We check out the house and all two floors of it. We make an initial assessment of all improvement requirements, then step outside to survey the grounds. Handal has lots of advice on how to make this place a home. Elise listens to him critically. I eye him questioningly. Our deal with him has long since been concluded. I'm beginning to wonder why he is still hanging about.

Seven days later, on yet another beautiful Saturday morning, I jolt out of bed to the sound of loud hammering at the front door. My phone is also ringing incessantly, and my computer is going out of its mind with message alerts.

All electronic communication devices are under attack, I realize, and there could be a burglar trying to break into my place.

My mind is groggy. I'm completely disoriented. I stumble out of bed, grabbing my smartphone from the bedside table as I take my first unsteady step toward the door. I raise the phone to my face and with half-closed eyes, peer at it. Elise is the caller. And it's only shortly past ten. *Who is trying to break down my front door? This is the one morning I get to sleep in!*

I trip on my bedroom chair and curse. My laptop is on the chair, and I spot Elise's name and picture on each of the message alerts. Ignoring the laptop, I decide to answer the phone as I make for the front door.

"Hi, Elise, what's up?" My voice is a toady croak.

"The sun is shining. It's such a beautiful day, David. Come outdoors."

The front door is rattling under a relentless barrage. I yank it open to find Elise standing there, phone in hand, giggling like a naughty kid.

"Oh, you naughty, rotten apple," I say in a low reprimanding voice.

She bursts out laughing as I drag her into the apartment.

We wrestle on the couch. I get in a good spank, and she lets out a jolly scream, threatening to report me to her mother. She is laughing so hard she mispronounces every last word out of her mouth. I tickle her till she begs for mercy. I tell her I would gladly give her this thing called mercy if only I knew what it was. We fool around for several minutes more, till tears of joy spring out of her eyes. It's almost thirty minutes later that a calm Elise tells me why she is here. She has planned a surprise picnic.

"Lovely," I tell her. But then she mentions the intended venue for the picnic.

"The White Rose Residence," she breathes excitedly. Her manner and the way she says it makes it sound like some highly romantic French version of "I love you."

I almost spank her all over again.

We arrive at the White Rose shortly thereafter. Not far away a black BMW 320d in tip-top condition is parked at the side of the road leading up to the White Rose. It appears to be unoccupied. We spot its apparent owners—a muscular man and beautiful, agile-looking woman, both in their late twenties—down by the river that flows beside the house. They seem to be sporty types. Both have short black hair and are dressed in simple jeans and T-shirts. A few feet from them, almost at the beach of the river, is a simple picnic that has been halfheartedly bitten into and long since forgotten. For now, the two lovebirds seem to have given in to the greater pleasure of marveling at Mother Nature.

"Looks like we're not the only ones keen on nature dining," I say to Elise.

She simply shrugs.

The two strangers check us out.

We wave politely.

Neither of them responds.

We decide it's in our best interest to let them be. Acting indifferent, we drive through the gate and onto the grounds of our new property.

Because the flora here has been neglected for so many years, it has acquired that peaceful and lovely appeal that one finds so often in pockets of nature as yet untouched by man. The air is sweet and clean. The foliage is richly green, and I could swear it appears almost prehistoric in nature. A variety of majestic trees and shrubs on either side of the overgrown driveway sway elegantly in the gentle breeze. Color blooms everywhere. It's like being in an enticingly cool enchanted forest.

Given today's magnificent weather, I am actually beginning to enjoy being here.

We park halfway up the driveway and forge left a handful of meters into the expansive, overgrown front yard. Here, underneath the canopy of an old ginkgo tree, where the air is pleasantly cool, do we at last stop and set up our picnic spread.

The spot we've picked for our al fresco meal is indeed a beauty. Fifty meters behind us is the unsightly structure that's soon to be our home, and thanks to all the trees in between, it's practically invisible to us. Not too far on our left is the clear sparkling water of the slightly effervescing river flowing through the tiny patch of woods. A cheery trickling can be heard emanating from it. It's a peaceful sound. I quickly forget the White Rose.

The contents of the picnic basket turn out to be as mouth-watering as Elise promised they would be—prosciutto-and-roasted-red-pepper sandwiches, chips, frozen grapes of various colors, licorice twists, a bottle of white wine, and four colas. It's a sizable spread. Far more than needed for a single sitting, but I keep my thought to myself. Since the lovely feast turns out to be quite tasty as well, I dig in with pleasure.

Time almost crawls to a standstill in this idyllic place. A flock of merrily tweeting goldcrest up in the branches above our heads hop about from one treetop to the next, as though excited about these two humans lounging out in their part of the world. We admire their graceful appearance. We eat. We engage in lighthearted banter. We even make out a little after the meal, and not surprisingly, I start entertaining thoughts of sex on the beach. I think I'm in the mood. Elise's quick to put on the brakes. Evidently, she has other plans.

At about twelve thirty, we walk along a meandering path in the ten-year-old wilderness. The smell of foliage lingers in my nostrils. The scent of fresh earth recalls to mind my Boy

Scouting days. I get to feel like a new-age explorer on a for-gotten island. How magical it would be to discover tropical wonders here.

Mother Nature's powers of reclamation are astounding. The cleanly cut pathways that once existed here are no longer discernible. The paved walkways are heavily overgrown, and the flower beds are all but nonexistent. It's a forest, unruly in every possible way. It's exhilarating.

Several minutes later we break through the thick foliage into a small clearing. There, before us, for the first time on this day, do I come face to face at last with our future residence. Fifty meters long, twenty wide, two stories high, peeling paint on practically all its cemented facade, and a multitude of broken windows wherever I look. My lips curl in disgust at the sight.

Elise takes my hand. Together, we walk into the building. Just inside its entrance is the largest assortment of garden tools I've ever seen.

"You sneaky little girl," I say to Elise.

She bursts out laughing.

"When did you plan all this?" I ask.

"Last week." She's brimming with mirth, and her eyes are full of mischief. "A little each day, a day at a time, all while you were holed up at Displaytek," Elise explains.

I look at the tools, still unbelieving.

"This place won't get into shape by itself, you know?" she says. "Time to get to work, lover boy."

"Good God," I say, realizing I am in for some hard, phys-ical labor.

Elise sets up a battery-powered radio in one corner of the building. She tunes it to a music station. Then she smiles, winks, and says, "Take me upstairs, darling. I'm in the mood."

"Sure, bidibeez, my queen bee. Your wish is my command."

She laughs gleefully.

I squeeze her hand and then lead her upstairs, both of us armed to the teeth with all manner of tools and brooms. Our plan is to start on the top floor and then work our way to the bottom.

THE CLEANUP exercise takes off on a good note. We sweep and collect for an hour, tossing discarded packaging materials into garbage bags and a large assortment of empty bottles into crates. I toil like a donkey. The rubbish begins to dwindle. Not surprisingly, my white T-shirt gets quickly drenched in sweat. I promptly discard it.

Elise gets rid of her blouse too, but keeps her black bra and matching frill skirt on. The two of us are prattling about topless when Handal makes an unexpected appearance.

"Hi," he calls out.

Startled right out of our socks, we turn around in disbelief. There he is, in a blue polyamide jogging suit and white sneakers. He makes his way toward us.

"What are you doing here?" Elise asks, walking over to her blouse and putting it back on.

"Just out for a jog in the neighborhood. Beautiful place for that, you know?"

I notice he's not sweating, despite the warm weather.

"Thought I could check out the place, make sure everything's okay. Imagine my surprise at finding you two here!"

We own the place. Plus, what's to check out? Trash? I keep my thoughts to myself.

"Just tidying up a little, in preparation for the architect's visit," Elise says sweetly.

Handal smiles even more sweetly than Elise. Since he doesn't make a move to leave, Elise gives him a wide broom. "Take up the rear; sweep in our wake," she says simply.

Handal gladly obeys.

This man is starting to freak me out. I decide then and there to keep a close eye on him.

We sweep and leave a clean wake behind us, all the way down to the ground floor. Sometime next week, the architect, Marcus Bellmann, will come. He'll draw up plans for turning this place into a respectable house. Meanwhile, Elise and I will work on plans to turn it into a beautiful home. Elise's excitement is beginning to rub off on me a little. Handal wants to hug. I keep my distance. I'm still suspicious about his sudden appearance.

At one thirty, we take a short break. I'm tired. I didn't realize just how famished I am until now. The three of us dine on leftovers from the earlier picnic. Every once in a while, I spot the occupants of the black BMW. They're still here.

Not once have they set foot on our property. If I'm not mistaken, they seem to be keeping tabs on us. I haven't caught them looking anywhere else but in toward our property. This is a bit unsettling. I try not to dwell on it.

Handal, it would seem, has spotted them too. Each time he looks their way, he shrinks a little and then tries to hide from their view altogether. Does he know them?

I study him closely. He's fighting to appear casual. He praises Elise nonstop for the prosciutto-and-pepper sandwiches, says he's never eaten anything tastier in his entire life, and even begs Elise for the recipe.

Elise enjoys this attention. She does her best to explain to him how to make the sandwiches. She needn't bother. Handal's barely listening. Like me, he's stealing repeated glances at the occupants of the black BMW. Something's off. Something's definitely got him bothered a great deal. I'm beginning to smell a rat. What's going on? Should I be worried?

Shortly before two, as Elise announces it's time to work on the garden, he excuses himself and quickly disappears. I pray he never comes back to our neck of the woods ever again. Still, I cannot shake off a rather unsettling feeling. I fear we haven't seen the last of him yet.

Seventeen

THE SUN is quickly disappearing over the tree line. Right on time, the charismatic Marcus Bellmann drives up to the White Rose in a fashionably black four-wheel-drive Land Rover Discovery.

From the doorway of our derelict mansion, we watch as he smartly jumps out of his car and briskly walks in our direction. The soft orange glow of the setting sun pulses lightly in his background. It's the perfect frame, forming a beautifully sharp contrast to his professional appearance; blue suit, light-blue shirt, and shimmering-gray tie. I estimate him to be about six-foot-one, and in his late thirties.

He critically surveys the property, the trees, and the clearings we've prepared for green lawns and flower beds. His narrow face lights up with a myriad of emotions as he glances once more at the bleak two-story building with its many broken windows.

"This is a goldmine!" He exclaims to my utter surprise.

"It is, isn't it?" Elise cries out immediately, completely overcome by his and her excitement. "Want to see the rest of it?"

"Thought you would never ask," Marcus replies, beaming at her.

She takes his arm. The three of us go off to rediscover the White Rose.

For about thirty minutes we walk and talk, stop and go, show him every nook and cranny inside and out, and fill him with details of all the fabulous parties we want to hold here in the near future.

He falls in love with the river and very nearly takes a dip in it. He praises our business acumen and can't believe we got this land for a song.

He asks Elise what her dreams for the place are.

Since Handal's encouragement, Elise has been dreaming without restrictions. Now, at Marcus's insistence, she holds nothing back. They come flooding out of her nonstop as she shares her every dream and fantasy for this place, and consults with Marcus at every juncture.

Marcus is elated at the prospect of work coming his way. He listens intently. He takes studious notes and complements these with a couple of photos, even making a handful of rough sketches for good measure.

Outside, darkness is quickly falling. We wind up our consultation and see Marcus to his car. He promises to deliver brilliant architectural plans before driving off into the darkness.

Elise's all smiles as she looks up at me. There's an expression on her face that says, *I told you so, David. This place has potential. Even Marcus sees it.*

It's nice to see her so full of wonderful expectation. I kiss her warmly and hold her close. Shortly after, we drive off in her mini to her apartment. There's romance in the air. I do not leave her side until late Sunday evening.

For nine days, Elise and I hear nothing from Marcus Bellmann. We know his firm is situated in the famous Jen Shop Towers in the middle of downtown. Obviously, he's still working on the blueprints. Though eager to know his progress, we resist the urge to pay him a visit.

Elise calls me at work on Tuesday afternoon to share with me some good news. "Marcus Bellmann was here," she says, barely able to contain her excitement. "He just presented me the much-awaited blueprints."

"Lovely," I reply.

"Indeed," she says. "You should see them, David. They're marvelous!"

"I'll take your word for it," I tell her with a slight chuckle. "So, what's next?"

"Project White Rose is a go," she says breathlessly.

"When are we breaking ground?"

"Right away," she says.

I listen to her talk excitedly for a while.

This is really happening, I grasp. We're making a home together. The notion of living with Elise under one roof is beginning to appeal to me more and more.

A foolish smile commandeers my face as soon as we say our goodbyes. I set down the receiver and stare blankly into empty space. I'm lost in sugar-coated daydreams.

For the past week, Elise has taken to calling me at work almost on a daily basis, and always early in the afternoon. She says it's essential to keep me up to date so that I don't get any nasty surprises when I turn up at the White Rose.

On this Wednesday, like so many of the other days before it, I get to hear a glorious and most uplifting progress report. The White Rose is a beehive of activity, she says. A demolition team made up of six young men is on the premises. All look alike, all massive packs of muscle wielding colossal demolition hammers. "You should see them, David."

I'm trying to figure out if she's referring to the hammers or the lads, but quickly give up and continue listening to her. She's talking again, spewing forth more details. "The walls marked for demolition came down in a cloud of dust two hours ago. I coughed for an hour before someone handed me an industrial mask. And the racket ... I wish you could have heard it, David."

Thank you but no thanks, princess.

"It was loud, darling. I think my ears are still ringing. Anyway, mercifully, the din is over now. All that's left of the walls is enough debris to raise the *Titanic*. The foreman tells me the foundation is solid and can remain in place. Clearing away the debris will take all of two days. We are having lots of fun, David. The guys even brought beer. Your favorite too. Are you sure you want to miss all this?"

The tree-chopping action Elise put me through at the White Rose still lingers in my mind. For now, buddy moments like wielding hammers to rock music while sipping beer just doesn't appeal to me. I tell Elise this, but in fewer words.

"Hm. Pity," she says and then quickly changes tone. "Oh, I almost forgot. That BMW has been here all day. Same occupants, same Peeping Tom mannerisms. What do you think their deal is?"

"No idea, Elise. But be careful all the same. Don't tread too near."

"Roger that, captain. Tonight, at five?" she asks.

"Sure thing, baby."

I say my goodbyes, hang up and slip into deep thought. The black BMW is starting to worry me somewhat. As yet, no crime has been committed. Nevertheless ... What could a man and a woman in a black BMW possibly have against us? What could they do to us? My brow furrows. My eyes squint. About a million possible criminal intentions race through my mind—everything from daylight robbery to BDSM scenarios. I shudder at a number of the former type. I slink in my chair at several of the latter, eyes darting right and left, hoping no one's seeing my embarrassed face.

It's a while before I get back to work.

Eighteen

AN AFTER-HOURS VISIT to the construction site reveals a pleasant surprise. Work on the raw structure is almost complete. The fifty offices that once took up space within these walls have been whittled down to eleven supersized rooms. These include seven self-contained bedrooms all carved out of the upper floor.

From left to right on the ground floor is a gigantic in-house garage, a grand living room, a spacious dining room, and a fabulous kitchen. The place is still an empty shell. And its walls are in dire need of a coat of paint. The White Rose is still a work in progress. There's plenty to be done. But it's taking shape. I think I'm beginning to like it.

Handal Hoams has been here every step of the way. So far, his reasons for showing up remain a mystery. On this day, like many others before it, he's dressed in a gray suit and trying to blend in with the walls. I notice him standing motionless while staring anxiously at a construction worker in gray overalls. The man is wielding a metal detector.

Handal, I realize, is not just nervous. *Could it be he's downright scared?* The hairs on my nape begin to rise as I watch him closely.

Meanwhile, the worker crisscrosses the living room in a sweeping motion. The metal detector swings this way and that. As he comes to a stop near the center of the living room,

Handal abruptly loses his resolve. He's unable to remain still anymore. He blanches fiercely, and while following every move the man in gray makes, starts to shake in livid fear.

This is surreal. My heart is beating wildly. I'm just as scared as Handal Hoams.

Suddenly he looks in my direction.

I duck through the nearby doorway and hide behind the dining room wall. There's a chisel a mere arm's length away. I pick it up and get busy seconds before Handal pokes his head through the doorway. The wall before me is flawless. Doesn't matter. I scrape away at it in earnest.

He screws his eyes in my direction for a second or two, cocks his head to one side as if deliberating my diligence, or honesty, or God knows what, then withdraws his head and is gone.

My heart is hammering like mad. *Why should I be so scared? This is my property, for crying out loud. If anything, it's Handal who should beat out of here with his tail between his legs. He doesn't own the White Rose. It's not for sale. Not anymore, at least.* But all this logic does nothing to calm my racing heart.

I inspect the wall critically to a count of five, then carefully lean over and look through the doorway again. His attention is once more on Mr. Gray Overalls. I'm of no further interest to him at this point. *Thank God!*

I lean out further and follow his gaze, which is now firmly fixated on a certain spot on the floor.

The metal detector passes over this very spot several times. Each time, Handal reaches for his heart as though his very life's about to be over. Just when I'm sure he's on the verge of a heart attack, the worker loses interest in Handal's spot and walks away.

The metal detector didn't beep even once. I am severely disappointed. I expected him to find something. I was certain he was seconds from raising the alarm. I look over at Handel who's still visibly shaking. One thing's for sure. Something's buried down there. And He doesn't want us finding it.

Two hours later after the crew has departed and night has fallen, I make my way with a beating heart to Handal's spot and examine it closely. An overpowering sense of danger comes over me as I study it for any clues to his bizarre behavior. No cracks, no openings, nothing. Just a smooth and seamless cement floor, waiting for a layer of parquet. I tap on it with my shoe. A solid sound reverberates throughout the empty room. There's absolutely nothing out of the ordinary. What did I expect? I'm almost disgusted with myself. I've been building mountains out of molehills. I've been clutching at straws, unnecessarily thinking the worst of Handal Hoams.

At this point, I recall his palpable fear earlier in the day. My suspicions spring back to life. Wouldn't hurt to be thorough, I decide. To this end, the construction team will help. I will ask them to look closely at that spot, ping it, tear it up, do whatever it takes to reveal its secrets. Let's see if they can bring up whatever is down there.

I leave the still-uninhabitable White Rose Residence seconds later. The sky is filled with a myriad of stars. They twinkle and glow against the black-velvet background of the young obscure night. Down below, darkness reigns. The trees are almost lost in the impenetrable gloom. At their base, just outside the property, a little way off the side of the road, is the black BMW. Both the night as well as the towering trees hide it well. I wouldn't have spotted it if it weren't for a sudden sliver of moonlight across its metallic hood. The two dark silhouettes within slink lower in their seats as I drive past. Alarm bells go off in my mind. I recall the day of the picnic. I remember Handal's strange reaction to the BMW's occupants. Recognition, fear, flight; all these and more, had played on his visage. Then, I had been amused by it all. At this moment, I am certainly not laughing. First, Handal's constant presence, then his strange preoccupation with the floor. Now this; the BMW. Why are these two parties orbiting our property? What in heaven's name is going on? I have a very bad feeling in the pit of my stomach. I need answers. I must know what's in that floor, one way or another, whatever it takes. *Tomorrow, at the very latest, I'll have my answers.*

Nineteen

MY FIRST ACT when I arrive at Displaytek the next day, is to place a call to the construction team at the White Rose. I give them my unusual request. They think it's crazy. They want to know why I'm requesting them to dig up the floor. I keep the reasons to myself. "Just tell me what you find," I say, and hang up. I'm a little on edge. I also didn't sleep well. Probably because of the fear that's been gripping me for most of last night and early this morning. I'm afraid of whatever it is that's buried down there beneath the White Rose. I try not to think about it.

HANS HARTMANN is finally responding to Christine Gay. He's flirting! Who would have thought this possible? This unexpected turn of events is doing something equally unexpected to Christine Gay.

As of this morning, she's been going about like a patas monkey in a banana field, as though completely overwhelmed with all the goodies in supply. each time her big deer eyes look through her thick glasses and land on dear Hans, she instantaneously goes into ecstasy, seeing yet unseeing, as the object of her desire goes through equally similar emotions.

Budding love is a fascinating thing to witness. Right now, it's just the sort of distraction I need. For most of the day, my concerns of the previous evening are all but forgotten.

The call I've been waiting for arrives early afternoon as I grapple with issues of takt time and lean production.

"Come quick," Say Elise urgently. The note in her voice makes me freeze for several seconds.

There's no mistaking her fear. I hear it. I feel it. I'm even shaking slightly as I ask, "What's wrong?"

"Can't say on the phone. Just get here quick. Please, hurry."

The phone goes dead in my hands. I stare at it for precious seconds more. Then I am up and running. First, into Kevin's office. "Family emergency. Got to go" is all I say. I bound out of his office and head for the exit before he can utter a word. *Might he be wondering what family? After all, I'm not married.* But that's of little consequence now. I'm out and away.

The drive from Displaytek to the White Rose usually takes about thirty minutes. Today, with my foot all the way down on the gas pedal, I make it in fifteen. I screech to a halt before the gate and instinctively look to my right. The black BMW is once again there, and the same man and woman are seated inside. Both occupants have a rapturous look of wonder on their faces as they marvel at the woods. Obviously, they are feigning interest in the woods, pretending to like the trees, and very much in love with the way they're growing so nicely. I stare at them, prompting a reaction. They give up the act and simply stare back at me.

My phone is in my hand. I think of calling the police. My thumb hovers millimeters over the speed dial number. It's my panic button. If the two so much as cough in my direction, my thumb falls, and the police will be on their way. I wait for them to move, cough, even sneeze a little, but neither of them so much as twitches. Seconds go by. Their stares waver. Time seems to stand still. Then very slowly, they turn away in unison. Once more, they are admiring the trees. In particular their crowns. I no longer am of any interest to them. *What nerve!*

I hesitate a fraction of a second and then jump out of the car and dash through the gates. I'm going mad with fear, trying to imagine what sort of horror awaits me inside.

The whole driveway, including the roundabout before the house, is full of small trucks and cars belonging to the construction company. As I race past them, I realize not a single person is on the grounds outside, not even the gardeners Elise hired to lay down lawns and flower beds.

I burst through the front door which is mysteriously ajar. I zip across the empty entrance hallway. I'm sweating as I burst through into the living room.

Here, at last, I find everyone. Elise, the construction workers, the gardeners, and their foremen. They're all gathered around the very spot of floor I checked out last night. A few are speaking in excited tones. Most are just standing there, as if unsure of what to do next. On each face is a strange mix of shock and curiosity.

I look around for Handal Hoams. He's nowhere to be seen. My heart starts beating wildly as I walk up to the group. How many people are there? Ten? Fifteen? What am I going to find in their midst? A cache of guns? Maybe a corpse? Fear of the unknown has me in a vise grip.

The crowd parts as I reach it. Before I know it, I am standing next to Elise. The construction team dug into the floor as they promised they would. In the next second, I'm looking down into a hole below. It's a meter wide on all sides and about two deep. In it is something I never thought I would see in my entire life—polythene bags, about a hundred of them, each roughly the size of a man's hand. In each is a white powdery substance I've never come across but still recognize from all the countless movies I've watched my entire life. With a sinking feeling of hopeless despair, I realize I am looking at cocaine.

I can't believe this. I am in shock and fighting to stay calm. The bags are filled to the brim. My mind balks and tries to shut down. Cocaine? On our property? How in the world did this ever happen to us? And to make matters worse, on top of the whole stash of illicit drugs are neatly stacked bundles of hundred-dollar bills, all tightly wrapped with transparent foil into a single massive bundle. My legs are weak. I think I need to sit down. I also need to think.

Elise and I are both law-abiding citizens. Of all the things in the world that we could find on our property, why did it have to be cocaine and drug money? I swoon a little. My head is extremely light. *God, please, not now. Not the fainting thing.*

"How much do you think is in there?" Elise asks, her voice shaky, almost inaudible.

"The drugs or the money?" My voice is not much better. My throat is parched. I'm badly in need of a drink.

"Both."

"I would say between five and ten million in drugs, a million in cash."

"What are we going to do?" she asks fearfully.

The gardeners and construction workers simply look on, listening to us talk. Not even one of them dares utter a word.

"I think we should call the police," I say.

No one speaks for a while. Finally, Elise wrings her hands. "Fine," she says in a defeated voice.

"Really?"

"Yes, David. Call the police."

Something drops unceremoniously to the floor with a heavy thud. I jump, look around and see it's Heartsflip. He's the gardening foreman. A tall, wiry lad with an oval face, short sandy hair and extra-bushy eyebrows, dressed in green gardening overalls. Obviously, he's scared as hell and because his spindly legs can't take the excitement anymore, they've given out under him. With little effort, he tries to gather himself together while still on the floor. Now he's unceremoniously seated with one leg tucked under him and the other under his chin. He's shaking slightly, entering into a full-scale panic attack. "The police," he murmurs to himself as though dying.

I wonder if he has a police record? Clearly, he's regretting the day he took on this job. In his eyes, this stint is turning into a jail sentence, maybe even a death sentence. Or both?

I watch Heartsflip closely. A premonition of doom comes over me. With a heavy heart, my finger finally drops on my panic button. The call to the police goes through.

In seconds, I am speaking to a police constable. I explain the situation carefully. More than once, I expressly stress the fact that we are all innocent. Heartsflip's color comes back a little bit on hearing this.

The police constable grunts and gruffs a lot. When he finally has all the essential facts, he promises to dispatch a team to us. At that, the line goes dead. For a while, I listen to the empty buzzing, unsure of what to do. Then I hang up.

In the ensuing moment of awkward silence, Mr. Heartsflip's mind buckles back to its original state. Untold horror is once more doing a nasty job to his face. He's still seated on the floor when he voices the question on everyone's mind. "Mr. Elbert, how did you know?" he asks, his voice squeaky, low, barely audible.

"Know what exactly?" I ask full of mistrust as though he's trying to frame me of some unspeakable crime.

"What's under the floor?"

"Handal Hoams," I reply quickly, very much eager to assert my innocence.

"The real estate agent?"

"Yes."

"He told you?"

"No. He kept showing up here, even though he didn't need to. I noticed him staring at this spot and became suspicious."

"You think it's his?" Elise asks in surprise.

"Who else can it belong to?"

She considers this new bit of information with a mixture of awe and dread. "He was here most of the day," she says quietly.

"Even made a terrible scene as I set about drilling the floor," says Hardclop, the construction foreman, a rock of a man in gray overalls. "At first, I thought he was the only one here with a sane mind. You know, what with you asking me to drill a hole in this majestically beautiful floor on a whim." He shakes his head, wondering how wrong he could have been. "But still, a job is a job. So, we got on with it. And that's when Handal Hoams happened. We had to physically restrain him in the end." He nods a bit and shows a little muscle as he says this. Quickly, however, he drops the act in light of our current plight and concludes by saying, "That's when we dug up this mess. I think my life is over." He slumps, as though indeed things will never be the same again.

"Where is he now?" I ask.

"Disappeared before we hit pay dirt," a construction worker standing somewhere behind me says.

That sounds just like him, I can't help thinking.

Within two minutes of my call to the police, pandemonium breaks out. Two out-of-uniform agents from the drug-enforcement agency barge into the house with all the flare usually only seen in big-budget action movies. The male agent identifies himself while flying through the air, gun cocked and ready to fire. The female agent skids across the floor toward the only visible cover in the whole room—a stack of paint cans about ten feet away from the doorway. She hits them with a resounding wham! Many of the paint cans scatter in all directions. The noise is deafening. Whereas we were scared before, now we are truly going out of our minds with fear. Terror is etched on every single face within the room. We are all rooted to our respective spots.

Both agents shout out commands. Their mouths are open wide, spewing forth nothing but chilling words. These are coming out of them with such bloodcurdling vigor that I swear I feel my blood do just that. Every drop of that precious liquid inside of me has turned to curdle. My whole system is completely clogged up. I am as good as paralyzed.

"Don't move!" the male agent shouts.

"Put down your weapons!" negates the female agent.

"Hands up," demands the man.

"Get down on the floor," challenges the woman.

All these contradictions from only two people? It's extremely unfair! I am practically frozen. I'll never again be able to move another muscle.

All around me, construction workers and gardeners scramble about in a vain attempt to comply with the agents' opposing wishes. No one knows whether to listen to the male or female agent. So, the only thing going on is the very last thing either agent wants—a lot of movement. Tools and gadgets come raining down, crashing to the floor as several hands go up in the air. Many of these same hands rush back down again, as their owners hit the ground, only to spring up once more, confused, uncertain, getting more desperate by the second. At this very moment, deciding whether to stand or hit the floor seems to be the hardest thing any of these people have ever attempted in their lives. The agents watch on in flabbergasted dismay.

Heartsflip and one of his fellow gardeners are especially hard-hit. The spades they're holding seem practically glued to their hands. This is probably due to all that unadulterated fear locking down every single muscle in their fists. Both are acutely aware of their lack of satisfactory compliance with the agents' wishes. Their mortified eyes lock onto the agents' weapons, which could go off at any second. This fact is slowly driving both of them around the bend. So now both are doing something akin to squats, stuck halfway between hitting the floor and standing up still. All the while, their arms flap about wildly. The spades refuse to drop.

A second gardener quite clearly considers cutting off his arms to save his life. He's busying himself against the blunt edge of the doorway, hoping this sawing movement will somehow get rid of at least one bloody appendage.

I see it all from the corner of my eye, even as incredulity clouds my face. *This is ridiculous!* I wish I could laugh at the scene, but I can't. I'm also scared shitless and have problems of my own. These come in the way of Elise. She's clinging to me for dear life. I think she's waiting for me to save her in the event bullets start to fly. Or, at the very least, hoping for a little comfort in this overly dark and dangerous moment. But not the slightest bit of spark, let alone a flaming warmth, is left inside of me. I'm frozen rock solid.

Both agents survey the pathetic scenes. I hear them chuckle and giggle. We see them settle back to watch the show, and before long, they're suffering bouts of uncontrollable laughter.

We listen to them howl like wolves for a while.

At last, after deciding that none of us could ever be a threat to them or national security, they come out of hiding and put their guns away.

Seeing this, Heartsflip melts to the ground in a heap. He's still alive. Relief and gratitude overcome him.

The agents flash their badges. We finally get a good look at them. Elise gasps, and my jaw drops. They are none other than the occupants of the infamous black BMW.

I shake my head in shock. I stammer at them as I start to make the connections. Now it's all beginning to make sense—Handal's crazy behavior over the last few weeks, the BMW, the drugs, and this final revelation. The two who've been stalking our home are agents. *And to think I almost called the police on them!*

We watch them closely as they walk up to us. As usual, both are in blue jeans and black T-shirts. The muscular man runs a hand through his short black hair and gives us a sinister smile. The agile female agent is beautiful. Her dirty-blonde hair is set in a charmingly low pixie hairstyle that's a little long at the front, and falls halfway down her elegant brow. She's wearing exquisite silver earrings. They glitter. She's endearing.

Once beside Elise and I, the agents take a look at the stash. Then in unison, as if on cue, they whistle softly, from the belly up.

"Somebody's in big trouble," the stunning lithe woman slowly drawls, head bobbing up and down, emphasizing each word.

At this, construction workers and gardeners slowly distance themselves from us. Eventually, only Elise and I are left standing next to the incriminating find. The agents move to cut off all escape routes.

"Special Agent Kirling," the man says.

"Special Agent Moneypot," the woman says. Her head never stops bobbing.

"And you must be Mr. Elbert, the one who called the police, right?" Kirling asks.

"Yes," I say, still partially frozen.

"Care to answer a few questions?"

"Do I need a lawyer?"

"If it's not yours, I don't see why," Kirling replies, jerking a thumb at the multimillion-dollar stash. He stares at me, daring me to ask for a lawyer. I think I need a doctor more.

"What do you want to know?"

"How long have you known Handal Hoams?"

"About two months."

"How did you get acquainted?"

"He's a real estate agent. We were looking for a home."

"How did you know where to find the stash?"

I explain it all to him. The two look bored and instead focus their attention on the others in the room. Six construction workers, four gardeners. And their foremen.

Heartsflip feels the heat of the agents' stare and slowly melts into jelly once more. He suffers a quick relapse and does a few more involuntary squats in rapid succession. It appears he's undecided: hit the floor and stay still, or remain on his feet ready to run for his life. The spade is still in place. It's firmly glued to his hands. I bet it will feature in his nightmares for months to come.

Several other workers raise their arms halfway in the air, tools notwithstanding, as uneasy restlessness spreads among them. Kirling and Moneypot study the workers' every move, half reaching for their guns again. I almost shut my eyes in fear of a bloodbath.

Agent Kirling suddenly interrupts my rumblings, saying, "We already know all this." Agent Moneypot bobs her head in confirmation.

"How?" I ask. "I'm positive you didn't get all this from the cops. You were here mere seconds after I called them. It's simply not possible to have received a detailed recap in that time."

"True," says Kirling. And that's when they drop the bombshell on us. They've had their suspicions for months and have been painstakingly gathering evidence. When they felt charges could stick, they got a search warrant for this place.

"When?" a shocked Elise asks.

"When it was still a pigsty, before you bought it," Moneypot says.

"You searched the place? What did you find?" Heartsflip asks, his voice trembling. I wonder how much of this he can take before he suffers a total nervous breakdown.

"Nothing of course," Agent Kirling says, exasperated. "Why else do you think we're still here? Damn thing was truly well hidden, as you can see."

We all look at the hole in the floor.

"Handal must have known we were closing in on him," Kirling says.

"He couldn't dig out the stash, couldn't relocate it," Moneypot says.

"Consequently, he got you to quickly buy up the place," Kirling says.

"You were meant to sit on it and keep it warm for him," Moneypot says.

"Just like a good cock and hen do on their unhatched eggs," Agent Kirling adds, laughing hysterically. Moneypot laughs too.

They are both beside themselves with laughter for a full minute. *The little twerps. If only I could rap on their heads and knock some sense into them.* But I am still partially frozen.

Agent Kirling suddenly gets serious and feels the need to expound on his words. "Yeah, that's what he needed you poor bastards for, to sit on forbidden goods till the heat died off."

"Then he would've come back," Moneypot says.

"For the goods," Agent Kirling elaborates.

"Probably would slit your throats in the process as well," Moneypot says. By now, her head has bobbed a kilometer and counting.

"Oh God," Elise gasps with intense feeling. All this has finally become too much for her. "Really? Murder?" She hugs me close. This time, she gets a little bit of comfort from my slowly thawing body.

"Oh yes," Moneypot says. "So is the nature of the business. We always catch them in the end, though, and they rot in jail for murder, so chin up. All's well that ends in jail."

I'm not a fan of her variation on "All's well that ends well." Personally, I prefer the original version. I would rather they catch him before anyone gets murdered. I stroke Elise's throat, reassuring her it's still very much intact.

Kirling and Moneypot explain the situation some more. It turns out that at first, the police thought we were in cahoots with Handal Hoams.

"Right after you bought this place, we installed listening devices in the walls. Sorry about that," Kirling says.

Elise goes extra pale on hearing this, and I find myself freezing solid all over again.

"But now we know your hands are clean," Moneypot says.

"Yeah. Never smoked a joint in your lives," Kirling says.

"We looked you up, you know? Just in case."

"And since we've now located the stash …" Kirling trails off with a shoulder shrug.

"No reason not to pull out the active bugs," Moneypot finishes.

I bet they always finish each other's sentences in poetic rhymes, these two.

"What about the inactive ones?" Elise asks.

"Destroyed when you brought down walls to whittle down the rooms," Kirling replies. There is a look of accusation in his eyes. It's as if he's implying we were deliberately trying to sabotage his James Bond espionage. I wish we had brought down all the walls just to spite him.

Before long, the rest of the drug-enforcement team arrives. A skid of tires can be heard halfway across the neighborhood as they draw to a stop outside the gate. They have extremely powerful megaphones, and it takes them no time at all to blast out to the whole neighborhood that there are drugs here. They advise everyone not somehow involved to keep his or her distance, saying that anyone found loitering anywhere near the property will be a suspect.

This is insane! I cringe horribly. I call passionately on the Yeti for justice. How nice would it be if the abominable snowman appeared out of thin air to scare these boys in blue out of existence? *They are ruining my life! There goes our neighborhood reputation. Forget friends, forget languid afternoon tea parties. Nobody-will-come! I think my life is over.*

The drugs and money are finally lifted out of the hole and quickly secured. The whole bundle is escorted out to a heavily armored van waiting just outside the gate.

Agents Kirling and Moneypot request that Elise and I drop in at the police headquarters tomorrow. "Just the little matter of an official statement remaining," Kirling says.

"And don't worry your little heads," Moneypot assures us. "We will issue an APB on Handal Hoams."

They leave us with a little bit of advice. Should Handal Hoams contact us, we are to notify them immediately. With that, they get off the property and disappear in their black BMW.

The whole entourage of agents starts up all at once. It's an impossible cacophony of revving engines. In seconds, they are out of sight.

Heartsflip wobbles severely on badly shaking legs. He too is making an exit. Speaking to no one in particular, he says that he's never coming back to the White Rose. "Nothing rosy here," he says. "I'll need a year to recover from today's scare." His gardeners wholeheartedly agree with him. Behind his back though, they quietly whisper to us that they will be back tomorrow, with Heartsflip in tow. All will be well. Work will continue, they reassure us. Then they too disappear.

Only the construction workers remain behind to tidy up. They putter about for fifteen minutes and do little. Mostly they talk earnestly about all that's transpired today. Eventually, they leave as well.

Elise and I remain in the empty shell of our future home. We talk for a bit at the brink of the massive hole, incoherently discussing the situation, and loudly wondering what has become of the world today. At nine, we are drained. She agrees to accompany me to my place. We barely speak till we get to my apartment. For an hour, we console each other as passionately as we can. At midnight, we finally fall into fitful sleep.

Twenty

My soft loan for the White Rose has thus far been partially granted. The terms and conditions for the remaining half still need to be ironed out. It's for this reason that I'm back here at the bank this Friday morning, on my own, without Elise, discussing pay-back models and trying to squeeze out better terms of repayment from an otherwise stoic Banker who's as hard to read as they come.

Negotiations last an hour. I gain little traction. At one point my dismay goes out of control when he suddenly mentions last night's drug bust.

Christ! Does everyone know about it already?

He tells me it's all over the media, and that he fastidiously read all about it on his way to work since it involves the same piece of property I'm acquiring. The very same one his bank is putting up money for, he gravely adds.

Aha! This explains why he's being a bitch, I realize. I find myself pleading my innocence for the second time since yesterday's awful discovery. Alex, my banker, doesn't care one bit for my story.

In the end, I walk out of the bank with more or less the same deal as I had before. Yes, I now have twice the amount to repay in the same time frame. But other than that, nothing's changed. I still have the same terms and conditions. The same interest rates. The same noose tightly around my neck. I want to scream.

For half an hour, I walk about in a stupor as I think. It's time to tighten the reins on needless expenditure. I sense dark days ahead.

EVIDENTLY, cocaine with a street value of $10 million is big news. True to my banker's word, the media's having a field day with the narrative. Newspapers and tabloids alike are awash with the story. I notice this as I stumble into the Paradise Train Station at the junction of Knebel and Am-Volksbad Street as I make my way to meet up with Elise. She and I have an appointment at the police station that's now the least of my worries given the frightening print media I'm staring at.

With my heart beating erratically, I peruse the bold headlines. *"Drug Lord Caught in the Act."* Says one. *"Millions in Loot Discovered in Up-and-Coming Celebrity-Style Residence."* Says another. *"Beware, Parents: Drugs Have Moved into Town."* Warns a third. Can they possibly scream bloody murder any louder?

It doesn't escape my attention that they all have a photo of the hole in my floor, with the drugs and money in it. Probably taken last evening by one of the construction crew and leaked out sometime during the night.

"This is bad," I mumble to myself.

I start to worry my picture's in the papers. With a sinking feeling, I buy one and just as I'm about to start reading, notice something familiar on a wall-mounted TV not too far away. It's an aerial view of the White Rose under siege from drug-enforcement agents who happen to be bellowing excitedly into powerful megaphones. *Damn! This is a scene from last evening!*

I duck as though caught red-handed doing something illicit. Then catch myself and slowly straighten up when I realize none of the commuters are paying any attention to me. Intrigued with the unfolding story, their eyes remain glued to the screen. They watch it intently while patiently waiting for the tram to arrive. An old lady shuffling behind a walker asks if anyone was shot in the process. No one responds. Everyone is caught up in the riveting broadcast.

Elise and I are mentioned as the owners of the crime scene. To hear my name in this context almost does it in for me. I start to see stars. Black fog moves in from the corners of my eyes. With my head held low, I start to backpedal away from the curious group.

"Watch out, mister!" an exasperated man shouts behind me.

I look back to see I'm standing on a pretty big foot. The bull of a man it belongs to towers over me. He is livid red and all but ready to charge.

Everyone turns and stares. The second lasts a lifetime. I wait with a racing heart for the inevitable to happen, but it doesn't come. The bull doesn't strike. The crowd doesn't recognize me. Then realization hits me: my picture hasn't been aired yet. I almost fall apart from the overwhelming sense of relief flooding my every vein and nerve ending. With any luck, my picture won't be aired at all during the entire course of this harrowing experience. Maybe it's too much to ask for? I surely hope not. I decide to remain hopeful.

Meanwhile, the newscaster is saying the drugs don't belong to the innocent and rather unwitting owners of the crime scene. Did I imagine hearing this? Was I just vindicated me on public television? The commentator repeats her broadcast in different words. I listen keenly, catching her every word, watching her every nuance, almost afraid to breathe, and then she's done talking, and there it is again, crystal clear, like writing on a wall.

This is the best news ever! I've just been exonerated of a crime I didn't commit!

A rush of exhilaration overcomes me. I cry out loud with joy and relief and completely startle the crowd around me, which by the way I'm no longer afraid of anymore, and most of which is now convinced I've absolutely lost it. I'm excited. This is great news. I can't wait to share it with my girl.

Elise shows up two minutes later and finds me this way, effervescing, uncontained, almost unruly. She's surprised yet happy as I overwhelm her with hugs and kisses. It's a beautiful moment.

We walk the two blocks to the police station. A slight feeling of apprehension tags at us as we go in through its doors. Neither of us has been looking forward to this moment. We try not to imagine the worst possible outcomes.

The statements are a breeze. The cops are friendly. We needn't have worried. At some point during our testimony, a blond female agent gives us lots of free advice on how to enjoy ourselves without ever turning to drugs. She's insistent, and her eyebrows keep flickering at us desperately. She seems to think the sight of last night's opioids might have corrupted us a little, hence the tough love.

I do my best to reassure her coffee's my favorite drug of choice.

In a flash, she's offering me a capper, plus a rich creamy doughnut to go with it, and begging Elise to accept the same. Caffeine addiction over cocaine? Now here's a surprising new twist in this age-old moral dilemma. But the choice is an easy one for our blond officer. She's radiating excitedly. Her eyes prompt us to say yes, coffee's good, and so are doughnuts. We do as asked and receive a copious serving of both.

Not once do we catch a glimpse of Kirling or Moneypot. I can't tell whether I'm disappointed about this, or relieved. I recall that they're outdoor types. Both are probably pursuing the drug dealer as we speak. Handal, I'm certain, must surely be halfway across the world by now.

NEWS OF THE RAID spreads like wildfire. I receive a hero's welcome and a million questions when I later walk into Displaytek at about nine in the morning. Was I tempted to keep some of that loot and get high? Asks Frank. What if there's more buried elsewhere within the property? Timothy wants to know. He poses with all his gums and canines completely visible until I answer the question. More cocaine still hidden at the White Rose? I hadn't thought of this possibility till this moment. I don't much care for its implications. I think I'll have to mention this to agent Kirling.

"Damn clever, using real estate business as a front for drug trafficking," Ludwig comments. "To bury the loot in unoccupied property and come back for it when the heat's off? Pretty damned ingenious, if you ask me."

"Only this time," Nick Neumann adds, "the drug-enforcement agency got wise."

"Yeah, and put a tail on his ass," Hans Hartmann finishes.

"Damn bastard almost turned you into a scapegoat," Timothy says with feeling and a valiant effort at a sneer which doesn't quite come out right, since all he'll ever look is funny and hilarious, and that's that.

"Pig," agrees party animal Frank Krueger. Unlike Timothy, his face is very flexible and ends up looking just like he wants it to, which at this very moment, is one very angry bulldog. Drugs, he likes. To him, they're the best thing in the universe. The idea of framing someone for them, however, completely irks him. "A real pig-dog," he adds vehemently, eyes wild and flaming with anger. Just like that, mankind's received its latest hybrid to the animal kingdom. *Thanks a lot, Frank.* Time itself will never expunge this horrifying creature from my dazzled mind.

ELISE'S UNUSUAL CALL later in the morning lets me know the drugs incident is far from over. About a dozen reporters have camped at the gates, she says. They've barri-caded the property. They're sticking microphones in people's faces and scaring half the neighborhood to death. It's horrible, David, she laments, and continues to elaborate just how much this is disrupting her lifestyle. She's cooped up; she can't leave the house, can't go out for a breath of fresh air, or enjoy the sunshine. She's desperately in need of a walk by the river. Will I come right away to rescue her? Will I take a walk down by the river with her? Will I?

"Come lunch hour, I'll dash over to your rescue," I in-form her.

THE TEAM OF REPORTERS I find gathered before the White Rose gates is much larger than I'd anticipated. About thirty in total. A sizable number of them are bellicose and rowdy. Some are shouting endlessly as though immedi-ately demanding some sort of appearance from those within the White Rose, or else, they'll switch to ballistic and the scene will go to the dogs. I shiver at the sight. It's a siege, no doubt. An all-out war. I wouldn't put it past them to tear down the gates and storm the house.

And what if they spot me? There's not a single doubt in my mind what would happen then. They'd make short work of me. They'd chew me up and spit me out within seconds. That'd be a disaster.

I try not to balk at the thought and instead look at the situation from another point of view. Why should I put my-self through the wringer? I don't need that, not now, not ever. Besides, I have no desire to be on tomorrow's news, so best thing to do? Simply give them the proverbial slip. That's my plan of action.

With my mind made up, I sneak undetected to the back of the property where, unfortunately, the brush is thickest. I hesitate for a second or two as I look at the dense mess apprehensively. Most of the twigs are tightly interwoven. They defensively wrap around the property, effectively shielding it off just like a fortress would. It's clearly an impenetrable jungle. What have I gotten myself into this time? But even as I think this, I know it's too late now. No time anymore for any second thoughts. I've made my bed. It's time to lie in it. Besides, Elise's waiting for me. With a sigh, I start to inch forward, not in the least bit fond of what comes next.

I plunge into the dense foliage and quickly find myself in a living nightmare. More than once, I could swear that branches reach out and grab me, almost slowing me down to a complete halt. Several saplings give me the whipping of a lifetime, and just when I think it can't get any worse, I run into a family of five extra-large and fully armored porcupines, who waste no time assessing my threat value. They want to charge. I'm standing stock still doing my best imitation of a tree when a gust of wind suddenly blows through the underbrush. Trees and shrubs sway like crazy, but I fail to move an inch, and, alas, my cover's blown.

In that instant, five huge porcupines realize I'm not a tree and start to show their displeasure. In the next, they're barreling through the underbrush at me, enraged, dark, and lethal. Their screams are deadly. The prospect of barbed quills buried deep within my flesh strikes fear inside my heart. I scream, jump straight up, and hit the ground running like mad. I'm crying for my life. I'm cursing the porcupines. And fighting a seemingly enchanted forest that appears out to get me.

By the time I break through the thick underbrush to other side, half my trousers and most of my shirt is gone. I'm wearing tatters, pieces that badly fit together. About a million of my skin cells are hanging on the branches and twigs I just plunged through, and I'm desperately out of breath.

The porcupines, thank goodness, are nowhere to be seen. Their deed is done. Their wooded turf if defended. They have no desire to come out into the open. My relief is immense.

Shaking slightly, I come to a stop before Elise. I'm scratched all over. I'm threadbare, bewildered, and wild-eyed, as I recount to her my near-death experience in the woods. She simply bursts out laughing. My desire to spank her is overwhelming. Instead, I narrow my eyes and stomp off to clean up.

SINCE WE haven't officially moved into the White Rose yet, my wardrobe's still at my apartment. This means I have nothing appropriate to wear back to work.

"Not to worry," says Elise. She immediately sends Heartsflip to buy me a decent pair of trousers and a shirt, but, remains vague on the overall look the garbs should have. "Something one can wear at the office," she simply tells him. The choice of style and color is left to him. Heartsflip has a big decision to make. I'm curious how this turns out.

While we wait for my change of clothes, Elise and I take a walk within the inner circle of the property. I'm treading about in borrowed shorts and a T-shirt. They fit badly. She's in jeans and a T-shirt. Hers fit like a second skin. She looks fantastic.

We munch on sandwiches while walking over rich green lawns.

"The garden is coming along beautifully," Elise remarks.

"Aye, I respond. "Especially the single-variety flower beds."

She smiles.

We admire roses and carnations, marvel over the chrysanthemums and tulips, and praise ourselves for the unfathomable wisdom of carefully choosing each one. It's a lovely sight. We both enjoy the walk immensely.

Heartsflip eventually arrives with my new set of clothes. Ceremoniously, he unwraps a light-brown pair of trousers and a ridiculously bright-yellow shirt. Both have unusually large and gleaming black pearl buttons. I stare at them in horror. They're way too funky, I protest in dismay. Certainly not meant for a career office, I clearly state. Which begs the question, what's Heartsflip's idea of an office?

With gleaming eyes, he tells me they are elegant, perfect, simply to die for.

"Clubbing outfits would be my best guess," counters Elise mischievously. She simply can't stop giggling at my mortification.

Eventually, I too realize the hopelessness of my situation. There's nothing to do, other than get on with the unthinkable. Reluctantly, I dress up. Then hit the road. Dread of the reception awaiting me fills me as I drive back to Displaytek. What will my colleagues at the office make of my clothing?

LUNCH IS SOON OVER as I arrive at Displaytek once more. The production manager, Matthias, ushers me into his office for an impromptu pep talk. I tentatively take the chair across from him. My colleagues, seated at the tight group of six desks out in the operations-scheduling section, watch Matthias and I closely through the glass wall, trying to discern the nature of our conversation. Kevin, in his own glass-walled office to the right of us, is looking in as well. By the level of his concentration, I would say he's trying to read our lips. I decide then and there to do weird things with mine. Something akin to alien speech for anyone who's watching. This might turn out to be fun after all.

Matthias Wolfgang is curious. It goes without saying I'm dressed in different clothing than what I had on this morning. And since I'm scratched all over as though just coming from a fierce catfight, he's regarding me with no little amount of suspicion.

I return the favor, inspecting his black hair, which is mostly gray over the ears. His mustache has practically gone white, and his eyebrows are well on their way down the same road. He's clean-shaven and wearing a shiny blue suit and blue tie. I appraise him, happy to see not a single incriminating scratch on him.

His mood, however, in light of my appearance, is slowly turning dark. Turns out, the mountain of drugs found on my property is still fresh on his mind, as he promptly asks, "Are you using?"

I am shocked. "No," I say vehemently, "Never!"

"Then why did you disappear over lunch?"

I tell him I had to dash back home for an emergency.

I can almost hear him think, *Oh God. Another drug bust?*

He stares suspiciously at my fresh lacerations, takes in my disco clothes, and then starts to tell me every known downside of illicit drugs of all kinds. He goes on and on, as though oblivious to the petrified expression taking charge of my visage.

If anything, this man is thorough. By the time he's done, a picture of me missing teeth and looking out of hollowed eyes while desperately trying to add simple numbers together in a cooked brain incapable of recognizing my own face in the mirror is burned so deep into my mind that I swear to him never to touch an illicit drug for the rest of my life.

He implores me with his eyes to be sincere about this. I swear to him with my eyes that I am. This silent conversation increases in intensity, quickly charging the air between us. But thankfully, no explosion happens. We talk for about a minute with our eyes before he decidedly turns back to words. He says the company's reputation is at stake here. My actions matter.

I wholeheartedly agree with him.

He then presents me with a urine-sample bottle that has my name in bold block letters across its side.

I almost fall off my chair in shock. A miserable yelp escapes my lips as he plants the bottle on the desk and pushes it in my direction. He suggestively looks at it and then at me.

His intent is obvious. Matthias Wolfgang wants my urine sample for science purposes. I fail to hide my astonishment and can't stop wondering, *"Should I not have expected this?"*

There shouldn't be a speck of cocaine in my veins, but honestly, at this point, I'm not sure anymore. Maybe I sniffed a little off the air as the drug-enforcement agents carried it away that fateful evening? After all, cocaine is powder. And powder has a way of taking to the air all on its own, doesn't it? I break into a cold sweat.

Matthias smiles apologetically. "Sorry, couldn't resist the prank." He then giggles like a little girl. And soon puts the bottle away.

I am a study of incredulity and enormous relief. Mixed reactions, yeah, but that's what's happening to my face.

"Seriously, though," he continues, "did seeing all that cocaine mess with your head?"

"I don't think so, sir."

"Honestly? No nasty thoughts lurking in there somewhere?"

"No, not that I know of, sir."

He doesn't look convinced. Seconds pass by. The way he's looking at my head, he appears to be contemplating subjecting me to a brain scan. Soon, this develops into a possible tomography, full-body X-ray, and an array of other scary procedures I care not to think of as his eyes travel lower on my lacerated person. If there's even the tiniest molecule of an illicit drug in my internal organs, I almost feel like he'll find it, just by looking at me.

I sit up straight. I try to look as solid as a block of stone. No space in me for drugs of any kind, I speechlessly portray to him.

Finally, he relents. "You're a nice lad," he says at last, quietly, thoughtfully, as though weighing the truth of this statement. "Wouldn't want to lose you, you know?"

"No, sir!" I agree eagerly.

"What?" He starts up and inches forward in his chair. His gray eyes look for the slightest bit of impertinence in me. "What did you just say?"

"I mean, yes, sir, of course, sir, you wouldn't want to lose me. I know that now, sir," I say quickly.

"Of course?"

"Sir?"

He digs holes in me with his gaze for several more seconds. Despite knowing his intention is to shake me and see what falls out, I still end up somewhat rattled. It dawns on me he's probably thinking I'm high on something and is desperate to prove this hypothesis. Finally, after gathering no conclusive evidence one way or the other, he dismisses me, and not a second too soon. I wobble out the door as though pumped full of drugs.

THE WHITE ROSE is still incomplete. We can't move in just yet. Like many other times before, Elise and I are chilling and relaxing in my modest student apartment, simply happy for the day, each other's company, and the strong unconditional love that binds the two of us together. At this moment, we are both reclined on my couch, watching the evening news. To our joy, the White Rose's connection to Handal Hoams is on the decline. The opposite is only too true of the man himself.

Busy investigative reporters have been looking into every known and unknown aspect of Handal's entire life since birth, unearthing every fact that can be unearthed and looking for new ones in the weirdest places. They're explorers. And for now, Handal Hoams is their mysterious landscape.

A lot of stuff about this secretive man has come to light in the past few days. It's now known for a fact that he's the extremely slippery boss of the infamous Cygnus crime syndicate, a smooth-talking lord of the dark who has his iron hands in everything from drugs, illicit trade in valuable art, to weapons and a whole lot more in between. This fierce cartel is rumored to span the entire globe. It's been in operation for a couple of decades, and woe unto anyone who crosses their path in any way, so it's said.

Handal Hoams has become quite notorious. The media loves him. The masses fear him. Hollywood is moving heaven and earth to make a movie in his honor. And we here in my apartment, are simply disgusted by it all.

Elise and I intently listen to all this talk and then discuss it for hours. We're both trying to hide our trepidation. Out of fear of Handal Hoams, we spend the whole weekend indoors.

ON WEDNESDAY, October 1st, a miracle happens. Matthias Wolfgang's urine-sample bottle lands in the garbage bin. I see this happen through his glass wall and whoop with joy. Ludwig, Hans, Tim, and Frank almost jump out of their skins from the sudden unexpected sound. I'm too happy to notice them.

It would appear Matthias is finally convinced of a fact I've known all along, namely, that I'm drugs free. *This is simply fantastic! Absolutely marvelous!* I feel like a new man already. In celebration of this momentous occasion, I get off work early and go out for a beer.

DUNCAN BEIKE, who's been missing in action since the cocaine incident kicked off, finally comes out of the woodwork on Thursday afternoon to show his support and belief in my innocence.

I'm flattered.

Anje Tille tells me he now trusts himself enough to be seen in my presence. No more lingering fear of guilt by implication, it would seem.

He even sets a new precedent by allowing himself to be immortalized beside me in a series of solidarity press photos in my honor. I am dressed in that same black suit I love so much for such occasions. He's standing next to me in an expensive Italian suit, silk, dark blue, open coat, white shirt, no tie. With chiseled jaw and full head of silky black hair, he stands tall, solid, and looks formidable. Today, he's in a pretty good mood.

"David is famous," he says to everyone standing behind us in the background. All the while, he's pointing meaningfully to the press, who are here doing a scoop on me about my close encounter with Handal Hoams. "What a truly amazing person we have in our ranks," he continues. "We're really lucky to have you, David," he says, smiling into the camera.

I feel like a ghost beside him, totally ignored and forgotten. *Maybe the camera is a new make called David? And he's really talking to it, not me?* I'm irredeemably baffled.

When the brilliant flashes of the said camera die down, Duncan finally remembers I exist. He shakes my hand, claps me on the back, and stands back to take me in with an ecstatic expression on his brightly glowing face. "Isn't this fantastic?" he asks.

The photo shoot? My so-called fame? Or the fact that I am now an amazing person in his eyes? What's fantastic? What's he referring to? By the way, does this mean the CEO and I are now best of buddies? The possibilities that come to mind at this thought are simply mind-boggling. I contemplate wheedling a high-powered job out of him. Something with a six-figure pay raise would be nice.

The dreamy look that starts forming on my face dies instantly in the next second as Duncan begins talking again. He's suddenly his old self again, scowling his face into a livid mess and speaking fast. He's showing reporters out the door while simultaneously barking at everyone else to get back to work. Anyone still standing about will be fired on the spot, he cries out in a war-like fashion, sending assembly workers scattering every which way in a jiffy. Managers follow suit. I hesitate but only a second. Then I too, vanish to my thesis study.

LATELY, I've been looking up successful people on the Internet trying to figure out what makes them tick. This is not simply out of curiosity but mainly because I need to know what their secret of success is.

The one thing they all seem to have in common is that they stuck to what they knew best. Since I'm yet to discover what it is I do best, I decide for the time being to concentrate on that which I do have, namely, my current professional engagement, that is, my thesis initiative.

I'm also hoping to sooner or later stumble upon that monster discovery on how to make my own millions someday, so, as you can probably tell, I'm truly passionate, focused, and single-minded in my current approach to my future career options. At this very moment, I'm tackling the sensitive issue of takt time. Until today, I've been putting this off, gathering knowledge and letting my wisdom grow.

It's taken a while. On this beautiful Friday morning, the pieces finally fall into place. I now know what to do. At last, I'm ready. And bridling with excitement.

I make myself comfortable at my desk as I dive into the preliminary calculations. The company would like to achieve a 400 percent increase in output. This means a total output of 4,400 units a month. In other words, 200 units a day. Is this a tall order? That's what I am here to find out.

Deducting all intervals taken up with coffee breaks and lunch results in eight available hours of hard-core work time, or 480 minutes' worth of daily production. So, the needed takt time at each workstation will be 480 minutes divided by 200 units. This translates to a takt time of 2.4 minutes. *Fantastic!* I'm smiling joyfully at this wonderful revelation.

Every 2.4 minutes, each workstation should hand over a partially processed unit to the next workstation, so I take a closer look at the X28. Some processes fall within my established takt. Others do not. I see the problem immediately. Process redefinition is called for.

Quickly, I list every X28 process in chronological order, write down in a new column the events within each process while paying attention to their chronology of sequence, and two hours later, end up with an impressive list over 160 lines long. I'm shaking with nervous excitement. I admire my work. A goofy smile is firmly planted on my face.

I look about at our tight pool of six desks. Hans and Ludwig have their heads stooped low over reading material. Timo is preparing a document of sorts. Even Frank is busy, and this prods me back into a state of industry.

My mind is once again racing. I zero in on the home run by noting event-times against each event, then chronologically add them into little groups from the first on the list to the last at the bottom. No group is more than 2.4 minutes long. *In other words, I've done it! I have created Takt-oriented processes!*

Excitement buzzes and courses through my veins. For the first time ever, I realize one-piece-flow production is indeed possible. "Wait until Matthias Wolfgang knows what I've discovered," I whisper to no one in particular. *Two hundred units a day! We can make it! This is simply priceless.*

I repeat these actions with every one of the remaining 85 percent of lean-line compatible products. Hours come and go. The day slowly unfolds. Optimal reassignment of events into logically takt-oriented processes keeps me joyfully busy for the rest of the day.

Twenty-one

Our progress back home is just as surprisingly phenomenal. We want a beautiful place to call our own. And guess what, it's happening! I can't believe it, but it's really happening! This is turning out better than I ever imagined it would. *The White Rose is fleshing out!*

By now, all the fixtures and fittings are complete, have been tested for functionality and deemed ready for use, cleaned, polished, and above all, carefully cleared for Elise's universally feared stringent inspections.

Everything from wardrobes, bathroom suites, plugs and kitchen units; it's got to be supremely upmarket, absolute top dollar, the very best of quality and nothing less, Elise says, and on this, she's not ready to compromise.

Perfect! Now this is going to be amazing! I cannot wait to see the outcome.

We spend the whole of Saturday with a middle-aged interior decorator whose mesmerizing world of compatible hues and exciting patterns captivate and inspire us to dream some more. She's brusque and to the point, full of ideas, and says there's much work to be done. We nod in agreement.

Each house is unique and requires certain colors to bring out the very best in it and make it a home, she knowingly lets us know, daring us to contradict her. We don't. Truth be told, we implicitly trust her. She's the expert.

And so, we let her set the pace. By Wednesday of the following week, most of her suggestions shall have been implemented. The White Rose will then take on its true substance, qualifying as an elite home ready for luxurious habitation. I'm excited. It won't be long now. We'll soon be moving in. I can barely wait for that moment.

MY initial framework for the written report requested by Matthias Wolfgang is almost done. In it is an outline of the current production method, a list of its hang-ups, several reasons explaining its ineffectiveness, and expected rewards to be gained from the changes I am suggesting. Matthias will love this. It's logical. It's reasonable. A tiny irrefutable glimpse of the future.

Throughout the day, the absence of the production manager and his second-in-command has not gone unnoticed. Every now and then, one or the other dashes back in, collects something, clicks away at his mouse or hurriedly peruses his screen before bolting away for the better part of an hour or two. A distinct sense of desperation hangs in the air.

My colleagues here in the operations-scheduling section seem to be faring no better. The usual intermittent fooling in the absence of Matthias is ostentatiously missing. In its stead, whispers interspersed by an eerie silence go back and forth with increasing earnestness. Nick is tense. Ludwig's actions are uncertain. Even Hans Hartmann has lost interest in his biceps developer. I smell fear. Including my own.

Hans, seated to my left, stoops low to whisper. He's itching to get something off his chest. I adjust myself slightly to get into this silent information super-highway, till I'm able to catch his words. He's imparting the latest intel, straight from the legal department. According to his girlfriend, Christine Gay, a crisis is looming. It's said that one of the company's best customers has finally blown its top and is demanding change in the way Displaytek does business.

In the wake of this, Displaytek received an ultimatum; "Cut down manufacturing lead time or lose us to the competition, that simple," the rebellious client is reputed to have disclosed.

Frank Krueger, who's seated across from me, bends forward in my direction and elaborates in a quiet whisper, "They're our biggest spender and happen to be Displaytek's very lifeline," he gravely reveals. "Everyone knows they are responsible for fifty to sixty percent of our total annual revenues. They walk, we sink," he concludes.

Timothy and Nick nod grimly. "It is what it is," says the latter.

"It would appear," says Ludwig, bald head gleaming as ever, "that a crisis meeting's in progress and our best and brightest are gathered to assess the situation."

This is a lot of scary information. Stunned, I bow my head and think it through. Careers and livelihoods, even lives seem suddenly at stake at this very moment. Are things really that bad? I know the current batch-production process consumes a lot of time. I also know how much we stand to gain should one-piece-flow production on a lean line be implemented. What I don't know is, how better off is the competition? Can our rebellious client find a better deal elsewhere?

A more disturbing thought crosses my mind. *What if Displaytek folds before I'm done? Having to look for another company and start all over from scratch would be a disaster!* Such an outcome would delay my graduation. I struggle with this for a while. The thought alone gives me a headache.

About midday, the phone rings. Ludwig Beck answers. He listens for a moment then turns to me and says, "It's for you, David."

"Who's calling?"

"Kevin," he says, handing me the phone in a businesslike manner.

I've been waiting for something like this to happen since the emergency meeting. Given Displaytek's predicament and the nature of my study, it was all but inevitable. I know why he's calling. I take the receiver, press it to my ear and announce my presence. "David speaking!"

"David, about your study ..." he falters.

I suffer a racing heart for a few seconds then prompt, "Yes?"

"There's no delaying this anymore. We need to take immediate action, which brings me to your work. How's it coming along?"

"Splendid!"

"You mean that?"

I play it safe and mention the need for more collaborative research, but basically, it'll be wrapped up in a month, I quickly add.

Kevin doesn't say a word. I wait with growing unease for his next words.

"Aaahhh," he sighs in one long draw.

I want to dwell on the meaning of this, but he's speaking again. "Matthias and I would like a detailed presentation from you. Everything you have to date."

"When?"

"Tomorrow morning, eight o'clock."

"Pretty short notice, don't you think? I'm only halfway through the written report. Besides, compiling a PowerPoint presentation will take a day, maybe two."

"Leave out the PowerPoint. Just you, me, Matthias, and your cold hard facts."

"That still boils down to a whole night's worth of preparation, and—"

"Thanks, David. I knew I could count on you, you know? That's why I backed you up for this, and that's why Matthias Wolfgang likes you so much," he explains rather tongue-in-cheek, clearly aware of Matthias' earlier cocaine suspicions against me. "Don't stay up too late. You need to be spry and fit tomorrow, okay?" Before I can voice an objection, he's gone.

I was expecting such an assignment, but not anytime soon, and certainly not to be carried out this very evening. Surprised, I stare at the dead receiver in my hand. Elise and I have plans tonight. What will she think of this new development? I fear she'll not like it one little bit.

ELISE'S WAITING for me at Holzmarkt Square when I get into town shortly after hours. She's quick to suggest ice cream at the Eiscafe Riva, to which I gladly say yes.

We walk in, find a table with a nice view overlooking the busy square, place our orders and soon settle in to enjoy sweet cooling ice cream, all the while watching the sea of humanity drift slowly by in pursuit of one errand or another. It's a serene moment, a peaceful interlude in the midst of bustling activity. I feel free and untouched by goals, pursuits, deadlines, and relentless expectations. Only one thing's on my mind. Elise can tell something's bothering me.

She broaches the subject.

"How's work?" she asks.

"Good," I respond.

"Something's on your mind," she states intuitively. "What's going on?"

I smile. "It's surprising how well you know me," I tell her.

She smiles but says nothing, instead waiting for me to speak.

"I'll need a raincheck on our evening together."

"Oh. Why?"

"Work, I say simply."

She digs into her tropical ice cream sundae, avoids the spicy papaya stuck into it, and raises an eyebrow in question.

"A client's threatening to walk if Displaytek doesn't come up with a new blueprint to improve efficiency in supply," I explain to her. "This issue falls within the purview of my study, and so a request has been made for me to make a presentation first thing tomorrow morning."

"Let me guess, and you fear you are not ready for the presentation?"

"Yes and no," I reply.

A look of confusion comes over her.

"Yes, I'm not ready, and no, I don't fear it. I've been given this evening to work on it. I'll be ready by tomorrow."

"You've been given?" asks Elise in consternation, now clearly aware where this conversation's headed. "What about our date tonight?"

"That's just it," I sigh. "You'll have to give me a raincheck on that."

She digs into her ice cream with a lowered head so that her face is hardly visible.

Concerned, I try to discern her emotions. "Elise?"

Slowly, she looks up and sighs. "Okay," she finally concedes. "A raincheck it is then, sweetheart."

"That's great darling," I respond in kind, before noticing the sudden flash of mischief sparkling in her eyes.

"Elise?" I know that look. I don't much care for its connotations.

"You are aware this is the third time this has happened? This time around, it will cost you, and boy, will you pay for this, lover-boy!" She giggles as some devious scheme of revenge begins to take root in her mind.

With a smile, I remind her of the last spanking I gave her for mischievous conduct, to which she only laughs louder and assures me what she's planning next will shake me to the core.

Elise's a prankster. A devout one at that. Sometime soon, she'll make good on her promise. Try as I might, I'm unable to figure out what form it will take.

BACK IN MY APARTMENT and for close to six hours, I belt out an impromptu presentation that even Matthias Wolfgang will be proud of, and at midnight, as my eyes begin to droop, a quick pot of coffee revitalizes me for another hour during which I put the finishing touches to the eloquent pros and cons of my leading argument. Later, I earnestly pour over my notes looking for anything I can add to round off my presentation. I come up with two new points. Finally, as the caffeine wears off, my head swoops and my eyes close. I'm fast asleep before my cheek hits the laptop.

SEVEN IN THE MORNING. Matthias Wolfgang's office. I'm standing before the imposing mahogany desk of the production manager who is not only intently listening to every word I say, but is also studying me closely. Perched on a chair rolled up beside the production manager's, is Kevin Koch. His right leg is swung over the other. It's oscillating in time to every third word out of my mouth.

My uninterrupted monologue on the virtues of takt-driven production is rolling out just as I'd planned. I'm lucid and expressive. I think I'm hitting note.

Next to me is a portable blackboard on which I've sketched a general lean-process flowchart. I learnt early in life that a visual aid is a powerful tool when faced with the task of presenting one's case. It's working! They're hanging on my every word.

Time and again, something I say piques their interest. When this happens, they jerk forward and lean close over the desk to scribble and scrawl hurriedly on their large notepads, then shoot their torsos up to stare at me some more.

I discredit batch production. But let them know this is only my opinion.

Matthias nods. He scratches the graying hair over his ears. Kevin shrugs.

Opinions are okay, they say. But facts are better. They demand some.

I fill half the blackboard with solid facts. I follow up with takt calculations so impressive that I stand back to admire them myself. My smile is unguarded. I want to laugh for sheer joy. This is fantastic! I really am an engineer!

Matthias and Kevin exchange glances, probably wondering if maybe this is all getting to my head a little too much. But I'm on the move again, so they cut me some slack. They're back to staring.

I give a list of accrued benefits to be expected in the event of one-piece-flow implementation, including time and efficiency improvements. The list is long. It takes five minutes.

I conclude by stating just how relatively easy this method is to manage and maintain, and just how much savings in money and time it will yield. "And did I mention substantial increase in revenue?" I ask, finally coming to the end of my presentation. "This, gentlemen, is the extent of my research thus far." I breathe in deep and clam up. For now, I'm done.

Kevin blinks rapidly several times as though something's in his eye. Wolfgang simply stares at me through his white eyebrows. They're hopelessly bushy, so it goes without saying, I can hardly see his eyes.

Neither of them applauds. Evidently, they have grave concerns.

My anxiety rises. "Ah … Any questions?" I ask.

The air is fraught with crackling tension.

I scan the office in the ensuing silence to keep myself busy. Though this is only my third time in his eminence's personal workspace, I am intimately familiar with its decor, fixtures, and fittings, thanks to the office's glass walls. There is nothing in here that I can't see from my regular desk out in the open office section.

In all honesty, there genuinely isn't much to see in this office. The chairs, a mahogany desk, an imposing bookshelf, and a side cabinet. That's all. The place would be blunt and uninteresting if it wasn't for the personality that occupies it. I know for a fact that Matthias has the most curious assortment of artifacts in his cabinet. Among them is a breathalyzer. He's very fond of using it on anyone he suspects to be inebriated, and then, of course, there's the strange incident with the urine sample bottle he eventually threw away. I wonder if he has more of the same stashed in here somewhere?

Right now, the way he's staring at his cabinet is sending shivers down my spine. My face turns crimson as he gets up. He walks around his desk and keeps going, toward said cabinets, at which point I almost buckle at the knees, before realizing he's looping around to eventually arrive back where he started, at his chair. With a last look at me, sits down again. There's a slight smirk curving his lips, as though he's aware of the scare he just gave me. But then the look is gone in a second as his gray eyes lose focus. He's moved on to contemplating the gist of my presentation.

Precious seconds vanish. I feel like my life is hanging in the balance.

Finally, Kevin looks up from his notes and breaks the silence. "Thinning out activities that don't add value to product is all okay. But getting rid of quality control measures?" He leans forward, impatient to hear what I have to say.

"Quality control doesn't add quality to a product, it merely confirms the presence or lack of it. So, carrying it out once, at the end of a unit's production, is all that's needed."

"So, get rid of all the other quality controls in between?" he asks.

"Yes."

You should see the look on Matthias's face. It's priceless. He's now sure I inhaled something illegal, probably sometime between last night and this morning.

I move quickly to explain myself. "Intermediate quality controls are a drain, not only on time, but resources as well, especially when experienced assembly workers know what they're doing. Since this is their work and they do it day in and day out, they are aware where mistakes could occur and naturally look out for them. All they need is that extra minute or so to control the quality of their own work. And since I believe you will concur with me that prevention is better than cure, this is the logical way to go for any company that wants to remain profitable in today's competitive world."

Matthias inhales deeply. "So only one general quality control procedure on each unit as it comes off the line?"

"Yes."

"And when blemishes are detected?" he asks.

"Then rework on the unit commences at the point of the blemish's occurrence. The affected process steps are carried out again."

He scratches the top of his head, which, thankfully, still has black hair.

Matthias bobs his head up and down. His eyes are half-closed, his brain cells churning away. Kevin tilts his head to one side as he weighs the pros and cons of my suggestions.

Beyond the glass walls, the picking team has given up all semblance of working. Since they can't hear a sound through the walls, they've settled for keenly watching the silent movie as it unfolds. They're not clueless as to what I am presenting though. I have debated many of these points with them over the last few days. They know just how radical my arguments are. They're on the very edges of their seats. They can barely wait to see how this turns out.

Meanwhile, Kevin and Matthias are done contemplating.

A short consultation ensues between them.

Finally, to my surprise, Kevin says, "Excellent presentation. Absolutely ingenious,"

"Yes," agrees Matthias. "Absolutely fantastic!" He says this repeatedly, like a valve venting out to prevent critical mass. He's excited. He's glowing. He's bursting over with energy.

I cannot believe my eyes. Am I really seeing this? So much praise has turned my legs to jelly. I urgently need to sit down.

Both turn and gaze at me.

"Okay," says Matthias. "Implementing one-piece-flow production on a lean line to eliminate transport distances and queue times ..."

"But can we make it work?" asks Kevin.

"With the prospect of achieving a target output of two hundred units a day? We simply have to try," Matthias answers. There is a dreamy look in his gray eyes. His bushy white eyebrows are fluttering. This is unusual coming from Matthias, and, I must admit, a little uncanny.

Kevin cautions lightly, "These takt calculations first have to be examined closely."

Matthias is unconcerned. The positive energy from him is almost palpable.

We discuss prickly issues and tricky hurdles for the next few minutes. Questions arise. Like how does one curb takt fluctuations between workstations? What are the resource-adjustment mechanisms at peak and ebb intervals? How does one deal with processes whose takt times fall well above the generally established norm? I strive to answer these to their satisfaction.

Finally, at ten-thirty, Matthias and Kevin believe it's all ironed out.

The two congratulate me on a marvelous strategy.

All I can do is smile weakly. I'm drained, in need coffee, with lots of cream, and cake. And maybe, just maybe, I'll find a dark corner on this day in which I can nap uninterrupted for a solid five hours. I think I need to talk to Frank. He's the resident expert in this field.

Shortly afterward Matthias and Kevin let me go.

Hopefully, the rest of the day will be mundane and boring.

I make a beeline for the cafeteria.

LATELY, I've been catching myself looking over my shoulder for no apparent reason. This mostly happens when I'm walking alone on busy streets or in the center of town. Shadows make me jump. Every person hanging in a doorway is a possible Handal Hoams.

I had a nightmare last night in which he told me he's coming for me. "I'll strangle you with my bare hands till you turn dark blue in the face," he'd said, all livid and revved up and looking like murder incarnate.

Could this be a warning? Could my subconscious be telling me something bad is about to happen? *Damn, how I hate nightmares!* In this very one, Handal solely blamed me for the loss of his precious drugs. He said I owe him ten million dollars, plus interest. I distinctly remember laughing hysterically. His answer was to pull out a gun. I peed in my dreams. I mean, in the dream, not in bed.

Anyway, that's beside the point. Thing is, I'll never know if he fired off a shot or not. The reason for this is plain and simple— My consciousness backed out. Just as his finger twitched on the trigger, I bolted wide awake to find myself crouched on the bed crying out for mercy, hands high up to protect my dear head.

Luckily, Elise was spending the night at her own place. It would simply have been too embarrassing for me if she were here to witness this. For her to see me crouching like that? I don't think I'd ever recover from the social stigma.

Even more relieving was seeing not the slightest hint of Handal Hoams anywhere in sight, around, or under the bed. I cried for joy.

Still, that nightmare has had a profound impact on me. Since it happened, I've become vigilant, always alert and watching out for any sort of trouble. In short, I'm on the lookout for the drug lord.

This evening while traveling on a tram on my way to see Elise, someone succeeds in creeping up on me and tapping my shoulder. I spring like a wild buck in contact with a live wire before turning around to face my adversary.

It's none other than an old acquaintance, Jack, someone I know from back on campus.

He takes in my deathly pale face and hooked fist. His eyes bulge in shock and surprise.

My heart is racing, my pulse elevated. Sometimes I'm sure if Handal doesn't get to me first, the adrenaline will. To say the least, living like this is truly exhausting.

It takes me a while to placate Jack, and even longer to explain things to him.

He's understanding, even sympathetic and caring.

We exchange numbers.

He makes me promise to stay in touch, before alighting at the next station.

Elise and I wine and dine at the cozy El-Sombrero in the company of several other ecstatic lovers.

I charm the socks off her.

As usual, her laughter rings out and her eyes sparkle like diamonds. She's radiant. She's warmth. She's resplendent. It's a beautiful thing to see.

About midnight, all my Handal Hoams' worries fall into the background of the quiet music and romantic atmosphere.

Twenty-two

Elise has something to tell me in person, she says on a call to me Wednesday afternoon. I suggest a meeting at a local pub and she panics. Too exposed, she says shortly. It has to be a place where she'll feel safe right now. A place teeming with young people. A place where a drug lord will stand out like a sore thumb. She suggests the local university library. Jena University library it is then, I say. We agree to meet there in an hour's time.

I walk into the library at four-thirty. Elise is cowering in a corner cubicle with a good view of the entrance. She's in a short silk dress. Flimsy shoulder straps, no hint of a bra underneath. It's deep autumn shades offer a beautiful contrast to her pure white skin, long scarlet hair and elegant shoulders. She looks ravishing. And obviously scared.

I take a seat across from her. "What's up?" I inquire with a worried look, my mind battling fears of the unknown.

"It's Cygnus," she hisses quietly. "They're back."

My fear now has form and substance. I don't like the sound of this. My mind won't accept it. "Are you sure?" I ask.

"Absolutely certain," she whispers. Obviously, her quiet voice has little to do with all the studying students about. Fear of bloodthirsty drug lords motivates her every action. Her eyes dart this way and that. They're filled with dread.

She lowers her head and leans toward me. "I know I'm being stalked." She looks at me, her eyes pleading for protection.

I'm in no position to help. "I think it's happening to me too," I say. I've had similar suspicions of being stalked, which is probably why I had that nightmare about Handal a short while ago. But since I spend most of my day at Displaytek, I suppose I'm no rich pickings for a stalker.

Elise, on the other hand, due to her ongoing sabbatical and her current engagement in the management of the White Rose's construction, is up and about, out in the open, completely exposed, and to my sudden consternation, quite vulnerable.

Neither of us has to mention Handal Hoams's obvious involvement in this suspected case of stalking. True, we haven't identified the goons that appear to be on our tail, but one thing is certain: they are Handal's men.

Elise takes a ragged breath. "What shall we do?"

"What can we do?" I ask.

She pauses a fraction of a second and then says, "Maybe…"

"Yeah?" I'm attentive, bending forward and eager to hear her next words.

"How about do the same thing as before when we discovered the cocaine?" she ventures tentatively.

"You mean call the police?" My eyebrows rise in question.

"Yes, yes," she confirms, nodding firmly.

I'm nodding to, albeit in a somewhat pensive and withdrawn manner, as I contemplate the possible repercussions of such a move.

Elise cautiously touches my arm.

I look up at her.

She's trying to act brave for my sake.

"This time though," she continues, "we should insist on their protection," she says in a weak but reassuring voice.

"And bulletproof vests," I add. "There's a trigger-happy drug lord out there, and he's set a target on our backs. In fact, why not throw an armored vehicle into the protection deal? Just for good measure. After all, we helped them get millions worth of cocaine off the streets."

Elise rolls her eyes at me. "I suppose you'll be asking for a sidearm as well?"

"Hey, Elise, not a bad idea at all! I say excitedly. That's brilliant!"

She sneers, shaking her head from side to side ever so slowly. "Do you even know how to use one?"

"How hard can it be? Aim. Fire. *Bang!* I watch a lot of movies," I inform her knowingly, bobbing my head up and down.

Elise shakes her head again and sighs heavily.

I ignore her. Just the thought of having a heavy piece to pull out and show off to dangerous drug lords is tickling me pink. Not only does it make me feel safe, but just as equally dangerous and not to be messed around with at all. "David, the new Rambo." *I like the sound of that immensely.* There's a faraway look in my eyes as I picture myself in the epic movie. I'm grinning profusely. It's a lovely daydream.

"Cut that out you awkward buffoon," says Elise finally.

"Okay, darling. You win. What now?"

She smiles, nods assertively and says, "Time to pay agent Kirling a visit."

WE DO ASK FOR and get police protection. But not in the form we imagined. The cops laugh heartily when I mention an armored vehicle. I don't even bother sharing with them my sidearm fantasies.

They let us know they are overworked, understaffed, running out of a steady supply of doughnuts since the last budget cuts, and are not amused by the prospect of babysitting two youngsters afraid of their own shadows.

All we get are two flimsy panic buttons. The little things look impossibly fragile. I fear they will break at the first sign of trouble. I express this to the police. They warn us to use them only in the event of a real emergency. That way they'll last longer, we're advised.

Super! Great! Absolutely fantastic! I'm disgusted.

When Elise asks what constitutes a real emergency, the answer she gets is "an honest-to-God, real life-threatening situation."

So that's it? If Handal visits us with the express purpose of merely slapping us around for the fun of it, we are on our own? I express these views and almost get frozen over by their hard, cold, stares. Best to clam up. And only open my ears. So, I listen keenly for anything that might be useful in keeping Handal at bay.

"At least they look like ordinary jewelry," Elise says, admiring the beautiful chains hanging down from the panic buttons. She compares them with the color of her dress. She loves the contrast. I can't believe my eyes. How can she even think of jewelry at such a precarious moment in our lives? Girls will be girls; that's for certain.

We are instructed to wear the delicate things around our necks at all times, even in the shower.

Some policeman deep within the precinct shouts, "Handal Hoams!"

It's a prank, but my mind doesn't know this. My thumb comes crashing down on my panic button. A resultant alarm goes off somewhere within the police precinct. Several cops, who've been watching me keenly and waiting for this moment, burst out laughing. My heart goes on thudding and racing for several minutes longer.

GIVEN the probable short life spans of the little gadgets, we decide to take a walk about town in hopes of luring Handal and his goons to attack us and force us to use our panic buttons when they are still fresh. Better now rather than wait for them to suddenly die from a quick and unpredictable onset of old age.

So, for an hour, we meander from one street to the next, present a pretty pair of targets, expose our heads and hearts to laser points of targeting weapons, but none land on us. Nothing happens. Neither Handal nor his goons show up.

Maybe they are not using laser points as targeting mechanisms but are certainly out there somewhere, trailing us? Maybe we just don't know what his goons look like? They could be standing right next to us, and we would never be the wiser. Or maybe the presence of these many eyewitnesses is scaring them off?

Elise and I earnestly debate all these possibilities. In the end, we decide to take an excruciatingly slow drive toward the White Rose Residence, hoping the bad guys will tail us into the outskirts of town where they'll feel safe enough to attack. And we get to use our panic buttons. Before their unknown expiry dates are upon us.

But this new ruse too, sadly, turns out to be a failure as well. Handal doesn't show. His goons don't appear. We're now in the hands of fate.

For now, a constant stream of GPS signals emanates from our flimsy panic buttons, letting the police know where we are at all times. Should Handal decide to attack, we'll get immediate assistance. All we can do is hope and pray the little electronic lifesavers hang in there long enough to do their jobs when and if the time comes.

Twenty-three

Displaytek Systems Ltd is now even more exciting than ever before. This is because I'm currently dealing with one of my most favorite subjects of all time; issues of ergonomics.

Just like a home, a workplace layout is of critical importance to the well-being and performance of those who use it. For this reason, and since the morning began on this wonderful Monday, I've been working out correlated human and workplace dimensions down to the very last detail.

It's a noble goal, a delicate balancing act. Enhancing work-health balance over extended time periods is a calling. I'm determined to get it right.

Several times Matthias or Kevin comes around to check on my progress. They criticize one point of view or another. They draw me into a discussion about various aspects of my endeavor. I listen to their useful advice. Together, we analyze everything ranging from Kanban methods, stocking quantities, work-in-progress quantities, to workplace structure and workflow organization.

In a few weeks, I'll have this wrapped up. Matthias likes the sound of that. He promises me a party, with champagne, maybe even an all-expenses-paid trip to a holiday destination of my choice. I like the sound of that.

Matthias and Kevin eventually report my promising progress to Duncan Beike. The CEO is delighted. If I keep this up, he says, not even the sky will limit my future success and career.

I'm inspired and motivated to carry on. I work nonstop for the rest of the day.

News this evening is vibrant and filled with a touch of mission impossible. It's about the Cygnus syndicate. The police raided a small cottage in the south of France, and what they discovered there still has them reeling in a state of shock. — drugs, a lot more than has ever been discovered anywhere, plus a more cash than they've ever seen at any place that's not a mint. The little house is also reported to have been harboring real bars of gold and glittering pools of blood diamonds, all buried under the floors of three bedrooms and a living room.

Ten smartly dressed, high-powered executive look-alikes were arrested on the spot. Naturally, they protested having any knowledge of the cottage's illicit treasures. They claimed they were merely renting the place for a little countryside vacationing.

Among them was a well-known confidant of Handal Hoams. He played the misunderstood executive for the better part of an hour before giving up the poor act. He's currently being interrogated. To date, Handal has successfully eluded the law enforcement agents. But now they're sure they'll have him in custody by the end of the week.

"About time," I say to Elise.

She nods her agreement.

Several times in the past week, she and I have received suspicious calls from someone who hangs up the minute we say hello. Honestly, it's been creeping us out. We suspect it's Handal Hoams fervently trying to scare us to death, possibly quite literally, in the hopes of enacting some sort of remote payback for perceived vexations against him and his Cygnus syndicate.

We never mentioned this to the police though, instead choosing to solemnly implore each other to be extra careful. Each night, we check our panic buttons to make sure they haven't died yet. As of now, they're still on standby and in good working order. Wonders never cease.

And now that law enforcement's in hot pursuit of Handal Hoams, I find myself breathing easy for the first time in a long while.

The newscaster exhorts anyone who knows of Handal's precise whereabouts to come forward with this information or risk a heavy fine for obstruction of justice. If it's a criminal coming clean, leniency will be granted. There's also a cash incentive. And a clear warning about prank calls from gold diggers. The latter will be dealt with severely.

Elise and I take in every word and discuss this new development excitedly. For us, this could mean possible closure, an end to the constant fear we've been living in since we found the drugs on our property.

We cheer the police on. We wish them good health and heartfelt success. But most of all, we wish them Godspeed. The sooner Handal is out of commission, the better for us.

BY THE END OF THE WEEK, we move into the White Rose and start our new lives as a coexisting couple. We let all our friends and acquaintances know about this. Even a couple of neighbors. It's a big moment.

This new exciting adventure couldn't have come at a more opportune point in time, since, for all intents and purposes, we're no longer in the crosshairs of criminals. Handal Hoams is ostensibly out of the way.

"As far as I'm concerned," I say to Elise," the Cygnus syndicate and its nefarious drug lord will never bother us again. How about that for good news?"

"You believe so?" she asks hopefully.

"I know so," I say confidently, kissing her gently.

"I sure hope you're right," she coos, dazzling smile and warm hug enveloping me as she returns the kiss.

It's a new era. The two of us are experiencing a rebirth in the art of love and companionship. Gone are all the fears that came with our real estate agent. It's time to live it up a little.

Twenty-four

"This can't be right, can it?" I peruse my results with unbelieving eyes. "Damned," I whisper, astounded by the results of my last hour's efforts. "This's far better than I ever hoped for!" I cry out loud, startling my workmates.

"Cool it down," will you?" calls out Ludwig.

Nick and Hans grumble just as loudly.

And Frank snorts, temporarily coming out of deep slumber before slipping back into it again.

I hardly hear their spirited lamentations. I certainly don't see them. This is because I'm terribly excited, and for the first time ever, with very good reason. *I've just done the impossible! I've created the perfect company on paper,* I think, as I stare at the many zeroes in the profit margin I just calculated.

From financial figures to corporate culture, the feasibility study staring me in the face is nothing short of a miracle. I sit back in wonder, my gaze never leaving the monitor for even a second.

Unbeknownst to me, Kevin has been watching my every move for some time now. He sees the look on my face and in five seconds flat is at my desk. "What's it, David? You look terribly excited. What's it?"

"Look," I say, practically beside myself with joy.

Kevin bends closer, studies my screen, and with a shaking hand, points while saying in an equally shaking voice, "Is that …?"

"Yes."

"And that ...?"

"Yes."

"No way!" Exclaims Kevin, eyes large, taking in the figures as if contemplating whether to believe them or not. "No absolute way!" He repeats, deciding at last not to trust his eyes.

"My previous sentiments exactly," I respond, "so, I checked them out twice."

"And got the same results?"

"Oh yes."

Kevin shakes his head in a daze. "Objective project time frame?" He asks.

"Within acceptable limits," I answer.

"Extrapolated customer absorption rate?"

"Levels off at way above 100 percent," I respond excitedly. "What's more? Even market-capture-rate is way above average," I tell him, clearly aware that no one within the company could ever have imagined anything as fantastic as this.

The two of us remain silent for several seconds, neither of us staring anywhere else but at my screen, not quite able to comprehend the astronomical figure staring us in the face.

Finally, Kevin pulls out a USB stick. He solemnly transfers a copy of my finished work onto it, and in the next instant, shoots out of the operations-scheduling section without so much as a goodbye in my direction.

I know where he's headed. He'll be visiting all the department heads in turn. First technical, then marketing, and eventually the legal and personnel departments. He'll ask each department head to go over my business plan and resulting strategy with a fine-tooth comb. If it stinks, he'll want to know it. If it's gold, he'll visit the CEO and insist they mine it.

If all goes well, by the end of the day, Kevin and the CEO will drink a glass of champagne in celebration, and within the month, this company will begin work to streamline its way of production and bring it into a new era of true corporate leadership. I can't help but feel proud of what I've accomplished. I've worked out a blueprint for success. I've contributed to this company's future wellbeing. No one can ever take that away from me.

IN ABOUT A WEEK, I format, print, and bind my findings, then deliver a copy of my finished work to my faculty at the university. After that, I present a similar copy to Matthias Wolfgang who, wonder of all wonders, is giving me the royal treatment. This is so completely out of character for him, that I hardly know what to make of it.

He starts off by shaking my hand. Then he half bows, dusts an otherwise clean seat and asks me to sit in it, all the while smiling sweetly.

He inquires if I would like anything at all. Whatever it is, he'll gladly fetch it. Lemonade? A cold beer? How about ice cream? He's smiling from ear to ear and can barely wait for me to give my order.

For obvious reasons, I say no thank you, I'm good. I mean, I know for a fact none of these things he's offering me are available at Displaytek. So, why's he asking? What would he do if I said yes? Dash into town for ice cream? A hospitable Matthias is indeed a scary beast. He puts on a bewildering freak show for several minutes. It's the damnedest thing I ever saw.

NOT LONG AFTERWARD, a date is set for my defense at the University of Jena: next week, Thursday afternoon, 2:00 p.m., six days from today. That gives me five days to prepare a PowerPoint presentation. It's got to be good. I have every intention of blowing everyone's mind away.

THURSDAY AFTERNOON EVENTUALLY ARRIVES. Once again, I'm at the University of Applied Sciences in Jena, nervous but doing my best to rally as I look about and gather my emotions. As expected, this little gathering is taking place in a small presentation room on the third floor. A line of windows to the left overlook the busy Carl Zeiss Promenade. Across from this and on the other side, is yet another university block whose several windows mirror ours. Through those windows, I can see students attending lectures in some halls, holding group discussions in other halls, and fooling about in many more.

The clock strikes 2:00 p.m. as I take my place before Professor Sigmund. The big man in gray trousers and white shirt is seated next to Kevin, who's dressed as usual in tight jeans and a checkered shirt. Both keep glancing at their watches every few seconds or so. Professor Staudinger is running late. I'm slightly grateful for this. I use the time to gain composure.

The current dean of faculty walks in at five past the hour. He's tall and clean-shaven with a jovial smile, uneven teeth, and well-kempt but rapidly graying hair. He quickly apologizes for not being on time. After a short round of greetings, he takes his seat beside Professor Sigmund and then leans back to stare at me challengingly.

The three gentlemen are my judge and jury on this very day.

I get my laptop up and running and connect it to the provided projector. A crystal-clear image of my presentation's cover page is projected onto the screen beside me. I'm ready to go. Now all I'm waiting for is the green light. The dean takes his time giving it, fidgets a little, flips pages in the file before him, then looks up and nods ever so slightly. With that, the clock is ticking. I quickly dive into my presentation.

I talk about Displaytek, its past and future, all facts and figures, logical plan and strategy, and even elucidate on profits and losses. Kevin listens gravely. Sigmund and Staudinger study me closely. For twenty minutes, neither one interrupts my train of thought. *Thank goodness,* I think to myself, as I safely sail through to the end.

Four long years of grueling work and study. All boil down to this very moment. I analyze the undiscernible dispositions of the three mentors before me as I realize one obvious fact. My fate lies in their hands.

Without a word, they turn their heads to face each other and begin to whisper. My knees almost buckle at this sight. My mind is like a train wreck. To cope with the moment, I fall into a trance.

The jury does eventually come back with a verdict. I did it, Professor Staudinger informs me while smiling broadly. My defense was successful. Considering this, there's no quarrel about arming me with a degree, setting me loose on the world and allowing me to partake in its economic activities.

I'm beaming uncontrollably and heaving with joy. This is the best news I've ever heard in four long years, probably in my entire life. Absolutely fantastic!

I CONVINCE Elise to go out with me on a Thursday night. We celebrate my good fortune till four in the morning, then taxi back to the White Rose for a wild morning of endless foreplay and mind-blowing sex.

For the first time this Friday, there's nothing on my calendar but endless time and limitless freedom. It's a beautiful feeling. I intend to enjoy this.

We sleep in till midday.

Twenty-five

A slight chill caresses my cheeks as I step out of a taxi onto the busy Loebdergraben Street. Pedestrians pour over the sidewalks. They're everywhere. Cars whiz past and high up, colorful crowns of nearby trees betray the changing season. Beneath my shoes lies Autumn's natural version of a bright and spongy red carpet. All around, more dazzling leaves float lazily to the ground.

I pull up the collar of my overcoat and begin to walk. Daylight's fading fast. Soon, JenTowers comes into view. I pause for a moment, taking in the brightly lit skyscraper. "Yes," I whisper excitedly, unable to suppress my steadily growing anticipation. "Yes, yes, yes. Let's do this!"

I walk into the building and into an elevator that carries me to the twenty-eighth floor. Its doors crack open, revealing a large ballroom already bustling with life. The atmosphere's inviting. Mysterious promise fills the air.

I walk in, swinging my head this way and that to capture the moment. Most of the black upholstered chairs on either side of the central aisle are long since occupied. Men are in tuxes. Ladies in ravishing dress.

Everyone here is either an academic, a scholar, a family member, or part of the TV crew filming the occasion for a documentary on the country's education system. No Handal Hoams or his scruffy gang in sight. I relax and breathe more easily.

An elevated stage at the front holds a narrow wooden podium behind which a good number of the university's administrative staff seats in a row of plush leather chairs. Most of them are engaged in lackluster conversations that seem to be boring them to smithereens. For them, it's just another day at work. For me, it's the start of a whole new chapter in my life. It's the day I get to graduate. *This is super exciting!* I'm almost shaking with pride.

It doesn't take me long to spot the primly seated Elise near the far wall. Like everyone else, she's patiently waiting for the ceremony to begin. An exquisite older version of herself to her left whispers something in her ear. She laughs heartily and turns to share the joke with the huge middle-aged man to her right. I watch them for a second and realize the obvious. The two must be her parents. Today, for the first time, I'll make their acquaintance. Elise prepped me a thousand times not to worry about this first encounter. I can't help it. One look at the lot and I'm jittery.

Across on the other side of the aisle are my heartily waving parents. I quickly walk over, hug, and take my place beside them.

Professor Staudinger's excited voice comes through the loudspeaker about two minutes later. With a few deft words, the dean of faculty introduces himself and is done as quickly as he started. Speeches scare him. Listening's more his thing. He calls on Maximillian Kaldrig to take over, and we watch as the university's president lumbers over to the podium.

Max Kaldrig loves ceremony. The white-haired man quickly gets down to the very serious business of welcoming the board of directors, members of staff, graduates, parents, and everyone else to this momentous occasion on such a wonderful and glorious day. He's deeply honored to be standing here before us in his capacity as elected university president and host of ceremony, a position he's held every year for the past five years, he proudly tells us, somehow also managing to insert an obvious pause which we duly fill with the expected animated handclaps. He's bursting with pleasure and nodding firmly. *"Yes, this's what he's made for,"* he seems to be thinking.

We, the audience, are loving every minute of it.

Without missing a beat, Maximillian moves on to handing out degrees and overzealous handshakes accompanied by little words of advice for the next half hour, amid deafening handclaps and the near blinding eruptions of flashlights from multiple cameras. The air pulsates with life and excitement. I do my best to add to it. I cheer myself hoarse.

Finally, after an epic speech full of words such as success, elite, best of the best, eye of the tiger, so on and so forth, he announces a ceremonial dinner awaits us a floor above, shouts "last one there is a kitty cat," then suddenly jumps off the stage and to the surprise of his audience, makes a mad dash for the door. Clearly, He intends to be the first one there. His audience roars with appreciative laughter.

Nice. You certainly got 'em this time, Max.

THE GREAT MOMENT, at last. Elise sweetly catches my attention and coyly beckons me over as we stream upstairs for the sumptuous meal above. "Come meet my parents," she mouths and gestures, points and hints, making sure I get the message.

"Mom, dad, I have to go," I say, turning to my parents.

"Already?" Mom is smiling knowingly.

"We talked about this, remember?"

"Yeah, yeah, you're meeting your girlfriend's parents for the first time today, and will probably spend the whole of dinner with them. We got the memo," says dad. "Don't mind us, we're only here for the food."

"Hey!" Mom pinches dad, giving him a scolding look. "Be nice, will you? Remember the first time you met my parents?" She giggles. "That was a…"

"Okay, okay, you win, sweetheart. Jeez, woman," interjects dad, smiling and teasing all at once. "why bring that up ever?

There's a story here I've never heard before.

Seeing the growing curiosity in my eyes, dad quickly moves to kill the question forming in my mind. "David?" he asks.

"Yes pops?" I'm eager, hopeful. Maybe he's about to open up and spill the beans.

"Break a leg, have fun, win their hearts and everything else in between. Just don't reverse engineer anything, okay? Otherwise, you'll lose them." He laughs crudely, pawing my shoulder to drive home his point.

"Argh! You guys will definitely be okay." Feigning disgust, I turn and make for Elise.

My heart's flattering as I draw up beside the picture-perfect family. Stories of would be sons-in-law's first run-in with future in-laws kept me up most of last night, and now that the moment of reckoning is finally here, I'm sort of numb and on autopilot. There's a silly smile on my face. I feel like a schmuck but doing my best to hide it.

Elise's overly passionate show of affection goes slightly overboard, taking me by surprise. She's intuitive, somehow always aware of my every thought and feeling. We hug like long lost lovers.

Introductions are quick and pleasant. Mrs. Amsel was once a bright upcoming star and cheerleader, Elise lets me know with a bright smile. Her eyes glow with unbridled pride.

Her mom melts on the spot, warming to me all at once. Nice touch, Elise.

Old-Man-Amsel mentions being a former athlete. He lets out a nasty growl that startles me, then looks poised as if ready to deliver a flying tackle in my direction. I picture an Eighteen-wheeler ramming into a mini. *Damned!* The aftermath in my mind's eye is a total disaster.

"He was probably the best linebacker in his prime," coos Mrs. Amsel, for a moment lost in a glorious past. Her eyes are brimming with admiration as she kisses her husband. A smile of sorts cracks on his large and puffy lips. He's heaving with joy. I get to hear him speak for the first time. His words are gentle. Sweet nothings of affection pass between the two, who almost seem to be unaware of our presence. It's a touching moment.

I get to learn that Mr. Amsel's essentially a sheep in wolf's clothing, a nice man who can't help the fact that his tough-guy appearance scares the living daylights out of strangers. Plus, he has a throat condition, something that makes him growl and grant a lot to clear his airway and nothing more, explains Mrs. Amsel sweetly.

Frankly, the man looks scary. But seems sweet at heart. This contrast will take some getting used to.

The three-course meal is exquisite. And delicious. Classical music plays in the background, punctuated by the constant clinking of silverware on china.

I'm enjoying myself immensely, when I notice my parents chatting happily away at Maximillian Kaldrig who's constantly stealing glances at me and dying of laughter. Mom and dad ignore my cautioning look and redouble their efforts. I dare not imagine what they are sharing with poor Maxi. At this rate, he might very well genuinely die of laughter. 'Death by violent joke' the autopsy report would read. And mom and dad would forever be termed criminals, murderers for life, and drag my name down with them. I shudder at this insane thought. Not about them being criminals, though. Just the part about Maxi's death. Imagine the implications of such an outcome? Lawyers and legislators frantically running about to iron out new legislation for this new trend, 'death by violent joke?' They'd hate my parents forever. And of course, by implication, me.

I stare at mom and dad, the same stare I always used when I was about to reverse engineer something of theirs and cannot believe they continue to ignore me. They're having fun and don't much care for consequences. Someday, I'll visit them. When that day comes, that life-size TV they cherish so much will get a makeover. I can't wait.

All around, constant murmur of animated banter fills the hall as people talk, laugh and make new friends, so I think to myself, why not? I put myself to the task of making friends with Elise's parents. At first, I'm making good progress but soon realize the tables have turned on me. I find myself answering questions about every aspect of my life— past, present and future, and don't know how this came to be.

I hang in there and fight it out but however hard I try, the tables just won't turn back to casual conversation. All I can hope for is that I've gotten to know them better. I wonder if they now know me too? I'd like to think we're now friends. Maybe, sometime in the future, I may successfully broach the topic of being in-laws?

An hour and a half go by, after which we relocate once more to the hall downstairs. This time, it's been fitted for a party. A jovial DJ up on stage throws a solid beat while colorful lights sweep across the darkened dance floor, to the joy of numerous couples having the time of their lives. While some dance, others surround a bar at the back of the hall. Laugher rings out. Screams of joy pierce the pulsating night. *This party's rocking!*

"Absolutely super," I shout to Elise.

She laughs out loud. We kiss and hug. Absolutely amazing.

For four straight hours, we clown and party, later inviting both sets of parents to spend the night at the White Rose.

"THIS IS AMAZING!" screams Mrs. Amsel shortly after 11:00 a.m. the next day. She hugs her black Jack-Wolfskin jacket tightly to her voluptuous body. It's Saturday. The weather's perfect. And we're in a hot air balloon. Slowly, we fly over Jena and its environs. A gust of wind tugs at her scarlet hair. Tufts of it fly in all directions and even completely cover her face. For some unknown reason, she refuses to put it in a ponytail like the other ladies have done. The hair's getting in the way. She's creaming and laughing, charged and hyperactive. This is turning out to be profoundly amusing since obviously, she's missing much of the incredible view below.

I tell her this. It doesn't bother her a little bit. She's high on thrill and danger, she lets me know in a shrill voice. Being so high up in flimsy balloon has stirred up the beast in her. Life, passion, consuming feeling and richness of expression. She's alive! I chuckle at her show of exuberance.

To my right Elise teases her dad who's cowering on the floor, too scared to trust his feet.

Almost 3000 meters below, a river glitters like a chain of diamonds as it meanders its way through the miniaturized city, surrounding stretches of green and a sizeable forest. Everything's tiny. Everything's fascinating. From so high up, it's all breathtaking. We stay up in the sky for two long hours. The endless jokes. Fun. Laughter. The rush of adrenaline. It's a memorable experience.

In the afternoon, my parents depart for home. Elise's parents stay on until the next day when they, too, filled with sorrow over the imminent departure, eventually leave as well. Once again, life goes back to normal.

Twenty-six

FOR A WHILE, I go through the motions of something that's slowly turning out to be my most dreaded task ever. Jobhunting! Yeah, this has now become circumstantially necessary, given that I'm now a graduate and all that, expected by society to earn my keep, pay the bills, refund my bank loans, and do whatever good I can in this global community as a way of saying thank you for all those years taking care of me as I was growing up and learning how to spread my wings so that I may one day fly. It seems that day's finally here. All I now need to help me soar is work.

For days, I've been sending out applications by the dozens and excitedly checking up all my emails expectantly, the minute they land in my inbox. Something has to give, right?

Elise sees how hard I'm working at it and joins me on the hunt, claiming two heads are better than one, and besides, birds of a feather must always flock together, she says rather convincingly, concluding there's always strength in numbers. I've learned never to argue with Elise's somewhat eccentric wisdom, so I go along with it. Who knows? She just might pull that proverbial rabbit out of a magical hat. We keep at it, hoping for a break.

As the first week ends, we begin to realize the obvious. Dream jobs such as those we're after, are few and far between. Locating one? Not much different from searching for a needle in a haystack. And for crying out loud, what's all this talk of five to ten years work experience? I'm just a twenty-four-year-old graduate trying to get a foot in the door. All I've done for the last four years is study. How the heck was I supposed to acquire so much work experience? In a parallel universe?

Two weeks of this is all Elise can take. She enrolls herself in a masters degree program because nothing or no one is going to stand in the way of her getting a dream job, she swears to me. If more credentials are called for, then so be it. She'll hit the books with a vengeance and come out a genius. Damned, she's tough. I love this girl.

I SPEND ABOUT a week thinking up alternative ways of making money and becoming rich. My beautifully written thesis internship comes to mind. What if I sold it? In my opinion, it's worth millions. But since I signed a confidentiality clause saying I would abstain from revealing company secrets to third parties, its quickly realize it's for all intents and purposes useless to me. Auctioning the same to the highest bidder is totally out of the question. Still, this doesn't stop me from daydreaming. I let my mind go wild on get-rich-quick-schemes.

I relentlessly torture myself with such thoughts for another week, somehow hesitant to make the only logical decision left. *Time is flying, and I'm procrastinating.*

Shortly thereafter, I finally come to the inevitable conclusion Elise did. With a heavy sigh, I get moving. It's time for a little more academic inspiration. I follow Elise back into the halls of knowledge.

THE FACULTY OF BUSINESS ENGINEERING is having a rather busy day when I walk in at half past ten in the morning. I take my place in a long queue filled with many other masters applicants and await my turn to see the dean, whose office is behind the door to the right at the far end of the corridor. Several more doors on either side of the hallway lead to other offices no one else wants to visit on this day.

A quiet rapport emanates from all the waiting students. It sort of reverberates off the walls within the closed space, reminding me of my student-club days.

Now and then, a member of staff silently emerges or quickly ducks into one of the neighboring offices. The students avoid eye contact. Some are wary of unbecoming questions. Most are lost in their fears, doubts, hopes, and dreams.

The line inches forward. I'm at the very back. Every ten minutes or so, I move forward another step or two. This will take a while. I sigh and give in to my fate.

The last time I saw Professor Staudinger, I told him I was off to conquer the world and make remarkable history. Implied in all of this, was big money too. Lots and lots of money. I remember seeing his glowing eyes filled with wonder. Then fast forward to the present day, and here I am, before his door, in need of a masters degree before making good on my earlier promises. I almost laugh out loud in disgust. I wish I wasn't here. I try to think of other things for almost an hour till finally, I'm through the door and inside his office.

There, in a white shirt, tall as ever, graying hair well-kempt as usual, clean-shaven as always, smiling jovially and showing uneven teeth, is the good old professor, sworn duty to the pure pursuit of knowledge and wisdom still completely intact.

I open with a simple greeting.

He nods, remaining seated at his huge desk.

Along the far wall behind him is a shelf filled with books. Two other shelves line the sidewalls of his rather simple office. The one to his left has all manner of labeled electronic gadgets in different stages of assembly. The one to his right is filled with countless trophies. Apart from his love of teaching brilliant young minds, Professor Staudinger is also a staunch rowing enthusiast. And to prove this, just in case one cannot read the small print on his trophies, is a sleek carbon-fiber rowing paddle right in the center row of his trophy shelf. I think he polishes it every day. It's gleaming.

Before I can attempt to explain my repeated presence in his eminence's much-cherished world of books and brooding about life and science, Kevin Koch calls, thereby creating an unforeseen dilemma. My application for a master's program is in my hand. And Kevin's on the phone. Should I answer the call or deal with the professor?

The dean insists I tend to my caller first. He passionately hates ringing phones.

Unlike professor Staudinger, I on the other hand, passionately hate the caller. He's ruining my elaborately planned entrance and what little credibility I have with the professor. *And why should he be calling me anyway? This is strange. My study is done! That means my relevance to Displaytek is old news, is it not?* Curious, and a little agitated, I answer the call.

"Kevin?"

"Hi, David." An awkward silence and then, "It's almost three weeks after your successful thesis defense."

"Indeed," I answer. Maybe I didn't return a company item? I rack my brain for answers.

Another awkward silence follows.

"Actually, I'm wondering how things are turning out for you?"

"Super," I say. *Couldn't get a dream job, so I am applying for a master's,* I think to myself.

"Landed a job yet?" Kevin asks.

There it is. The big fat elephant in the room. He just had to bring it up. *Kevin, Kevin, dear Kevin, Why? Why be the thorn in my tender ravaged flesh?* "Jobs are a dime a dozen," I respond. "I'm only interested in the best though. So, I am thinking of taking on a master's."

Professor Staudinger's shock at my choice of words causes him to gasp. "Thinking?" he asks loudly in abhorrence. His face is twisted in horror.

I cringe, realizing he's been listening to every word out of my mouth.

Kevin, no doubt hears him clearly and asks, "Who is that?"

But I cannot answer him. Not just yet, anyway. I'm busy trying to appease the palpitating professor. "Sorry," I say to Professor Staudinger.

He in turn just stares at me, blinking every few seconds and shaking his head ruefully. His hands are halfway up, palms skyward. I think he's imploring me to carry on with my apology. I really want to, but Kevin's urgent voice suddenly grabs all of my attention.

"Are you by any chance in the dean's office?" he shrieks into the phone, evidently recalling the professor's voice from my thesis defense not too long ago.

Is he palpitating too? And why?

I have no trouble envisioning Kevin firmly gripping the phone, knuckles turning white, but somehow can't figure out why this is happening. *Boy, oh boy! I have a crisis on my hands!*

Kevin's breathing's coming in loud and clear through my earpiece. Temporarily, I ignore him.

As I continue my apology to the professor, letting him know I intend to take the master's program head-on, Kevin screams "Nooooo!"

I shriek from the burst of sound in my ear. Kevin heard every word I just said to the professor. His cry is so much like that of a fan whose team has just conceded an impossibly ridiculous goal that I almost believe he's watching a game this very minute. At his desk. In the office. Within Displaytek. While making a polite follow-up call to a lost-cause thesis student. I almost hang up on him in disgust.

"Don't do it," he screams.

"Do what?" Now I'm really confused and on the verge of losing my mind as well.

"We have a dream job for you," Kevin says hurriedly, tongue tripping over words.

His voice comes and goes so fast, I'm left doubting my ears. "Did he just say…"

"Yes, yes, I did. A job. A great one. Something we would normally give a Ph.D graduate. But alas, time is slowly slipping away. You, on the other hand, are well versed in the subject matter. We want you, able-minded tiger, go-getter, slayer of dragons and conqueror of kingdoms. What do you say?"

I burst out laughing at his theatrics, temporarily forgetting where I am.

Incomprehensible disbelief contorts professor Staudinger's face. "Inconceivable!" he exclaims, then a miserable sound escapes him, then "David? … David?"

I gather from his expression no student ever behaved like this in his office before.

He seems to be thinking. He peers at me, eyes reduced to narrow slits. I think I notice a little change in his facial complexion. Could it be his temperature's rising?

Quickly, I apologize.

The good Professor now stares at me as though looking for clues to my mental health.

Kevin tells me he wasn't offended.

My apology wasn't meant for him. What's next? Dear goodness gracious me, these lines of communication are hopelessly crossed. I think I'm having a mind bender.

"Honestly, David," Kevin continues. "Tear up your master's application. Come work for us. You'll love it. You'll never regret it, I promise and swear to you, now and for all time."

I'm completely beside myself with joy. *This is truly happening! Kevin is dead serious! He's offering me a job! How great is that? Damned! Finally!* I break out into a broad smile.

Meanwhile, professor Staudinger is fuming. "Such cheek," he mutters, screwing his eyes to stare at something which appears to be lost in a faraway place. 'Thinking'?" He shakes his head. "Knowledge is power. We offer it to them. We say, 'Take, fill yourself with it, go out and get rich.' And how do they answer us? 'We are thinking of taking.' And this, right in my face." He shakes his head woefully, seemingly lost in eternal misery. "Preposterous!" he suddenly cries out. "Unbelievable," he adds after a few seconds. "Then laughing like a hyena in my office? Unheard of ..." he says, trailing off. "Children nowadays need a good firm hand, that's what they need," he says, nodding firmly, convinced he has the cure to beat all cures. "A solid spanking. One powerful knock on the head. Something like that. Jar them back to reality, is what I would do. I would—"

"Professor Staudinger?" I say tentatively. I'm a little bit concerned. I'm thinking of Dr. Freud's friend, the one who cured my parents back in the day when they were having a mind bender. Do I still have his number? Should I call him?

Professor Staudinger hears his name and snaps back to reality. The good old professor slowly rises from his seat and towers over me. I swear there is lightning in his eyes. He takes an ominous step toward me, and that's it. I wait no more.

I am at the threshold of his office, though I don't know how I got there. "A million apologies," I say to the distraught man, making sure my line of escape is clear. "Change of plans. Got to go!" I tear out of his office, spanking phobia haunting me and pumping my legs like pistons. I tear down the hall past startled master's-degree applicants and only look back several minutes later when I'm well and truly out of the university building.

I'm breathing hard as I look behind. To my enormous relief, my wake is completely clear. No ominous professor wielding a paddle in sight. I'm completely ruffled, but safe. I almost drop to my knees and kiss the ground. My heart's still pumping like mad. It takes a while for my fight or flight response to power down. A little longer still, for the adrenaline coursing through my system to wear off. I can relax.

I CALL ELISE at the White Rose and excitedly share my good news with her.

She absolutely loves it. "Go get 'em, tiger." She says in a breathy voice, leaving me just as breathless.

Thrilled to the bone, I do just that. I am at Displaytek in twenty minutes flat.

KEVIN RUSHES ME INTO HIS OFFICE ON MY ARRIVAL. Within seconds, he's getting me up to speed. He spends ten minutes repeating much of what I already know. A top Displaytek client wants to bail out. Displaytek cannot afford to lose his business. My thesis is a winner. Displaytek wants to implement it. And since I am its author, they want me involved in the project from the very word go. In fact, there's talk of making me the project leader. How do I feel about this? He wants to know.

My feelings are all over the place. I'm honored. Scared. Overjoyed. Grateful. Happy. Confused. Damned, why did it take so long? I go with my first reaction, which I then express to Kevin.

"Don't mention it David." He says. "But here's what you should know." He goes on to elaborate the situation, facts and figures, dates and times, places and names.

I sit ramrod straight and listen attentively.

He's using lots of big words. I think I'll have to look up three or four of them when I walk out of here. For now, I nod eagerly, maybe a little too aggressively. After all, I might be a power executive soon. My heart's fluttering way too fast. I'm too excited.

Kevin realizes he might have laid it on a bit too thick. He switches tactics to stress that above all, I should be a team player. I practically grew on everyone's heart in the last few weeks. So, they all want me back, but just the way I was, with no new unexplainable airs or anything.

I'm the dictionary definition of total agreement. I don't like airs. Have always hated them. Can't stand them. Don't know them. No time for them.

Kevin smiles. Of course, it's of paramount importance that I get started right away. "Hit the road running" are his exact words. "Can you do that?" he asks.

"Definitely my good Bentley," I answer confidently, regretting my remark immediately and wishing I could kick myself in the sheen.

Luckily, no harm was done. Kevin is beaming. Heck, forget beaming. The man's downright glowing. He gets up, dashes out of his office, and says over his shoulder, "Follow me."

IT'S A HARD act trying to keep up with Kevin when he's on one of his Marathon-walk-race-moods. He tears down the corridor and takes the stairs as though running from a hurricane.

I'm fighting to catch up.

Up we go to the executive floor, and in we march to the personnel office. It's been a while since I was here.

Christine Gay peeks up at us from behind a wide folder that she is purportedly perusing. I know what's coming. I've been down this road before. I can't wait for the show to begin.

Anje Tille's happy to see me, and no, she doesn't disappoint. She's as robust as always, as erratic as the last time, and as energetic as never before as she gets into her startlingly chaotic routine. Bless this woman, I think Hollywood should make a movie about her. Would kill the box-office with it, I'm certainly sure.

Overjoyed to be handing me my new work contract, she whistles as she mentions my starting salary—a whopping $180,000 a year. I am dumbstruck.

Kevin smiles knowingly and says simply, "Welcome to the club."

And what's running through my mind? *I am rich!—I can slowly work off the whole of my bank loan—I can afford everything I ever wanted in life,—and everything I never knew I wanted in life,—plus a whole lot of other stuff I'll probably never know I'll want in my future life or thereafter. This-is-fantastic!* I'm smiling from ear to ear. Thankfully, nobody knows what embarrassing things are going on in my mind but me. *Okay. Time to get serious.*

I straighten my face as I sign the contract. It's noon. A Kodak moment.

Christine Gay suddenly springs up from behind her folder and is beside me in two seconds.

What the heck? This makes me nervous.

She begins to analyze my elaborate scrawl to make sure it's not a fake.

Now this is confusing. Why would I fake my own signature? I look at her funny.

She looks at me funnier. "Work contracts are a big deal," she says with clear distrust as she regards my chicken-like scrawling. "As the company's legal representative, I have to carefully read every single word on every single contract. And since you've just added a new unintelligible word of sorts into this contract here, I'm obligated to proofread the whole thing once again," she concludes, frowning at me and then at the contract, as though one of us is surely up to no good. She looks at my scrawl from all angles while turning the document this way and that.

Her demeanor scares me. I'm thinking of jail time. Maybe I've been writing something illegal all my life each time as I sign my signature, and I'm only getting to learn of this now? *Oh, dear people. Oh, help.* She's about to call the cops.

I swallow hard and await her verdict.

Finally, Christine straightens up and says with great conviction, "Gibberish."

"I beg your pardon? Is everything okay?" I inquire timidly.

"Yeah, it's all good. Just stating a fact. Your signature's gibberish.

"You mean unintelligible?"

"That, yes of course, but also gibberish. Trust me. I've scrutinized many."

God bless her heart, she's clever. For one, I'm grateful my signature won't be flagged by Interpol. Secondly, and most importantly, I've zero intention of telling her what my signature actually means. If she finds out, I fear she may faint on the spot.

Twenty-seven

AS OF THIS Monday in this last week of September, Displaytek has become my employer, my second home away from home, a new family, a friend in need, and as such, a friend indeed. The company's counting on me. I am grinning like a cat that's just caught a big fat fish. I'm already started counting my dollars.

At this moment, I am in the room across the narrow corridor from Kevin's and Matthias's offices. Before this day, it doubled as an odds-and-ends storage room. It has since been transformed into my very first office ever.

I look up through the highly polished glass walls to see Kevin. He's in a yellow sweater vest and white shirt, tapping furiously away at his keyboard. Matthias Wolfgang is behind his own desk in the adjoining office, trademark silk suit and all, lost in the intricacies of intriguing production-report analysis. His intense show of industrious endeavor finally brings home to me the reality of my situation.

I'm here to help form and shape this company's new future. It's a lot of responsibility. There'll be hard work involved, and I assume, long hours of suffering in lengthy consultations. From this point on, life will not be a walk in the park. I shiver a little. I try to focus on other things.

My desk is a simple yet elegant affair—modern, spacious aluminum framework with a laminated-plywood top. A cool shade of gray, solemn and radiant with power. The only thing on it right now is my laptop. And this, I'm not ready to power up just yet. For now, I am settling in, checking out the dynamics of my new plush leather chair as I swivel this way and that. It moves like a dream. The office is fantastic. *This is simply super. I'm certainly going to love it here.*

It's a while before I start up my computer.

Matthias waits till I glance through the glass wall into his office late in the afternoon of this, my first day, and then proceeds to summon me over with a wave of his hand. *The phone could have done perfectly,* I can't help thinking as I comply.

"We are sending you to Dr. Magnus Schaefer," he says the minute I am seated across his desk.

"Who is Dr. Magnus Schaefer?"

"Who?" exclaims a surprised production manager, bushy white eyebrows shooting up on his forehead. "Only the best project manager on the continent, that's who. How can you not know this?" Incredulity rearranges his face in a way that steals my words for a moment. "Four years of studies, and you never heard of him?"

I have heard of Einstein. I've heard of several other greats who have long since perished. Maybe Matthias should ask me this question a hundred years from now, long after Magnus Schaefer is dead? With any luck, this Magnus fellow will make it into the history books by then. I want to tell Matthias all this, but the way he's running his hands over the white hairs on his temples makes me think twice. So all I say is "Sorry, the name doesn't ring a bell."

Matthias scoffs. He twiddles his white mustache and then says, "We sent your thesis as a project proposal to him. He's been looking it over and says it's in the right direction. But theory is one thing, practice another. So, we asked him to polish you up."

"I thought I was good to go?"

He tilts his head and looks at me quizzically. "You have to be very fit for the job," he growls.

"Okay. I'm game. Where do I find Magnus Schaefer?"

"He's set up shop as a consultant in Stuttgart."

"When do I leave?"

"Tomorrow."

"Travel arrangements?"

"All done. Speak with Caroline Henke. She will fill you in. And one last thing, David."

"Yes, Matthias?"

"Make the most of this opportunity, will you?"

"Sure thing, sir."

He quickly dismisses me on that note, and I go in search of Caroline Henke. She's at her post in the reception area. After a short talk with her, I walk off with my travel plans.

My journey to Stuttgart sets off promptly at 9:38 Tuesday morning. The Intercity-Express shoots off like a bullet out of Jena and guns for Erfurt. We make good time and arrive, as expected, on schedule. A short connecting taxi ride brings me to the main airport in the city. Preflight check-in is a breeze. The service here is lovely. I am in the air a short while later.

While flying business class, a fine young man working for Safetek Engineering Systems draws me into an exciting conversation. That is to say, current technology advancement in the field of aerodynamics. Yeah, a real nerd. Just my luck. Our heads remain huddled together for most of the flight as the miles slip swiftly past. All in all, it's a pleasant trip.

In Stuttgart, a young taxi driver who fancies himself a rally driver brings me at breakneck speed to the Steigenberger Graf Zeppelin hotel on the famous Arnulf-Klett-Platz, where he then brakes to a stop as though only just avoiding a horrendous tumble over a very high and precarious bridge. I am shaking like a leaf in high wind as I pay him and climb out.

A pleasant evening in the hotel's recreational facilities winds me down somewhat. Afterward, I fall asleep like a baby. I also manage to invent interstellar travel in my dreams.

MAGNUS SCHAEFER'S consulting firm is only a couple of blocks away from the lovely Steigenberger Graf Zeppelin. I walk over, arriving punctually at 7:00 a.m.

A secretary shows me to a large conference hall. I walk through hand-carved double doors and find myself looking into the open end of a large U-shaped conference table made of wood, and realize it's shining just like the glossy wooden paneling on the walls. Magnus Schaefer, I presume, dominates the outward curve, enjoying a dead-on view of the hall's entrance.

He looks up and smiles on seeing me. "David Elbert from Displaytek?" asks the firm's founder and CEO.

"Yes," I respond. "That's me."

"Come on in. Have a seat." He points to his left.

He doesn't have to ask twice. Three members of his consulting team are to his right. About fifteen places on either arm of the U are unoccupied, their swivel chairs neatly tucked under the table.

We spend a minute on polite pleasantries. Then, without warning, the grizzly-haired, elderly CEO initiates a quick question-and-answer session. He and his consulting team fire away. I do my best to answer.

They want to know how well grounded my knowledge is. Minutes pass into an hour. The clock keeps ticking as they hack away at me. I get to talk about principles such as Six Sigma, 5S, pull codes, process time, event time, capacity planning, manufacturing lead time, and the kanban system, to name a few. It's a brutal pace.

Two hours later they know all my strengths. They also know my weaknesses and prejudices. These, they promise me solemnly, will be history by the end of the day. Do I like the sound of that? They ask.

All I know for sure is that I'm drained. I need a minute to catch my breath.

We take a tea break in the dining hall next door. Afterward, Magnus Schaefer and his team take on the task of straightening my analytical thinking. They leave no stone unturned. We thoroughly work over the intricacies of project planning, execution, monitoring, steering, and reporting. A lot of this I already know, so I goad Marcus Schaefer and his team to take it up a notch. After all, Displaytek is paying good money for this. I want to be the very best I can.

Lunch comes and goes. By this time, the grooming is no longer for the fainthearted. I grapple with issues of computerized simulations. My mentors watch me closely for the better part of an hour.

"Excellent," says Magnus Schaefer to me at exactly five o'clock. "You've nailed it! My boy, you're now ready to take on the world," he concludes, punching me lightly on the shoulder.

I'm beaming with pride and satisfaction as I leave Schaefer Consulting LTD.

Back at the Steigenberger Graf Zeppelin, I spend thirty minutes in the sauna before taking a quick shower followed by ten minutes of cooling off in the indoor pool. Afterward, feeling relaxed and refreshed, I head up for dinner.

Twenty-eight

MY VEHICLE'S AFFLICTIONS have gotten worse. This student-budget acquisition not only has to endure a busted ventilation system but now also stutters and sputters so much, that I'm now certain this happens at least three times for every kilometer I spend on the road. The racket is impossible. Even worse, I feel this environmental hazard is on the verge of giving up on me altogether.

Several times, Duncan's elegant white Mercedes-Maybach Pullman limousine has whizzed past me on the way to work. On one such occasion, my car saw fit to retaliate. Oh yes, it belched out a cloud of fumes and vapor so dense, and acrid, that for a fraction of a second, Duncan Beike and his limousine were totally covered in it.

He's never mentioned this incident to date.

I've never been able to live off the shame.

At about nine O'clock on Thursday morning, my desk phone starts ringing. I find it hemmed in between stacks of books and pick up the receiver. It's Duncan Beike. The CEO wants to see me.

I go up to the third floor, rap lightly on the door to Duncan's office, and crack it open, revealing a large anteroom. A single brunette secretary sits at an arc desk on the far side of the room. She asks if I am David Elbert.

"In the flesh," I respond.

"The boss is waiting," she says simply, gesturing to the door in the wall behind her.

It takes me about ten steps to reach her desk and about five more to the said door. The place is large.

I walk through into a spacious office. My first thought is *Wow!* On the wall to the left, a Van Gogh. To the right, a Picasso. *Surely the two alone must be worth millions?* A crystal chandelier filled with bulbs provides soft electrical light. This is actually superfluous, as daylight is streaming in through the large windows behind Duncan. He is seated at an ultramodern glass-top desk, eyeing me as I cross the floor to him.

"Hello, Mr. Elbert. Please, do come in." He gets up and comes around his desk.

I walk up to him. Today, the tall, heavyset man is dressed in a Giorgio Armani suit. We shake hands.

"Nice to have you on board," he says in a strong voice.

"Nice of you to let me aboard," I reply.

He lets out a robust chuckle. It fills the room. I simply smile.

"Let's sit down, shall we?" he says.

He sits back behind his desk, and I settle into a red Italian designer chair placed before it.

"So, Mr. Elbert, I read your thesis."

"And?" I ask.

"Must say I am buzzing with excitement at what it could do for this company." He pauses.

I wait for him to say more.

"Are you ready to turn your words into action?"

The difficult part was researching the thesis and then tailoring it to fit the company's needs. With the necessary assistance from the rest of the team, implementation shouldn't be that hard. "I believe I am, Mr. Beike."

"Good, good." He pauses for a while, rubbing his day-old stubby chin as though contemplating the next course of action. "Project manager of lean-production implementations. That's the position you are filling. Am I right?"

"Yes, Mr. Beike, it is."

"You do know this is a position of authority and great responsibility?"

"Yes, I am aware of this, sir."

"We are counting on you, young man." He looks at me inquisitively.

I feel the need to say something. "I will give it my very best shot, Mr. Beike. Rest assured of this."

"Good. Very good." He rakes a hand through his jet-black hair before proceeding. "The position is also a reflection on the company's image."

"No doubt about it, sir."

"Nice of you to be so agreeable. I believe you will also agree the ramshackle you drive does nothing good for our image?"

My car's attempt at choking him to death comes flooding back to me. I choke on my apology.

"Obviously you are thinking about a new car?"

"I am?" Surprise oozes out of me. I was thinking more of a quick service session at the local auto-repair shop and then getting on with life.

"After all, we are paying you a king's ransom."

Now that he mentions it, the prospect of a new car is like early Christmas.

He sees the idea growing on me, so he adds, "Tell you what. Take Friday off. Go shopping. See what's on the market. Get yourself what you like. And if it's out of your budget, come to me. I will put up a quarter of its asking price."

"You will do that for me?"

"Yes, just as I have for a handful of other productive members of this company."

"Awesome. That's really nice of you, sir."

"Just promise me one thing."

"Yes, sir?"

"You will be productive?"

I swallow hard. A promise is one thing. Delivering is another. "I will do my best, Mr. Beike."

"That's all I needed to hear." He smiles pleasantly.

In the next instant, I am dismissed.

ELISE AND I visit countless flamboyant dealerships. Mercedes, BMW, Opel, Lexus, Porsche, and many more. The offers are enticing. The cars are breathtaking. Everyone's friendly. At about five o'clock we settle for a black Audi Q7 on a monthly payment plan. I must say we couldn't have made a better choice. I am pleased.

Twenty-nine

AN EERIE SILENCE fills Displaytek as I walk through the building's lavish corridors at the beginning of this new week. A quick time check lets me know it's only six O'clock in the morning. No one's here yet. And it's a little bit dark. This, for some unknown reason, has me slightly on edge and a little bit jumpy. I sneak around corners and tiptoe as I advance toward my office. More than once, I look behind me. Not once do I run into a monster. No grisly shadows tailing me. I pinch my arm to remind myself I'm not in a horror movie.

It was my express intention to be here before anyone on this Monday morning. After all, this is what I wanted—the silence, the complete and utter lack of interruptions. I have a project to plan. I need my whole mind on it.

I walk into my office and sit at my desk, somewhat relieved at having not encountered anything otherworldly. Before me is a single document, "The Project Order." Matthias Wolfgang probably placed it there sometime on Friday, while I was out shopping for my Audi. I pick it up and read the project's name. A short description of the project's nature follows and covers three lines. Below that is my name, as well as my position as project manager. There we go. My accountability is as clear as writing on a wall.

The rest of the sheet is filled with an impressive list of all my duties and responsibilities, which include project planning. There is a battery of guidelines to aid me in this noble task, such as cost-benefit analysis, expected results, disposable funds, known risks, and many more. Every one of these is a vital piece of valuable information. I'm grateful. They will come in handy.

I turn my attention back to the project order. In big brilliant red is the deadline: November 28. The lean production line should be operational on this date. This is also the date Displaytek's biggest client, Lux Cars Ltd., intends to abandon ship if we cannot convince them otherwise. Manufacturing-lead-time improvements are urgently needed.

My heart almost skips a beat. I wanted responsibility, and now I have it.

Today is November 8. I have two days to plan the project. Communicating with contractors to clinch contractual obligations will take about a week. Thereafter, assembly-floor renovation will gobble up yet another seven days. My eyes travel to the bottom of the document. "Signed by the CEO, Mr. Duncan Beike."

I set the document aside and take a deep breath. Time is of the essence. Planning should never be rash, but rather, detailed. To complicate matters, this undertaking is intricate. Professor Staudinger always said, "Better plan several times over than dive right into it and face a multitude of problems from the word go."

That's right, the famous catch-22. Time versus detail. I groan out loud.

Eighty percent of project management is planning. Plan the timely availability of raw materials, components, and skilled personnel in their required quantities, quality, and acceptable price range. Then plan to direct all these into creating the desired end-state, without losing sight of the project's stated overall cost, time limit, and quality specifications.

Trying to do all this without a plan is like shooting at an apple on a man's head with one's eyes tightly shut, and trust me, I know the feeling. Horror scenarios such as inadequate task coordination, time loss, inept performance, and cost explosion fill my mind for a minute. I shudder at these involuntarily and tell myself none of them should come to pass. With my mind made up, I quickly get to work. I'll be at it for a solid hour before this place fills with life.

Displaytek is now teeming with people, most of whom have answered my questionnaires on various topics ranging from ergonomics, procurement, quality, costs, risks, hopes and fears, and many more. I gather these into mutually accepted considerations for the intended project and as the day ends, my very first document, the statement of scope, comes into being. This was a breeze. I'm beginning to myself.

Tuesday brings with it delivery planning issues, determination of manpower distribution and project process flowcharting. After three hours and to my extreme joy, I realize my initial project plan is complete. I am ecstatic! The network plan is a marvel. I waste no time transferring expected process durations onto a Microsoft Project calendar.

Not too long after this, someone knocks on my door and enters. I'm still elbow-deep in planning and not too keen on interruptions. I look up to see Duncan Beike before me.

"Good afternoon, sir. What can I do for you?"

"Good afternoon, project meeting in an hour." He pauses and then adds dramatically, "Be there or be square."

What the heck? My smile dies.

He breaks into laughter. "Relax. Just kidding."

"About the meeting?"

"No. About being square. Just bring along your initial plan, and everything will be fine."

My hesitation is evident.

"You do have an initial project plan by now, don't you?"

"Certainly, sir. Just finished it."

"There you go." He chuckles. "Nothing to worry about. One hour. Conference hall B."

He shuts the door on his way to the executive floor.

AT THE APPOINTED hour, I gather my laptop plus an assortment of documents and leave in a mad dash. I turn right, out of the scheduling department, and then left, into a corridor with large magnificent bay windows. I look through them as I walk past. Dark clouds are slowly sailing in. Soon, the orange sky will be no more. Probably a storm brewing. A weather station on the wall places outside temperature at just above thirty degrees Fahrenheit. Soon, the bay windows are behind me.

Up the stairs I go to the third floor, where seconds later, I walk into conference hall B.

All eighty of Displaytek's souls are already gathered before Duncan, Matthias, and Kevin. The place is jammed to capacity.

Matthias spots me and beckons me over. I'm at his side in a heartbeat.

As the CEO prepares to address the crowd, I study it. Funny how birds of a feather always seem to flock together. Even here, departmental lines are clearly visible. I spot the picking team huddled together, research and development not far off, and most of the assemblers somewhere in the middle. An exception to the rule is, of course, Hans Hartmann and Christine Gay. The two lovebirds are seated in the very last row, tightly squeezed together even though they practically have the whole row to themselves. Since I walked in, they have been whispering and petting each other nonstop. I try not to look.

"Ladies and gentlemen," Duncan Beike says and then pauses for breath. The coat of his black pin-striped suit is open to reveal his starched white shirt. For some reason, he is not wearing a tie today. "In the last couple of weeks, many of you have probably heard unsettling whispers, disquieting talk as to the company's future. True, we're in a precarious position right now, but hopefully, that will change."

The throng mumbles its discomfort.

Hans and Christine kiss passionately. They are oblivious to the world. Duncan ignores them.

"Change can bring with it new opportunities," he continues, "The chance to improve one's self, one's position, and production," he says, with great emphasis on the word 'production'.

Pin-drop silence. Everyone's listening, apart from the lovers.

"Today, we see the future," Duncan says, peering skywards as though literally waiting for a revelation.

His audience claps, whistles, and cheers.

Satisfied and beaming brightly, Duncan steps back. He's done for the day.

As appointed project leader, I am next on the podium. Unlike the CEO, it's my first time addressing a crowd this big. Roughly half the employees are watching me keenly. The other half have their eyes on Kevin, whom by now, has been singled out as my second-in-command for the project's duration.

"I introduce the project by name, accept a handful of questions, then picking up steam, spend the next couple of minutes bolstering general interest for the work that lies ahead. Everyone has a role to play. We are a team. I'm in charge. True corporate success is just around the corner.

Due to time constraints, we have decided upon the strong-matrix organization structure."

There are many confused looks, so Kevin explains, "Those directly involved in the project will be spending more of their time and effort on it, than on their usual duties."

Sounds of comprehension echoes throughout the audience.

Kevin proceeds to call out the core project team members, asks them to head out to the conference room A, then ends the meeting and dismisses everybody else.

This second inner-group meeting between Kevin and I, Henrik Wang from IT, John Nwosu from total quality management, Lars Roeske from materials procurement and Philipp Kuehn from product documentation, is mostly a hierarchy transfer of information from me down to my team. In it, I explain that the project officially takes off on the twelfth of November and ends on the fifth of December, hand out copies of the network plan to keep everyone on the same page, call their attention to the project's very short time span and make sure that every single one of them understands the urgency of the situation.

Questions arise. I do my best to answer them. In the end, duties and responsibilities do become clear, and they all begin to relax. First thing tomorrow, I will conduct one-on-one meetings with every single one of them. I will focus on questions of what, how, when, and where. They will want relevant examples. I have all my prior work, notes and pictures ready. The momentum's picking up. I guess we're on a roll.

I pop into a jewelry store after work and on a whim, decide to buy Elise something elegant. Handcrafted crystal earrings with a matching necklace catch my eye and win my heart. The three pieces of jewelry glitter and twinkle like a million stars in a brightly lit miniature galaxy.

That night, I present them to Elise, who excitedly covers me with kisses for half the night, and guess what? She also makes love to me for the other half. Life is beautiful.

Thirty

I've never been to Cloud Elevators Ltd., nor as far as I know, have they ever been to our premises at all. A few minutes ago, Susie Morgan, their receptionist, was kind enough to patch me through to Christian Weber, their sales representative, who, I believe, under the erroneous assumption that I'm simply pursuing idle banter, has decided to put me on hold.

After nearly five full minutes of waiting, I hear a click on the line, and then, "Christian Weber, Cloud Elevators. How can I help you?"

"Hello, Mr. Weber. Remember me? David Elbert from Displaytek?"

"Of course, Mr. Elbert. How can I forget? How did it turn out? Were my tips useful?"

"I could never have done it without your help, so yeah, you were amazing! But I guess you already know that, don't you?"

"Glad to hear it." He chuckles graciously, then adds, "So do tell, what can I do for you today?"

"Sell me an elevator, that's would be lovely."

"Are you kidding me?"

"Oh no, sir. I would never dream of kidding about something like this. This has now evolved into a project, and guess what? It's you I'd love to do business with, you know?"

"Fantastic!" He cries out excitedly.

I agree with a laugh.

He's beside himself with joy and wants to know when the project starts.

I tell him.

"And how about the elevator? When do you want this installed?"

"The nineteenth."

"Pretty short notice, don't you think?"

"Can't help it. We have a deadline to beat."

"That will cost you extra," he tells me.

We discuss net price, optional assembly fees, then haggle over the initial operation and adjustment expenses before rounding off with a detailed look at training and maintenance costs. Within the hour, we agree on a contract. My first business deal on behalf of Displaytek Systems is a roaring success.

Similar scenes play out in the offices of Kevin Koch, Lars Roeske, and Henrik Wang. I call each one, in turn, asking for progress updates and receive the same good news. No one is having any difficulties. Henrik expects to wrap up by the end of the day. Kevin tomorrow, and Lars still needs a little more time. All in all, perfect. I couldn't be any happier.

Thirty-one

Not once in the last couple of weeks have we run into Handal Hoams. For this, I am eternally grateful. According to police reports, he's gone into hiding, and, quite effectively, has erased all traces of himself and his activities from the face of the earth. It's as if he never existed. This is truly baffling. Law enforcement authorities, many of whom admit they've never dealt with such a case as this before, have no clue as to where he may be. Indeed, the king of drugs is turning out to be a formidable challenge.

The fact that the police can't find him scares me immensely. But one thing does console me a little: he's on the run. In other words, surely, he can't be stalking us anymore? I try to convince myself this is the case, that I can breathe easier, and that there's no reason to worry about him any longer. Still, for some inexplicable reason, I can't help but feel I haven't seen the last of him.

ACTUAL PROJECT kickoff takes place right on schedule Wednesday morning just as planned. As expected, Duncan Beike shows up and for the first one hour, paces up and down for the most part, and somehow manages to present the image of a caged tiger dying to break out and maul the terrified sheep.

He's in pain, with good reason. As long as the project runs, no regular work will be carried out, no product assembled, no money made. To Mr. Beike, this is worse than losing a pint of blood by the minute.

I chuckle and try a handful of jokes to lighten his mood.

Like a lost soul, his eyes frantically take in the dynamic transformation taking place in every direction, clearly shocked by the depth and extent of the mess. His production department is no longer recognizable. A major overhaul is underway. Chaos, tools, gadgets, and people, it's a madhouse.

"Things are looking up," I say to him.

He opens his mouth as if to speak, then simply turns around and heads out the door.

Good God, don't let us botch this up. We need a win. I redouble my efforts in leading the team.

BY TEN O'CLOCK, several of the old workstations have been dismantled and cleared away. By noon, we move on to the next task, and as late afternoon comes to an end, relocation of the remaining workstations along the hall's walls successfully comes to conclusion.

Across from the production hall, evident changes within the operations-scheduling section are also happening. The open office space is now clear. Its little island of tables and chairs is gone, and the shelves and filing cabinets that once lined its walls are no more. The hall stands empty.

This is great! We've reached a milestone! Tomorrow morning, workmen can move in to carry out the next task in the sequence of renovations. I'm glowing as a result of this little success. The rate of progress is better than expected. What's more? We've encountered no problems whatsoever. With any luck, we will encounter none. I'm suddenly hopeful. If we keep this up, we will make the deadline for sure.

In celebration of this steady progress, Elise and I go out for a candlelight-dinner followed by a late-night city walk and a theater visit. It's almost midnight when we get back home.

THE SOUND OF MY RINGING CELL PHONE draws me out of deep sleep and into a state of semi-wakefulness. Beside me, Elise fidgets and moans in consternation. My head feels like a ball of lead. Carefully, I crack an eye open. A painful squint at the clock on the bedside drawer reveals the time. *Five thirty? For crying out loud! Who on earth is calling at this ungodly hour?*

I reach for the phone and place it to my ear. "Hello?" My voice doesn't sound like my own.

"David Elbert?" asks a strange voice.

"Speaking," I say. In all honesty, I am almost growling.

"Christian Weber, sales representative, Cloud Elevators. Sorry to bother you at this hour. It's necessary."

Elise asks in a dreamlike state, eyes still tightly shut, "Is something wrong, sweetheart?"

"No, honey," I croak. "Just work. Go back to sleep, okay?"

She mumbles something about the unsocial behavior of leaving cell phones on standby overnight and then drifts back into slumber.

"Just a second," I growl into the cell. There is now a gruffer edge to my voice. I'm hoping this will compel Christian Weber to hang up, but he doesn't. Moonlight filters through the trees outside and streams in through the glass wall of the master bedroom. Elise and I had the glass specially fitted in so that we could better admire our beautiful garden from our innermost sanctuary. As a bonus, the bedroom is usually bathed in a faint enchanting gloom when the moon is up. As it is right now. It's romantic. But that's the last thing on my mind right now.

I get up and walk out of the bedroom so as not to disturb Elise. "Okay," I ask while sinking into the couch of the neighboring guestroom, "what's up?"

"It's about our contract," he says.

A knot forms in the pit of my stomach at the sound of his despairing voice. "What about it?"

"The team was scheduled to drive off for your premises at this hour ..."

"Was?"

"Well ... Yes ..." He goes silent.

"And?" I prompt gently, worry and fear rising inside me with every second.

"We have the new elevator parts loaded up, including all tools and equipment. Six of the eight-man team are ready for action."

"Six?" I ask, not liking the sound of this at all.

"Yeah," he sighs.

"What happened to the other two?"

Again, he sighs heavily. "It's a long story."

Yeah, right. To me, that sounds like the onset of a breach of contract. Should I sue? I picture the eight men in my mind's eye. Two pneumatic drill experts, three elevator assembly technicians, an electrical engineer, and two hands for heavy lifting. The last two are easy to replace. I cross my fingers and hope they are the problem. "Which two?" I ask quietly, aware of the crisp note in my voice, but somehow unable to help myself.

"The drill experts," Christian solemnly replies.

Cold constricts around my lungs to the point I cannot breathe anymore. How could this happen to my best-laid plans? It's always those circumstances beyond one's control that are the most dangerous. This is a project manager's worst nightmare. My first project, my career debut, my opportunity to build up managerial collateral and show what I can do, then this? My heart starts beating without rhythm. I am in a daze. Sound comes to my ear as though traveling from a long way off. It's Christian's voice. His long story's unfolding.

"It all started on Wednesday afternoon during an inter-company football match," he says. "The opposing team is our archenemy. Our two drill boys, needless to say, were playing. Over the course of time, they have become as thick as thieves and will do anything and everything for each other, you know? Have each other's backs, cover for each other when one is absent, so on."

I feel sick. I want to ask him to cut to the chase, but my lungs are acting up again. I cannot breathe, let alone speak. I suffer his rendition in silence.

"The smaller drill boy is also our soccer star and, as such, has been the victim of many a horrendous foul over the years." His voice fills with zest.

Great! He loves telling stories. Now I know I'm doomed.

"Sadly, this game was no different, and as you might have already guessed by now, one such foul was so nasty, that Emil, the said soccer star, suddenly ended up with a severely sprained ankle. Our big pneumatic driller, Leon, couldn't take that, and what a lack of surprise when he finally exploded!" says Christian with a loud groan, obviously reliving the scene as it plays out in his mind's eye.

I'm caught up in this tale. I'm dying to hear more.

"You see," Christian continues, "Leon is built like a bear. So, when his well-planted left hook sank into the jaw of the perpetrator of this horrendous crime, it sounded like a really heavy 18-wheeler plowing into a stationary mini."

I hate Christian Weber, but I am riveted to his story. "What happened next?" I inquire.

"A wild brawl suddenly broke out," he replies. "Can you see it? The fists and kicks flying this way and that?"

"Yes, I…"

"Then the referee jumped into this milieu, whistle firmly planted between his lips, and as his cheeks filled up with air for a good blow, Leon's right hook suddenly appeared out of the blue, and plowed into the side of his face with a mighty crunch."

"Ouch!" I exclaim.

"Oh yeah, it was bad," agrees Christian Weber, sounding relieved at how much I'm feeling his story with my heart, hopeful I'll be lenient for the excuse he's about to give. "The referee's lower lip tore wide open! Can you believe that?"

"That must have been it for Leon, yes? Game over?"

"Oh no. The pain-riddled referee didn't even bother with a red card! He simply called the police on the spot and burned with anger until they arrived. According to his statement, Leon punched him on purpose. Leon refuted this, of course. His intended victim ducked out of the way at the last second, and suddenly, there was the referee's face, making contact with his fist. No one was more surprised than he, he swore to this fact."

Christian chuckles.

I can't help laughing.

"This didn't stop the enraged referee from pressing charges, though. You can imagine how shocked I was when Leon was shuffled away in handcuffs. So, there we are, that's the whole story." He draws in a deep breath, replenishing his starving lungs.

I exhale loudly, feeling defeated and a little disgusted. This situation is hopeless. How can we salvage it?

Christian Weber finds his tongue again and recaps the obvious. "Emil's right foot is now in a cast. He can barely stand, let alone walk. Leon is behind bars. Posting bail will take at least a full day. You need two drill boys today, in three hours. I have gotten in touch with my contacts, called up every favor owed to me, searched high and low for pneumatic drillers on short notice, all in vain. I am really sorry," he concludes, the pauses and waits for me to say something.

I jog my brain cells. Where can I get two demolition experts on such short notice?

Christian can't stand the silence anymore and asks, "Can you get two demolition experts on short notice?"

"Give me twenty minutes. I'll call you back."

He apologizes once more and hangs up.

It's not Christian's fault that we're in this mess, and I try to keep this in mind as I call Kevin. As expected, he reacts the same way I did to being called at this ungodly hour. I recount Christian's words to Kevin, almost word for word. He punctuates my narrative with heartfelt curses. I'm not certain if they're directed at me or the insufferable situation. After all, I did ruin his sleep, didn't I?

In clipped words, he tells me some of our boys do indeed have pneumatic drill training. It's up to me to find out who, though, and barely are these words out of his mouth, when the line goes dead. No goodbye, no goodnight, nothing. Clearly, I'm not his favorite person right now.

Finesse now flows through my bloodstream as I call the boys one after the other. I tear them out of sleep and grill them on their drilling expertise. Yes, they're bewildered. It's an ungodly hour to call, they let me know. But they're quickly placated. And minutes later, I have what I need: two drill boys, Hans Hartmann and Timothy Lang.

Christian Weber is happy to hear the good news. He's elated as well as immensely relieved.

"The two, however, are a bit rusty and in need of mentoring," I let him know.

"What do you have in mind?" he inquires.

"Send the injured boy over. We'll just prop him up in a chair. He can give our boys quick refresher course whenever the need arises."

"I suppose we can fit him up with a wheelchair and send him over. Beware though," warns Christian, "Emil's heavily sedated to counteract his unbearable pain."

"Don't worry. We will take good care of him," I say reassuringly. "ETA still eight thirty?"

"Yes. I believe they can make it."

"Perfect!"

Fortunately, Christian has no more shocking news. A few seconds of niceties later, he lets me get back to slumber.

Thirty-two

AT NOON ON THE FOLLOWING DAY, I WALK INTO THE LEAN-LINE REPLENISHMENT POINT and immediately realize something is seriously wrong. Ludwig Beck, who has been in charge in my absence, is pacing up and down and wringing his hands. In the far corner of the room, a slight twentysomething man with a crew cut is slouched in a wheelchair. He's dressed in orange overalls, the right trouser leg of which is pulled up to reveal a heavy white cast. Emil, I deduct. Not only is his right foot in a cast, but his toes, which should be exposed, are bandaged up as well. He appears extremely groggy. His head is swaying from side to side, back and forth, in constant motion. I look at the baby-like face beneath the crew cut. It's severely contorted and strained. Now there's a man in unbearable pain.

Both Hans and Timothy are dressed in orange overalls as well, provided by Cloud Elevators. The two are wielding massive power drills. I watch as the muscular man and his puny colleague attack the wall in earnest. Thankfully, the small goods elevator is gone. They are now widening the aperture in readiness for the new one, which is a whole lot larger. A short distance away, the wall seems to have been drilled through. The spot has been patched up, but, unlike the rest of the light-blue walls, it still needs a paint job. This extra drill action wasn't sanctioned. Plus, they are two hours behind schedule. What's happened? What went wrong? I want answers.

I walk up to the pacing Ludwig and indicate we should talk. He nods and then taps the drill boys on their shoulders. Ludwig moves his flat hand knifelike across his throat, the famous pantomime for kill-action, and the boys respond accordingly, shutting off their power drills. The loud chug peters out. Silence reigns.

As if on cue, Emil breaks into the most pitiful moan I've ever heard. It's a bloodcurdling sound. A chill runs down my spine. Horrified, I turn to Ludwig. "What in goodness' name happened here?" My face is the embodiment of one big question mark.

He sighs heavily and looks defeated. "A disaster, David. A long, appalling story. Do you really want to hear it?"

Two rubble boys in blue workman's overalls come in. A yellow rubble container dangles between them. As they pass by, I see "Cloud Elevators" embossed in bold white letters across their backs. I watch as they start to shovel freshly drilled rubble into the container.

It's clear from the expression on my face that I need to hear this story. So, Ludwig gets on with it. "We started off on a good note," he explains. "Emil here, bless his heart, gave Hans, Timo, and Frank, a quick and impeccable refresher course on pneumatic drilling. Quite competently, I might add, despite being heavily sedated."

Ludwig's clean-shaven head doesn't glisten today, I notice. I attribute this to all the drilled-up dust sitting on it. We all look in the direction of Emil as the said man moans forlornly at the mention of his name. The pitiful pining evokes different emotions on different faces. Timo's own is a riot of contradicting emotions ranging from heartfelt empathy to an expression that seems to say, *For Pete's sake, why won't you just shut the hell up?* An apology must be whirling somewhere in there too, for he presently says, "I am truly sorry, Emil."

"Oooohhhhh!" goes Emil, for nearly a full minute.

Unbelievable! I have goosebumps all over. At this point, I know Timothy is somehow responsible for the dreadful sound Emil is making. My curiosity is intensely piqued.

Ludwig continues. "Hans and Timo then got off to a good start. Each worked one side of the old goods elevator, digging it out, so to speak. Frank must have partied nonstop last night, as he presently mysteriously disappeared. Without a doubt, we knew he was sleeping it off somewhere."

Typical, I think to myself. *That's Frank.*

"Timo was a bit shaky, being so rusty and all," says Ludwig. "Still, his contribution mattered. So, Emil—"

Emil screams.

I cry out, jump a clear meter in the air, then hurtle back down to the floor and look about in fright. There's Emil in his wheelchair, mouth ajar, head hanging to the side, the last wisps of his horrible scream still emanating from his open mouth.

I'm shaking.

Though a living livid mass of pain, Emil apparently can still hear his own name whenever it is spoken, and clearly attempts to respond to it. Could it be that in that morphine-infused head, he believes he's responding with a simple yes? Whatever the case may be, his powerful wail is simply not natural. It can't be. It's supernatural. I don't want to hear it again.

Ludwig is as white as a sheet. The particles of dust on his clean-shaven scalp are beautifully aligned, as though a heavy magnetic disturbance is taking place deep within his brain. He hesitates a second, looks at me questioningly, then carries on. "Timo's contribution mattered. He was allowed to continue. Shortly afterward, Hans got a phone call and paused his work to take it, disappearing for half an hour."

We all look at Hans. "It was really urgent," he tells us in earnest defense. A twitching eye gives him away. He was probably on the phone with Christine Gay, singing one of his many love duets to her.

Ludwig wipes a nervous hand across his dust-covered scalp. A gleaming strip of scalp, totally free of dust, appears.

Several of us stare. But no one laughs.

"Time slipped away," Ludwig continues. "Hans didn't come back, and our emergency substitute, Frank Krueger, was nowhere to be found."

"Did you try all the restrooms and dark corners?" I ask.

"Yes," answers Ludwig. "But all in vain. Anyway, with looming breach of contract, Emil got nervous and took matters into his own hands."

As if right on cue, Emil screams.

The painful yowl tears through the air, shattering the silence.

We need seconds to recover.

I caution Ludwig not to mention Emil's name.

Heads bob up and down in eager agreement. No one wants to hear that sound again.

Timo, who for the most part has been cowering a little, now looks downright miserable and is obviously not looking forward to what Ludwig has to say next.

"*He,*" continues Ludwig, now pointing at Emil rather than voicing his name, "took Hans's place." With eyes full of admiration, he looks at the boy in the wheelchair. "You should have seen him, balanced on his left foot, working Hans's power drill, determined, in pain, making slow but steady progress, doing his best to ignore his sprained ankle. A real hero," Ludwig says in awe.

"Until Timo lost control of his power drill …" adds Nick Neumann.

"And sprung sky-high…" interrupts Hans.

"Only to land squarely on those exposed toes, sending the man screaming in pain," Ludwig concludes.

"I thought you were nowhere to be found?" I ask Hans.

"I came in just in time to witness it all," he answers.

"And what happened to the wall? I look at the damage, not believing my eyes.

"The result of our injured friend's pain-reflex," says Ludwig.

"Yeah, was a bomber," Hans lets me know. "Pneumatic drill digging into the wall and careening to the far left, severing the main power duct, causing a total blackout." He shakes his head in dismay. "It was bad."

Ludwig too is shaking his head. "We had no power for an hour."

"Really sorry," says the embarrassed Timothy.

"So, that's how we spent the first hour," Ludwig says in conclusion. "A total disaster."

"What happened after that?" I ask.

"We had to get Emi— eh … the power drill operator to the hospital," answers Ludwig.

I have a nervous eye on Emil. He doesn't stir. I breathe out in relief. "I assume the CEO already knows all this?"

"Certainly." Replies Ludwig. "He came looking for answers the minute his computer lost juice. Luckily, Cerltek Electronics was on site installing cables and offered to fix the power disruption. Mr. Beike let them do so. He's expecting a report from you on probable impacts to our deadline."

"Well then, let's not keep him waiting, shall we?

They get back to work.

I WALK OUT of the lean-line replenishment point into the production hall. Along the walls, batch production is ongoing, just like in the old days.

And thanks to Cerltek Electronics, a new network of electrical sockets lies embedded in the floor or hangs from the ceiling within the hall's spacious center, ready for use. Our project's still in the clear. And we're ready for the next step.

I put all these facts into my report, mention that the new workstations will be installed within the next two days, and give the CEO a copy. Whether he chooses to punish Frank Krueger's unexcused absence, Hans Hartmann's personal phone call, or Timothy Lang's clumsiness, remains to be seen.

Thirty-three

TIMOTHY COMES IN TO SEE ME shortly before lunch hour. His every inch from head to foot is covered in fine drill dirt. He sits across from me with a whoosh and is suddenly surrounded by a halo of dust.

"Do you have kids?" he asks.

"No, Timo, I don't." I act busy, try to put across the point that I have lots to do, no time to chat, but he doesn't take the hint.

"I have one coming up," he says.

"What?" I ask.

"A child."

"Oh." The way he put it, I thought he'd just ordered a pizza and was expecting delivery any minute now.

He leans back contentedly, as though on his couch at home, totally relaxed, just like a man waiting for his soon-to-be-born baby to spring onto his lap.

I shake my head and close my eyes to get rid of the insufferable apparition.

"Our obstetrician says it's a baby girl."

"Good for you," I say. "Any point in telling me this?"

"Yeah, sure." He acts grave, but, with all that dust on him, manages only to look utterly ridiculous. "Do you know how much it costs to bring up a baby girl these days?" The creases on his brow deepen.

Aha! Timothy is living through a moment of job insecurity. He's reaching out, looking for reassurance. With a warm smile I say, "Look, Timo, the project is well thought out. Each process is falling into place and is still right on schedule, despite today's mishap. We will complete successfully. We will have greater production capacity and improved manufacturing lead time after that. Our future's bright. So, will you quit worrying?"

He watches me, cool, composed, head cocked to one side, struggling with doubt for a little bit, but finally caves in. "Okay, David," he says quietly. "If you are so sure ..." Suddenly he jerks forward. A cloud of dust tries to keep up with him. Now he's leaning over my desk, eyes sparkling, face inches away from mine, burning with eagerness.

I find myself in his halo of dust, coughing uncontrollably.

"We are done drilling," he says excitedly.

"The elevator assembly technicians?" I ask.

"They've taken over," he informs me with an exuberant amount of confidence. "Installation of the new elevator is ongoing as we speak," he happily adds.

"Perfect!" I exclaim.

He sits back and smiles, dust-riddled trouser legs crossed over each other, and talks for five more minutes before letting me know the CEO wants to see me. Couldn't he just have started off with this?

Duncan Beike's happy. It's all coming together quite splendidly, he agrees, tells me to keep up the good work, rein in the boys, avoid further mishaps, and constantly update him on all new incidents and changes. I promise to do all the above.

AFTER A hard day's work, while sauntering out of the production department on our way to the parking lot, Kevin tells me we need to talk and quickly invites me for a beer. I say yes, but all I can think about is food. I am famished to the point of starvation. He, on the other hand, is clearly worried about something.

It's five O'clock. Darkness is falling. "A big football game is on tonight," Kevin says. We agree to head for the sports bar on Johannisplatz 9.

A festive atmosphere greets us the minute we arrive at our destination. We walk into the bar and settle at a table. Kevin immediately catches up on the game as I take a good look at the cheering crowd—students, career types, simple workers and young girls, all looking to score a big date or have some fun. The mixed crowd churns and broils with unbridled energy as a mere handful spurs it on with football war songs. It's unbelievably loud. Sound reverberates off the walls and comes crashing back in on the patrons, many of whom, undaunted by the high acoustic level, are also attempting to carry out intelligent conversations with each other. Shouted questions, comments, and replies add to the maddening cacophony. The game streaming on the various wall-mounted monitors is hardly audible. I sigh, as I look at Kevin. *The things I do for friendship!*

Seated behind the bar is a burly man whose intense pleasure at the unfolding sights and sounds unmistakably betrays him as the establishment's proprietor. Beer is flowing, cash is changing hands, business is booming, and his bar is crowded. He's the very image of a man going out of his mind with joy.

As if by magic, a stunning little waitress in a clinging red T-shirt appears at our table the second normal conversation is possible. I order Texas roast beef and French fries. Kevin eyeballs her and asks for a malt beer. She winks and goes off to do our bidding.

"Cute, isn't she?" I comment, smiling.

"I'm married," Kevin says.

"Yeah?"

He shows me his wedding ring. Gold band, dazzling green stone of medium size. Just then his team almost concedes a goal, sending him and countless others into a roaring frenzy. The danger passes, the noise subsides, and Kevin starts to tell me about his wife, Doreen, who is a doctor. I get to hear how they met and fell in love and grew as one to become inseparable. It's an exciting story. "But that is not why we are here," he lets me know.

On the big screens, the referee blows the whistle for half-time. The game is still tied. Null to null. The fans are once more civilized. Conversation is easier.

"Are you aware of the Lux Cars situation?" Kevin asks.

"Yeah, sure am. The top client threatening to bolt if we don't increase output sufficiently to meet their growing demand?"

"Exactly!"

"What about it?"

"I have been looking through the company's financial reports and mission statements and following various press releases for months now," he says.

"And?"

"To a schooled eye, such information can be truly revealing. The direction a company is headed, upcoming management upheavals, and so on. What I have managed to piece together is quite astounding." His face is deathly serious.

"Yes?" is all I manage to say. A feeling of dread is slowly creeping over me.

More guests walk into the now overflowing bar. Several remain standing. There is nowhere to sit. Kevin contemplates his next words carefully and then proceeds. "You do know Lux Cars is a subsidiary to the much bigger and more powerful Kenen Automobiles?"

"Yes, I do. Ludwig mentioned it once. According to him, Lux Cars became a share-limited company about eight years ago. Within a year, Kenen became majority stakeholder, and in five, they assumed total control of Lux Cars. Is this more or less right?"

"Dead-on," confirms Kevin, head bobbing up and down furiously. "Kenen deemed Lux Cars unprofitable. They issued an ultimatum. Step up output by twenty percent, or suffer permanent closure. Two days later, Lux Cars came knocking on our doors with their own ultimatum."

"Yeah," I say, my voice a little apprehensive. "Step up output by one hundred units, or goodbye."

"Hence the reason for your project," says Kevin, stating the obvious. "Lately, the press has been full of stories about a series of closed-door meetings between Kenen and Lux Cars. And know what I found out?"

"No," I reply, now practically on the edge of my seat. "What did you find."

"Lux Cars' liquidity has sunk drastically in the last few weeks. In other words, they have incurred unusually massive expenditures. But what's truly amazing is that these have been counterbalanced by a substantial increase in plant and machinery. Just yesterday, the company's CEO made a public statement indicating they were on the lookout for highly skilled labor." He pauses for effect.

I am scared out of my wits and don't know why. "What are you getting at?"

"Lux Cars is gearing up for a step up in production far in excess of twenty percent."

He waits for me to comment. I take a few seconds to digest his deductions. "All this, just from financial statements?"

"As I said, financial statements, press releases, mission statements, the works."

Again, I am silent for a while before asking, "What does it all mean?"

"Lux Cars will soon be barking up our tree. Trust me; they will be looking to shake loose much more than a hundred units a day from us. Fail to cope, get the ax."

My heart is beating erratically as we fall back into thought. On the big screens, the commercials run out. The commentator's voice comes on and booms out in excitement. Fans get thrown back into football frenzy. Just then, reruns of the futile goal-attempts, splash over the screens. Jeering fills the air. Copious drinking sets forth. Just a normal soccer evening at a bar.

I order a non-alcoholic drink and take a swig from it. "You know what?" I finally say, brightening up a little after a minute's thought.

"What's to know?"

"I think we will be fine."

"How can you be so sure?"

"I included futuristic capacity within the project's parameters."

"You did?"

"Yes."

"How much?"

"Two hundred percent."

Kevin simply stares in amazement, totally perplexed. "How did you anticipate Lux Cars?"

"To tell you the truth, I didn't."

"Then how?" he asks, genuinely bewildered.

"It's my job to anticipate futuristic capacity," I say. "Every project manager worth his salt does it."

"Damn!" lets out Kevin. "You mean to tell me I worried for nothing?"

"Maybe not," I respond solemnly. "Let's hope Lux's upcoming onslaught stays within the expected futuristic capacity."

Kevin nods just as solemnly. Neither of us dares mention the obvious. It would be a disaster if Lux Cars demanded more than we could offer. They would walk out on us. We would be done for.

On screen, the whistle blows once more to set off the second half's action. The patrons cheer. The chanting resumes. I get swept up in it all and become just as frenzied as everyone else. No worries for now. No lingering fears. For the moment, I'm happy.

Thirty-four

AN EVENING WALK through the heart of town with Elise helps me clear my mind. We amble along without a care in the world. Cool breeze, sweet banter, brightly lit showcase windows, —it's all fantastic! And I'm feeling fabulous. This is wonderful.

We weave in and out of pedestrians. High above us, a helicopter flies in lazy circles with no apparent destination in mind. It's just there, droning on, like an added accessory to the town. No one pays it any attention. I haven't looked up once.

At this hour, Johannis Street looks docile and normal. Colorful clubs, cozy bars, glitz and glamor, the usual. The nightlife is just coming to life. And party people are streaming in and out of everywhere, including pouring all over the sidewalks.

I take Elise's hand in mine and squeeze it slightly. She smiles radiantly up at me, those gorgeous eyes drawing me in, till I lose all sense of time and place. This love I'm sure, will consume me forever.

Someone roughly bumps into me from behind. It happens a second time. I curse with great feeling and look over my shoulder. Two muscular men in casual jeans and black jackets, staring back at me. Their cold eyes are suddenly very familiar. Despite the red caps pulled low over their faces, I immediately recognize them from pictures I've seen on TV. And my heart goes cold. *Handal's associates!* My heart begins to hammer. These very two men have been at the center of a police APB that has so far dredged up nothing for the last couple of days, and now, out of the blue, they're in my face. In that very moment, as the realization of our predicament sinks in, one of them presses the muzzle of a pistol into my side.

Oh dear God! Oh my dear God! I think over and over as a cold chill runs down my spine. *I'm done for. I'm finished! This is the end.*

Elise sees the expression on my face, turns back, and freezes.

"Put your hands where we can see them. Understand?"

I nod, but only barely.

"Don't make a sound," continues the same thug. "Don't alert anyone. Do as we say, and nobody gets hurt, okay?"

I don't believe him.

Elise seems to share my opinion too. She sees the gun sticking in my side and begins to moan, eyes growing larger as they fill up with dread. Goodness gracious me, is she about to scream? Thoughts of bullets tearing through my rib cage send my hand flying up to her mouth, which, to my amazement, is continually opening wider than I've ever seen it go, a clear indication she's getting ready for one terrific blast of sound that'll very likely be a Guinness World Record attempt at waking up the dead. Just in time, my fingers clamp over her trembling lips. So, the action in her body goes elsewhere. She is now shaking. Violently. All over.

"It's okay, Elise. Everything will be fine. We'll do as they say. We'll be fine. Trust me," I urge and cajole her, wink and trying to smile, but sadly, miserably failing at even convincing myself. Our situation is dire. I know this. Elise knows this. Neither of us has a clue as to what's about to happen.

"Walk," the second man orders.

We stumble forward on shaky legs. I can't help but think we're sheep being led to the slaughter. How blind can all these pedestrians be? Not a single person here notices our predicament? A few empty stares from one or two onlookers is all we get.

My throat constricts with the overwhelming urge to shout out for help. I know this would be foolish. I do my best to stifle it.

Resistance is futile. With growing despair, we walk down the street as directed, certain that this is the last day we'll ever see the light. We shuffle past Titty-Twister and Rosenkeller. Further down, late-night revelers sit at numerous sidewalk tables filled with tall drinks and mugs of beer which they now and again lift up and sip as they catch up on the goings-on in each other's lives. Everyone's happy. And carefree. No one discerns our desperation. Which is increasing with every moment that goes by.

Up ahead, a group of teenagers boisterously celebrating life closes in on us. A young lady in their midst offers me a slug from her wine bottle. The assailant behind me roughly shoves her away. She swears. Cold steel digs into my back with renewed vigor. The wine-girl doesn't sense anything's amiss. She doesn't alert the police, no sirens, nothing dramatic happens. I want to curse. I feel like crying. I do neither.

Clearly, our attackers are pros. Not once does anyone spot their guns, — which, for now, they've chosen to conceal beneath their flimsy newspapers. I bet the news on them dates back to last week. *I laugh at this in my mind. How cliché. I hate these thugs. I hate their guts.* But all these thoughts do not help me in the least bit. The fear in my own gut is growing exponentially. I am barely keeping it together. I keep my mouth shut and walk on.

A single black SUV with darkened windows parked fifteen meters down the block catches my eye. The driver's door opens a tiny crack. My overly strained heart begins to race wildly. An irrational fear grips me as the crack ever so slowly widens.

What now?

My assailant jams his pistol into the small of my back. I'm forced forward. Beside me, Elise suffers the same fate. Suddenly, the last man we were expecting to meet again, sticks his head outside the car, glimmers at the two of us. And that's when Elise loses it. She screams in shock. She screams again. The sound tears through the night, loud, shrill, deafening, paralyzing, and utterly terrifying.

All at once, all hell breaks loose. The helicopter that has been droning up there all along is suddenly very near. Extremely near, powerful searchlights turning the surrounding darkness into day. At the same time, a voice in earnest competition with Elise's horrendous scream booms out of a megaphone, "This is the police! You are surrounded! Drop your weapons! Get out of the car! Hands up! I repeat: hands up! Now!"

My hands shoot skywards.

A dozen men in drug-enforcement-agency uniforms materialize from the surrounding side streets and converge upon us. More come streaming in from the nearby parking lot, all charging like a rugby team and I'm the ball. Several pedestrians scatter and run for dear life. I want to run. Others scream hysterically. I want to scream. And agents, god bless their sweet hearts, close in from all directions, as if headed right for me. And I'm frozen, rooted to the spot. Completely immobilized. Terrified beyond measure. Simply waiting for death.

In seconds we are hopelessly surrounded.

In his attempt to get away, Handal puts his foot down on the gas pedal. Tires squeal. The pungent smell of burning rubber fills the air. The SUV shoots forward as agents take aim and fire in rapid succession. A volley of bullets thuds into the car's wheels which deflate with a loud pop. Handal loses control. The SUV skids dangerously toward mortified onlookers, before flipping into the air. In slow motion, it moves, hangs in the air for an unusually long second, then plunges, turns upside down, and with a mighty bang, crashes back onto the ground on its roof. Shards of glass fly everywhere as its windows burst outward. With unspent momentum, it careens on its roof away from Elise and I. The screeching of metal scraping on tarmac fills the air and the surrounding night sky, forcing everyone with free fingers to plug their ears and wince. Finally, the shattered vehicle comes to a rest a good distance away from us, in the nearby flower bed.

Handal Hoams is plainly visible. The clearly bewildered drug lord is just lying against the SUV's roof, motionless, folded in half with his legs over his chest, a big fat question mark written all over his unbelieving face. He certainly didn't see this coming. To be fair to him, I didn't either, but still, the moment is undeniably priceless. I burn it into my memory.

Out of the blue, Special Agents Kirling and Moneypot are once again in our lives. The two are zipping down cords hanging from either side of the helicopter, swiftly rushing toward the ground like avenging eagles. Just like last time at the White Rose, they do not disappoint. Intent on terrifying everyone within earshot, they proceed to shout out a volley of commands at the top of their voices.

Oh boy. Here we go again.

Kirling's facial expression is deathly menacing.

Moneypot's contorted face looks like something out of a horror movie.

The effect these two have on me is completely electrifying. Like last time, I am frozen and rooted to the spot, if anything, this time more than ever.

Beside me, a puppy whine escapes Elise's trembling lips.

Kirling's scary appearance is the final straw that pushes me over the edge and into full-blown panic. It's at this moment that I remember my panic button for the first time since the ordeal began. There's a look of surprise mingled with a little bit of hope on my face doing havoc to my face.

I've been wearing this flimsy gadget every single day without fail and even begun taking it for granted. Right now, it's dangling from my frozen neck, under my fully buttoned-up shirt, pressed up against my frozen chest, waiting for action. My equally frozen hand is in the same vicinity, trying ever so desperately to calm my totally frozen heart. Though my index finger is just as stiff with fear as the rest of me, I manage to move it slightly and reach my panic button. Then I start to press. And by George, I am pressing. I press it for all I am worth, then press it some more. I press and press, and as if this were not enough, press and press and simply continue pressing. There's a look of frenzy on my face that's just as frozen as the rest of me. I continue pressing even as I finally realize just how redundant this action is, I mean, law enforcement is already here, is it not? No need to call for them again. Or is there? But panic has me in a vise grip. And I have a panic button. So, I guess I'm stuck on press overdrive, and quite frankly, I'm beginning to fear just how much physiotherapy my poor finger will need after this.

A lightning-quick reassessment of the situation brings our would-be captors to an astonishing realization. Their quest is over. The ship is sinking, and it's time to bail out. In the blink of an eye, they lose their pistols in the nearby bushes and try to act like they were just reading newspapers, you know, trying to catch up on the day's news, when suddenly, the sky is lighting up and sh** is going down.

About two dozen highly skeptical agents watch their every move.

Thug One and Thug Two take to acting like two simply unlucky guys who somehow ended up caught in a sudden crossfire. It's a tough act to sell. One sinks to the floor in a heap, feigning mortal pedestrian fear. Two whistles something out of a *Tom and Jerry* cartoon. He looks so amazingly innocent, that I almost forget the guns in the bush.

Elise finds this utterly ridiculous and bursts out in hysterical laughter.

Lucky her. She can afford to laugh. Me, I am still frozen solid. Only my button-pressing finger is moving. I think the rest of my joints are starting to creak.

Meanwhile, Special Agent Kirling makes it down from the helicopter in one piece. On touching down, he half crawls, half crouches toward the SUV, gun cocked, action ready, helmet firmly in place, eyes fixed on the driver's door and vocal cords ready for extreme sound.

The minute Special Agent Moneypot's feet strike the pavement, she wastes no time adopting a snake approach.

What the... How can this be? My eyes bulge in wonder at the impossible spectacle before me. Seeing an officer of the law slither on the ground like a poisonous puff adder takes some getting used to. In fact, this defreezes my neck, and to my surprise, I notice my head begin to move, swing, more like it, fully in her direction. I watch avidly as she zips across the earth like an eel during happy hour and zeroes in on the other side of the SUV, successfully cutting off Handal's line of retreat.

This is unbelievable. Such flexibility? If my eyes get any larger, I think they will pop.

"Get! Out! Now!" shouts Special Agent Kirling.

I cringe, even though this command isn't directed at me.

"Don't move! Or I shoot!" cries out the slithering Special Agent Moneypot.

Handal, processing both commands with growing horror, remains frozen, folded in half, legs over his chest, and begins to shake. First, he looks at Kirling. Then, at Moneypot. Their unrelenting demeanors dare him to defy them. Stay where he is? Or crawl out? Which of these decisions will earn him a bullet? It's at this point he realizes he's in the wrong business altogether. Being a drug lord is pretty damn hard, and right now, it's just turned into a total nightmare. Poor chap. Poor, poor chap.

It takes a while and lots of confusion, but eventually all three criminals give up, are duly handcuffed, and whisked away. The guns are recovered from the bushes.

Elise and I spend a few minutes talking to the agents. They fill us in on what will happen sometime in the future; lawyers, trials, testimonies, that kind of stuff. For now, they have lots of paperwork to handle, so, without much ado, they finally excuse themselves.

We thank them and watch them go.

Pedestrians discuss the living daylights out of the incident, till there is nothing more to discuss. They, too, eventually disperse.

Elise and I stay in town a while longer. We are both in urgent need of a beer. After an hour, color comes back in our faces. Once again, life is worth living.

"Phew! That-Was-Awesome!" I'm looking at Elise, eyes shifty, attempting a smile.

"She glares at me and snarls."

I shut up for good.

Thirty-five

A BARRAGE OF OVERZEALOUS REPORTERS rush to the White Rose on Friday morning. Every single news network is keen for inside scoop on the story. Elise and I are under siege. I can't leave. I can't go to work. The perfect excuse I needed. I call in sick.

Lucky for me, Duncan is quite understanding. He saw some of last night's action on this morning's news and still can't believe I made it out alive. I convince him that very nearly didn't happen. He's all sympathy, telling me to take the whole day off. The project can cope for so long without me, he says.

He wishes me a quick recovery before adding he expects to see me in the office bright and early on Monday morning.

"It's a deal, boss," I assure him.

No sooner's he off the phone, when I'm up in the air, whooping and chasing Elise about the house in dead earnest. She cries out in joy and dares me to catch her. We go off screaming, laughing, and giggling from one room to the other, fit as fiddles and bristling with energy. Yes, that's right; we are both in tip-top form. Never been better. Nobody needs to recover from anything here.

ABOUT MIDDAY, the reporters start to disperse. Shortly thereafter my phone rings. It's Duncan Beike. I start to fret. *What happened to recovery time?*

"How are you doing?" he asks.

"Still woozy," I respond in my best groggy voice. "But I will be as good as new tomorrow."

"Nice to hear that," says the CEO.

Elise starts to giggle.

I admonish her. In all truth, I am indeed feeling woozy. Chasing her about is hard work. But that's the least of my concerns right now. A rather disturbing note in Duncan's voice has set me on the path of worry. It's obvious a pressing issue has come up. There's something on the tip of his tongue. I hold my breath and wait for him to get this load off his chest.

"Something's happened," he finally says, his voice quiet and brooding. "We need to meet and discuss it."

"Oh. Okay." I make a sad face to Elise.

She acts bewildered.

"Of course," Duncan adds, "since you cannot come to work, we'll come to you."

"Here?" The surprise in my voice is clearly audible.

"Yes, why not?"

"I'm at home!"

"The White Rose isn't it?" He inquires expectantly.

I'm speechless for a second. I've been bragging a lot at work about my new designer home, and, now that there's a reason to come over, Duncan doesn't hesitate. He wants to see where I live and how I live. I'm warming up to the idea, feverishly looking forward to it. It's time to show and tell.

He lets me know he's not coming over alone.

The more, the better, I say to him.

All of Displaytek's think tank will be accompanying him.

Super, boss. Bring them all. I can't wait. I cordially invite them to lunch at the White Rose.

SHORTLY BEFORE TWO O'CLOCK, Duncan and company make it through the electronic front gates and into the outer circle of forest around the White Rose. The elegant white Mercedes-Maybach Pullman limousine emerges into the inner circle covered with flower beds and green lawns. It moves along the curving driveway, right up to the roundabout before the house, negotiating it before finally pulling to a stop at the foot of the grand staircase leading up to the house.

His driver gets the door. Duncan steps out. So do his passengers. They all admire the vast estate, then take in the exquisite nakedness of the female statue in the middle of the roundabout, and ask if it's fashioned after my girlfriend, Elise.

"Absolutely not," I respond.

"Okay, Madonna, perhaps?" Asks Kevin with a cheeky smile.

I stand tall and proud and never stop smiling. Eventually, I invite them indoors. We make straight for the dining room.

The White Rose dining room is large, with lovely pictures of abstract art hanging on its light-cream walls. Its table can seat a total of eighteen people. Lars, Kevin, Elise, and I, sink into four seats in the middle of one side of the table. Henrik, Christine, Matthias, and Duncan, sink into the four chairs across from us. Sunlight streams in through huge windows. It's slightly warm. The mood is pleasant.

Our cook, who's barely a week old on the job, has been extremely efficient. As expected, lunch is served at two on the dot; grilled salmon with avocado salsa and a light wine to ease digestion. It's delicious. As we bite into it, the meeting commences.

The CEO mentions our gravest concern. "Got a call from Lux Cars this morning," he begins. Suddenly, everyone is all ears. "They are demanding one hundred units more or no deal," he says with a pained look on his face. "That totals to two hundred units just for them, which as you are all aware, practically amounts to all the output increase we set out to attain."

Kevin temporarily stops chewing and fixes me with a stare that says, *I told you this was coming, didn't I?*

A mixture of incredulity and concern flares across the faces of Henrik and Lars.

"That's preposterous!" Cries out Matthias, white eyebrows and white mustache dancing in fury. "They promised to stick with us if we stepped up deliveries to one hundred units a day. Now they are demanding two hundred a day overnight? Who do they think we are, Santa Claus?" His steel-gray eyes blaze with anger.

"Contractual obligations cannot be demanded in the event of impossibility to perform," Christine offers with legal authority. "We could plead insurmountable obstacles and be let off the hook." She adjusts her huge black-rimmed glasses for effect, light-brown hair glimmering and cascading all about her torso.

Seconds pass as we digest her comment.

"Wouldn't that mean losing the contract?" Lars asks.

Duncan stares at the sandy-haired Lars with cold, steely, unforgiving eyes. The message is loud and clear: Displaytek is not losing a client. Not today, not tomorrow. In fact, not ever. "Could anyone tell me how we can hold on to Lux Cars?" His booming voice comes through partially gritted teeth. The scent of imminent danger creeps into our corporate jungle.

With my wits about me, I carefully form an answer. "Lux Cars wants two hundred units a day, right?"

"Yes, they do," replies the CEO, eyes rolling in exasperation. I have just repeated the obvious.

"I was asked to develop a strategy for producing two hundred units a day," I press on, confident of what I'm about to say. "This, might I add, I successfully did."

"Yeah, yeah, get on with the point," Kevin comments, his impatience getting the better of him.

"I chose a lean line approach as you all know. As is written in my project proposal, lean engineering advocates futuristic capacity in new installations."

"I beg your pardon?" Across from me, Duncan's burly frame rises an inch taller. His chiseled jaw flexes.

"I doubled the capacity to four hundred units," I say, calm, collected, looking him in the eye, daring him to fire me. And earnestly praying he doesn't.

"Are you saying we can produce four hundred units a day?" Christine asks in surprise.

"Yes, that's exactly what I'm saying," I confidently respond while sneaking a sideways glance at Duncan, our sometimes stoic and often hard to predict CEO.

Another pin-drop silence follows suit. This one though is laced with hope.

Lars Roeske rubs his sandy goatee excitedly.

Henrik Wang's oriental eyes do a little dance.

Christine smiles happily, and Duncan simply stares at me for long moments. He loosens his tie and takes it off. Presently he undoes a button or two of his starched white shirt and tries to relax. His coat stays on. A slight smile begins to form on his face. "Well, David, I take it we can comfortably accommodate this unexpected influx of business from Lux Cars?"

"Certainly," I respond, "without so much as breaking a sweat."

He tilts his head, suddenly stiff again. "What of our other clients' needs?" he asks.

"Business as usual," Kevin says, swiping a speck of salsa off his burgundy sweater vest. It lands squarely on the long sleeve of his green shirt. He curses bitterly and then looks up at us. "With a futuristic capacity of four hundred units a day, any reasonable increase in output-demand made by our other clients will be easily met, no strain whatsoever."

"Perfect!" exclaims Duncan. He briefly allows a bright smile to play on his face for a second or two. Then promptly kills it. Once more he's the unpredictable CEO we all have come to know, fear and love. "Okay," he says, squinting at us. The cold eyes of steel have returned. "Here's the deal. Today is the twenty-eighth of November. We have until the third of December to convince Lux Cars that we are up to the task. Words won't work. Concrete facts and figures will. We need to convince them. Any suggestions?"

Kevin clears his throat and says, "We could prepare a detailed projection of expected production capacity and show it to Lux Cars. What do you think?" He fixes Matthias with a questioning gaze.

"That might help," the gray-haired production manager says solemnly before adding, "Any suggestions? David?"

"A production simulation, perhaps?"

"Why?" Henrik asks.

"Simulations are a beauty," I reply. "Not only are such demonstrations crystal clear, but also depict conditional branching and rework looping. Besides, they are easy to analyze, concise, and detailed. Probably the best thing about them is the way they reveal our invested energy and indicate just how well prepared we are."

"Excellent," Duncan booms out excitedly. "Production simulation it is then. Any further comments?"

"Yeah," says Henrik, long twang clearly evident. This draws a rather nasty stare from the CEO. His request for comments was rhetorical and not meant to be answered. He slits his eyes at Henrik, daring our IT manager to douse his flames of hope. "We have no production-simulation software, boss," reveals the young man.

"That's preposterous," cries out Duncan. "Why?"

Henrik Wang stutters and sputters, his Asian accent more pronounced than ever before. "Eh, we have never needed one, boss."

"Are you kidding me?" Duncan growls. Henrik slinks lower in his chair. The rest of us suddenly remember to eat. Cutlery sinks into food with renewed earnest. No one wants to look up.

"Okay," Duncan takes a deep breath and lets it out slowly. "How long would it take you to acquire one?" he asks.

"A day. Maybe two. After that, setting up the software and making necessary adjustments could take another day. Then there is the issue of getting acquainted with it…"

"How long in total?"

"Three, maybe four business days," spells out Henrik.

"Jumping kangaroos," breathes out Duncan. "Unacceptable!" The thick vein in his neck pulses.

I shudder.

No one dares to speak.

After a while, a deeply disturbed Duncan resumes talking. "I want this production simulation to be ready by Monday. How can we make this happen?" He glares at us.

We search our brains for a solution.

An idea comes to me. "Well …" I start.

"Yes, David? Speak up, boy."

I hesitate a second. What the heck. If he wants to jump kangaroos at me, so be it. I spill the beans. "Jena's University of Applied Sciences offers such software to students in its engineering labs."

"Yes?"

"Ah, yeah, and… well, I have used it before."

Pin-drop silence follows these words, which I'm now regretting. Where they foolish?

Everyone stares at me.

Finally, Duncan breaks into a sunny smile and booms out, "Excellent!" He beams and says, "David, Kevin, you will both sneak into that student lab and prepare a production simulation. Is that understood?"

"Sneak?" Kevin's completely bamboozled. The look on his face? Priceless. I'd be laughing right now if it wasn't for the fact that I'm just as concerned about all this sneak-talk as Kevin is.

"Get a hold of yourself, boy!" Duncan exclaims indignantly. "Were you expecting me to loan you an army too? Maybe take the place by storm in the process?"

"What? No!" Cries out a most horrified Kevin, not quite believing any of the things he's hearing on this very unusual day at work. Has the world gone mad? Has Duncan?

"So, no army? Good! Sneak it is!" Duncan laughs. He slaps the dining table, totally happy with the way the meeting is turning out.

Kevin and I look at each other. I shrug. He sighs. Our fates are sealed.

"One more thing," Duncan adds.

"Yes, boss?" we reply in unison.

"Remember to dress like students. If you get thrown out of that lab, you're fired! Capish?"

"Oh, boss," Kevin groans, a splendid show of dismay on display across his features.

We all break out in boisterous laughter.

The rest of lunch is pleasant.

We enjoy the meal and have a good time amidst jokes and laughter, each of us now fully savoring the promising taste of the great future about to come.

Duncan asks how recovery from my near-death experience is coming along. I tell him slow, but steady... I'm on the mend.

He allows me to stay home.

At three, my guests depart for Displaytek. No sooner do they drive off, when Elise and I resume our recovery regimen. We frolic about like teenagers for most of the weekend.

Thirty-six

THIS MORNING'S breakfast of bacon and eggs is made a dash more palatable by the incident analysis on the dramatic arrest of the now-infamous drug lord Handal Hoams, streaming live, from the thirty-six-inch TV embedded into the kitchen wall before us. I lift my giant mug of green tea and take a thoughtful sip. Elise, who's also seated beside me at the kitchen counter, twitches noticeably when we learn the drug-enforcement agency had an eye on us the whole time.

Of course, they only mobilized a strike force and moved into position the minute they received a tip that Handal was not only in the country but in our immediate vicinity.

The beautiful incident analyst has it from good authority (Special Agent Kirling), that yes, Elise and I were bait, but no, we were never in any real danger.

What the heck? I want to scream blue murder. *Never in any grave danger, they say? I very nearly died!* I look from the analyst to Elise in vehement protest, but the nasty snarl curling up her upper lip makes me shut up and keep still. She's boiling with indignation more than I am. I turn back to the TV. I try my eggs. Then take another sip from my mug. I keep watching.

Handal Hoams's notoriety for carrying a grudge is well known. So, the drug-enforcement agency, assisted by the police, had us well covered we duly learn. Of course, we were not allowed to know this, says the analyst, with very good reason. According to Special Agent Moneypot, Handal may have tapped our phones and may have been listening or watching every move we made. Tipping him off would have been a disaster. He might have disappeared into the woodwork, never to be heard from again. So, keeping us in the dark was a necessary evil, she concludes. Finally, a couple of photos from the incident air in sequence.

The agents' antics Thursday night still haunt us. Elise says her blood is still not flowing properly after the incident. I dare not question this strange remark. Instead, I suggest a massage. She smiles indulgently.

As for me, the minute Special Agent Kirling's image splashes onto the screen, strange things happen to my emotions. I feel the need to panic. I hiss at the TV while reaching for my no-longer-present panic button. My eyes are dancing wildly. Elise very nearly dies of laughter.

At eight, I head out for work.

SIMULATING a production sequence of processes isn't really that difficult. All one needs are appropriate simulation software, intricate knowledge of actual production parameters, and a reasonable degree of software deftness. I can't for the life of me figure out why Displaytek doesn't have the necessary software yet. To think this company has never created a production simulation? Unbelievable! By the last count, there isn't a better way to troubleshoot or push the frontiers of continuous-improvement processes. Simulations are beautiful, unadulterated genius, true works of wonder, and today, Monday, first of December, Kevin and I head out to create Displaytek's first-ever inaugural simulation.

We speed off in light traffic and arrive minutes later at the bustling University of Applied Sciences. It all comes back to me as we negotiate the corridors of knowledge. The many hours of hard study. Countless moments of daydreaming. Endless nights of brazen parties. They all fill my head in a flash, leaving me a little overwhelmed. Had I chosen to do a master's, I would still be living this life. How I miss it.

It's only been a few weeks since I was last here. Nevertheless, it feels like ages. I spot a few new changes, like a yellow-and-blue information kiosk in the main building's entryway. We quickly slip through into an adjoining corridor.

I guide Kevin through the lesser-known passageways as I answer some of his questions about my student life. One person I'm fervently hoping not to run into is Professor Sigmund. He's the university's leading authority on production, technology, and operations management. He also taught me how to make production simulations. I was the apple of his eye.

We make it to the high-tech computer room without running into anyone I know. Timidly, I poke my head through the door, expecting to find a class in session. Kevin does the same, exclaiming with joy at what he sees; no lecturer up front, only a couple of random students seated at ten rows of tables. No authority figure in sight. Beautiful!

Before each student is a thirty-two-inch monitor showing simulations in various stages of preparation. It's practice hour, we realize. This means there is nothing to stop us from doing what needs to be done. So, in keeping with Duncan Beike's order, we sneak into the room undetected. James Bond music plays in my head as we quietly slouch into the seats nearest the door. *This is exciting!* I can hardly believe just how much I'm enjoying this secret-agent lifestyle.

We act like a couple of regulars, as if we have been here the whole time, just popped out for a coffee or a pee. Now we are back. Don't mind us, students; just keep on working. Your diligence is bound to pay off.

The charade is unnecessary. No student looks in our direction. They couldn't care less who just walked in the door. They all have their own headaches to deal with.

Hardly have I switched on the monitor before me than someone comes in the door and startles me clear out of my skin as he shouts, "Elbert? David Elbert?"

My heart stops and then starts thudding inside my rib cage like a runaway bull. I would know that overly confident, boisterous voice anywhere, anytime, anyhow. Professor Sigmund, the very one who evaluated my thesis presentation, who was present during my graduation, who helped mold me into the man I am today, and the very last person I wanted to run into on this very day. He must have stepped out for a pee or maybe a cup of coffee. Or both? Now he's back. And zeroing in on me. Like a dart to a dartboard.

Sigmund is more than just your average simulation professor. More than anything, he's a know-how geek with an undying penchant for the new. I attended his classes almost two years back, during my fourth semester, and never once did he conclude a lesson without colorful mention of the innovation industry. Sigmund wanted us spearheading cutting-edge technology. He wanted this so badly he could taste it. And since I was his ace student, he would stare at me when beseeching the class to take jobs in the said sector, and I would actively ponder this, letting him know just how actively I was pondering it.

After a few months in his class, ...well, ...I caught the bug. I remember telling him on many occasions that I would invent the next generation of simulation software. How I enjoyed telling him this. And how he loved hearing it.

At this moment, like so many times in the past, the big man is standing before me in his favorite checkered suit with matching hat, both of which are the very same color as his copious brown hair, his face still as hairy as a grizzly bear's. He's staring at me, waiting for me to speak.

"Hello, Professor Sigmund," I say with a smile. But my head's in turmoil. My beloved professor is about to find out I'm not spearheading the birth of new technology. "How are you?"

"Fine, fine, thank you," he says. His eyes dazzle as he looks at me, his one and only star in a world full of mundane people. "And how about you?"

"I am good," I reply.

Curiosity burns inside of him, eating him inside out. He tries to hold his tongue. The muscles on his face twitch erratically with so much unrelenting strain, that for a minute, I really do believe he's going to explode. Pressure builds to critical mass. Finally, it bursts. Out pops the question, the one he just couldn't hold back. He's talking fast, as though trying to get it all out before the heart attack strikes. The words tumble over each other. "What are you up to these days?"

"Working."

"Where?"

"Displaytek."

"As?"

"Project manager."

This is a fully-fledged interrogation. I break into a sweat.

The good old Professor Sigmund doesn't notice. He's beside himself with excitement. "Software development?"

"Actually, lean production design," I say with a cough, trying to muffle my voice. Don't get me wrong. I am extremely proud of my job. I love it so fiercely I would be willing to fight a grizzly bear to prove it. I know good things are in store for me. All I have to do is work diligently, and it will all come together. If I pull this project off, I will get Displaytek into the big leagues. When this is done, trust me, I'll be a made man.

I just know it. Companies will come knocking on my door, looking for my services. I will be able to take my pick, name my price, state my working hours, and even open up shop as a private consultant. One day, I will be rich beyond my wildest dreams. I tell you, I will be swimming in money.

However, at this moment, Professor Sigmund's perspective is not lost on me. According to him and the slowly dying light in his eyes, I am now a lost cause, a statistic, a fallen genius, a tragic loss of inventive talent. The grieving bear of a man sweeps me along into his sinking mood. I start to feel like someone dear just passed away and didn't even leave me a penny. Blistering barnacles! I need consolation.

Kevin, who, for the first time since I've known him, is not wearing a sweater vest and is dressed like a typical student, stares incomprehensibly from me to Professor Sigmund, earnestly trying to figure out what's going on here. Failing to make it all out, he nudges me for an explanation.

Professor Sigmund sees this from the corner of his eye, sighs pitifully, and then asks, "So who's your friend?"

"Kevin Koch, my workmate," I say in introduction.

"I see," Sigmund replies. There is a faraway look in his eyes. His shoulders sag so dangerously low, I fear he might dislocate them. He looks forlornly at me.

I'm barely hanging on to my sense of self-worth. *Please, professor, just go away. Go pick on a student.*

To show him there's hope for me yet, I stand up tall, square my shoulders, and try to sound impossibly important as I say, "We are here to prepare a production simulation for a major, extremely vital client. He's big, this client." I stress heavily on the words major, extremely vital, client, big, this client. My voice is deep, almost as resonating as his.

"Sure," croaks Sigmund, barely impressed. He wallows in bereavement for a second, sighs in quick succession for another two, then like a lost soul, quietly adds, "I will let you get on with it then, my boy." Slowly, he turns about, muttering under his breath. We watch in amazement as he reenacts a one-man funeral procession all the way to his desk up front. The way he's acting, I might as well be truly dead. I really do feel sorry for him. Or for me? Oh boy! This is very confusing.

The Professor settles down to drown his sorrows in a novel. He's on standby. If a student needs his help, he'll be up in a beat. That's Sigmund.

"What in goodness' name was all that?" Kevin is stumped.

In a nutshell, I explain to him what just went down. He laughs. Then we settle down to the task at hand.

For the past five minutes, I've been going at it with little to no results. I'm just discovering that bustling up a simulation after two years without practice can be unpleasantly tricky. As if this were not enough, Kevin is now breathing down my neck. He's watched me click on several rubrics, one after the other, in vain. He's followed the cursor with narrowed eyes as I've meandered through the options. Time and again, I've closed these very rubrics almost immediately and tried my luck elsewhere on the screen, only to go back to the former rubrics. Now, his nerves are shot. And thanks to all that squinting, his eyes are bloodshot too. *"What the heck's he doing?"* he seems to be thinking, while looking at me. Finally, he can't take it anymore. He opens his mouth and asks, "What's wrong?" His voice is loud. Hushed conversations break up and heads swing in our direction. Hanging over a blackboard behind the professor is a single sign that says "Silence."

"Shh!" I whisper. "Keep your voice down." I look to Professor Sigmund. If he heard Kevin and decides to come over, I will surely die of shame.

"What's wrong?" Kevin asks in a quiet whisper this time.

"Nothing. Just trying to get a feel for it."

"Is the software new?" he asks, pushing for clarification.

"No. Been a while; that's all." I click on a few more symbols on the screen. Just as many warning tones get thrown back at me.

For two minutes more, as Kevin watches this sick action, he drums his pencil-thin fingers on the wooden desk. I feel his agitation climbing. His color changes from white to red and almost crosses over into a dark purple. Suddenly, he stoops low and whispers, "So I gather Sigmund was your simulation professor?"

"Yes."

"Is he good?" he asks.

"The best," I reply.

At this, he straightens up and looks dead ahead, then, suddenly, "Professor Sigmund?" he yells out.

In shock, I look up at Kevin, who's now busily beckoning the professor over as though he were a long-lost friend. Almost immediately, Sigmund slaps his novel down, as if this is what he's been waiting for all along. This, I know from past experience, is what Sigmund lives for. Intelligent conversation, scintillating classroom action, the transfer of knowledge. Such moments are the very highlight of his every day, the one true life force that courses through his veins. And now, it appears, at this very minute, he's about to get some. With a dazzling smile, he strides over, almost skidding to a stop beside my desk. "Do you two need any help?" he asks brightly.

"No," I say.

"Yes," Kevin counters.

"Perfect," replies Sigmund. He draws up a chair and sits. "What seems to be the problem?"

"The software! It's acting up," Kevin laments.

Sigmund can't believe his ears. Of all the lame excuses ever given, this one must surely top them all. The professor opens his mouth to speak and then thinks better of it. Instead, he rolls his chair between us and goes to work. "What you boys need is a quick crash course," he says in the authoritative voice of a confident genius.

I sigh.

Kevin squares his shoulders in growing excitement.

And so, a private lecture begins.

From one rubric to the next, Sigmund shows us the ropes, explains fundamental sequences, shoots test questions to gauge our level of attentiveness, and lets us work out a few examples. He's a brilliant star, this professor. In no time at all, he gets me back in shape, then stands up and smiles profusely as he wishes us luck. Quickly, he retreats to his novel. A second later he's once again engrossed in it.

This time around, things are different. No warning sounds come back at me. No crazy pings. No heartaches. Kevin and I work steadily for an hour. At nine, we take a coffee break. A short excursion outside helps us clear our hyperactive minds. Then in we go again for the second round. We kick new ideas back and forth and implement several of them. Gradually, the simulation starts to take fantastic shape. It's growing beautifully. We eye it admiringly. And smile an awful lot.

In great detail, we include materials input and then move on to plan accruement of value. The energy coursing through our veins is indescribable. I love it. Kevin is charged. I am supercharged. It's like playing an awesome video game. We're having a ball.

At eleven, we come to an end. About half an hour of rigorous testing follows. Eventually, we get rid of all the tiny little bugs, leaving behind nothing but sweet, pure victory in their wake. At last, our creation is ready. And boy, do we have a masterpiece. I give Kevin a high five and laugh as he beams with joy. I knew we could do it. We're prepared. Lux Cars? Here we come.

Thirty-seven

ELISE AND I get a formal invitation to appear as witnesses in the trial of Handal Hoams. A date for the hearing has been set and confirmed. A month from now, we will face him in court. I expect we will run into the colorful and highly volatile Special Agents Kirling and Moneypot on the said date. I shudder at the prospect. Wherever they go, crazy action and mortal fear seems to follow. I pray the courtroom environment will keep them docile. Living on the edge is dangerous. I've had more than my fair share of scary moments.

On Tuesday the second day of December, at exactly 8:30 in the morning, Duncan Beike flags off Kevin's trip to Lux Cars' headquarters in the neighboring town of Berlin. Kevin's mission is simple and complex all at once. "Keep Lux Cars' from bolting. Present the production simulation to the car manufacturer, win them over, and come back victorious, or not at all," were Duncan Beike's exact words to the poor lad.

Boy, does he have a task.

To be fair, we don't expect him to have any trouble. Still, his presentation is vital to Displaytek's future and continued growth. We try not to worry. I work like a donkey to stay calm. It will be a long day.

With a team of twelve, I set to work on the newly assembled workstations in the center of the production hall. The sense of purpose is invigorating. A feeling of brotherhood sizzles between us as we lay out our plan and get started. We map out item placement locations on and about the workstations. We stick name labels within these borders. By the time we're done, everything has a specific place. Fixtures, fittings, hardware installations, equipment, machines, kanban containers for raw materials, you name it. By this time, it's almost three o'clock. I stand back and admire it all. The finish line is at hand. We are almost there.

Kevin returns from Berlin late in the afternoon and appears to have a dark cloud hanging over his head. The minute I see him, a sinking feeling forms in the pit of my stomach and knots my intestines. On his face is a frantic expression. He looks haggard and scared. An overwhelming sense of foreboding overcomes me at once. He starts spilling his guts the minute he walks through my office door. "We're in trouble," he says in a cracking voice.

I dare not breathe as I wait for him to continue.

"Nils Eisenberger wants to be here on D-day," he says, haunted eyes darting every which way, trying to determine how close to completion we are.

"What?" I ask in surprise.

"He's coming to production kickoff," Kevin says hopelessly.

My world feels like it's coming to an end. "Why?" I ask. But of course, deep down inside, I know the answer.

"He wants to compare actual production to our clever simulation."

And at this remark, I almost crumble to pieces on the spot. Newly acquired systems and technology don't always run according to plan on the first day. Problems usually arise, and when that happens, solutions have to be found. Sometimes this leads to a tricky process of trial and error, chance and luck, and a whole lot of messy things can happen before things get better. It's no day for a client to visit. I tell Kevin this. He vigorously agrees with me.

"Why didn't you dissuade Nils Eisenberger then?"

"The bastard was adamant," replies Kevin. "He's coming, and that's that."

I moan. "Should actual production not match simulated target figures at kickoff?" I think out loud and ask Kevin at the same time, once again fully knowing the bleak answer.

"Then he walks. That's what he said. No more Lux Cars, no more big money, no more top client. He will leave us high and dry, David, of this, he's assured me. He'll go over to another supplier."

This is a nightmare. The primary goal of this project is to keep Lux Cars on board. With Lux Cars' CEO threatening to ditch us, what will become of this initiative? For the first time since we started, and despite our best efforts, I realize we're in grave danger. I take a minute to think and then reach a decision. This is not over yet. We are not going down without a fight. "It's time to prep the workers," I tell Kevin. "We need to finish the project ahead of time. We will go into elaborate systems testing a day after tomorrow. That's one whole day before schedule. If Nils Eisenberger is expecting us to give up that easy, he's in for a big surprise."

Kevin loves this and quickly goes out to inform everyone. The team's a sport. Everyone readily agrees to overtime. We stay on and work frantically until seven thirty in the evening.

On Wednesday, the third day of December, I walk into my office at seven, as usual, to work on my management progress reports. A memo on my desk catches my attention. It's from the CEO, probably placed here a few minutes ago. According to it, after lengthy deliberations, Timothy Lang has been placed in charge of materials replenishment. He is to take over his new responsibilities effective immediately.

I grip my heart in shock. The memo slips from my fingers and lazily glides to the floor. This turn of events spells danger for my best-laid plans. Timo? He's okay, but wouldn't Nick Neumann have been a better fit? I fall back into my seat and ponder my options with a knitted brow. Can I argue with Duncan about this? Or, can I check out Timothy, see if he's up to the job? I decide to do the latter.

I walk out of my office and directly into the materials-replenishment point. The place has been refurbished. Five massive silver metal shelves run the room's length from wall to wall, separated by wide aisles. They tower toward the ceiling, falling only a foot shy of it. Black twin containers stapled in piggyback fashion fill each tier. Larger containers at the bottom, smaller ones higher up the shelves. Each is filled with raw materials. There are about a thousand to twelve thousand parts in each, depending on part size. More importantly, each container has just enough material for a month's worth of production. I know this because that's how I planned it.

I walk through the shelves, admiring them. Presently, I run into Timo. The young lad is whistling a ballad while carrying out his new duties. He spots me coming and grows an inch taller.

"How's it coming along?" I ask.

"Super, boss," he replies, trademark toothy grin in place, all gums visible.

"No difficulties of any kind?"

"None that I can't handle," he says proudly.

"And the boys?"

"All doing great," he adds. "They are professionals." He beams at me and then points at Nick Neumann and Ludwig Beck. "See those two over there?"

I turn and look. Both are wearing elegant suits. They are dressed like twins and look like twins. The only difference is, one has a full head of black hair combed forward, styled to just fall short of forming a curtain over his eyes, while the other has a shiny, clean-shaven scalp. The two men are in the act of skillfully steering hydraulic work platforms in between the long rows of shelves. They are picking materials. I nod at Timothy, letting him know I see them. "What about them?" I ask.

"See the stacks of containers on their hydraulic work platforms?"

Most of the multicolored containers are a foot long and a foot wide. Some are smaller; others, slightly bigger. All in all, regular workstation containers. Nothing amazing, nothing out of the ordinary. Curious, I ask why he wants me to see them.

"Each container has a unique label," he says.

"The labels are known as pull codes," I tell him with a smile.

Unfazed, he continues, "Each pull code has picking and placement information."

"Care to give details?" My voice is nonchalant, my eyes piercing.

He takes a deep breath and then plunges into explaining pull codes. With each word, his excitement increases. He talks about their ingenuity. He tells me how they specify the quantity of material to fill into the container. The pitch of his voice slowly rises. His voice is filled with awe. Pull codes this. Pull codes that. Would I like to know their advantages? Without waiting for my reply, he starts to reel them off, counting on his fingers. I'm impressed by the depth of his understanding. He talks nonstop. I nod forever. He makes vivid comparisons. I do my best to picture each one, his lecture coming at me faster and faster. It's hard to keep up with the ever-changing scenes. Still, he zips from one to the next.

At one time, he compares pull codes to destination addresses. "Each pull code has two addresses," he says excitedly. One is a specific cubicle of a particular shelf in the materials-replenishment point. The other bears the number of a precise spot at a unique workstation. "Nick or Ludwig travel to the first address, where they fill up the container. Frank or Hans travel to the other, where they deposit the full container. It's a concerted effort. See for yourself," he says, his joy spilling over. He points to his left. This time, we are looking at Frank. "Thank God the party animal had a good night's sleep," says Timo. "Not once has he winked off since the action begun."

Good for you, Frank. Bravo! I follow the black-haired man with my eyes. He's rolling a trolley up against Ludwig's hydraulic work platform. As we watch, he picks up containers of raw materials from the hydraulic work platform and loads them, one after the other, onto his trolley. In two minutes, he's guiding his trolley into the production hall, which is just across the way, and bearing down on destination addresses to off-load containers on workstations. Both teams are well-oiled machines. Each man is aware we are racing against time. They all know what's at stake. I know what's at stake. Tomorrow, Thursday, fourth of December, we will carry out a systems test. The day after, lean-line production will kick off in the presence of Nils Eisenberger. Either we make it, or we don't. Everything must be perfect. There is no margin for error. I'm jittery and doing my best not to show it. At least Timothy and his boys seem to know what they are doing. I'm grateful.

Back in my office, I evaluate the project plan with a fine-tooth comb. My bases seem to be covered. Apart from the materials action going on and the forthcoming testing, no other part of the project remains outstanding. So, I focus on reporting updates. Every single party concerned with the project wants to know if we are in the clear. We might be nearing the end. But somehow, the end appears to be only the beginning. My nerves are on fire. I'm aware of every passing minute in this deathly quiet countdown.

Thirty-eight

THE MOMENT we've all been waiting for is finally here: the first day of lean-line operations. It goes without saying that management is overly optimistic. With good reason. Every possible scenario likely to pop up has been studied, analyzed, and in the end, adequately accounted for. Still, I find myself exceedingly nervous. As is always the case in such undertakings, about a million other unexpected things could still go wrong. So, obviously, my heart is racing. My blood is rushing through my veins and roaring in my ears. I twirl a penny through my shaking fingers just to give myself something else to focus on other than this unbearable suspense before kickoff. This only helps me a little. I'm barely calm.

My gaze roves the production hall as I look this way and that. Visual confirmation is critical. Is everything as it should be? Along the walls are the batch workstations. On each of them, business unfolds as usual. A different scene meets the eye along the center length of the production hall. Two compact rows, each containing ten state-of-the-art workstations interconnected by a series of electric conveyors. Every single one is fully stocked up and ready for the impending action on this decisive Friday. For now, they are unoccupied. But that will change presently. Other than this, nothing seems to be out of place. Still, I can't stop worrying. I'm a nervous wreck.

Assembly workers charge in at precisely this moment. Unlike me, they're engaged in that type of excited chatter that signals the dawn of a new era. They walk up confidently to their brand-new workstations and take their places. Watching them bolsters my confidence somewhat. "All will go well," I quietly tell myself. Everything's as it should be. We're in the clear.

Alongside the workstations is a temporary observation post—a simple long table with a line of chairs on its far side—set up early this morning. It's occupied by Matthias, Lars Roeske, me, and Duncan, in that order. To Duncan's left are four more empty places. We are expecting company any minute now.

As we wait for our honorable guests, we take in the assembly workers, who by now are firing up several computers and machines, thereby bringing the whole system to life. It's preparation time. The hour of action is almost upon us. I'm charged. This feeling is almost tangible.

At seven-fifteen on the dot, the Lux Cars delegation arrives. For the first time ever, I set eyes on their CEO, Dr. Nils Eisenberger. The man is a towering hulk with the presence of an Aztec warrior. He advances on stealthy feet toward us, looking every bit like a lion ready to pounce on its helpless prey. A foreboding severity hangs about his person, thick as a fog, sending cold chills down my spine. I make out his features and try to size him up. Mid-forties; black hair, thinning at the front, thick at the back; lean face; narrow hawk nose; trimmed, centimeter-long facial hair. He looks like a dangerous man; the type you don't mess around with under any circumstances. Probably would have made a good secret agent during the Cold War. Or a striking action hero in a big-budget sci-fi movie. I will go for the latter. The first one scares me to smithereens.

Mr. Action Hero is accompanied by three top-ranking Lux Cars officials—Brook Shields, Felix Flink, and Mark Davidson. All four are in expensive Giorgio Armani suits. The shortest of them, Felix, is built like a pit bull and carrying a rather large briefcase. The other three have their hands in their trouser pockets and are trying to look cool. For some reason, I am reminded of Mafia thugs. I watch them bear down on us like bad weather on a cold winter day, half expecting them to draw out guns and start shooting at us. My blood pressure is way off the charts as they come to a stop before me. We shake hands. My grasp is firm. My eye is roving all over their faces. I can't help it. I sense danger.

They introduce themselves as doctors, and boy, do they have titles. Doctor of Engineering for this, Doctor of Business for that, and so on. *Has any of them ever been in a gunfight?* I want to ask but think better of it. Instead, I sink back to my seat in relief, simply happy that none of them pulled a gun on me.

Dr. Nils Eisenberger quickly gets down to business. "This is it?" he asks in a deep, resonating voice. He's staring at the line of workstations before him.

I watch him with incredulous intensity as he takes his seat on Duncan's left. "The journey of a thousand miles begins with a single step, Dr. Nils," I say, trying to sound important, full of promise. *Why does he forget that he too probably had humble beginnings?*

His boys gape at our lean assembly line with stricken eyes. They are acting as if they've just discovered the bubonic plague and Ebola in one place at the same time and don't know whether to laugh or cry or call the government's health department at once.

"By this time next year," says Duncan, who's dressed in another one of his favorite metallic-gray Italian suits, "we will have a fully-fledged automatic production plant capable of churning out thousands of products in a single day, I promise you. This is just the beginning of great things to come, Dr. Eisenberger. We have great plans. Stick with us. It'll be worth your while."

Nils Eisenberger mumbles under his breath.

Just then, Kevin appears from the depths of Displaytek, engulfed in an aura of purpose and intensity. He makes his way across the production hall toward the two rows of lean production lines at the center, ever so careful to keep his eyes directly in front of him. His strides are well spaced. In his up-turned palms is a stack of glossy sequencing cards—no doubt, today's intended production volume.

Nils Eisenberger slips to the edge of his seat. He's waiting to see action.

A nearly ceremonial atmosphere hangs in the air as Kevin smiles. He's like a great magician about to reveal an amazing trick. We watch almost breathlessly as he showcases the sequencing cards, points at them, and draws our attention to details. "Each card has the product's name, product's picture, and the desired quantity to be produced," he says excitedly to his keenly attentive audience, then asks, "Any questions?"

No one speaks, so he places about four cards into the start trays at the head of each production line and then twirls about to face his appreciative audience once more. "Sequencing is now complete. Production will now commence in the same order I've placed the cards, from the first at the top to the last at the bottom. This show is now on the road, gentlemen," Kevin concludes with a broad smile and a slight bow.

True to his word, we watch as the athletic-bodied Bianca Winkler picks up the first card in her start tray, quickly sets an electronic counter to the desired production quantity of two hundred units, and then reaches for the colorful manual of assembly instructions fastened an arm's length away at eye level. She opens it to the relevant page. A winning smile springs up on her face. Countless wrinkles blossom beside each eye. She tucks a tuft of blonde hair behind her left ear and then passes the card to the next workstation in the line. From station to station, the assembly workers repeat the same actions until finally everyone is ready for assembly. Twenty-four highly trained professionals put on their business faces. It's time to show Lux Cars what we're made of. It's time to create real value.

Silence falls at our observation table. Bianca swings into action. With nimble fingers born of dexterous practice, she makes short work of building the day's first lean-line subassembly. The Lux Cars delegation is impressed. In two minutes and twenty seconds flat, she places it on the conveyor belt to her left. A sensor detects it, and the electronic counter drops by one: 199 units to go on this line. Simultaneously, the electric conveyor automatically powers up. With that, the first subassembly is in motion. It makes its way down the line, coming to a halt at the new-arrivals pad of the second workstation. Jonas Haas, a twentysomething lad with short hair a shade of burnt umber, promptly picks it up and makes his contribution to it. By this time, Bianca is already hard at work on her second piece. It's a good start. The race against time is on.

I wonder what Lux Cars thinks of the show. Do they appreciate our initiative? I look in their direction. Nothing seems to escape their attention. The four watchful doctors compare every aspect of our actual production with the initial simulation, down to the tiniest detail. Given his doctorate in manufacturing engineering, Brook Shields has me the most worried. I watch the redheaded man closely. More than once, he ducks his head into a disconcerting secret discussion with Nils Eisenberger. Every time this happens, they shake their heads woefully as though contemplating the incomprehensible, or the end of the world, or both. I watch and fret. And fall slowly apart.

Out of the blue, an excruciatingly loud bang rings through the air. My hand flies to my chest. I think my heart has stopped beating. Pandemonium breaks loose as screaming assembly workers dive for cover under their workstations. I strain for focus, fight to regain my orientation, and train my eyes at the electric conveyors which are now grinding to a complete halt. My heart starts to beat unbelievably fast as I think to myself, *this is bad! This is really, very, bad!* All at once, thick smoke pours out of the programmable logic controller standing not more than five feet away. Brook Shields jumps in shock, losing his thick glasses in the process. He stares through horror-stricken eyes at the smoke, and then, just like the assembly workers, he too screams hysterically and hits the floor. I hear him sobbing ridiculously somewhere under the table. I'm unable to laugh. "This is it," he says between heaves. "Armageddon is finally here." I'm on the verge of agreeing with him, when sudden movement at the corner of my eye catches my attention. It's Nils Eisenberger. This suddenly agile CEO of Lux Cars springs to his feet, turns about wildly, cries out for a fire escape, and ultimately crashes into Duncan Beike, who happens to be the only person still seated at the table. It takes me a second to realize Duncan Beike is not only stock-still, but gradually turning as white as a sheet.

This is a disaster! I feel the urge to crawl away. Quickly, I realize this urge is in fact prompted by the fact that I am literally on all fours. It's from this awkward position that I've been straining my neck every which way to catch the action. *How did I get here? Never mind that. It's time to act normal.* Embarrassed, I get up. And since I'm rattled to the bone, I waste no time dialing up Henrik.

He double-times it in, yelling and shouting frantically to everyone within the hall. "Just a short circuit, you wimps. No one's going to die, okay? Relax. Stay calm. Everything's under control; believe me. I'm here!"

I wish I could wring his neck. How could this happen in the first place? I glare at him as he walks confidently to the PLC. Several pairs of eyes completely lost in deep mistrust follow him closely. Brook Shields snarls at him from under our table but dares not come up.

The minute Henrik starts poking instruments at the PLC, we hold our breath and wait for the end of all time.

I crack an eye open two minutes later. No one has been blown to pieces. We're all still here. I'm thankful for small favors.

To my overwhelming relief, Henrik's tinkering finally breathes new life into the lean production line. Conveyors suddenly jerk back into swift beautiful motion. It's music to my ears. A resounding cheer from the assembly workers rings through the hall. They resume their places. We're back in business.

Henrik Wang saunters over to us and offers an apology. "Sorry guys. Technology is man-made," he starts to say, gets interrupted by Brook Shields, who lets out such a malevolent snarl, that Henrik jumps and splits from the scene in a jiffy.

We get a glimpse of Brook's red hair sticking out from under the table, and that's it. Nothing we say will draw him out. He doesn't trust us as far as he can throw us. I'm on the brink of a nervous breakdown. If anything else goes wrong, I am done for.

About twenty-five minutes later, the first X28 automobile head unit rolls off the other end of the line. It's a complete product. It's also fully packaged and ready for transport. A round of applause rises at the observation table. Twenty-five minutes! Not bad, considering the six minutes blown away during the PLC-explosion incident. That means nineteen minutes per piece for a disaster-free production. With any luck, there will be no rework, no scrapping. Should this pace remain as steady as it is, we will have a complete, fully packaged and transport-ready product coming off the line every 2.4 minutes. Now how fantastic is that?

Hope creeps into me at this realization. I tell the others my deductions. Their built-up tension dissipates somewhat. We all begin to relax a little.

SOMETIME THEREAFTER, Brook Shields resurfaces from underneath the table. The explosion is still fresh on his mind, and his fear is evident. With renewed fury and unparalleled zest, he goes back to whispering in Nils Eisenberger's ear.

I'm looking at a man dying for payback. We gave him a pretty big scare. Now he's out for blood.

Nils's color and breathing change dramatically as the whispers continue. After several minutes of this, he turns to me with a list of concerns so grave in nature, I simply don't know where to start addressing them. As he rubs his week-old facial hair, he draws me into a spirited debate. We discuss the pros and cons of production strategies and expected results. Nils is no fool. He knows his stuff. I give him a run for his money, though.

After about a quarter of an hour, he turns back to Brook Shields and pats him on the back. "Relax, comrade," he tells his employee. "Things are not as bad as they look. David here seems to know what he's doing. It's under control."

Brook, unconvinced, simply growls and bares his teeth at me. I think he's wishing he were a four-legged creature of some sort, probably a Wolf-Doberman hybrid, vicious to the bone and looking for a thigh to bite. Right now, the way he's staring at me, I can't quite shake off the feeling that he's marking me for a future rabid-dog attack. I covertly look elsewhere and say a little prayer. Eventually, he slumps in his chair and plays dead. I love it! Heck, I even afford a little smile. The atmosphere at the observation table quickly improves.

THIRTY MINUTES GO BY. I'm in need of a coffee. The Doctors become fidgety. It occurs to me I don't know how long they intend to evaluate us. Will they be here the whole day? Though I don't smoke, I would give anything to do so right now. A big fat cigar would be nice, just a little bit of poison to make me feel a little bit more human.

Nils taps me on the shoulder just then and asks, "Your simulation mentioned management by walking around?"

I brighten up. "Yes, it did."

He shoots up, sending his chair scraping across the floor two feet behind him. "Show me how that works." In the next instant, he's walking in the direction of the assembly line.

I get up and give chase. Duncan is hot on my heels. The other doctors are not too far behind.

"Management by walking around, huh?" Nils says, turning his head to throw his voice back in my direction. He breaks stride a few feet from the assembly line. We catch up with him. As a tight bunch, we veer left and continue down the line.

I'm talking as we go, giving pointers, keeping it short, simple, and to the point. All the while, I have one eye on Dr. Brook Shields. He's a dangerous whisperer. Dr. Felix Flink, who is short and stout and happens to be Lux Cars' total-quality expert, wants to know how we keep a lid on takt.

I explain the new-arrivals pads at the end of each conveyor belt. I let him know these are nothing more than in-process kanbans, a term they're all very much familiar with and are happy to hear. Ahs and ohs of recognition emanate from each of them. Even Brook brightens up at the use of this familiar terminology.

"At any given time, there should be no more than one work in progress in each new-arrivals pad," I elaborate. "If you find two or more, you should investigate."

"And what might one discover?" Felix asks excitedly. I notice the ridge of his nose has seen more than its fair share of breakings. He must've been athletic in his college days but is now more fat than muscle. I bet he and Hans would have many rugby-war stories to share if they ever got the chance. He peers at me, eager, waiting for an answer.

"Sometimes the problem is at the workstation with the pileup at its new-arrivals pad. Maybe due to a slow assembly worker. Or an efficient but nevertheless swamped one. Other times, the problem is at the preceding workstation. An over-zealous assembly worker moving too fast and trying to set a new assembly record is a dangerous thing. The result is always the same: a pileup of works in progress in the new-arrivals pad of the following workstation."

"Solutions?" Dr. Mark Davidson, a tall, slim man with a mole on his left cheek, speaks up for the first time. He has a singsong voice that's barely audible. Probably the reason he prefers to keep quiet, even in the presence of mortal danger. Or maybe we just didn't hear this soft-spoken man in all that screaming a while ago?

I turn to find him centimeters behind me, a far-off look in his eye as he tries to anticipate my answer. "Solutions … well, simple, really. For one, ask the slow worker to step up his or her game. Two, provide additional manpower to the efficient but overworked assembly worker, or three, ask the speedster at the preceding workstation to slow down."

"Sounds more like common sense to me," says Felix the pit bull.

"Indeed," adds Brook, squinting his myopic eyes in my direction.

"And that's the beauty of it all," I say. "Simplicity of management."

"Aha!" Rings out the chorus of agreements.

We walk farther. I explain ergonomics, *kaizen*, 5S, the two-bin kanban system, internal materials replenishment, and just-in-time materials sourcing. Everything has a specific place. Nothing foreign should ever find a place here. Keeping an eye out for order in the production plant is about the most basic rule of management by walking around.

We arrive at the end of the line. An end controller inspects a newly completed X28 head unit. Nothing's amiss. He's all smiles. He places the piece on a conveyor belt to his left. The belt springs to life with a torturous whir I only usually hear when two cats fight. It's not loud, just over fifty decibels. Still, it takes some getting used to.

By now, the product has traveled on this belt and arrived in the glass-enclosed packaging area. Matthias taps on the glass. "Cartons tend to flake," he tells our guests.

"And a producer of sensitive equipment must work in a clean environment?" Nils muses.

"Exactly," Matthias says.

"Interesting!" exclaims Felix. He too taps on the glass with suddenly knowing eyes. "Helps keep the rest of the production hall free of dust. Ingenious!"

"Which," I add, "prevents dust-related product malfunctions. In other words, no lawsuits."

Nils smiles at this. Suddenly, he whips about and asks, "Packaged units reach the downstairs loading bay through that little elevator an arm's length away from the packaging team?"

"Yes, that's correct," I say.

"Four hundred units a day is the maximum output?" he asks once more.

"Precisely," I answer. "Half of which you will claim every day."

"What if I want more?"

"That would depend on available capacity," Matthias replies.

"Besides, impromptu orders cost a pretty penny," Duncan adds.

Obviously, money isn't an issue at this point, so Dr. Eisenberger ignores this comment. His dark eyes seem to turn pitch-black as he fixes me with his gaze. "And all this optimism is based on the fluid functionality of your one-piece-flow production strategy?"

I hesitate for a second as I look at the batch-production workstations and then hesitantly answer with a yes. Though the lean production lines are our primary sales pitch, we do indeed have a secret weapon. Should the production lines grind to a halt for whatever reasons, we still have the batch production stations along the walls. These are my trump card in the event of dire circumstances. Mr. Beike wants Lux Cars' business. I wholeheartedly agree that we need it, and my budding career depends on it. At this point, I will gladly pass off batch work as lean-line produce if I can get away with it.

Come rain, come sunshine, Lux Cars is mine. I look again at my secret weapon.

Dr. Eisenberger follows my line of sight to the batch workstations. I only looked at them for a second, but the damage is done. My thoughts are betrayed. I think my trump card is in deep trouble.

Dr. Eisenberger stares with ever growing suspicion at the batch-production stations along the walls.

I look at them one last time, then at him. As I again focus on him, I realize he is now fully aware of my intentions with this backup plan. I sigh.

Seconds tick by. We apprehensively wait for him to say something.

Finally, he turns in my direction and says, "According to Kevin Koch, you intend to phase out batch workstations soon. Is that correct?"

"Yes," I answer. "The minute our remaining product models are lean-line compatible, we will do away with the old system of production."

He nods, then starts to think. He twirls the hairs on his chin. Furrows appear on his brow, and his eyes squint in growing concentration. "How many fully assembled X28s do you have in store?"

Finished-goods storage is situated downstairs. I call them and relay this question. A quick chat later, I hang up. "Twenty-five units," I let Dr. Eisenberger know.

"Have they been reserved for anyone else?" he asks.

"No."

"Good, good." He pauses, once again lost in thought.

Both Mr. Beike and I watch him closely.

"Production ends at four o'clock today, does it not?"

The doctors turn to Mr. Beike, who promptly answers, "Four fifteen actually, due to this morning's explosive incident."

"Ah, yes, of course. And by that time, two hundred units of X28 should be available for delivery to my company?"

The doctors turn in my direction. No smiles. No friendly gazes. Just hard business stares and unrelenting tenacity. My eyes never leave Felix Flink as I answer in the affirmative. He is the scariest of them all, what with his bullish look, broken nose, and football stature. I cannot help thinking the pit bull is poised and ready to tackle. I feel my muscles cringe.

"Three hours," Dr. Eisenberger states.

"I beg your pardon?" I barely heard him, and I'm also having trouble tearing my eyes away from Felix.

"Three hours," Dr. Eisenberger repeats for my benefit. "That's how long it takes by truck from here to my company's premises."

Felix Flink is momentarily forgotten. I swing my head back in the direction of Dr. Eisenberger. I'm lightheaded with anticipation. Could this be the breakthrough I've been waiting for all along? I focus my attention on Dr. Nils Eisenberger, who is already speaking again.

"I'll provide a truck and driver," Nils says. His deep voice resonates with ironclad authority. "You, of course, will provide the goods. As for transport quantity, here's the deal. On this first day, I want nothing but X28 automobile head units. The twenty-five from your store, the promised two hundred units from your first lean production line, and an additional two hundred units from your second production line."

Matthias, Duncan, and I cannot believe our ears. My eyes bulge. My mouth opens, but not a single word comes forth.

Finally understanding our dilemma, Nils addresses the issue. "Name your price for the extra two hundred. I will pay it. Does this settle your concerns?"

Duncan nods, so I nod. But neither of us dares to speak.

"Good," says Dr. Eisenberger, rubbing his hands excitedly, staring at us intensely. "This is a onetime deal. I expect four hundred and twenty-five units of X28 at my company's doorstep by 7:00 p.m. today. Not a unit less. Not a minute later. Not one product sneaked in from your batch workstations. Since your future deliveries to me will depend on this one-piece-flow system's performance, today's outcome will determine my decision. Fail on any one of these conditions, and the deal is off." He lets the bomb sink in and then throws in nerve gas for good measure. "Felix will remain here till 4:00 p.m. to make sure what I receive at the end of the day doesn't come from those walls over there." He points accusingly at our batch workstations.

I moan. I look forlornly at the perimeter workstations, knowing getting additional X28s from them is now out of the question. Gone is my only trump card. Sadly, I have no other tricks up my sleeve. And a pit bull will be watching my every move. We will have to make it fair and square after all. *Damned!*

"Do we have a deal?" Nils asks.

Duncan stares at me. Kevin and Matthias do too. Why should I be the one to make this decision? I think of the unexpected explosion this morning. Calculated risk or not, this is a gamble. Nothing can diminish this fact. Logic says we should make it. The figures support this notion. But as this morning proved, the systems have barely been tried and tested. Another minor but nevertheless time-consuming explosion could happen at any time. Then we would really be in trouble. What happens now? Should I err on the side of caution and lose the deal at this point? Or be optimistic and fight to the end? These and many other thoughts fire through my neurons in milliseconds. *I have to speak. I have to say something.* I don't recognize my voice as I finally breathe out, "Yes, we have a deal."

"Excellent," exclaims Dr. Eisenberger with a big smile planted on his face. The other doctors sigh in relief. They all fail to notice the deathlike expression on my face.

IN AN INSTANT, it becomes clear what Felix Flink is carrying in his briefcase. He undoes the latch and, to my utter surprise, pulls out three champagne bottles and a handful of champagne glasses.

"Oh-my-goodness! It's a clean-room environment for crying out loud," Matthias mutters in a wretched voice to no one in particular. He watches in horror as Felix pops open the first bottle. "Eating is not allowed," Matthias continues. "Neither is drinking, and ... *Oh dear heavens no!*" Standing stock-still, he stares in disbelief at the sight unfolding before him.

Despite all the no-smoking signs visible all over, Felix pulls out a truly fat Cuban cigar and goes on to stick it between his lips. Stunned, we watch as he fumbles in his trouser pockets. Is he reaching for a lighter?

A weird eerie moan escapes Matthias at this point.

Felix hears it too, as he promptly stiffens for a second. His hand stops digging about inside his pocket. Then up it comes, fingers spread out, no lighter in sight. An I-gotcha smile spreads across his face. But the cigar stays clamped between his jaws.

Nevertheless, Matthias reacts in relief, then focuses on eyeing the champagne bottles. Maybe if he stares at them hard enough Felix will relent with another I-gotcha smile again?

But this doesn't happen. As cool as a cucumber, Felix pops open a bottle. A fountain of champagne springs into the air.

Matthias screams.

Felix laughs. And proceeds to serve out the champagne. "It's an auspicious moment," says the bull of a man while handing out glasses of the precious bubbly.

Duncan frowns for a second. I too am resigned.

Matthias, indignant as ever, refuses to accept the offered glass, opting instead to glare malevolently at Felix, who deftly ignores him. The latter is making a toast to better times and good business, encouraging the clinking of glasses, smiles, handshakes, and small gossip.

I sip my champagne, watch Matthias closely from the corner of my eye as he quickly approaches critical mass. Finally, unable to bear it any more, he stomps off to his office where I believe he will spend several minutes screaming at the walls.

Felix, mark my words, you are a marked man. Breathalyzers and urine sample bottles are on their way.

Dr. Eisenberger gets up. He announces it's time for him to leave. We say our goodbyes and then watch him march off in the company of Brook Shields and Mark Davidson.

The inspection is finally over. I breathe a sigh of relief. Still, we are a long way from home. We have a mission to fulfill, a target to meet, and the clock is ticking.

THE FIRST TWO HOURS are touch and go. Despite their intensive training, several assembly workers turn to their instruction manuals a couple of times. It's the jitters, I suppose. This, of course, eats up many precious minutes of the valuable time we have left. I try not to worry.

By eleven, five faulty partial assemblies result in three re-assemblies and two scrapped assemblies. The rework devours yet another ten minutes. Bianca starts two fresh assemblies to replace the scrapped ones. All these put our estimated time of completion off by twenty-eight minutes. As we break for lunch, I am a nervous wreck.

Felix Flink dashes outside to enjoy his cigar during the lunch break.

Thirty minutes later, we are all once again at our places. Two hundred units of X28s to go. By now, Dr. Felix Flink might as well be in a pub. Much of the champagne is gone, and so is his sobriety. He starts to talk freely. Soon, he's crying about his love life, the girlfriends he's had, the ones that got away, and the one that broke his heart the most. It's highly explosive stuff, not the kind of thing one repeats to someone else. I listen and grunt and say, "Aha," "Yes," and "I know how that feels," the usual. Despite the entertaining nature of his lamentations, my thoughts wander elsewhere. *Maybe I can secretly commission the batch workstations to quietly cook up thirty units of X28 on the sly? That would surely help us regain lost time,* I muse in silence. *Besides, the pit bull surely wouldn't notice.* Or would he? He is plastered and groggy, slurring and sluggish like a skunk at the tip of a volcano overcome by volcanic fumes. He wouldn't notice, I decide.

I try to get away to set my evil plan in motion.

He grabs my arm for dear life and tells me he's not yet finished. He's got more secrets. He holds me in place with a viselike grip and pours out more scandalous material into my ears. I nod in defeat and resign myself to his endless whispers.

AT TWO, the truck Dr. Eisenberger promised to send us, arrives. It's a massive eighteen-wheeler with a double cab, painted in brilliant red and white streaks. No sooner does it come to a stop, when loading of the morning's completed X28s begins in earnest. Hans and Timothy graciously pitch in, happy to be of service on this critical day. In an hour, the deed's done. And afterward, every new box of X28s coming from the production hall immediately finds its way into the truck without further delay.

The last X28 is completed at 4:45 p.m. I snatch the collective delivery slip as it comes out of the printer and dash through the double doors to the parking lot. Felix is already on board, stretched out in the backseat of the truck's cab. He's snoring deeply. The alcohol finally got to him.

"Hit it," I cry out frantically to the driver as I take my place beside him. He needs no second bidding. We lurch into motion. It's a three-hour drive to Berlin, and we have only two hours and fifteen minutes to the deadline. I badger the driver into a frenzied dash across the state.

WE ARRIVE at 7:20 p.m. Lux Cars' impressive sprawl of real estate, situated on the east side of Berlin, is roughly two-thousand acres large. This parcel of land is filled with assembly plants, administrative buildings, test-driving courses, storage facilities, and parking lots. Almost every structure is coated in red, the company's favorite color. The place is massive, practically a little world in its own right.

Numerous information boards give directions, and a sea of traffic signs and lights regulate the extensive network of roads. The buildings are bathed in the light of neon signs and security lamps. The glow of electric light glitters against the background of impending night.

The truck comes to a screeching halt before the executive building. Most of it is in darkness, but light burns on the ground floor and on the third floor. Nils Eisenberger promised to wait until seven. It's now twenty minutes past the hour.

I jump out of the truck anxiously and make for the stairs. Thankfully, the door is not locked. Surprisingly, the receptionist is still at her place. Her coat is draped over her shoulders, and her purse is in her hand. She stands up the minute she spots me, almost breaths fire in my face.

"The boss is waiting for you," she says curtly. "Third floor, straight ahead." With that, she smartly turns about and hurries out of the building. My heart goes out to her. Two hours overtime spent just waiting for me goes well over the call of duty.

On the brighter side, however, and contrary to my worst fears, Nils Eisenberger is still here. If he is still waiting, it means he wants to make this business happen as badly as we do. I'm almost beside myself with joy. I believe my journey of a thousand miles is just about to come to an agreeable end. Success is within reach. I bound up the stairs and gun for his office.

Thirty-nine

Winter has finally set in. Snow is falling. Within Displaytek, a warm smile plays on every face as we usher in a new era of brilliant excellence. We did it! We truly pulled it off! Lux Cars is staying put, and thanks to this, all of our jobs are now secure. Furthermore, profits are expected to increase tenfold. Never in a million years could I have envisioned such a wonderful outcome.

On December 18th, a week before Christmas, we hold a business party at Displaytek in commemoration of our resounding success. Food and laughter, champagne and caviar, music and group photos. It's a beautiful sight. We fill our minds with endless joy and countless memories.

ELISE AND I INVITE both our parents over on Christmas Eve. They stay for several long, pleasurable days, then leave.

A DAY before New Year's Eve, Elise and I travel to Bacardi Island for our first real vacation together. It's late afternoon when we arrive at this beautiful tropical paradise. The weather is superb, so we head straight for the beach and warm water. A feverish thrill attributable to all the exotic sights and sounds quickly overcomes us. We give in to it and before long, we are splashing and fooling about like kids.

As dusk falls, the parties begin, taking us by storm and sweeping us along right into the very dead of night. In the wee hours of the morning, Elise and I sneak out onto the beach undetected by anyone. My heart is pounding. She is just as wired up as I am. Eventually, and under cover of the last few wisps of darkness, we sink to the ground in a fiery passion of unbridled intimacy. The warm air, the scent of the ocean, our lovemaking, and Elise's moans… Simply, fantastic! For now, I'm the happiest man on earth.

We will live in this idyllic state for a good solid week. Afterward, we will go back home, where I will take on a master to help prepare me for my next great conquest: Duncan Beike wants a fully automated production plant costing $300 million, and he wants me to spearhead its acquisition. I smell seriously big money coming my way soon.

About the Author

Kenn Oddeck is a business engineer. Through his education, he gained thorough knowledge of the topics he has written on. He wrote this novel in his free time and on weekends over a period of three years. He currently lives in Germany, and dreams of relocating to the United States of America. His deepest desire is to travel the world, and become a full-time author.

www.ingramcontent.com/pod-product-compliance
Lightning Source LLC
Chambersburg PA
CBHW021035030726
47496CB00006B/1545